"Tell me, pauper son," said the witch Nimiane. "Before I harvest the faeren, before I rouse your father to watch his seventh son die, why did you come? You have many portals. You could flee through the worlds and live a while. Why come to your death?"

Henry shifted, clenching the grip on his sword. "You know why," he said. "I come because of the words spoken when I received my name. I come because you are the darkness, and I am dandelion fire. You have seen me in your dreams. You know what I can do to you."

ALSO BY N. D. WILSON

Leepike Ridge

The Books of the 100 CUPBOARDS Series

100 Cupboards
Dandelion Fire
The Chestnut King

N. D. WILSON

THE CHESTNUT KING

→ BOOK 3 OF THE **100** CUPBOARDS ←

BLUEFIRE

Text copyright © 2010 by N. D. Wilson
Cover art copyright © 2010 by Jeff Nentrup

All rights reserved. Published in the United States by Bluefire, an imprint of Random House
Children's Books, a division of Random House, Inc., New York. Originally published in hardcover
in the United States by Random House Children's Books, New York, in 2010.

Bluefire and the colophon are trademarks of Random House, Inc.

The frontispiece illustration by Jeff Nentrup, copyright © 2007 by Jeff Nentrup,
was originally published in *100 Cupboards* by N. D. Wilson.

Visit us on the Web! www.randomhouse.com/kids

Visit 100Cupboards.com for news and fun activities!

Educators and librarians, for a variety of teaching tools, visit us at
www.randomhouse.com/teachers

The Library of Congress has cataloged the hardcover edition of this work as follows:
Wilson, Nathan D.
The Chestnut King / by N. D. Wilson. — 1st ed.
p. cm. — (100 Cupboards ; 3)
Summary: Twelve-year-old Henry York, finally reunited with his family,
works with them and the Chestnut King, the long-deposed and mythic leader of
the faeren people, to destroy Nimiane and her forces of evil.
ISBN 978-0-375-83885-9 (trade) — ISBN 978-0-375-93885-6 (lib. bdg.) —
ISBN 978-0-375-89320-9 (ebook)
[1. Magic—Fiction. 2. Space and time—Fiction. 3. Kings, queens, rulers, etc.—Fiction.
4. Fairies—Fiction. 5. Doors—Fiction. 6. Family life—Kansas—Fiction. 7. Cousins—Fiction.
8. Kansas—Fiction.] I. Title.
PZ7.W69744Che 2010 [Fic]—dc22 2008032748

ISBN 978-0-375-83886-6 (tr. pbk.)

RL: 5.7

Printed in the United States of America

11 10 9 8 7 6 5 4 3

First Bluefire Edition 2011

For my mother and father
(who never lost me)

1. Library/Adria/Lost
2. Cylinder/Aksum/Alt Pres
3. Wall/Mistra/CCM back
4. CV/Telmar/Alt Pas
5. Square/Ur/Damage
6. Barrou/Lindis/Pres
7. C. Lane/Yarnton/Vary delay?
8.   /Endor/
9. Vestibule/Buda/Pre-war
10. Balcony/Fontevrault/apprx. C loss
11. Larder/Milan/Alt?
12. Lunar A./Carnassus/Alt Pas?
13. Spiral/Lahore/Ruin
14. Kastra/Damascus/III
15. Litter/Napata/Alt Pres
16. Stern/Tortuga/Static
17. Rail/Arizona/Now
18. Treb/Actium/Constant
19. Hutch/FitzFaeren/Alt Pas?
20. Closet/Reba/Pres
21. Friez/Karatep/Broken
22. Deep Shaft/Masada/Varies
23. Viper/Edom/Alt
24.   /Cleave/
25. Falls/Rauros/Alt
26. Drop/Ein Gedi/Alt 2M back?
27. Sealed/Daqin-Fulin/?
28. Bom J./Goa/Pres
29. Dome/Sintra/Alt pas
30. Hall/Cush/Damage
31. Partition/Globe, H-let/True pas? Alt?
32. Garden/H. Sophia/Pre-minaret alt
33. Wet/Henneth Annun/Alt
34. Encyc./Uqbar/Partial Pres
35. Lower Castile/Transito/Sealed pres?
36. Rotten/Heriot/?
37. Water Tunnel/Germa/Varies
38. Tempore/   /Alt pres?
39. Lake/Acacus/Now
40. Bowl/Skara Brae/Now
41. Lab/Knoss/Alt Pas. back 4M?
42. Inner p./Arcturus/Surging
43. Mound/Lerna/Now
44. Sewer/Topkapi/back 5 C, true
45. Mouth/Marmara/Alt ?
46. ?/Angkor/Varies
47. Hall/Midge/Other
48. Fern/Bootes/Damage
49.   /Cleave/
50. Peat/Grus/Trailing
51. Hole/Nara/Alt now
52. Konya/Huyuk/Shifting alt
53. Granary/Mohenjo/Lost
54. Pool/Basra/Slowing alt
55. Grave/Lagash/Damage
56. Commonwealth/Badon Hill/Same
57. Hostel?/Bovill/Now
58. Hollow/Iguazu/Shifting Now
59. Narbonne/Carcassone/back 3C
60. Daxiong/Ningbo/Now
61. Barn/Lower Sol/Alt pres
62. Gate/Procyon/Flux
63. Lighthouse/Alex/Alt Pres
64. Sheer/Henge/Never
65. Moss/Morte/Surging pres
66. ?/Kappa Crucis/Lost
67. Nave/Dochia/Alt Fut
68. Column/Thucyd/Alt
69. Corrund. shaft/Myanmar?/?
70. Pump/Rayfe/Fast
71. Vat/Kimber/Alt now
72. Southern Cit./Boghazk/Alt pas. back 3M
73. Bank/Amster/yesterday
74. Wells/Premier Cullinan/Lost
75. Yellow Pine/Tindrill/?
76. Temp/Mysore/Alt pas. back 4 C
77. Post/Byzanthamum/When?
78. Shifting/San I.O./Shift spring
79. Gunnery/Brush/Static
80. Crush/Corvus/Dead
81. W.house/Cam?/Bubon
82. Mill/Gilroy/Alt trailing L
83. Reka/Skocjan/Back? Alt?
84. Bell/Delphi/Other
85. Base/Massis/Alt back 3C
86. Canal/Tenochtitlan/Alt pres
87. Bog/Malden/Damage
88. Blue/Cataldo/Alt fut
89. Loft/Strickne/Now
90. Sub Pill. 56/Persepolis/Alt pas. back M
91. Frame/Tana Kirkos/Partial Lost
92. ?/Ellora/Damage
93. Mine Spurr/Tordrillo/Now
94. Mid/Izamel/Flux Alt
95. Veranda/Millbank, Rhod./Alt pas
96. Model/Saqqara/Lost
97. Cliff/Achill/Now
98. Offs./Epidauros/Constat Aristo

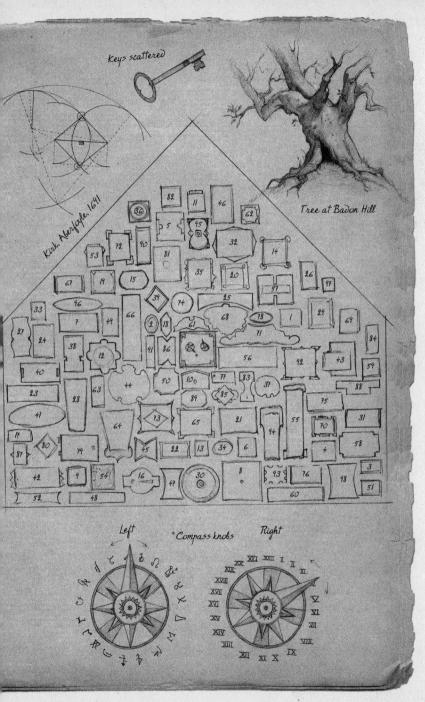

Keys scattered

Tree at Badon Hill

Kirk Aberfoyle. 1691

*Compass knobs

Left

Right

THE CHESTNUT KING

PRELUDE

In a world tangled in places with this one, both near and far from where we stand, near and far from where our grandfathers are standing as children, near and far from our past, from our now, from our never, there are two seas separated only by a long and strong belt of land. To the north, the belt widens and a continent divides the waters. To the south, another. But here, the two seas mingle in rivers and canals, in inlets and streams, in the bodies of fish and water beasts that creep through the mazes from sea to sea. Here, there is a city possessing the channels and canals, possessing the seas and the lands both north and south. Here, the streets wind like tangled veins, carrying the lives of thousands with their pulsing. Here, there are walls built on walls built on walls built on forgotten kings and wars and countries and cast-up coral bones. Streets and houses and gardens nest on the broad-backed stone and overlook the sprawling waters. Here, there are palaces and temples heaped up to kings and empresses and gods, known to the dead, forgotten by the living.

In this city, great gates open to the lands both north

and south, and greater sea gates, broader and taller than five-tiered galleys, shelter harbors both east and west.

Here, in the center of this city, with rounded stone peaks and shaded fountains, one palace stands peacefully, walled within the walls, carving out silence for itself. Here, tucked beneath a palace shoulder, there hangs a towered garden.

In the garden, there sits a woman. In her arms, there sits a cat.

CHAPTER ONE

Every year, Kansas watches the world die. Civilizations of wheat grow tall and green; they grow old and golden, and then men shaped from the same earth as the crop cut those lives down. And when the grain is threshed, and the dances and festivals have come and gone, then the fields are given over to fire, and the wheat stubble ascends into the Kansas sky, and the moon swells to bursting above a blackened earth.

The fields around Henry, Kansas, had given up their gold and were charred. Some had already been tilled under, waiting for the promised life of new seed. Waiting for winter, and for spring, and another black death.

The harvest had been good. Men and women, boys and girls had found work, and Henry Days had been all hot dogs and laughter, even without Frank Willis's old brown truck in the parade.

The truck was over on the edge of town, by a lonely barn decorated with new No Trespassing signs and a hole in the ground where the Willis house had been in the spring and the early summer. Late summer had now faded into fall, and the pale blue farmhouse was gone. Kansas would never forget it.

Dry grass rustled against the barn doors and stretched up the sides of the mud-colored truck. Behind the barn, in the tall rattling grass, Henry York was crouching beside the irrigation ditch. Sweat eased down his forehead from beneath the bill of his baseball hat. A long piece of grass dangled between his teeth, and a worn glove hung on his right hand.

The field across the ditch was as black as any parking lot, and the sky above him held only the smoky haze that had so recently been wheat and the late-afternoon sun, proud to have baked the world.

Henry slapped a fist into his glove, shifted in his crouch, and flashed two fingers down between his legs.

"Again?" Zeke Johnson asked.

Henry smiled and nodded. It was his favorite pitch to catch. He watched the tall boy wind up, arms tight, leg high, and then Zeke uncoiled, striding forward, arm extending, and the ball—string wrapped tight around a rubber core, all stitched up in leather—came spinning toward him.

Zeke was throwing hard, and Henry, crouched with his left arm behind him and his right arm stretched out, tracing the ball, had no mask, no shin guards, no chest protector, no catcher's mitt. He didn't care. He didn't even notice.

People who had known Henry in Boston would have had trouble recognizing him, even though his looks hadn't changed that drastically. To Kansas, he was the same boy who'd once been plucked crying out of an attic cupboard by an old man, who had returned twelve years later, fragile and afraid. But to Kansas, a tadpole is the same thing as a frog. Henry was a little taller, his shoulders were a little wider, and his jaw was scarred, but it was the boy inside the body that had really changed. And his eyes. His eyes would go the color of midnight when they really wanted to see. When he let them. When he couldn't stop them.

They were black now, following Zeke's curve ball as it carved through the air. To Henry's eyes, strings of force trailed the ball, connecting with Zeke's hand and fingers, straggling into his shoulder and back and hips. The air bent around the spinning ball, and pushed. In an instant, the ball shifted, as Henry knew it would. High and inside on any right-handed batter, it broke down and across the imaginary plate. With a snap, it stopped in the old leather web of Henry's glove. The forces, the threads, the crackling trails all tattered and faded, sliced and destroyed by the grass, swallowed by the world.

Henry called the strike and jumped to his feet, cocking his arm. Zeke waved him off.

"I'm done. You wear me out."

Henry laughed. "It's not been that long." He looked at his watch, the watch on his right wrist. He had another on his left.

"Two hours," Zeke said. "We've been pitching for two hours. I'll have to ice my elbow if I want to throw to-morrow. But I'll catch one more for you." Zeke dropped into a catcher's stance. "A heater. And this time as hard as you can."

"Really?" Henry asked. He wiped his forehead on his wrist and pushed back his hat.

"Really," Zeke said, and flashed one finger down. "Just throw it straight."

"You know it doesn't always go straight."

"Try."

Henry sniffed, bumped his feet together, and brought his glove up to his face. He shook his left hand loose, squinted at Zeke, and then he nodded slightly, pretending to take the sign. His eyes went dark, and he felt the burn on his palm heat up inside his glove.

And then he rocked his right foot back and twisted his left, slipping it in front of the invisible pitching rubber. Something inside him reached out and tangled with the grass, digging strength from their roots, from the deep, rich earth—the slightest spark of force from the skin of a spinning planet. His right leg was up, and he was seeing nothing but Zeke's glove. He wasn't taking life or energy or strength away from anything. He channeled it, shaped it, directed its stinging heat through himself. It came out of his hand.

Zeke couldn't see anything other than a boy pitching hard. And then the ball came straight at him, blink-fast. He reached for it and winced, waiting for the sting, but the pitch tailed away, rising briefly, bending around the barn, and disappearing in the tall grass.

Zeke burst out laughing and sat down.

Henry grinned, threw off his hat and kicked it.

"Straight!" he yelled. "Why can't I throw straight?" He flopped onto his back and slapped his glove over his face.

With dirt clods in his shoulder blades, Henry shut his eyes and filled his lungs with the scent of his old leather glove, the glove Uncle Frank had purchased for a worried boy from Boston. Every time Henry put on that glove, he added to its scent, to its story. Every time his uncle swiped it and worked more oil into the old leather, the glove grew richer, and felt better on Henry's hand, better in his lungs. It even tasted good, though Henry had never let himself chew more than one of the loose leather ties at the end of the thumb.

Henry's glove was an anchor. It was the same in both of his worlds. Picking at it, smelling it, chewing it kept him from clawing at the itching scar on his jaw.

"How's school?" Zeke asked. Henry couldn't see anything but leather and shards of hazy sky between the oversize fingers.

"Horrible," Henry said. "I have to learn three languages, and the math is harder than anything I've ever done. And I don't have a calculator."

Zeke laughed. Henry pushed his glove off and stared at the sky. "My dad was teaching me . . ." Henry paused. It still felt weird referring to Mordecai as his dad. The things they talked about, the things he'd started to learn how to do made it even weirder. "Well, you know." Henry turned and looked at Zeke. "His stuff."

Zeke nodded. "The dreams. They still comin'?"

Henry flicked something crawling and ticklish off his forehead. He shouldn't have told Zeke about the dreams. He didn't want to think about them. He tried not to while the sun was up. "Yeah. They're still comin'."

"What did your dad say?"

Henry levered himself up and looked out over the blackened fields. "He's been gone for a while. He and Uncle Caleb have been all over the place trying to track . . ." He drifted away again, and his fingernails found the pock on his jaw.

"Her," Zeke finished.

"Right. They were supposed to be back today. I don't know if they will be."

"I saw your uncle."

"What?" Henry spun around. Zeke had taken his hat off and was rubbing his head, loosening up his short hair.

"He came by our house early this morning."

"Here? In Henry?"

Zeke smiled and worked his hat back in place. "We don't have any other houses."

"My uncle Caleb? He just walked down the street with his big boots and his bow?"

"He was wearing some of Frank's old clothes—a John Deere shirt and a pair of ripped-up jeans. They were way too small for him. No bow, just his huge dog."

Henry was confused, but he couldn't help smiling. "Why?" he asked.

"He invited us to your birthday. Had breakfast and left when I left for school." Zeke picked himself up and stretched his tan arms above his head. White shoulders slid out from under his shirtsleeves. "I gotta find a drink and some shade. It's too hot for fall."

"Are you gonna come?" Henry asked. He tried to sound uninterested, casual. But that was stupid. He wanted Zeke to come. "I hope you can."

Zeke looked at him, his face blank.

Henry shrugged. "If you don't, I'll just be stuck with Richard and a bunch of girls."

Zeke half-smiled. "Mom says we'll go. I'll get you a calculator. But what's wrong with Richard?"

Henry puffed out his cheeks. "What's right with him?" He ripped out a clump of grass and dropped it on his glove. "Actually, I like him just fine. Or I was starting to, I mean, I did. But he's way too good at this awful math. My mom actually asked him to tutor me." Henry clambered to his knees, found his hat and then his feet. "I can't stand him right now."

Zeke's smile was wide. Henry sighed. "I mean, he used to be pretty bad. Now I think he'd be willing to die if he thought it would make me better at geometry. But there is one good thing."

Henry grinned. Zeke waited.

"He's tutoring Henrietta, too. And she's way worse than I am."

"Zeke Johnson!" The voice was big. Both boys jerked in

surprise. "Who you with back there? Can't you read or
don't you know what trespassin' means?"

Henry grabbed his glove, ducked over to the barn, and
pressed his back against the flaking paint. Zeke glanced at
him and stepped around the corner.

"Sorry, officer," Zeke said. "I was a friend of the family.
I didn't think it was trespassing."

The voice was growing closer. "Don't you know what
happened here?"

"Does anyone?" Zeke asked.

Henry crept to the opposite corner and waited. He
wanted to make sure the cop was beside the barn before he
made his dash for the kitchen doorway.

"A whole house disappeared, and a car owned by the
Kansas Highway Patrol along with its sergeant, and now
there's nothing left but a hole full of salt water."

"Didn't the sergeant come back?" Zeke sounded confused.

"With amnesia, some burns, and a bullet hole in his
foot. Would you like amnesia?"

"No, sir."

"Burns?"

"No, sir."

"A bullet hole? Or maybe you'd like to be sucked away
by a mystery twister, or swallowed by a mystery sinkhole,
or abducted by some space weirdies in their saucer."

He sounded close now.

"No, sir."

"How about just a ride in my car?"

Henry took a deep breath, clutched his glove, and slipped quickly around the corner of the barn.

His head collided with a startled police officer's chin, and then, with eyes blurry, he was flat on his back.

Henry didn't have time to think. He rolled onto his belly and tried to stand. Hands were grabbing at him. Long fingers gripped his shirt and then his right arm. The cop was yelling. Henry's glove was gone. He lunged, kicked, and tore free, scrambling back behind the barn. Another officer stood, potbellied, beside Zeke.

Henry turned, jumped the irrigation ditch, and ran into the black field, kicking up ash as he went.

"Hold it, son!" the fat one yelled. "Nothin' out that way!"

Henry glanced back and slowed. Then he pulled the bill of his hat low to shade his face and turned around. He didn't stand tall. He crouched. He didn't want anything about him to be memorable.

The lanky cop picked up Henry's glove and waved it. "You want this back? Come on over." He beckoned with a long arm. His own trooper's hat was on the ground. The fat one still had his on.

"What's your name?" the fat one asked. His hand was on Zeke's shoulder.

"Don't tell 'em, Gil!" Zeke yelled. Both officers looked surprised.

The fat one snorted. "Do you think we're stupid?" He shoved Zeke to his partner and grabbed the glove. "Well," he said, "you're a lefty. And your name is . . ." He rolled the glove around, scanning for ink.

Henry's heart sank. His name was on it. Sort of. Richard had tried to label all of Henry's things in his most important handwriting. He'd started with schoolbooks and ended with Henry's baseball and his glove. Henry had caught him before he'd finished.

"What kind of writing is this? You should do wedding invitations." The officer looked up and squinted at Henry. "Henry Yo. Henry Yo?" His eyes widened. "Don't tell me you're Henry York?"

Henry didn't have many options. Running farther away from the house and the little doors in the attic wouldn't help him get home. Waiting until they came after him wouldn't do much, either. The chase had to happen sometime.

Henry came out of his crouch and ran straight at them. The ground was too rough for real speed, but he pushed as hard as he could. The tall officer let go of Zeke, and both men stepped toward the ditch, surprised, bracing themselves for an impact. Henry veered to the fat one's outside shoulder, and he jumped.

Zeke stuck out his leg.

Henry broke through the arm tackle as the policeman fell. He staggered, kept his feet, and plowed through the tall grass beside the barn, past the sleeping, mud-colored truck and into the dandelion jungle that had once been the backyard. He turned toward the hole, surrounded by tattered police tape. A thin slice of doorway hung in thin air, propped open by his bat. His hands found the invisible knob, and he pushed through into a tired, out-of-place kitchen and skidded across the linoleum floor.

Zeke heard a door slam. The officers were yelling, and he followed them as they searched, tromping through the tall grass, peering into the hole, testing the barn doors. He could have run away, but running wouldn't help. They knew where he lived. At least this way they could give him a ride home. But he'd need a good story. At least a good enough story. Maybe no story would be better.

He looked over at the hole, at the space that had once held a house. And he saw a shimmer. The kitchen doorway was becoming slightly visible, just a crack.

Henry stared at the two cops, at the lanky one, who kept rubbing his chin, at the fat one, who was carrying Henry's glove. Henry wanted that glove. He needed it. He could explode out of nowhere and attack. He might be able to get it. He might be able to get it and still make it back through the doorway. Not likely.

Henry sighed and glanced down at the watch on his left wrist, the watch set to Hylfing time. He would already be late, and he didn't want to have to explain all this. Not even to his mother. Zeke was looking at him. He nodded. Henry nodded back at his friend, at Kansas, at his glove, at that other world where he had spent most of his life, where the people he had called parents still lived and worried.

Where the two policemen were wondering if they'd just seen the missing boy. Where they were probably wondering exactly how much Zeke knew.

Henry shut the door. He would see it all again. Right now, he had to hurry. Outside the gapped and shattered kitchen windows, a flat and empty world sprawled to the horizon. Grass, thin and still green, shifted slowly beneath a breeze.

Henry hurried into the dining room, scattering a group of fat gerbils. He hurried through the living room, past the carpet of shriveled mushrooms. And then he was on the stairs, climbing two at a time, up to the room that had been his, up to a wall full of doors.

CHAPTER TWO

Henry stood in the doorway of the small attic room. His old bed, filthy and disheveled, angled awkwardly away from the wall of doors. Salt crust, a reminder of the strange sea that had poured into the house, ground under Henry's feet like sand. He sniffed nervously and checked his watch. The time wouldn't be exactly right, the watch always got a little confused shifting worlds, but it was right enough.

This was the hard part.

Standing in front of the cupboard wall had always been unnerving. Now that Henry could see, really see, what was going on, it was worse. Each door was like a drain. Swirling threads of life, strands connected to the walls, to the air and the wood in the floor, spun slowly around the open mouths and disappeared. Dozens of open mouths sucking in whatever would come to them. Not always sucking. At times the swirling would stop, and things, scents, flavors, traces, influences, would burble into the room followed by wind or voices, even living things—snails, insects, mice.

"Witches," Henry said out loud. "Or babies."

The door to Badon Hill wobbled on its one remaining hinge, letting in a cold sea breeze. His door. The door that had been his first entrance to Kansas. The compass locks in the central door were still set to Badon Hill. That would be the way that Caleb had come. It had been the only way, at least at first. But Henry had something new, his own door arrangement. For now, he was the only one who knew about it.

On the left side of the wall, there had been two doors that connected to each other. Numbers 24 and 49. Henry still remembered the numbers, even though Grandfather's journal was at the bottom of the harbor, at least if it hadn't washed out to sea. And he remembered what they had been called. Cleave. That had been their only name, one word for both of them. Number 24 was open above his bed. Number 49 was gone. He had torn it out.

With a deep breath, Henry stepped closer to the wall. An angry voice trickled out of a door near the top. Somewhere else, somewhere distant, a woman screamed. A barrage of smells, good and bad, surrounded him. Henry's throat tightened. This was a much faster way to get home than traveling to Badon Hill and then hopping through faerie mounds, but it still made his head throb, and he always ended up with a bloody nose.

Where Number 49 had been, there was only a hole in the wall. The wood was splintered around it, and the rusted crowbar Henry had used was on the floor, pushed halfway under the bed. The ninety-nine cupboards had been reduced to ninety-eight.

Henry knelt on his bed and relaxed the focus in his eyes, letting the wall swirl in front of him, watching only the motion, the drain and burble of gaping mouths. Staring straight ahead, he lifted his right hand. The scar was heating up on his palm, but he couldn't see it. He couldn't see past the bright, writhing dandelion fire between his wrist and his fingers. The room brightened. The swirlings shifted. Trails and strands moved toward his hand.

Tears ran down Henry's cheeks. His pulse beat painfully in his temples. He couldn't let himself blink. He lost everything when he blinked. Henry flattened his hand on the edge of Number 24 and moved it around the cupboard mouth in a slow circle. The swirl grew. It swallowed the cupboards next to it, and Henry moved his hand a little faster. His mind groped around for help, for strength in the old plank floors, in the rock and sand of concrete plaster, and in the cool air outside the attic roof. It all flowed out of his hand.

The current thickened, mixing elements. Colors changed, and smells blended, but all of it was tinted gold. All of it answered to the dandelion. The wall had found a single motion. The other cupboard doors had been forgotten.

Henry could feel the pull now. He was going to flush himself.

Ignoring the physical wall, the wood of the doors, and the metal of the knobs, ignoring his own size, Henry shut his eyes, held his breath, and leaned into the funnel.

His ribs popped and compressed. His teeth ground together, and something warm ran down his lip. His fingers found cool stone, and he fell into fading daylight. Blinking,

Henry lay on his back, a small gapped roof above him. The view was cut off by a face, dark and serious, and two eyes looked down at him from around a blunt horn. A coarse tongue licked Henry's nose and swabbed his lip.

"Sick," Henry said, and both his calves cramped. "Ow!" He jerked up, banged into a rickety wall, knocked over a heavy clay pot, and grabbed his toes. The raggant staggered and bellowed, offended. Then the fat animal flared its wings, restoring its dignity, and walked away.

When his calves relented, Henry climbed to his feet. He was standing in a tiny shed, smaller than an outhouse. Old pots leaned in stacked towers in one corner. A spade with a cracked handle leaned in another. Behind him, a rotten bench hunkered over Number 49, the simple-looking cupboard that Henry had freed from the old farmhouse. Its door was open. Henry kicked it shut and wobbled out of the shed, onto the upper roof of his mother's house. Hylfing, pale in places with new cut stone, charred in others, spread out beneath him. He could see the walls, framed up with scaffolding. He could see the bridge, straddling the river where Eli FitzFaeren had died to save him. Where Darius, the tall, insecure wizard of Byzanthamum, the witch's pawn, had fallen with the Arrow of Chance in his throat. He could see the harbor, purpled in the early twilight, and he could hear the pounding sea beyond it.

Henry hurried to the little stairs that would take him down to the lower roof, and then down again into the upper sun rooms of the house. But at the top of the stairs he stopped, suddenly dizzy. Leaning against the parapet, breathing slowly, he tried to calm the storm in his body. His stomach was churning from the violent world shift, and his joints felt loose. His left eyelid twitched spastically.

"Henry?"

Henry turned and blinked, trying to focus. But his eyes felt abused, and they refused to cooperate. The world was nothing but purple, and then a shape walked up the stairs toward him.

"Henry?" The voice was his cousin's. "Where did you come from?" Henrietta asked. "I was just up there, and then I heard something break when I was going back inside. Your nose is bleeding. It's smeared all over your cheek. What happened?"

"Is my dad back?" Henry asked. "Have they started?"

"No. But Uncle Caleb is. He said your dad would be late. Something about Franklin Fat-Faerie. And—" Henrietta stopped. She was slowly blinking into focus. Her curls were loose around her shoulders, held back by some kind of band. She was wearing a white linen shirt, or maybe a dress, all embroidered and gathered at her waist. Not a dress. There were tan trousers underneath.

Henry normally would have smiled and made some kind of comment about becoming a lady, or looking lovely, but he wasn't interested in getting a reaction right now. Or in getting slapped. Henrietta grabbed Henry's hands and pulled him to his feet.

"You need to clean up."

Henry nodded and began working his way down the stairs. "And?" he asked.

"And what?" Henrietta was following behind him.

"You said *and*. And?"

"Oh. Right." Henry heard her sniff. She was trying to be casual. "And your brother's here. That's his ship in the harbor. That huge galley."

Henry looked up. He hadn't noticed a new ship when he'd first tumbled out of the shed, but there it was, anchored farther out than any of the others. Henrietta was right. It was huge. Five masts—three towering—five rows of oar banks. A flag he didn't recognize rippled slowly above the stern— white with a red emblem, long, and three-pronged at the fly.

"James?" Henry asked. James was the sixth son, one up from Henry, one of the four still alive. Nervousness forced away the last of Henry's dizziness, giving his stomach a new reason to burble. He had been an only child for twelve years. He didn't know how to be with siblings, how to act or talk or touch. He was still closer to his cousins than his two sisters. And it wasn't his sisters' fault.

Henrietta stepped past him and turned around. "Just be normal," she said. "You'll be fine. And now tell me where you were. Because I know you can't have been in that shed."

Henry licked his lips. Crusting blood. "I have to clean up."

"Were you in Badon Hill?"

Henry shook his head, put his hand on his cousin's shoulder, and stepped past her. "I need to hurry."

Henrietta didn't follow him. "You do that," she said. "I'm going to have a look around."

Henry sighed and moved across the roof to the low, arched doorway that held more stairs. The raggant, no longer offended, snored in the shadows behind him.

In his room, Henry dipped his hands in a porcelain bowl on his dresser and splashed his face. Then, looking in his small mirror, he rubbed at the blood. Had it been worth it? He'd seen Zeke. He'd pitched. But now his head was drumming, he'd lost his glove, and Henrietta was suspicious. And when Henrietta was suspicious, life could be terrible.

Blinking away water, he leaned forward and examined his face. First, his eyes. A little bloodshot but fine. His hair had been cropped short a month ago, but now brown tufts stood out awkwardly above his ears and on the back of his head, where his baseball hat had left a crease. Where was his hat? Had it fallen off in Kansas? Was it on the roof? He didn't have another one.

Henry reached up and touched his jaw, where the witch's blood had marked him. For a moment, he let his eyes relax, and he watched the gray spiderwebs float out of the scar, twisting slowly. And then he pressed his palm against it and shut his eyes. Inside, his bone grew cold, and his teeth ached. But his skin was hot. A shifting, twisting, growing warmth pushed in, struggling against the witch's deathless trace, forcing her cold away. The brand on his palm, the mark of his second sight, the mark given to him behind a barn in Kansas, where his blood had mingled with the soul of a dandelion, turned his itch into pain. A better pain. For a moment, the pleasant burning was all he felt, and then he dropped his hand, his warm jaw cooled, and the gray death strands reappeared, Nimiane's strands, trailing away from his face in their slow dance. His scar had been growing, the strands had been thickening, and Henry didn't want to think about what that might mean.

Shivering, he turned from the mirror, pulled off his T-shirt, and kicked away his jeans. Someone, probably his mother, had laid a white shirt with half a collar on his bed. Dark trousers and a matching coat lay beside it. He hadn't seen them before, and they looked new, a change from all the altered clothes his brothers had outgrown. His brothers. He hadn't met any of them. Three of them, he never would. He had seen the dead trees in his mother's orchard, where his own sapling had been planted. One he would meet tonight.

Henry swallowed and jumped quickly into his clothes. His white socks were dirty, and cheatgrass seeds pricked his skin through the ankles, but he didn't bother to change them. He forced his feet into the brown leather things that he'd been given for shoes and hurried out his door.

In the hall, he was met by laughter. His sisters'. His cousins'. He could hear his aunt Dotty, his uncle Frank, and then the big voice of his uncle Caleb. His father's laugh was absent. One more flight of stairs lay between him and a brother. He tried to descend them with confidence, but Henrietta was leaning against the wall at the bottom. She looked up at him, and her eyes were sparkling. Her brows went up, and she flashed him a tight smile. She was holding Henry's hat.

"You look nice," she said.

"Shut up." His voice was flat.

"Great socks."

Henry stopped beside her. "Shut up," he said again. He hadn't seen her look this happy in a month.

She leaned over to him and whispered in his ear. "I can't believe you. Does your mom know you've been going to Kansas?"

Henry didn't answer.

"Your dad?" Henrietta examined his face. "Fine." She turned, grabbed his arm, and pulled him into the room. "Come meet your brother."

The room was full, and James was seated at the far end of it, beyond the long table. His hair was the same shade of brown as Henry's, but his jaw was much broader. His skin was dark and sea-cured, though he still looked young. Barely eighteen.

Henry's sisters were clinging to him. Isa, tall, with straight, shimmering auburn hair, stood at his shoulder, laughing. Una, with her black hair piled up on her small head, sat on her brother's lap.

Henry stopped and ignored Henrietta's tugging. He wanted to take in the room. He loved it when the table was set, when people, his family and friends, gathered around it and seasoned the meat with laughter. Uncle Frank stood by the door, looking as he always had, though his clothes had changed and his eyes were more focused. A heavy gold chain hung around his neck. A plain carving knife stuck out of the wall above the doorway beside him. Caleb leaned against the wall on the other side of his brother, wine in his hand. Henry wondered if Frank liked the chain. He didn't think so, but he had to wear it now. This whole evening would be a celebration of that gold around his uncle's shoulders. Monmouth, the pale, young wizard, sat limp and smiling in a chair against the wall. Richard, with his thin legs crossed, sat perfectly upright to one side of him. He waved at Henry. Penelope and Anastasia, his other Kansas cousins, were bustling around with drinks and aprons and shining, oven-warmed faces that reminded Henry of Aunt Dotty. Anastasia's hair was even straggling out of its braid. Penny smiled at Henry and dropped into a chair on the other side of Monmouth. Various strangers and couples that Henry had seen before but could not name milled through the room, picking at the table's offerings and filling plates. His mother and aunt must have been in the kitchen. Grandmother Anastasia slept soundly in a corner chair, buried beneath a patched-together blanket. Her mouth was open, and thin white hair clung to her cheeks. She spent most days asleep, resting her blind eyes, and when she was awake, she rarely spoke, instead passing the time pinching and kissing whomever was closest. She had given Henry York Maccabee his new name in this room, at this table, and Henry loved her.

The smells were as varied as the voices, the smiles as broad as the table. Henry felt hungry and somehow already fed. This was his tree. He loved Kansas and parts of his other life. But his branch, cut off from this trunk for twelve years, had been grafted back in. That didn't mean he was used to it. Henry sighed and turned toward the kitchen. He would see his mother before meeting James.

"Henry?" A hand gripped his shoulder and twisted him back around. He was suddenly looking into a hard, friendly face in some ways like his own. Apparently, he would meet his brother now.

Henry smiled and realized that his brother's other hand was hanging in the air, waiting to be clasped. He gripped it, winced at the sudden pain in his fingers, and then coughed as his brother wrapped him up. Henry's already sore ribs creaked, and a series of pops rolled up his spine. Henry slid his arms around his brother and held on, grimacing, waiting to be put down, inhaling salt and sea from the cloth of his shirt. Muscled knots moved beneath his fingers, knots he wasn't sure that he would ever have over his own ribs.

And then he was free and breathing again. James stepped back and looked him over.

"So, you're the seventh, the one with double eyes. Our sisters say we resemble, but I can't see it. What do you think, little brother, are we alike?" James lifted his eyebrows, strained his neck, and preened, turning his head side to side. Isa smiled, demure like her cousin Penelope. Una burst out laughing. Even Monmouth's smile grew.

"A little," Henry said.

"A lot," Hyacinth said behind him. "All of my sons are cast from the same earth and shaped by the same hands." She kissed Henry's cheek, and then James's, and put her arms around their shoulders, bringing their heads together

25

with her own. "You may look like your brother, Henry," she said quietly. "But you are not so much the rooster."

James laughed and pulled away. Henry smiled. "I saw your ship," he said suddenly. "It's huge."

"Oh." James turned to the table and began piling cold meat and olives and spiced apples onto a plate. "Well, it's not mine. I was taken from my own ship and ordered on this one."

"Why?" The voice was Caleb's. He no longer leaned on the wall, and his pale eyes had sharpened. "That flag has not been in this sea since my childhood. Not since your father and I went into the south as boys." Caleb looked at Grandmother Anastasia in the corner. Henry was surprised to see her blind eyes open, her smile gone. "Not since the sea rose and took your grandsire."

The feel of the room had changed. Henry stepped backward. Caleb looked a great deal like Mordecai, Henry's own father. He was tall and dark-haired with light eyes—blue with green centers when the light was bright. He could laugh as easily as he could breathe, but there was a hardness inside him, in his bones, that could make him seem as tough and unbreakable as one of the ancient trees he tended in the hills. For the first time, Henry wondered if Caleb and his father were twins.

James was the only one eating in the room. A few of the guests sipped nervously at their wine.

"I was summoned to one of the imperial galleys," James said quietly, "and the commander told me that my father lived. But the word that Mordecai had returned was already being whispered in every inn and in every harbor along the continent. Green man to the northern imps, keeper of Hylfing, barbarian, savage, ape, witch-bane, what have you. The rumor men and storytellers flavored it as they liked. Mother tells me that she sent a letter, but I never received it. A dozen different times, and in a dozen different ways, I heard old sailors entertain the mess with tales of how you, Uncle Caleb, and my father imprisoned Nimroth's heir when you were only children. I heard every breed of lie and truth and mythic tale that could be told. And then I began to hear a new story about Mordecai's return and his missing son and a wizard shattering the walls of my mother city and the golden flight of a magical arrow. Some said it was the Arrow of Chance, the shaft of Ramoth Gilead itself, and others that Mordecai had woven it from lightning and fitted it to his brother's bow. All told of how the earth shook and the mountains heaved up fire when the arrow found the wizard's throat. I had already resolved to request early leave to return to Hylfing when the emperor's men came aboard in Lahore and claimed me for their own service." James grinned. "The mates and crew—some tale-tellers themselves—were shocked to learn my pedigree. Only the captain had known."

Caleb had not looked away from his nephew's face. His voice was quiet but stone-hard. "What service did they require?"

"Delivery and introduction," James said. "The stories were not only about my father's return. There were dark stories about Endor and a new life for it as well—the return of the deathless queen. I have a parchment with the emperor's seal to give to my father. And I was to introduce him to an imperial liaison, but the man was not on our ship. He may arrive within the week."

Caleb said nothing. Uncle Frank smacked his lips. "Hard to imagine anything that needs a warship to deliver it being good news. How many slaves are chained to oars out in the harbor right now?"

James had been cheerful throughout the conversation. Now his smile faded. "I know," he said. "I've only ever served on free ships. I'd hoped to be given leave to sleep ashore, but the captain won't grant it."

Hyacinth stepped over to her son and wrapped her arms around him. "The harbor is still the closest you've been this year."

Outside, bells began ringing. Uncle Frank set down his glass and plate and yawned slowly. Aunt Dotty bustled out of the kitchen and began fussing with Frank's shirt, fiddling with the collar and the chain on his shoulders.

"I don't suppose I can get out of this?" Frank asked. The room laughed. Dotty pretended to be offended.

Caleb slapped his shoulder. "Not a chance, Francis. You're the oldest."

Uncle Frank looked across the table at Henry and grimaced, contorting his lips.

"Frank," Dotty said sharply, but her voice didn't match the smile on her face. "If you want to be taken seriously as mayor, you can't act like a child."

Frank snorted. "Lord Mayor to you. And if you think I want to be taken serious, then you haven't been paying much mind to your husband all these years."

The bells rang on, and the leaded-glass windows shivered with each peal. Dotty finished with her husband and stepped back to admire her work. As she did, the front door opened, and Henry's father, Mordecai, stepped in. Franklin Fat-Faerie, knob-nosed and bleary-eyed, squeezed in beside him. Henry tried to catch his eye, but the faerie hurried straight through the room and into the kitchen without looking up. Mordecai grinned at Uncle Frank and gave the chain a little tug.

"You like the city collar?" he asked.

Frank snorted. "You want it? We might be able to melt it down and make something useful—a bookend maybe. Or a shoehorn."

"Mordecai," Hyacinth said. She walked to her husband. "James is here."

The last peal of the bells faded slowly. Mordecai turned, and Henry watched him take in his son. He stepped around the table and wrapped James up in his arms, and James seemed small beside him. Then he held James away, with a hand on each shoulder, and stared into his son's eyes. The moment was frozen. The room was silent. Hyacinth wiped her eyes, and Henry felt his own growing hot, his throat tightening. He looked down at his hands, at his arms. He seemed so weak, next to his father and his brother, next to his uncles.

Mordecai reached out and pulled Henry to his side.

"You and I should get to know this James of ours." He turned back to the door and gestured to Frank.

"Lead us, brother. The streets are full and waiting."

Henry watched Uncle Frank take Aunt Dotty's arm, and the two of them faced the door. Frank leaned over and gave his wife a quick kiss on the head. Dotty panicked, struggled out of her apron, and threw it into a corner. And then they stepped into the street. While the crowd in the room began to funnel after them, Henry ducked away from his father and brother and slipped into the kitchen.

It was a big kitchen, with stone chimneys and grates, a jungle of pots hanging from the beamed ceiling, and firewood stacked in a corner. In the center of the room, a square table of rough planks squatted on ship-timber legs. One end of it was occupied with knives and vegetable ends and apple peels, bowls and pots and an oversize rolling pin. At the other end, on a tall stool, with his head down and his hands around a towering mug, sat Franklin, the fat faerie.

He sniffed loudly when Henry walked in. "Begone, boy," he said, and lifted his mug. "Leave me to my brew."

"Frank?" Henry moved over to the faerie, lifted a hand to set on his shoulder, and then thought better of it, letting it drop on the table. "What's wrong? Aren't you coming? You love ceremonies."

Frank looked up. His eyes were bloodshot. His nose was running and tear tracks glimmered on his cheeks. He pulled at a thick earlobe "Do I? I don't know what I love or what I'm allowed to love. I don't know what I am, is, or will be." He pulled at his mug. "All I know is was. I know what I was. Your father was there with me. That's all I could ask."

Henry licked his lips. He didn't understand what was going on, but he didn't think the faerie was drunk. He wasn't sure if it was possible for Frank to get drunk.

"I need to hurry," Henry said. "But can you just tell me what happened?"

Fat Frank moaned and shifted his short legs on the stool. "What happened is the committee. That's what happened. Had a hearing today. All proper. All duly called and treble notarized. I thought it would be motions and tablings just to get to my exception. But no. No exception for Franklin of Badon Hill, who saved your life more than just once, who saw the faeren brought about straight, who dragged you safe to a christening and saw Mordecai, God green him, walk through that door, and a blade thrown and the mound magic of the faeren broken. No exception for me."

"What did you do?" Henry asked.

The faerie slid off his stool and walked to a cask against the wall. He refilled his mug, braced his belly with one arm, threw his head back, and drank deeply. Then he turned and threw it into the kitchen fireplace, sending shards out the grate and across the kitchen floor.

"I told," Frank said. "I broke the first article in the *Book of Faeren*. I told a human." He looked into Henry's eyes and pointed up into his face. "I told you how to break a faeren spell. I told you to throw the knife that freed your father."

"So what?" Henry said. "The committee had betrayed my father. They were trying to kill me."

Frank shrugged. "Rules is rules, or so they say, the new shiny-faced cud-chewers on the committee. There was a time I'd have been killed outright, jellied and fed to foxes or something like. Might have liked that. Would have known where I was."

Henry blinked. The faerie had begun sobbing. "I'm not faeren, Henry York. Not anymore. They unselfed me. Right then, banging the gavel and in front of a crowd, they said the words not said in a lifetime. I'm unpeopled. Franklin Fat Nothin'."

"Come on, Frank," Henry said. "You're still a faerie, and I don't care what they said. They can't change that."

Frank's eyebrows shot up. "Can't they? You should know better than to doubt the mound magic, Henry. Should know better." He sighed. "The frost's coming to Fat Frank. My blood's chilled, and the green will die. Have a look. Trust your pauper eyes if you can't trust me."

The round faerie hopped back up onto his stool and thumped his round head into his hands, tugging at his crazy mop of faeren hair.

Henry's eyes relaxed, and the world began to spin. He focused in on his friend, on the green vines of strength that always surrounded him.

At first nothing seemed to have changed beyond the faerie's mood. And then Henry caught his breath. He could still vividly remember the first time he had seen Fat Frank with his second sight—tumbling around the bottom of a boat, fighting a wizard to the death. His green strands had been wild and strong then, and they could snap and lash around like lightning when he was angry. Now, in his sadness, they wove slowly, tangling and disappearing in the air. But at the end of each strand the color had changed. Green was now tipped with yellow.

Henry shook his head and blinked it away. He didn't know what to say. He didn't know what it meant.

"Am I brown and twisted?" Fat Frank asked. His voice was sullen. "My autumn is here. Every faerie's magic grows out from the mound where he was born, and I've been root-lopped. Frank the faerie husk. Frank the magickless dwarf. I'm a waned faerie, doomed to end as a bit of dead, chalky nothing."

"It's only a little yellow at the tips," Henry said. He wanted to sound confident, but he couldn't. "That can't mean anything. It can't. Can it? What does it mean? What will happen?"

Frank sighed and hopped off the stool. "Couldn't say. Haven't rotted before. Ask a dying tree."

"Can't you appeal?" Henry asked. "Who's above the district committee? Can't my dad overturn them?"

Frank laughed. "Not even your dad can rewrite the *Book of Faeren* or stand the mound magic on its head. Above the committees, there's only the queene, and she's just a pretty idea that couldn't be shed. It's all decentered and parliamental. She doesn't do, she just is. Nothing but a mascot."

Suddenly, the faerie puffed out his chest and cheeks

and knuckled his eyes. When he'd pulled himself together, he poked Henry in the stomach and glared.

"Not a word, Henry York. Not a word. Not to no one but your father." And then he turned on his heel, pushed through a swinging door, and disappeared into the back of the house.

Henry watched the door swing to a stop. He looked at the mug shards on the floor, and he thought about sweeping. But he knew he was already desperately late. His mother would be wondering where he was. He might have already missed the entire processional.

Biting his lip, Henry ran into the front room, threw open the door, and staggered onto the cobbled street. He'd run this city before, and in the night. He found the center of the street, filled his lungs with the cool air crawling in from the sea, and felt his legs accelerate down the hill, down toward the old stone bridge, and then to the square and the cathedral.

Old Grandmother Anastasia opened her blind eyes. The front room was empty, and the heavy door creaked on its hinges, pushed with breeze breath.

"Henry York Maccabee," she said quietly. "Ten fingers will find you. Two are tapping at the gate."

Shivering, the old woman pulled up her blanket and shut her eyes tight.

CHAPTER THREE

Henry sprawled on his bed, staring at his shadowed ceiling. A lantern flicked light on a small table beside him. It had been a long day, his head was hurting again, and he was hungry. Massaging his eyebrows, he tried to remember if he had eaten anything before or after Uncle Frank's ceremony. He didn't think so. He'd been too distracted before, too tired after.

Henry's eyes fluttered, and he fought them. He didn't want to sleep. He didn't want to dream. But sleep came, as inevitable as the sunset, and like a slow wave it pounded him down. His body relaxed, his joints loosened, his quaking eyelids stilled. Beneath them, Henry's eyes darkened, ready to see.

Again, Henry was in the city square, catching up to the back of the crowd. Men and women sang, swaying and swinging lanterns with colored panes—red, green, orange, yellow, blue—while young girls danced and spun in the stained-glass light.

Henry pushed through to the cathedral doors and walked between the city guards.

The cathedral was tightly packed with bodies, shoulder to shoulder, all shifting and leaning, trying to get a view of the front, some with children perched high, others bouncing infants and humming quietly.

Henry reached the long pews, loaded with people. He wouldn't be sitting with his family.

He could make out his mother in the front, and his father and Caleb. But his sisters and cousins had been swallowed by the sea of heads.

Uncle Frank was standing in front, facing the crowd. Behind him three men and two women were seated, all wearing silver chains. Frank looked up and nodded at Henry. That hadn't happened. Henry's mind jarred as it slipped away from memory and into something new. He knew he was dreaming now. Beside Uncle Frank there stood a bishop in a bulbous hat and a blue robe. With one hand on Frank's shoulder, he was chanting unintelligibly in some ancient language. And then he changed. The robe and hat disappeared. He grew taller. His shoulders broadened. His skin, pale as sea foam, glistened in the cathedral's candlelight; his hair, oiled black, was pulled into a tight knot at the back of his head. Three notches stood out in the top of his left ear.

"Down," he said to Frank, and his voice was the voice of a woman. Frank knelt in front of him and dropped his chin to his chest. The man drew a silver knife from his belt and set the point on Frank's neck, at the base of his skull. Henry's head throbbed. He couldn't move. He couldn't interfere. He couldn't change the vision. Holding the knife in place with his left hand, the man raised his right, palm flat, poised above the hilt. He looked up. He looked into Henry's eyes. Without expression, he drove his hand down.

Henry tried to scream, but his throat wouldn't open. He tried to push forward, clawing through the image fog even as it faded.

The world became bright. He was back in memory, sitting on a warm balcony overlooking the fume-trapped city of Byzanthamum. An old man and his wife sat next to each other, smiling at him. Ron and Nella. The woman, white-haired with beautiful eyes and dark, lined skin, leaned forward and gazed into Henry's face.

"Are you here?" Henry asked. "You're a dream-walker. Are you here?"

"Believe your dreams, Henry," the woman said. "Yours tell you no lies."

"No," Henry said. "I won't. No one is going to kill Uncle Frank. The ceremony already happened. No one stabbed him."

But Nella was gone. Byzanthamum was gone.

Henry was barefoot, standing in a black pool in the center of a walled garden. He was facing a white statue, a man tangled in vines, frozen in his struggle to break free. Water poured out of his stone, yell-widened mouth. Henry turned, slowly, shifting his feet on the slick bottom. The tall walls were shaped from a reddish stone, and outside of them Henry could see the spires and towers of a great city.

The garden was full of vined arbors and slender, silver-leaved trees. Between the trees and in the arbors, there were set brightly colored rugs and chairs and backless couches.

Somewhere, a man was sobbing.

Henry walked forward, and his splashing made no noise. He stepped out of the water and onto the grass. The lawns were wrong. They were weedless, uniformly green, uniformly shorn. Too perfect. Vibrantly dead. The trees as well. Branches were overbalanced, symmetrical to the last leaf. There were no insects, no birds, nothing to live in and love the garden.

The sobbing grew louder. Henry pushed through trees and stepped into an oval clearing.

The sobbing stopped.

Ten men lay facedown on the ground, evenly spaced around the clearing, arms stretched to the center. Some were taller than others, some broader. All lay perfectly still. All wore black. All, though they had different tints of skin, had long hair, oiled blackness spread loose on the grass. All had a small circle shorn bald on the back of the scalp, and in the circle, a small drop of blood, steaming. The man closest to Henry had three notches in his left ear.

Henry wanted to run. He wanted to jump in the pool, splash water on his face, and wake up. But he couldn't. His eyes kept seeing, and his body followed them.

On the other side of the clearing, there were four trees, planted in a square. They were the only real-looking trees Henry had seen, tall, with trunk scars and thick overhead branches. Between the two closest, there stood an eleventh man. His hair was blond, his cheeks were wet. His head lolled on his shoulders. Henry stepped closer. Both of the man's arms were outstretched, and his hands were on the tree trunks on either side of him. Henry blinked. The man had no hands, or at least no fingers. Just after the wrists, his arms had grown into the trees. His feet were missing as well. They'd been buried. Grass surrounded his shins.

Behind the man, centered between the four trees, there was a red couch. On it, Henry could see the shape of a woman, a tall woman with smooth olive skin.

"Welcome, pauper son," the woman said. "There is space for another between my trees."

He had to run. He had to run now. Behind him, ten men rose slowly to their feet.

The man between the trees looked up. "I have a problem, Henry." It was Richard's voice. "I'm quite deeply in love with both. I need you to pick."

Henry's legs pushed and bent in place. He was rooted to the spot.

"Henry?" The man even cocked his head the way Richard did.

Panicking, Henry crouched, dug his toes into the turf, and jumped.

This time, he moved.

Henry opened his eyes as he flew off the bed. His toes, finally gripping sheets, propelled him into Richard where he sat beside the lantern, and propelled Richard and his chair into the bedroom wall. The chair splintered as the two boys slammed off the plaster and onto the floor. And then they were still, breathing hard, gasping.

"Ow," Henry said. He was facedown, and bits of grit on the plank floor were grinding into his cheek. His right arm was tangled in Richard's chair.

"I apologize," Richard said from somewhere beneath and behind him. "I had not anticipated your response."

Henry rolled onto his back. He hated dreams. "What are you talking about, Richard?"

Richard sat up. His face loomed into view. Narrow, thick-lipped, and usually friendly, it looked more offended now. His eyebrows had climbed high above his large eyes.

"Your sister. Don't tell me you haven't noticed?"

"My sister?"

"Una. I love her. And your cousin. Anastasia. I love them both."

Henry shut his eyes and slapped his hands over them. "Richard—" So much was built up inside him, so much that he was trying to understand and avoid understanding. And then this. Suddenly, Henry was laughing, rib-quaking, stomach-cramping laughter. The oppressiveness of the dream, the fear, came burbling out as he shook; it ran down his cheeks in hot tears. Henry propped himself to sitting, breathing slowly, trying to control his jaw and the spasms in his diaphragm. "Richard," he said again, wiping his eyes on the backs of his hands. "You can't marry them both. And you're barely eleven."

Richard sniffed, embarrassed. "I am aware of my age."

"And Anastasia hates you."

Richard's eyes grew, making him look even more fish-like than usual. "You don't think she's covering another emotion?"

"No." Henry bit his lip, trying not to laugh again. "No, I don't."

"So, then, you recommend your sister? Wouldn't you mind having me for a brother? I've never been sure if you've cared for me."

Henry sighed, and all temptation to laughter was gone. Henry had felt oppressed by his adoptive parents. He had felt bubble-wrapped, closeted, and ignored. But his life had been nothing compared to Richard's—a runaway mother, a dead father, and servant-trustees to keep him curtained, contained, pale and sickly, but alive while they controlled the estate. And his clothes—velvet suits and button boots. Henry had never felt bad for bringing him into Kansas and then to Hylfing. At times, he did feel bad for how annoyed he was by him.

He looked into Richard's big eyes. "Richard, if my sister wanted to marry you, I would be happy to be your brother."

Richard grinned. His eyes sparkled. Henry didn't know what he'd do if Richard started crying. Hopefully, he wouldn't want to hug.

"Would you talk to her for me?" Richard asked.

Henry grimaced. "No."

"Would you talk to your father for me?"

"No. Richard—" Henry's door opened and Mordecai stepped into the room. The raggant followed between his legs. "Talk to him yourself."

Henry looked up at his father. "I was dreaming. I jumped off the bed on Richard."

Mordecai nodded. "Your mother told me about your dreamings. I'm sorry I haven't been here to talk with you about them." He looked at Richard. "Would you mind if I spoke with my son?"

Richard scrambled to his feet and stood poker-straight. "Sir, before I leave, I need to ask for an audience myself. Soon if possible. It's regarding your daughter Una."

For a moment, Henry saw confusion on his father's face, and then amusement. "I'd be happy to speak with you, Richard. When things have quieted."

Richard bobbed his head, said, "Thank you, sir," in his most proper voice, hurried out the door without so much as glancing at Henry, and then shut it quietly behind him.

Henry stood up and sat on his bed. Mordecai nudged the broken chair with his foot, and then sat down beside him. The bed dipped, and Henry had to scoot away to avoid sliding into his father's side.

Mordecai reached across him, turned the lantern up, and then shifted so he could face Henry. The raggant scrambled up onto the bed behind them.

His jaw was unshaven; his skin, normally sun-dark, was even darker in the lantern light. His eyes shown. He only lacked Caleb's temple scar and the trail of white hair that it left on his brother's scalp.

"Are you and Uncle Caleb twins?" Henry asked.

Mordecai smiled and nodded. "Separated in birth by less than one hour. He the sixth son, I the seventh. We have grown more alike in our age." He lifted his hand to Henry's face, just as his mother always did, and touched the burn on his jaw. Henry felt a tingle, and then scratching heat. He blinked, but he did not move.

"The rot is growing," his father said.

Henry licked his lips and nodded. He could feel his throat constricting. "I don't know how to stop it. I try sometimes." He held out his right hand and flattened the palm. His eyes shifted, and he sat, with his father's hand on his face, watching the twisting of the fiery, living, changing word, the gold and green and gray of dandelion life and dandelion death. "Do you know how to stop it?"

Mordecai lifted Henry's face and stared into his eyes. He shook his head slowly. Henry's eyes were still dark. He was seeing all of his father, the green man, Mordecai Westmore. Thick strength twined around him, forming his arms, guiding his eyes. His father was a human tapestry, held together with the strength and glory of grapevines. Henry shut his eyes and waited for a moment. When he opened them again, his father was still, no longer a cacophony of twisting life.

"What do you see when you look at me?" Henry asked. "I've tried in a mirror, but I can only see the spiderweb things twirling out of my face."

"I see fire." Mordecai smiled. "Near unquenchable. Your strength comes from a fast multiplying weed, servant to the sun, named for the lion. I have never seen nor heard of it rooting in flesh until I saw it in my son. To you, it is only in your hand, branding its entry. But I see that fire in your eyes, I see it winding through your bones and building a gold and green bonfever of protection in your mind." He traced the burn pocks on Henry's face. "Around these wounds, it burns hottest, dies, and reseeds itself. The fire there is too bright for my eyes."

Henry stared at his father, blinking. Mordecai dropped his hand to Henry's shoulder, and then to the bed.

"I won't lie to you, Henry. You are strong enough to know the truth. If that death vintage had dripped on my face, I would already be dead. The slow, potent strength of grapes and their vines would do nothing to protect me. Monmouth's aspens would have browned and fallen. And truthfully, if that creeping decay had rooted in your arm or leg, we would have already sacrificed the limb." He smiled, but there was sadness in his eyes. "We cannot sacrifice your head."

Henry swallowed hard, processing what he'd just been told. "You mean, it's just going to keep growing? It's going to grow until it kills me?" Cold fear crawled through Henry's veins. He could see himself with the burn scar sprawling across his face, spreading from ear to ear, around lifeless eyes. His stomach churned. His head sagged, dizzy. He was going to pass out.

Mordecai lifted his head with both hands and leaned forward until he and Henry were eye to eye. "What I mean,

Henry, is that what you have survived, I could not. I mean that your fire is fast and bright and finds life again when beaten down. It would be easier to crush quicksilver, that scattering and reuniting liquid, than to stamp out the flame in your veins. But the blood that wormed into your jaw is death itself; it is the devouring blood of the undying. It will die only when she dies, when death finds the immortal. No one has ever done more than entrap Nimroth's breed, even when they were mad and gibbering helplessly in Endor's ashen streets. Caleb and I snared her once, but only with luck and a tomb prepared for her kind. Even that would not help you now." He leaned his forehead against Henry's and shut his eyes. "We must do what has never been done. I will find her. She has gone to ground and left no trace that I can sense, though your uncle and I have wandered far. But she must show herself. She cannot gather strength and hide forever. And she will always gather strength. Nimiane will fall or I will." He opened his eyes again. "Or we will."

Henry was numb. A switch inside him had flipped, a switch that made it impossible to feel. Somewhere deep inside, his mind had decided that feeling was not a good idea right now. "She was in my dream. Tonight." Henry's voice was quiet. "It wasn't the first time."

Mordecai sat up. "Tell me. But in the air, beneath the stars. Come." He stood and pulled Henry up with him. "The roof will better suit us."

*　　*　　*

The night air was sharp, and the breeze tightened the skin on Henry's arms and numbed his cheeks. He leaned on the wall between his father and the perching raggant and stared out over the recovering city, out at the harbor and the moon-glistening sea.

Henry couldn't retell his dreams well. He described everything he could and always felt as if he were forgetting something, something that might be essential. But his father was patient, listening, occasionally prompting when Henry lost focus, occasionally asking questions. In the telling, his dream seemed childish, and his fear unreasonable. But the horror of it remained fresh for all of that. A strange man had executed Uncle Frank. The witch had spoken to him.

Henry stopped, opened his mouth to say more, and then stopped again. He'd said everything.

"The witch is in a garden?" his father asked. "In every dream? Not merely tonight's?"

"Yes. Always in a walled garden. I think it's the same one every time. Everything seems fake. But she's always been alone before."

"No men?"

Henry shivered and shook his head. "No. And no one has ever killed Uncle Frank before. I've died once. You've—" Henry looked up. "You've died." He hurried on. "What does the garden mean? Does it tell you anything?"

Mordecai met Henry's eyes and then turned back to the harbor. "I'm sorry, Henry. I couldn't say. Perhaps she hides herself in a garden, but there are many gardens in the world. The men, I expect, tell us that she is growing in strength. They may be actual servants of hers, tools to replace the fallen Darius."

Henry leaned against the wall beside his father, waiting for more, hoping there would be more. The sea's chilled breath swirled around him, and he shivered.

"In your own death dream," Mordecai said quietly, "in what way were you killed?"

Henry laughed. It seemed almost comic now. "I was eaten by dandelions. I mean, they rooted all over me. I yelled and screamed, and they grew out of my mouth and nose. I suffocated, and then I was dead, watching my body shrink away, burning up with dandelions. When I was gone, they all went to seed and blew away like ash."

Mordecai's profile was stark in the moonlight, set against the bottomless sky. His brows were down.

"What does it mean?" Henry asked. "Is it bad?"

Mordecai looked at him and smiled. "It means that you had a dream in which you were eaten by dandelions. I can tell you no more than that."

Henry was confused. "How do I know when a dream means something?"

His father sighed. "Men rattle bones and bathe in smoke and blink at the stars, hoping for an answer to that question. I will tell you some part of what I know." Mordecai turned and leaned his side against the wall. "Some dreamings are visions, pictures rooted in reality as it is or as it could be. Your dreams tonight may be of this sort. Others are nothing more than the imaginings of a wandering, uncontrolled mind and are built on exhaustion or wine or overspiced meats. These, too, may have some role in your restless nights."

The raggant snored, and his head dipped and sank. Mordecai, smiling, reached in front of Henry and grabbed the loose skin between the animal's wings, kneading it slowly. A long, low, sputtering groan rumbled in the creature's chest, and it seemed to go limp, wobbling in enjoyment. Henry wondered if it would fall.

Still kneading, Mordecai continued. "A dream-walker may study visions of their own, or, if they are strong, they may enter the visions or sausage dreams of another mind. If they do, their own mind tends to meddle and interfere." Mordecai rubbed the raggant's ribs, sliding thick skin over the bony washboard, and then he slapped the animal's side and straightened. "Most difficult, Henry, is what you did in the faeren mound. You dream-walked free of your body around the waking world, listening to the conversations of traitors, and leaving a weed sprouting from the clay of a faerie wall. It is not your mind that wanders. It is your soul, and once wandering, it can be kept out. It is dangerous but powerful. You should not try it again, not unless another danger is greater."

Henry shivered once more, and this time, his teeth clacked sharply together before he muffled them with his lips.

"A cloak?" Mordecai asked. He had none and seemed unaffected by the wind or its bite.

Henry shook his head and stepped closer to his father, hoping for a shadow in the breeze.

"I must leave again," Mordecai said suddenly. "Tonight. I cannot wait for the witch to play her hand. But I will speak to my mother. She will watch your dreams."

"What can Grandmother do?" Henry asked.

Mordecai filled his lungs and slowly released his breath back into the night. "Your grandmother's eyes are not blind. Her mind is not addled. For twelve years, she sent her soul searching for her son, every night while she slept." He paused. "In the end, she found me in my prison sleep. She struggled to worm into my walled mind, and she succeeded, but only by tearing away from her own. Your grandmother found me, but could tell no one. She wandered too far, and there are rifts between soul and body that cannot be healed. She stayed with me. I returned, but she could not. She stays with me still. When her eyes are closed, they see. She will be with you now, my son, and she is a true comfort when the night's mares come calling." He put his hand on Henry's head and let it slide down to his shoulder. "A quieter time will come. I would learn your game. I would walk with you in that other world. But now, Caleb and I must hunt on." He looked down at Henry. "I may miss your birthday. Thirteen next week's end."

"It doesn't feel like my birthday. I always thought I was born right after Christmas."

Reaching down the neck of his shirt, Mordecai lifted something over his head. He held it out in the moonlight for Henry to see. A polished metal square twisted slowly on the end of a thick string. Diagonal notches had been cut into the square's corners.

"The leather thong is from a common cow. As for the rest"—he slipped it over Henry's head—"the shard is the last remaining piece of a sword carried by the Old King, and after his sleep, carried by our family through the wars of generations. With it, your grandfather took the witch's eyes before she took his life. It was with me in Endor when we entombed the witch."

Henry rubbed the smooth metal between his fingers and for a moment forgot the cold breeze.

"The metal has no power of its own," Mordecai said. "But much is now vested in it. It has a memory of courage and strength well used and knows the patterns both of bravery and goodness. Perhaps it shall guide you. Best of all, unlike your flesh and mine, it knows no fear in the darkest of places. It has a rich story. You shall make it richer."

"Mordecai?" The voice was Hyacinth's. Henry and his father turned and watched three shapes rise out of a doorway and onto the roof. Uncle Frank stood beside Franklin Fat-Faerie. In front of them both stood Henry's mother. She looked like her daughters. She looked like something made from trees and starlight. The breeze combed her dark hair. Her eyes caught the moon's light and threw it back into the world.

She walked to Henry's father. "Caleb is in the street with horses. Three of his men ride with you." She kissed him. "You cannot stay one night?"

Mordecai shook his head. The faerie flopped silently onto his back and shut his eyes. Uncle Frank winked at Henry and leaned against the wall, staring out at the harbor. "Don't care much for that ship," he said. "Not a lick."

Mordecai looked out at the galley masts, stark silhouettes. Lanterns glowed around the ship's rail. "Nor do I. But James says the captain has no ill intentions, and we live in the empire's frontier. This is no time for petty resistance. Treat them well."

"What was the message James brought?" Henry asked.

"The emperor requested that your father return with the ship," Hyacinth answered. "He has need of his service."

"Is that where you're going?" Henry looked at his father and then back to his mother. She looked up into Mordecai's face.

Mordecai shook his head. "I will attend him as soon as I am able."

"Oh, ho," Fat Frank said suddenly. Henry had thought he was sleeping. "He won't take kindly to that. No, he won't, the power-drunk puppy. He'll piddle his satin trousers."

"Franklin—" Mordecai said, but the faerie sat up and continued.

"The lord of the eastern and western seas, the lord of all the fishes and the peoples and the planets. Last I heard, he was only letting God have a go every second Tuesday." He flopped backward and splayed his limbs. "The little throne monkey."

Uncle Frank laughed. "Didn't know you were an anarchist, Frank. No surprise we get along."

The faerie snorted. "That from the Lord Mayor of Hylfing with his shiny chain. In a fortnight, you'll be regulating donkey behavings and tariffing figs. I'm a free creature, free as the Chestnut King himself, though he probably fears his mother. Free as rubbish in the road. I give account to no one." Still lying on his back, the faerie crossed his arms. "No one will have me," he added.

"Franklin," Mordecai said again. "Stand up and come here."

After a moment, the faerie obeyed, but slowly.

Mordecai crouched. The faerie adjusted his belt and sniffed loudly. "You are no longer a mound member, no longer a citizen of the district, nor a subject to the queene!"

"Do I need reminding?" Fat Frank muttered. "My spark's been doused."

"Not doused," Mordecai said. "Your strength's not ashen yet. I must ask you to do something, but I am no longer your bonded green man. I live because of you, my son lives because of you, and many others in this city as well. And so I ask you to do something freely, as a friend."

Fat Frank shifted his feet and squared his small shoulders. He said nothing, and so Mordecai continued.

"My brother and I leave in a dangerous time, looking for an even greater danger. Keep this house safe while I am gone, and my family in it. *The Book of Faeren* no longer constrains what remains of your magic. Use it all in their defense if you must."

Henry looked from his father's face to the faerie's.

Frank gave a little nod, and his jaw crept out. His nostrils flared, widening his round nose.

Mordecai rose, hugged his wife, kissed Henry on the head, and then ruffled his hair. "Soon," he said. "The storm must break soon, and we will be done with the waiting."

Henry watched his father disappear into the black mouth of the stairs. His mother followed him. Shivering, he looked at one Frank and then the other. Behind him, the raggant snored.

"Odd," Uncle Frank said, "having a brother like that. Makes me feel like a hen hatched in a hawk's nest."

Voices rose up from the street. Hooves clattered on cobblestones. Henry looked down at Fat Frank, rubbing his nose. The faerie wasn't much of a replacement for Mordecai.

"Good night," Henry said. And he walked to the stairs.

As the sky pinked with the dawn, Henry dreamed. Ten gray threads ran out of the scar in his face, and ten men in black held the ends, tracking Henry wherever he ran, wherever he hid.

And then his grandmother snipped the threads with sewing scissors and wound them into a braid.

CHAPTER FOUR

Henry jerked in his bed and opened his eyes. The room was blurry. He blinked hard, and the world slowly came into focus. His curtains had been pulled back, and gray daylight crawled sideways into his room. The sun wasn't high.

He yawned, stretching. It was too early to be awake.

"Henry. Get up. Something's going on." Henrietta poked him.

Henry blinked again and looked down over his blankets. His room was crowded. Richard stood by the doorway in some kind of nightshirt, bare-legged and wide-eyed. Isa and Penelope, the two oldest, stood next to each other, both dressed, both clearly worried. Penelope was pulling nervously at her hair. Una was leaning against her sister and chewing on her lip. Anastasia was bouncing, and her hair, undone, straggled in every direction. Henrietta jerked back Henry's blankets, and he was grateful for the linen pants his mother had given him, even if they were too big. With Henrietta and Anastasia around, it never paid to sleep in your underwear. He only wished that he was wearing a shirt.

Henry levered his elbows against the mattress and sat up. "What is it?"

Isa's hair was more red than auburn in the morning light. She stepped forward, and the other girls all turned toward her. "Father and Uncle Caleb left in the night."

"Yeah, I know." Henry swung his legs off the bed. "They're witch-hunting. I don't know where."

"I do," Una said. "Father told me they were going to Endor."

Henry coughed. He'd never thought they might do that. But where had he expected them to search? They weren't vacationing. Had they gone through the little black door in the old farmhouse? Was there a way through the old wizard doors in the hills? A familiar sickness crept into his gut. He tried to push it away. "What happened to them?" he asked.

"It's not about them," Henrietta said. "It's just they're not here to help. We're the ones with the problem."

"We shouldn't rush to conclusions," Richard said.

Anastasia stamped her foot. "Yes, we should. They took Dad and Aunt Hyacinth, and Monmouth called them names, so they took him, too. And Mom is on the roof crying."

Henry stood up, holding his pants with one hand. The girls' eyes all went to his stomach, where the glyph of a tree stood out in pink scars against his skin. "Will someone just tell me what happened?" He looked back to Isa, but Henrietta was the one who answered.

"Two more ships were in the harbor this morning.

They were both galleys like the first one, but not as big. All three unloaded soldiers on the dock, and one of the captains marched them up here and banged on the front door—that's when I woke up—and then they asked for your dad. When your mom said that he'd gone, they took her away, and our dad, too. From the roof you can see a bunch of soldiers in the square and on the walls and patrolling all over. We don't know what's going to happen."

Henry looked around at all the worried faces. Henrietta popped her thumbnail between her teeth. They'd come to him. All of them. His sisters, cousins, and Richard. What could *he* do?

"Where's the faerie?" Henry asked.

Isa answered. "He was in Mother's room a few minutes ago."

"He won't talk to us," Henrietta said.

"You were rude," said Anastasia. "I wouldn't talk to you, either."

Henrietta rolled her eyes. "I wasn't rude. I was in a hurry."

Anastasia put her hands on her hips. "Penny?" she asked.

Penelope sighed. "Anastasia, you're not being helpful."

"Listen," Henry said. "It doesn't matter. Everybody out. I need to get dressed. If you see Fat Frank, ask him to come here." He looked at Henrietta. "Ask him nicely."

"What are you going to do?" Una asked.

Henry snorted. "I don't know. But I'll start by trying to figure out what's going on."

*   *   *

Henry stepped into the street, shrugging on a brown oilskin cloak. Fat Frank stood beside him. The day was cold and overcast. Occasional drops shattered in dust on the cobbles, but the clouds seemed halfhearted. He hadn't known what to bring, if anything, and so he had only a small knife and his baseball tucked into an oversize pocket for good luck. It was hard to know what to bring when you didn't know what you were doing. For now, they would try to find his uncle and his mother. He didn't want to think about what might come next. Hopefully, nothing. The adults were just answering some questions and would be home by lunch. Easy enough. Somehow, he didn't believe that.

Henry turned and looked at Henrietta, standing in the doorway with her arms crossed.

"Don't let anyone leave the house," Henry said. "And don't let anyone in."

"Not that she could stop them," the faerie muttered.

"Why are you visible?" Henry asked.

The faerie seemed surprised. "Your uncle Caleb made a rule."

"I don't care," Henry said. "And neither would he."

"Well—" The faerie huffed up his belly and held his breath. Henry watched his cheeks turn red and then purple. The faerie gasped for air and then grinned. His edges shimmered in the sunlight.

"Are you invisible?" Henry asked.

Frank sniffed. "Yes, I'm invisible, and you can stop

being so smug about yourself." The faerie began walking quickly down the cobbled hill, toward the river and the bridge, toward the square and whatever was in it.

"Fine," Henry said, and he hurried to catch up.

"No one listens to Fat Frank," he heard the faerie say. " 'Guard the house!' says Mordecai. What good is a guard when no one listens? Don't answer the door. Don't go with the troopers. Oh, never you mind. Do what you like. Fat Frank doesn't have any worries of his own. He'll mop yer mess."

Henrietta blinked when the faerie disappeared. She watched her cousin turn and jog down the street, and then she shut and bolted the door.

In the front room, Grandmother Anastasia was feeling her way carefully toward her chair with a blanket over her arm. Her blind eyes were open, but there was no smile on her face. Henrietta kissed her cheek, smelling human age, fermenting life.

Her grandmother squeezed her arm and winked. "Her memory is long," she said. "She has made fingerlings." She extended her hand, fingers spread, and fluttered them. "Little daughter, grow wings and fly away." She shuffled to her chair and collapsed into it. Henrietta spread the blanket over her legs, but her grandmother was asleep before she'd finished.

Fingerlings? She hurried to the stairs and climbed them two at a time. The others would be on the roof, clustered around her mother. Except for the raggant. Henry had shut the raggant in his closet before he left. Henrietta could hear its muffled bellowing on the second-story landing. She hesitated but then moved quickly on. She couldn't risk letting it out. The little barrel-shaped creature would bite and butt its way free of her arms for sure. And then Henry would be all pompous about her mistake. She climbed to the third floor, twisted down a narrow hall, and found the stairs to the roof.

The few townspeople in the street quietly hurried past Henry, though one or two glanced at the muttering patch of air beside him. They passed three small groups of soldiers on their way to the bridge, and another on the bridge itself. All wore red tunics marked with the same symbol that flew over the galleys—three serpents braided into one, sharing a single head—and white trousers tucked into boots. Most carried crossbows; some pikes, double-headed with curved blades; and others wore short swords, always sheathed. All seemed nervous, chewing lips or nails, watching doorways and alleys with their backs against windowless walls.

"Are they afraid of the people?" Henry whispered.

"More likely they're afraid of your father," the faerie answered. "Or didn't you know that he's a demon what could suck your soul straight out your nose?"

Henry tried to watch the soldiers' faces without catching any eyes, but he didn't do well. They all seemed to look at him right when he took his glance. Each time, he put his head down and hurried on, but he knew they were watching his back, and that made his skin tingle.

As they reached the square, Fat Frank stopped. Two soldiers were standing on a corner with their backs to the wall just beneath a stone ledge. Frank looked them over, sniffed, and then grinned at Henry.

"Pretty little popinjays. So handsome in red."

Before Henry could say anything, the faerie skipped toward the two men, and then, in an explosion of balance and speed, he ran up the wall and perched on the stone ledge between their heads.

Henry stood motionless, slack-jawed, staring. Both soldiers slowly turned toward him, staring back. One lowered his brows and opened his mouth to speak, but Fat Frank had already swabbed thick forefingers through the insides of his cheeks. He crouched down and poked his findings into the soldiers' ears.

Both men jumped and yelped and slapped at their faces, spinning, looking behind them, above them, looking for any culprit. And then they both, each still with one hand over an ear, turned and looked at Henry.

Suddenly, he was very aware that his eyebrows were up, and that he was grinning.

"Come here, boy," one of them said, and he reached for his sword. Henry erased his smile and took a step backward. Fat Frank rolled his eyes and shook his head. Then he pushed up his sleeves, leaned over, winked at Henry, and hooked both soldiers by the nostrils.

Henry saw the pulse of magic flick out of the faerie, too fast for him to understand, and he saw the faerie jerk both men's heads back into the stone wall. For a moment, they were scrambling on their toes, trying to ease the pressure of the faerie's pulling, and then they went limp and tumbled to the street, limbs entwined, eyes shut in total sleep. White liquid, lots of white liquid, streamed out of their noses and pooled beneath them.

Frank jumped down beside Henry. "You ever have milk come out your nose?" he asked, wiping his hands on his trousers.

"Once actually," Henry said.

"Ah," said Frank. "But not that much."

"Hoy!" Three soldiers at the top of the street were running toward them.

"Right, then," Frank said. "They'll blame that one on your father. Let them think he's lurking on every ledge. We're off." Laughing, he grabbed Henry's sleeve and dragged him around the corner and into the square. "Violation," he said. "Unnecessary Human Engagement and/or Conflict. *Book of Faeren,* II.ii. Let's see the committee call up Fat Franklin now, hey? Petty gavel-bangers."

At one end of the square hulked the cathedral. On the other side, beyond a simple fountain, a building with round roofs heaped up in three tiers squatted symmetrically. The Hall of Governance. A white flag with the red serpent emblem flew at its crown, and soldiers blocked the steps in even lines. Perpendicular to them, arranged in three squares, stood the usual city guard. Not one of them was armed. The weapons that had been theirs were in a large pile beside the fountain. Townspeople milled around the group and chattered. Men stood in circles with arms crossed, and one or two occasionally cupped their hands and shouted some insult or other at the men in red.

"Lovely," Frank said. He jerked Henry into the next small side alley, hurried to a mound of trash, and shoved him behind a stack of crates brimful of rotting vegetables. He sat down next to him, rubbed his belly, and chuckled. "And Overt Bovinization. I'd forgotten that one. *B.O.F.* Appendix XII. Oh, this *is* a holiday."

"Bovinization?" Henry asked.

"That's right," Frank said. "Cattle spells, human use. Sometimes irreversible. Sometimes fatal."

"Frank!" Henry said.

Fat Frank jumped to his feet. "Oh, it's just milk. They'll have headaches and the odd gush for a moon or two and nothing more." He moved back toward the alley mouth. "Wait here, Henry York Maccabee. Snack if you like."

The rogue faerie disappeared around the corner, and Henry climbed to his feet. He walked slowly forward until he could see out into the square, and then more. He could see the soldiers in formation in front of the hall. A small shape ran toward them, twisted through the lines, and reached the stairs.

Henry sighed. He shouldn't have come at all. The faerie didn't need him. Fat Frank could find everyone alone. He reached up and scratched his jaw. His burn was prickling.

The skin around it was cold, almost numb. Shivering, he turned, and a yell froze in his throat.

Not ten feet behind him, a man stood. Tall, cloakless, dressed in black. His unnaturally dark hair was pulled into a tight knot at the back of his head. At the top of his left ear, there were three deep notches.

The man lifted a long arm and pointed at Henry's face, at the burn. "You and I share the same blood." His voice was strained, as if speaking were difficult. Henry couldn't look away from the pale face and its hollow eyes. "In a way," the man said slowly, "we are brothers."

He smiled.

Henry stepped backward.

"I am Coradin," the man said. He held out his hand. "Come. I will take you to our mother."

Henry turned and ran into the square. In an instant, the man was on him. A strong hand gripped the back of his neck, and a heavy body drove him down into the cobbles. Henry didn't notice the pain. He twisted onto his right side and kicked hard while the man's hand shifted to his throat. Henry's teeth found a wrist, salty skin, and the grip loosened. Yelling as loud and as long as he could, Henry rolled onto his back, freeing his right arm. His dandelion was burning. His blood was burning. His bones crackled inside him. His eyes went black. This man had killed Uncle Frank, even if only in a dream. In someplace deeper than Henry's mind, deeper than any logic, he wanted this fight. He wanted to finish it.

Henry forced his dandelion hand into the cold face, searing icy skin. Yelling, the big man rolled off and scrambled to his feet. Henry jumped up and glanced around the square. To his eyes, it was slow with twisting stone and crawling wind. The men in red were running toward him.

The city guard had broken ranks and were racing to their piled weapons.

"Henry Maccabee!" someone was yelling. "They attack Mordecai's son!"

Henry looked back to his enemy. The man stood still with his head tipped slightly down. He expected to see strength, angry strength winding its way out of the man, but he was nothing but coldness, and the life inside him, the soul's spark, was tiny and slow. Something else, a great gray serpentine mass swirled behind his head. He looked up.

"Pauper son," he said, but the voice was another's. "Pauper son," he said again. "My blood is in you. You cannot run."

Henry reached into his pocket and gripped his small knife. His mind reached into the ground and gripped the earth's breathing. He grabbed at the cobbles and the sky, and with the yelling of guards approaching and the bright shirts of the emperor's men blurring in the background, his tongue shaped words he did not know, and he ran at his enemy.

Frank Willis sat by the window. Technically, this was his office, though it hadn't felt like it. It felt even less like it now. His sister-in-law, Hyacinth, sat beside him, and James was beside her. Monmouth was in the corner. None of them had been tied up, but clearly, they would be the instant they caused trouble.

The room was big. Five soldiers stood with backs against the wall on the far side. Closer, seated, rubbing his head and leaning over, clearly not enjoying himself, sat the captain of the great galley in the harbor. Beside him sat a character that was far more unnerving. At least to Frank. He was large and dressed in black. Both his cheeks were scarred, and his hair, oiled darker than it already was, had been pulled into a tight knot at the back of his head.

His eyes, deep and empty, studied each of the pseudo-captives in turn. He hadn't spoken.

The captain looked up. "I am sorry," he said. "But you have no choice. You and all of yours must come aboard." He looked at Hyacinth. "Unless your husband comes alone."

"My husband is away." Her voice was crisp.

"So you've said." The captain straightened. "You have no choice. I have no choice. You're to be brought aboard. Those are the orders."

Frank licked his lips. "Can't say yes." He wished he knew how to be diplomatic. Was there a special smile? "And I'd like to see the orders. If our emperor stuck his seal on something special for you, there's no reason to be shy. Show it around."

"My orders are verbal," the captain said. "And the emperor did set his seal to something. He summoned your brother, and your brother ignored the summons. These are the consequences."

"Right," said Frank. "I did see that. He requested that my brother head on down as he had particular expertise in a current rumored situation or somesuch. And my brother sealed up a reply—and I don't mean to be rude, but it seems that someone up and read the emperor's mail— saying that he would come as soon as he could. And— here's the kicker—he will."

The big man in black drew in a slow breath, and then he spoke. "The witch-queen rises. The emperor commands your brother's presence. He must answer charges about his family's involvement in loosing that curse on the empire. He must suffer justice. He will come, and quickly. He will come for his family."

"There was nothing about any charges," James said suddenly.

"Then why did he run, James?" the captain asked.

James flushed. "He did not run. He's hunting the witch now. He and my uncle are traveling into Endor itself in search of her. Is that running?"

"James," Hyacinth said, and she shut her eyes.

"Oh, stop," Monmouth said from the corner. The young man stretched his legs and sat up straight in his chair. His pale eyes sparked in irritation, and he ran his hands through his dark hair. His recovery after the siege of Hylfing had been slow, and his strength still was not what it had been when he had first met Henry. "The way of all kings," he continued. "Lie and connive and order and seal and complain of dishonor and disrespect and treason. Rule by designs and plots, never by honesty." He looked from Frank to Hyacinth. "Can't you see that they'll have us one way or another? They have their designs to look after. Do not reason with them. They will lay a snare for the great Mordecai, and they cannot be dissuaded. Invite him politely or charge him with treason or kidnap his blood and bone. Mordecai will stand before the emperor, oh, and he will slip, for the floor will be greased with lies."

"You disrespect your emperor." James's voice was cold.

"My emperor?" Monmouth laughed. "I have no fealty to him. My father is a king in the west. He is petty but unconquered, and he is no better."

"Enough," the captain said. He looked at Frank. "Shall it be pleasant, with the ladies of the city tossing flowers at your departure? Or shall we take you trussed up in a wagon?"

Frank smiled. "Flowers make me sneeze. But I should warn you, the folk in this town aren't over-sophisticants when it comes to trussing up the mayor and his family— no mentioning the family of their favorite hero. They might not realize that it's all friendly and diplomatic and get a bit testy."

The big man snorted. "Fishermen and farmers do not concern us."

A yelling erupted outside in the square. Frank turned to the window and looked down three stories at two bodies rolling on the ground. A boy and a man dressed in black. Hyacinth stood up behind Frank.

"Henry?" she asked. The bodies separated. She gripped Frank's shoulder. "That's Henry."

The yelling grew to a roar as the city guard broke ranks and rushed to their weapons. Soldiers in red moved forward to meet them.

The big man in black rose from his chair. "Now," he said to the captain. "We do it now." He turned to the soldiers along the wall. "Tie them."

Monmouth leapt from his chair and a blade flicked from his fingers, but the big man cupped his head in one hand and slammed him against the wall. The young wizard slumped to the floor, unconscious, but his knife was buried in the man's gut. He picked it out and dropped it on the floor. "Only the boy must be taken alive. Get all you can of the rest, but kill any who resist too long. We must be on the ships before the anthill swarms."

In the south, nearer to the world's belt, a woman rose from her dreaming and stepped out from between four trees. She walked into the sun, a cat in her arms, her eyes unfocused. A man, suspended between two trees, moaned softly behind her.

"Mordecai," she whispered, smiling. "You would walk again in Endor?"

Near a black pool, a woman waited, kneeling with her head down. A velvet chair had been set on the grass. Beside it, a wicker cage busily peeped with young birds.

Nimiane sat. "This is for the emperor," she said, and dropped a small scroll in front of the woman.

"Mistress." The woman crawled away backward before standing and hurrying through the arbors.

The heir to Nimroth the Devouring, Blackstar, half-human, reached into the wicker cage and pulled out a bird. It blinked in the sun, wobbled, and slumped on her palm. She closed her fingers around it.

"The boy has grown," she said. "But not enough."

She opened her hand and released a small pile of ash into the wind. It swirled and descended, dusting the surface of the lifeless pond. It was a small life, but she savored it. Greater lives would come.

Inhaling slowly, she reached for another bird.

CHAPTER FIVE

HENRY slumped into a doorway, panting. His second sight was gone, his head was throbbing, and something sharp had nicked his calf. His jaw was ice-cold. Henry touched it, and his fingers came away sticky and red. The old burn was bleeding.

He hadn't been able to touch the man again. Coradin, or the one who worked through him, had been far too strong. Henry thought about what he'd seen, the thick, gray, spinning ropes on the back of the man's head. They were like his own, like the fine webs that twisted out of his jaw. Is that what his would look like in the end—huge, braiding serpents? Would the witch be able to control him, too?

Henry knew Coradin could have killed him. But he hadn't. He'd wanted to take Henry alive. And he would have succeeded if the city guard hadn't swept over them both in their rush to meet the soldiers.

In the square, the guardsmen were drawing back now, scattering. The soldiers, disciplined in the extreme, moved through them in a dense phalanx, guarding a small group in their core.

Henry sat up, straining to see. A lean man bobbed along in the center. Uncle Frank? It was his uncle, and his mother was beside him. Henry scrambled to his feet and limped forward. But what could he do? They were surrounded by more than two hundred men.

He didn't care. He had to do something. And then, pushing out from the soldiers, came two tall men, both in black. Both looked straight at him.

Henry turned, and with tears of anger in his eyes, he bit back the pain in his leg, and he ran. He had to get to the house, to his sisters and his cousins.

From the roof, Henrietta watched the wagon roll up the street and stop. She watched soldiers take up positions at every door and every window.

"What are they doing?" Anastasia asked.

Dotty sighed. Her arms were wrapped around Penelope. She wasn't crying. There was no use in it. "They are coming to get us," she said.

Una glanced over the wall. "I don't want to go," she said, and leaned against her sister.

"I don't think we have much choice." Isa's voice was surprisingly calm. Henrietta looked at her and then back down at the street.

"We can fight," she said.

"And we can be killed." Richard still wore his night-shirt. "It is in our best interest to go peaceably."

"Mom?" Penelope asked. "What are we going to do?"

Dotty buried her face in her daughter's hair. "I

don't know," she said. "Maybe they will take us to your father."

In the street, two men with axes walked to the front door.

Henry heard the shouting before he could see the house. The rain was still spotty but falling enough to make the cobbles slick. He had ducked through side alleys after crossing back over the bridge, and he knew it had slowed him down. But it had also kept him out of sight.

Once again, breathing hard and digging a knuckle into the stitch in his side, Henry glanced over his shoulder. No one was following him. At least no one he could see.

He staggered on. Another corner. A final crooked alley, and he slowed down. He was at the top of the hill, approaching his own street.

Angry voices shouted insults. He could hear glass breaking and a man giving orders. A mob of men and women pressed toward his house. Some were throwing stones. Others carried simple weapons, and others merely shouted. These were not guardsmen or soldiers. These were townspeople, pushing against the red of the emperor's fighting men.

Henry dug into the back of the crowd, worming his way forward. His house was surrounded by a double row of soldiers. Inside them, a wagon was being loaded. Dotty sat in the front, with her arms tied behind her back. Anastasia and Penelope sat beside her. Anastasia was yelling at the soldiers. Penelope was crying. Richard, with a swollen eye and a cut lip, sat perfectly upright. Isa and Una, both bound, were led from the house, lifted up, and shoved roughly in. A wave of anger rolled through the crowd, and they surged forward but broke against the pike fence of the soldiers.

Two more soldiers stepped out of the house, carrying a tied Henrietta between them. Twisting, she managed to pull a leg free and kicked one of the men in the chin. The crowd cheered while she got her footing and drove her head into the other man's stomach. Henry squeezed out from the front of the mob and tried to duck under a soldier's pike. He cracked Henry on the head, knocked him to his knees, and kicked him backward into the press of bodies.

"Leave her!" a big voice said, and two men in black stepped out of the crowd across from Henry. The frustrated soldiers picked Henrietta up, one clubbed her on the head with the butt of his sword, and they threw her limp body back into the house, pulling the front door closed.

While Henry watched, they ran to the wagon. Six other soldiers joined them, all huddling together, receiving orders from the men in black. Flame sprang up between them, and the eight men in red turned back to the house, carrying lit torches. Women screamed, and men pried cobbles up from the road and heaved them at the fence of redshirts, at the fire bearers. Three townspeople with short swords broke through the circle and were pushed back.

Henry looked at his sisters, both sitting straight and proud, both with their eyes on their home and tears on their cheeks. One of the men in black climbed onto the wagon. Henry didn't care where the other one had gone. Panic froze his limbs, his mind. His sisters, his aunt, and his cousins were being carted away.

Henrietta was being burned alive.

Flames licked out of every window, and still the soldiers held their circle. The planks of the old front door crackled.

Where was his grandmother?

The world went silent. From his knees, Henry saw the angry crowd surging against the pikes, but noiselessly. He saw cobbles bounce and flames lick and two soldiers stumble under blows and fall. He saw his sisters crying and Aunt Dotty writhing, now fighting her ropes, struggling to fall from the wagon, to go to her daughter through the fire. He saw the wind rise up above his burning house, and he saw blue sky crack between the clouds.

But he heard nothing. The blood and panic in him calmed. He knew what he needed to do. A man in black stepped in front of him. A big man, with a deep scar on each cheek.

Henry jumped to his feet and pushed backward into the crowd. The man shoved through the soldiers and came after him, but Henry was smaller and could move faster through the seams.

And he wasn't being pummeled by an angry mob. The man in black was like an earwig among ants. Stones and clubs and fists all found their marks, and Henry doubled back, back toward the line of soldiers but closer to the house. This time, no soldier's pike would stop him.

He pulled a stone from a woman's hand and slipped to the front. Breathing slowly, he gathered strength, his muscles overflowed, and the world changed in front of him. He changed it.

The stone hit the serpent on a soldier's chest, and an explosion of blades and tongues both gold and green drove him to the ground. The men on either side of him staggered and fell, and the line was broken. In shock, the crowd held back.

Henry stepped through a dense, rising cloud of dandelion down and rushed to the burning house. Flipping up the hood of his cloak, he slammed into the crackling door and tumbled through the flames.

At the foot of the stairs, Henrietta lay on her side. Grandmother Anastasia, on her knees, rocked and sang beside her, drowned out by the angry death of burning timbers.

The heat hit Henry like a solid force. He scrambled forward, feeling his body lose its moisture, his lungs filling with poisonous heat.

Was Henrietta dead? It didn't matter. Henry grabbed her under the arms and, holding his breath, began dragging her toward the stairs.

"Grandmother!" he yelled. "Upstairs! We have to get upstairs!"

But his grandmother still swayed with her pale eyes

open, her skin red, every thin white hair curling out from her head. "The puppet's strings," she said. "Cut the puppet's strings. Take his finger."

"What?" Henry yelled. He had Henrietta halfway onto the stairs. He dropped her and jumped over her body, down to his grandmother. "Come now!" he yelled, and he dragged her to her feet. "Upstairs! Upstairs!" He was shouting in her ear.

"The strings," she said.

And a black shape stepped through the burning doorway.

"No!" Henry yelled. "No!" He pushed his grandmother toward Henrietta, but before he could turn back around, thick arms wrapped around his waist and lifted him to a shoulder. He grabbed for his grandmother, he grabbed for the beamed ceiling, but he was moving away too quickly. Henrietta's body slumped on the stairs, where she would burn. His grandmother stood blind and helpless beside her.

"No!" Henry yelled again, and he pounded at the man's back. He tore at the man's hair, ripping his black knot loose, trying to reach back for his eyes. They were in the flaming doorway. He was almost outside. Henry rolled and hooked his left arm on the top of the door. Beside his elbow, sticking out from the wall with a blackened blade and smoking handle, there was a simple carving knife, the knife Henry had thrown at his christening. In a single motion, Henry ripped it free and plunged it into the big man's back. The man didn't flinch. His grip tightened, and he jerked Henry down and forward, but not quite loose.

"The strings!" Grandmother shouted. "Take his finger!"

Scrambling to free his legs, to brace his arms, Henry saw it. Nested in the oiled black hair where the knot had been, a single, pale finger twitched, as if in pain. There was no time to wonder, no time for confusion or revulsion. Henry unhooked his arm and grabbed the finger. Henry raised the blade, and flesh seared as he jerked the hot edge down through scalp, through the fusion of finger and skull. Together, he and the man burst into air and wind and sunlight and tumbled to the ground.

But the man was limp. Henry stood, and in the split second before he turned and lunged back into the smoke, he looked down into blinking, confused eyes set above scarred cheeks, and he saw the life leave, carried away with the ash of his father's house.

Inside, Grandmother had climbed over Henrietta and was straining at her arms. She was staring up and smiling.

Henry clambered over his cousin and pushed his grandmother up the flight. "The roof!" he shouted. Then, grabbing his cousin and trying to hold his breath, he dragged her quickly up to the second-story landing and around to the next flight of stairs. Passing his bedroom, the door rattled, and a bellow like a whole flock of angry geese echoed behind it.

Twisting the knob and shoving it open, Henry moved

on as quickly as he could. The raggant plowed into the hall with red, angry eyes. His nose and face were scratched and cut from breaking through a closet door, but his voice was louder than ever.

"Sorry," Henry said, backing into the next stairwell. "I'm sorry, I didn't want you getting in the way." Henry grunted his way up and up onto the top floor, licking sweat and ash off his lips as he pulled. The raggant followed Henrietta's feet with its wings flared, bleating and groaning in irritation.

"Last flight," Henry said. The door to the roof was open at the top, and he could already see the blackened sky. Willing his legs enough strength for another reverse climb, he pulled himself and his cousin up onto the rooftop. His grandmother stood waiting for him, wobbling on her feet with her face toward the clouds, ignoring the exertion, the smoke and flames, the roar of the crowd in the street.

Henry lowered Henrietta to her back. She groaned and then coughed, the sweetest sound Henry could remember hearing in a long time, but he couldn't wait and hope she'd come to. He looked at the stairs to the upper roof and knew that his legs were done. He couldn't get Henrietta up there.

Smoke surrounded the walls. The one patch of blue sky was gone. Raindrops, not nearly enough raindrops, were falling. Henry staggered up the narrow stairs to the shed. He kicked the boards free around the little cupboard, picked it up, and hurried back down.

"Another puppet comes," his grandmother said.

Henry's heart sank. He ran to the doorway, saw nothing but smoke, and slammed it shut. He had to be quick.

He shoved the cupboard into a corner beside Henrietta and knelt in front of it. The roof was hot beneath his knees. Vibrations shivered up into his bones as beams and timbers weakened in the floors below. How was he supposed to concentrate? He wasn't good at this by himself in a quiet attic, let alone now. He slapped his own face and stared at the little door. Nothing.

"Do it or die, Henry," he said aloud. "Do it or they die."

He could see. He could see the magic of the world, the living, changing words that made it all. Great towering souls of flame swung around him, battling with the cool breeze, chasing away the salty breath of the sea. Tangled anger and grief rose up from the unseen crowd and blended with their cries. In front of him, in all the madness, he could see the tiny swirling drain, a seam between two worlds held in place by a cupboard, by the small, twisting magic of wood and its grains.

He reached into the drain with both hands, with his mind, with his self, and he forced the swirl to grow, to push against the fire strength and smoke, to use it. He had to make the world-seam bigger than he ever had, big enough for three.

Henry's head throbbed. His mind felt crushed. He shut his eyes, and still he could see. He could see nothing but the hurricane of elements in front of him, a galaxy of smoke and dandelions and anger and stone widening a hole, a doorway into a battered old farmhouse and a world of grass.

His eyes were still closed, but his grandmother's strands came slowly into view. She swirled in front of him, between him and the doorway. Her threads were old and tired, like the roots of a tree grown on a cliff. They were slow and unafraid. Some were dead, gray and stiff. And then he could see it, a rift inside of her, a wound between her soul and her body, a split in the ancient tree that would never heal.

In a moment, all of her stepped into the eye of the storm, and she was gone.

Henry opened his stinging eyes, blinking, and looked at Henrietta. She was trying to sit up. He'd seen her before; he wasn't tempted to study her threads. They were all fast and bright and as curly as her hair. He jumped up and hooked his arms under hers, boosting her to her knees.

"Quick!" he said. "Crawl in the cupboard." She moved forward, but not enough. The hole was already shrinking. Henry dropped behind her and put his shoulder in her backside. She kicked him hard and crawled on her own.

She was gone.

Henry turned to the raggant. "Go," he said. But he knew it was hopeless. The animal would never go without him. It would only follow. Henry turned back to the cupboard. The seam he'd stretched was still larger than any he'd ever done, but much smaller than when his grandmother had walked through. He lunged for it but caught himself, hesitating.

The cupboard would burn behind him. He could still get back to Hylfing, going through Badon Hill and then through faerie mounds, but he didn't want to lose his own door. He looked around the roof, and his eyes found the cistern, hopefully full. The cupboard would have a better chance in there.

Behind him, the doorway swung open, and a column of smoke snaked above the roof. Henry exploded toward it before Coradin even stepped out with his blackened face and smoking hair.

Henry jumped and put both feet in the man's stomach, folding him over and sending him tumbling back down the narrow stairs. Henry landed on his side and felt a rib crack on the top step. His breath was gone. Gasping, he clambered back onto the roof, slamming the door behind him. Wincing in pain, coughing for air, he bent over to pick up the cupboard, but he'd forgotten the pull. It was sucking him in. Holding it in front of him, he staggered toward the cistern's red clay back set into the roof. Kicking the narrow lid open, he dropped to his knees, shoved the cupboard inside, and squeezed in headfirst behind it.

Warm water slid up his arms and splashed around his face. Black pressure crushed his head and slid down to his chest, down to his cracked rib. Henry screamed silently, and the pressure grew. It wasn't sliding down his body. He wasn't moving forward. He kicked his legs slowly, underwater, and his feet found the cistern wall. He could push.

But he didn't. He didn't do anything. His body went limp, and his mind left the pain behind. It left the darkness and walked into a sunlit garden.

Coradin stood in the center of the roof. His eyes stung. His skin was burned and blistered, and his hair was singed. His lungs were in raw agony. The roof cracked and shifted beneath him. Who was he? What was he doing? Why was he here? Memories jerked slowly into place. A family, his wife and sons, killed. He put his hand up to his notched ear— one for each master, two warlords and the king who'd freed him, whom he had loved. A bloody battlefield and the emperor's men. But where was he now?

He was in chains again, half-naked, struggling before the imperial throne. Red-shirts were dragging and pushing, pricking him with blades. Men and women, as brightly colored as jungle birds, chattered and laughed, pointing at his scars and tattoos. And then the cage, and the huge tusked tiger. He shut his eyes.

He'd killed the tiger. Chains again, and a garden at night. A woman. A beautiful, horrible woman.

The ritual.

He moved his hand slowly to the back of his head. The finger twitched when he touched it. He wanted to tear it off, to dig out the blood that rooted it to his skull. The roof cracked, and flames rose up beside him. He didn't care if he was consumed. But not with the finger still bound to him. He would rip it off and burn it first. Gripping it tight, he filled his lungs and opened his mouth to yell.

Coradin.

Peace flowed into him through the finger. He was content. He had a new master. His pain was gone—his lungs and eyes and skin, all soothed with something softer and sweeter than the hearts of desert plants. His arms dropped to his sides, and his eyes focused on something beyond the smoke and the flames. His ears ignored the crackling. They could hear only the voice inside him.

Coradin.

"Mother."

Do you resist my love?

"No."

Where is the boy?

Coradin flared his nostrils and inhaled, ignoring the flames, the smoke, the slowly collapsing roof.

"He is gone."

Find him.

The raggant stuck his nose out of the cistern and watched the stranger. Inasmuch as a raggant can hate, it hated the man. It hated him because to its senses, the man was as much the witch as he was himself. And the witch was as much faraway as she was near. And both of those things were very, very wrong and must be stopped. Short legs scrambled against the cistern sides and clawed uselessly through the hot water. Something inside the raggant needed to bite and horn-search the near-far-witch-man for fragile bones and soft spots until he had stopped being anything at all.

But the man turned away and walked slowly through the smoke until he reached the wall at the back of the house. He threw one leg over it and jumped, without hesitating, through the smoke.

Pulling its head back down into the cistern, the raggant focused on the bigger problem. The cupboard was cock-eyed at the bottom of three feet of water. Bobbing and wing-paddling and chuffing in irritation, the raggant spun in circles, unable to sink.

CHAPTER SIX

The wagon bounced and rocked through the streets, surrounded by a thick hedge of soldiers. The trailing crowd grew as they went, pressing after the wagon and its guards, jostling, shouting, clogging narrow streets, flooding the bridge where Darius had fallen.

Anastasia didn't cry. She couldn't. She was in complete shock. And Penelope was crying enough for both of them.

Henrietta couldn't be dead. She couldn't. It just wasn't possible. And Grandmother. And Henry.

The soldiers had stayed at the house, guarding the wagon, holding back the crowd, until flames licked the walls out of every window on every story and had sent up spiked tongues above the roof. The soldiers had stayed until a rescue had been impossible.

A raindrop ran down Anastasia's forehead and found the corner of her eye. The angry faces in the crowd had become a single unit, a weather system of people. And they stayed back now. When five soldiers had been dragged to the ground and clubbed, the rest had fired crossbows into the front of the crowd and then pushed the press back with bladed pikes. Behind the froth and din of the mob, Anastasia could still see a trail of wounded being tended and five bodies in red shirts. Closer to fifteen townspeople lay in the street, covered by cloaks.

They were nearing the harbor now, and the gate that would lead to ships that would lead to somewhere unknown—a life or a death.

Without Henrietta. Without Henry or her grandmother.

She was cold, numb inside and out, and she couldn't shut her dry eyes. She couldn't stop staring past the shouting and the perpetual skirmish behind their parade, past the smoke and the clouds and the sky. She couldn't stop staring at nothing.

"Anas," Una said.

Anastasia looked at her cousin, at both of her cousins, sitting up straight and strong, swaying with the motion of the wagon. Richard was doing his best imitation of bravery beside them, but his nightshirt worked against him.

"They aren't dead," Una said. "They aren't." She shook her head.

"Who?" Anastasia asked.

"Hetti and Grandmother," her cousin said. "Henry got them. I'm sure he did."

Hetti. Una shortened everything. Always. And Henrietta liked the name. She'd never liked any of Anastasia's choices.

Anastasia looked away, blinking. Why couldn't she cry? She looked down at the soldiers walking tight against the low wagon walls, at the two sitting on the end. She felt lost. Confused. She looked at her mother, frozen, silent, with her head down on Penny's and her eyes clamped shut. She wished that Penny would sit up and tell her what to think and what to say and what would happen. She could argue with Penny. She couldn't argue with Una.

She looked up at the pillar of smoke, towering on the hill behind them. "They didn't come back out," she said. She couldn't believe that Henry had saved anyone. She couldn't believe that he hadn't.

Irritation burbled up inside her. She wished she had a knife or a baseball bat. She'd swing at these red soldiers till her arms fell off.

"Hey," she said to the nearest one, and she leaned over the side. "You're in trouble. My uncles are going to be mad, and when they're mad, they're like . . ." She faded out. Her heart wasn't in it. Her heart wasn't in anything. She sat back up. "You're just in trouble," she said quietly.

The man sneered at her.

"And your teeth look like dead corn," she added. "I bet your mom doesn't even like you."

The wagon stopped. They'd reached the harbor gate.

"We'll gut your mum," the soldier said. With her arms tied, Anastasia spun on her bench seat and threw a leg over the side to kick the man. But she couldn't reach, and something else was happening. Something loud.

Crouching on a stable roof, Fat Frank watched the wagon crawl. He could see the four girls and Dotty, and he could see the scrawny big-lipped boy, but no Henry and no Henrietta.

He pulled his earlobes. That was either really good or right awful. He'd run into the soldiers and the mob on his dash back to the house, and that had changed his plans. The smoke crawling off the hilltop told him what he needed to know—Franklin Fat had failed Mordecai. Not as a servant or a loyal subject or an ally or a bonded faerie. He'd failed him as a friend.

He'd still been sneaking through halls and listening at doors when Hyacinth, Frank, Monmouth, and James had been carted off. The city guard had quickly been splintered apart by the red phalanx, and the fat faerie hadn't had much chance to do anything more than knock down the occasional soldier.

This time would be different. He ground his teeth slowly. With just fifty faeren, just a dozen, this all could have been different.

"You reach the wagon or you die right here, Franklin," he muttered. "What's there to lose? If you can't cut through those soldiers, you're not worth your own fingernails. Might as well be sold for glue."

The wagon grew closer. It would pass through the road beneath him on its way through the gate. The soldiers were pushing the pace as much as they could in the narrow streets, forcing their way through the mob. They were smelling safety—the city gate and their galleys.

Frank crept closer to the edge. He wouldn't bother with being invisible. That strength could be better used, and he needed the girls to spot him.

Soldiers in red lined the open gate, the stairs, and the broad dock that led to the longboats.

With a yell, men in brown and gray, carrying bows and swords and axes, poured out of side streets and clambered onto the wall. The red-shirted soldiers of the empire were thrown down from the walls into the crowd, or flipped over the battlements. Archers poured a volley down into the formations of red and received crossbow bolts in return.

The wagon stopped. Fat Frank jumped.

Wood splintered, and the wagon rocked. The soldiers at the tail slipped off, and the faerie bowled into Richard, flipping him into the street. Frank jumped to his feet and spun in place.

Pikes lunged at him from three sides, but the round faerie bobbed and twisted and wove his way easily between the blades. He grabbed an overextended shaft, ripped it away from its owner, and spun it above his head.

The weapon, more than twice his height, was well balanced, and the double blades at the end pleased him. He jumped and lunged and swung the pike like a windmill, clearing soldiers back from the wagon on all sides. Una flung a leg over the edge, rolled herself up, and dropped into the street. Anastasia quickly did the same.

Frank didn't notice. Sweat dripped from his face. Strength bubbled inside him.

"There once was a man named Red!" he shouted, and sent three soldiers sprawling, "Who was terribly proud of his head!" He caught another in the face with the butt of the pike. "Poor Red loved a brawlin', then I came a callin'." He knocked away a thrust. "And now an old stone marks his bed."

The wagon began to move. Frank turned. The soldiers had regained the city gate.

"Up now!" he yelled. "Off the back!" Dotty and Isa and Penelope all tried to stand. Fat Frank dropped his pike and grabbed at their hands. A crossbow bolt sliced across his thigh. He fell backward, and a pike blow knocked him out of the wagon onto the street. Before he landed, he caught his breath, blocked his pain, and focused his strength. Wincing and invisible, he was kicked and stomped by the now-rushing soldiers and the pursuing crowd, until he managed to roll to the side of the street. And when he sat up and looked, panting, the wagon was gone, and the dock and gate were solid with soldiers. He flopped onto his back and put his hands over his eyes.

"Franklin Fat Nothin'," he said, and he began to cry.

"Frank! Fat Frank!" Anastasia dropped to her knees beside the faerie. "Are you okay?"

Frank looked at her. He looked at Una, being untied by a guard, and Richard, holding a rag to his bloody nose. He looked up at the smoke in the sky.

"What are we going to do?" Anastasia asked. "Where are they taking them?"

He lay back down and covered his eyes.

* * *

The cat stood over Henry, looking down into his face.

Where have you gone? Do you have more doorways, even in Hylfing?

Henry shut his eyes. "I'm dead."

The cat, black with a white face, cocked its head and laughed. *No. You are not dead.* It licked him. *You would taste differently.* It licked his jaw, scraping its rough tongue around the scar. *I would have tasted all of you.*

The cat sat up on Henry's chest. *You cannot hide. Not with my blood in your flesh. It draws me. I could smell it through all the worlds.*

"Go!" Henry said. He swung at the cat, but his arms were slow and useless.

You killed a fingerling, one of your blood brothers. The ten are now nine. You shall make up the number. A finger for the pauper son, but it cannot be hidden away in your hair. It will root in your jaw.

Something scratched against Henry's face. He could feel it digging into his bone.

"No!" he yelled, and he slapped at it. No. Where was it? He would rip it out. He would tear the skin down to his jaw.

Two soft hands touched his face. The cat was gone. His grandmother smiled at him and pinched his nose.

"Was that real?" he asked. "Can the witch talk to me in my dreams?"

His grandmother shrugged, and then she beckoned for him to sit up.

*   *   *

Henry stretched and yawned.

"Henry? Are you awake?"

He opened his eyes and sat up. His clothes were wet, and he was in the old Kansas farmhouse, on the bed in his grandfather's room. The windows on either side were smashed, and sunlight poured through. The curtains were on the floor, and the bedding beneath him was filthy. Beside him, warm and wide, his grandmother was snoring beneath Henry's oilskin cloak.

Henrietta scooted a chair closer to the bed. Her face was smeared with soot. "You've been out for a while. A few hours, probably. I don't have a watch. You only just started yelling."

Henry scratched his jaw. His skin felt greasy. "I can't believe I made it through."

Henrietta smiled. "Well, you didn't actually. I pulled you."

"Thanks," Henry said. He needed to try to stand. He winced in anticipation of the pain in his joints and slid his feet to the floor. They were bare, and the glass and grit stuck to them. Glancing down, to avoid slicing himself, he froze.

"My toenails are all purple."

Henrietta nodded.

Henry pulled up his damp pant legs. Pale green splotches circled around his ankles. Putting all his weight on them, he pushed off the bed and stood, breathing a sigh of relief. "They look nasty, but they don't feel that bad."

"You should have seen your face."

Henry looked up at his cousin. She pulled at her own greasy hair, grimaced, and tucked it behind her ears. "Your nose was bleeding like crazy."

"It always bleeds."

"Do your eyes?" Henrietta asked. "And your ears? And your, uh—" She tapped her jaw. "All gushing."

Henry put his hands to his ears.

"Oh, I got most of it off," Henrietta said. "Lucky me. I would have left it, but it was pretty gross just sitting here watching it scab. Grandmother was no help. She went to sleep right when you did."

Henry moved tentatively toward the door. "How'd you get me downstairs?"

"How do you think?" Henrietta laughed. "I dragged you. Your little bed in the attic was all drenched—you came gushing through with ten thousand gallons of water. Plus I couldn't stand being by all those doors." She shivered. "Not right now."

"Did Rags come through?" Henry looked around to see if he'd missed a sleeping raggant.

Henrietta shook her head. "No, but I'm sure he's fine. He has wings."

Henry felt a knot growing in his stomach. The stubborn animal would have followed if he was fine. He was small enough to fit through the cupboard without any of Henry's swirlings. "Maybe he's just mad at me for shutting him in the closet."

"He'll show up sometime," Henrietta said, and she smiled. "He likes to let people know when he's mad."

Grandmother slowly rolled toward her side of the bed and sat up. Henry hurry-hobbled over to her. Her face was red where it wasn't soot-stained, and her already white hair had been singed off in places. She found Henry's face with her hands and pulled it down to hers.

"Here, I speak," she said slowly. Then she tapped his temple. "There, I see." She pinched his cheek, kissed his forehead, and let him go. "You must begin. You must hurry into the darkness and the three-mace trees."

"We need to go back," Henrietta said. "As soon as Henry's strong enough." She moved around the bed and sat beside her grandmother. "They took everyone," she said quietly. "They took them to those ships."

"Supper first, before the race," Grandmother said. "Food for the dark paths."

Henry and Henrietta looked at each other. Henrietta shrugged.

"Where are my shoes?" Henry asked. "I'm starving, too."

Henry and Henrietta led their grandmother between them. Through every gaping window, they could see green seas of grass stretching to the horizon. Henry wondered what season it was, or if this place had seasons. The grass was as green as when he'd first seen it, and the sweet-smelling air never seemed to age. Curtains ruffled in a breeze that was neither hot nor cold. In the dining room, dust tumbled slowly into clumps on the table, leaving little tracks behind them.

Henry couldn't help but think of tumbleweed. He couldn't help but think of Kansas.

"What time will it be?" Henrietta asked suddenly.

"I don't know," Henry said. "I tried to keep track of the differences, at least for a while, but it got really complicated. I even tried keeping a Kansas watch. But it's not like time zones at all. Sometimes it's hours ahead and sometimes it's hours behind, but the difference is never too crazy. One day to me is never two to Zeke, or anything like that."

Grandmother walked with her face pointed up, like she was smelling her way. In the kitchen, she began humming.

"Okay," Henry said when they reached the back door. An old baseball bat lay on the floor to be used as a doorstop. "Here we go." He put his hand on the knob and pulled the door open.

The two girls giggled. After all, they were being very, very grown-up. They'd even snuck out of their bedroom windows in the middle of the night, and if that wasn't grown-up, then nothing was. They were shivering now, nearly frozen in the tall grass. But that didn't matter. The two boys, one small and scrawny, one tall, freckled, and fleshy, sat with their legs crossed, facing them. They looked very serious in the moonlight, very important. Very sixth grade. Especially the bigger one. He was a new arrival in town, fresh from Wichita and an expert on cities. Rumor was, he'd been shaving for two years.

"Aren't you afraid of this place?" one of the girls asked.

"The whole family and the whole house just gone? People say it was aliens."

"I ain't afraid of nothin," the freckled boy said.

"Nothin," added the smaller boy.

"Not even aliens?" the girl asked.

"Aliens ain't nothin." Freckles pulled a cigarette out from behind his ear and offered it to the girls. "Smoke?"

They both shook their heads. "Those aren't good for you," one of them said, and she scratched her nose. The other nodded.

"Yeah?" Freckles asked. "What's gonna happen?"

The girls looked at each other, shivering in the cold. "Uh, you could die?"

"Death ain't nothin," said Freckles.

"Nothin," said the sidekick.

Suddenly, a doorway opened in the sky. Blinding light poured out of it; it poured around a shape.

The girls screamed and ran, tripping through the darkness, faster than they had ever run before. Sidekick fell onto his back, gurgled terror, righted himself, and disappeared into the fields. Freckles tried to stand, but slipped. He tried to run, but caught his toe on a dandelion clump, grabbed police tape, and tumbled down into the muddy hole. The alien hole. The hole where, if you get too close, you get sucked off to Pluto.

Quaking, squeezing his eyes tight, waiting for the light to pulse him into the stars, Freckles wet himself.

*　　*　　*

"Are they gone?" Henrietta asked. Then she laughed. "Those poor girls. I'd scream, too."

"Come on," Henry said, and he stepped into Kansas, into the cold breath of an autumn night.

The streets were quiet in Henry, and they moved through them as quickly as they could. The houses were all dark, all but one, where the blue flicking light of a television lit up the curtains.

Grandmother began humming again, softly, humming with the night air and the crisp breeze. The moon was full and bright, making the already infrequent streetlights useless, and it lit up Grandmother's hair like snow. She seemed to see the moon somehow. Despite her blindness, she seemed to sense the light and love it. Henry smiled. It was strange to think that this was the first time his grandmother, blind or not, had met this moon. She was becoming acquainted, making herself a new friend.

"Right here," Henry said, and he and his cousin turned their grandmother and helped her up the cracked curb. The three of them made their way up the broken walk toward the sleeping green house. Henry unlatched the screen door, and its hinges squealed at him. He made a fist to knock, but Henrietta reached out and pushed the glowing orange button by the door. After a moment, she pushed it again. A light flicked on inside.

The door opened a crack, and Zeke's mom peeked out. Her eyes widened, and she threw open the door. She was wearing an oversize tropical blue bathrobe.

"Henry? Henrietta?" She tightened her robe. "What happened to you? What's going on?" She pushed straying blond hair out of her face.

"I'm sorry, Mrs. Johnson," Henry said. "I don't know what time it is. We've had some trouble."

"Come in, come in." She took Grandmother's hands and led her into the house. The living room had wood paneling and thick brown carpet. A plaid couch guarded one wall, and two balding, mint-colored recliners faced a television.

"Mrs. Johnson," Grandmother said, tasting the name.

"Oh, don't call me that. Call me Tilly." Tilly Johnson lowered Grandmother into a recliner. "Antilly Johnson. My parents honeymooned in the Antilles, and apparently I was, well . . . They called me Ann."

Grandmother shut her eyes and put her hand on Tilly's face. "I've seen you," she said. "Laughing. My son showed me in his dream. Wheat hair, sky eyes."

Mrs. Antilly Johnson blushed. Grandmother dropped her hand and rocked slowly in her mint chair. "Ooh," she said. "This I love."

"The handle's on the side," Tilly said.

"Handle?" Grandmother found the lever, pulled it, and yelped as the foot rest swung up and the back dropped. "Ooh," she said again. "Ooh." And she shut her eyes.

"Henry?" Zeke stepped into the living room, pulling on a shirt. "It's two in the morning." He squinted at the visitors. "What happened to you?'

Henry looked at Henrietta's soot-polished face and her

flat, grease-covered curls, her burned and ripped clothes. Where should he start? James with his summons from the emperor? His father and Caleb leaving again? The fire? Fingerlings? His mother and sisters and brother, everyone gone?

"Well," he said. "Well . . ." The reality of it all suddenly collapsed on him. He'd been holding it off, refusing to comprehend. His legs felt weak, and a pressure built up in his chest. He dropped into the other recliner and covered his face with his hands. He couldn't let himself throw up or cry. Not in front of Zeke. Not in front of Henrietta. What was he doing back in Kansas? What was he supposed to do? Where would the ships take his family?

Without opening her eyes, his grandmother reached over and squeezed his arm.

"Peace," she said. "Peace. For now."

Henry looked back at Zeke and his mother. "My dad's house got torched."

"Soldiers did it," Henrietta said. "Henry got us through the cupboard in time."

Mrs. Johnson put her arms around Zeke. "The rest of the family?"

"My dad and Uncle Caleb were gone," Henry said. "The rest got taken by soldiers."

"Oh, kids." Henry felt a hand on his head. "What are you going to do?"

"If we could eat something," Henrietta said. "And maybe take showers? That would help."

"Of course. I can make eggs? There's some lasagna I

could microwave." Mrs. Johnson hurried into the kitchen and opened the fridge. "Cereal?"

Zeke dropped onto the couch and looked at Henry. "Soldiers?" he asked.

Henry sat up. "Not just soldiers."

"Her?"

Henry shook his head. "But people from her." He clenched and unclenched his hand, remembering the finger he had gripped and severed from a skull. He opened his mouth to explain and then shivered. He didn't understand it all himself.

"Cereal, Henry?" Mrs. Johnson held up a box. Henrietta was already shoveling down a bowl.

"Please," Henry said, and he levered himself out of his chair. His grandmother, as charred as Henrietta, snored beside him. Henry pulled a Technicolor afghan off the back of the couch and spread it over her. Already, he knew what he had to do, and his whole body felt clammy. Licking his lips, he wiped cool sweat off his forehead. Then he walked into the kitchen.

Strength. He needed strength for the dark paths.

And maybe something he could throw up.

"Henry?" Henrietta set down her spoon. "What? What is it? You look like you're going to pass out."

Henry sat down and poked a round, whole-grain, honey-flavored island below the white surface. He missed cereal. He missed this kind of milk. Thinner. Colder. Consistent.

"I'm going to Endor," he said quietly.

Henrietta laughed. "How? Why? Do you even know where it is?"

Henry looked up into Henrietta's eyes and watched her smile disappear.

"I have a door," he said. "You remember."

CHAPTER SEVEN

In the shower, Henry's eyes went black watching the water stream and steam from the nozzle. So he shut them, slumped down into the tub, and let the hot, pressurized rain soothe his body and rinse his filth away. It couldn't soothe his mind.

He needed to find his father and Caleb. There was nothing Henry could do about the ships and the soldiers, and he didn't want to face any more fingerlings by himself. But his father had gone to Endor, looking for the witch. Could the faeren help? Where was Fat Frank? Where was the witch? Maybe faeries knew how to kill her. He didn't think so. Was his mother okay? Where had his family been taken? Not to Endor. To the emperor? Who was the emperor, and why would he do this to Mordecai's family? Where were the ships sailing?

To a garden. A garden where fingerlings grew and a man hung between two trees. He could see it. He didn't want to, but he did. Henry's tired mind staggered and slipped into dreaming, while his tired body slept, huddled up in a Kansas shower, water pouring down his head, his eyelashes and cheeks, pooling in his open mouth, dribbling down his chin.

*   *   *

A pale, blond man held up his hands. One finger turned to ash and faded. The rest blackened and grew, swaying and slithering like snakes. They wrapped around the man, and he was no more. They grew further, and Henry stood in the sky, watching the fingers coil around a great city like dark snakes of fog until the city had disappeared.

Someone took Henry's hand. The city and the blackness were gone. His grandmother was beside him now. The two of them stood on a hill overlooking another city, a towering, sprawling city, a gray city, a ruin, a graveyard where huge houses marked each tomb, where palaces with black stone windows loomed over streets paved with ash. There was no life around the place, outside the walls or in the hills. Inside the walls, behind sealed doors and windows, deep in the ground, entombed in lifeless rock, were the lives without end—the undying breed of Nimroth.

Endor.

Henry looked at his grandmother. She was younger in her dreams. Her eyes were focused and sharp. Her white hair was thick and pulled back into a braid.

"This is where my dad is?" Henry asked. "Can't you just find his dreams and tell him what happened, tell him to go home now?"

Grandmother pursed her lips, and her eyes were sad. She shook her head slowly and then tapped her temple with a weathered finger. She reached over and tapped Henry's temple.

"My dreams," said Henry, and he sighed. "My dreams. I

know. My dad told me. You attached yourself to his dreams to keep him company, but now you're attached to mine." He looked back down at the ashen ruin. "I really have to go, don't I? But what if *I* found my dad's dreams? Could I do it? Could I find them?"

A cat appeared on the hill beside them, a black cat with a white face.

"No," Henry said, and thrust it out of his mind. The cat was gone. He stared into his grandmother's seeing eyes. "Could I?"

Grandmother looked from Henry to where the cat had been. She shrugged and cocked her head.

"Okay," Henry said, facing the city. "I don't want this." He waved his hand at it and shut his dream eyes. "I want to see my father. Take me to my father." That was wrong. There wasn't any dream magic to take him anywhere. There wasn't a guide. He had to find his own way.

He thought of his father. He thought of the way he smelled of leather and forests and the cliffs by the sea. He thought of his laugh and the deep blackness in his eyes. He thought of the awkward wonderful moment when his unknown father had first kissed him on the head, and the scratching of his jaw.

He opened his eyes, and he knew that he was not in his father's dream. He was in a different kind. His father was in it.

Henry stood on the side of a street. He had no body. He was part of a wall. Five men and five horses lay motionless, with limbs splayed in the dust. Ash drifted in the air above them. From a gaping doorway stepped eight men in black, with their hair in oiled knots. Between them they carried a glossy gray stone box, open and empty, the color of death, the length of a man. Black symbols had been inlaid along its sides, symbols that made Henry feel a sickness creeping over him, a cold sucking pulling at his strength. Into the end a black skull had been set, and black vines twisted out of its mouth and eyes and nose—the skull of a green man.

The box was lowered into the street, and dust swirled slowly away from it. The eight fingerlings picked up a man, and as they lowered him into the box, Henry saw his face.

Henry had no mouth to yell, no body to use in a fight. And then he did. He stepped out of the wall, ready to kill, ready to be killed.

The fingerlings looked at him, and the world went black.

Pauper son, a soft voice said. *You would enter my dreams? You would brush your sour mortal soul against my immortal essence?*

Henry saw nothing. He sensed nothing but the voice. And then he was in pain.

I had thought to save you for last, the voice said. *To wait until your father was ash in my hands, but you die now, pauper son, dream-walker, pup to mongrels. You die now.*

Henry struggled, but he had no arms to flail. A flash of gold spun in front of him, a living word, a defiant war cry, a weed. It twisted with green.

I can see, Henry thought. And then he heard, not the witch's voice, not her anger or her deathly bitterness, he heard the dandelion's burning song—a song of life, of laughter and death and life again, of wind and rain and sun, of ash and birth, of triumph and tragedy and victory in every defeat. He watched and he heard and he ached, not with a physical pain but with desire, with a yearning for everything the dandelion was, for everything it promised. Henry and the witch together watched the fire that guarded his soul, the place where a weed had taken root. Thick gray threads, arms, serpentine beams wrapped around the dandelion fire; they wrapped and contracted and smothered the burning weed song.

While Henry watched, the dandelion died. The green went gray and joined the strands. The golden fire slowed and stopped and drifted away in ash.

Grief, overwhelming loss, surged ice-cold over Henry as he watched the ash settle onto the witch's gray rot. But then, while he watched, each spot greened where it landed. One hundred plants spun themselves leaves and burst into fiery bloom.

Henry laughed, and the great, grinding death fought the noise and the heat and the life. A flower had become a choir, a flame had become a blaze. As more were killed, more bloomed, and suddenly, the gray serpents were gone. Henry, bodiless Henry, watched a single, slowly twisting flower say its name, and that name was a poem, and that poem was the history of the world—of all the worlds.

The dream was his again.

"Nimiane," Henry said. Could the witch hear his mind's

words? Had she gone? The words of his christening, spoken by his grandmother, flooded back to him. "I shall be your curse."

A queen, a witch, rose from her bed between the trees and gathered up a cat in her arms. She was feeling something new. Was this fear? No. This was . . . urgency. The boy could not be allowed to grow.

She walked into an oval clearing and passed through it. She walked beside a black pool and its fountain. It was time to begin bigger things. The fingerlings would bring her Mordecai, or he would bring himself, pursuing the bait of his family. The witch smiled. She looked forward to meeting his wife.

There was no more reason to hide since the galleys had fallen on Hylfing. She had shown herself, and she was ready. She had made her fingerlings, and armies and fleets waited on her. She stood behind the throne of the empire.

Old enemies would die. A new world would bow.

"I just think there has to be a better way," Henrietta said. Three backpacks sat on the kitchen table.

Only one looked even slightly new.

Zeke handed her a red plastic flashlight, now with fresh batteries. "Maybe," he said. "But it's not like Henry would want to go if he could think of anything else."

Mrs. Johnson was making a loaf of peanut butter and jelly sandwiches. "How bad is this place?" she asked.

"Bad," said Henrietta. "Super creep."

Zeke turned around and faced his mom. "But Henry's dad and Caleb are there. And they don't know what happened."

Tilly Johnson bit her lip. She didn't like seeing knives and a hatchet going into backpacks, especially not when she wasn't sure how they'd be used. "You all at least need to get some sleep first," she said.

Henrietta pulled her wet hair back tight and rubber-banded it into a ponytail. "Maybe," she said. "See if you can talk Henry into it."

"Henry," Grandmother said. She kicked the afghan to the floor, but she was still asleep. "Henry? She has him. Henry?"

Tilly hurried to the chair, grabbed Grandmother's hand, and felt her forehead.

Henrietta ran to the bathroom.

"Henry?" She banged on the door. "Henry!" She tried the knob, but it was locked.

Zeke swiped a straightened paper clip off the top of the door jam and stuck it in the small hole centered in the knob. With a pop, the door was unlocked, and Henrietta threw it open.

The bathroom was cool, despite the shower. The mirror over the sink was perfectly clear, no steam.

"Henry?" Henrietta asked, and she rattled the shower curtain. "Henry!"

She pulled the curtain back.

Henry was curled up with his knees to his chest. His

eyes were shut, and his mouth was frozen open. His skin was the color of paper. A thick black liquid, unaffected by the water, had oozed out of the center of the burn on his jaw.

Henrietta dropped to her knees and grabbed her cousin's arm. The water was frigid. Henry's right arm flopped limply over the side of the tub, and his hand opened. A fat wad of wet dandelion down fell out onto the floor. The same fuzz had mounded up around the drain.

"C'mon, Henry," she said. She slapped his hand; she slapped his cheek. She stuck two fingers on his neck, but she wasn't patient enough to feel around for a pulse. "Wake up!" she yelled. "Wake up!" She reached out and tried to wipe the black goop off Henry's jaw.

He jerked and knocked her hand away.

Blinking in the cold water, he looked from Henrietta to Zeke. Mrs. Johnson stepped into the bathroom behind them.

Henry snatched at the curtain and threw it closed. "What are you doing? What?"

Shivering, he managed to slide forward and turn off the water. Then he slipped to his feet, wincing. His ankles were tender.

"Um," Henrietta said. "Well, you looked dead."

Henry's irritation warmed him slightly. His embarrassment warmed him more. "How'd you know how I looked?" he asked, shivering. "Until you looked? Would someone hand me a towel, or I might really die."

Henrietta sniffed and shoved one in. "Grandmother

started yelling for you in her sleep, Henry. She sounded scared. I knocked, I yelled, I even shook the shower curtain first."

Henry didn't say anything. The bathroom door shut, and he was left in cold silence. The towel was rough and felt even rougher against his goose bumps. He cinched it tight around his waist and threw back the dripping plastic curtain.

Facing himself in a wide mirror, Henry stepped out of the tub and moved closer.

He couldn't take his eyes off his own face. He looked tired and thinner. Dark circles framed his eyes, and his cheeks had sunk. How could this much change in two days? Slick his hair back and notch his ear . . .

"I look like Coradin," Henry whispered, and he turned his head to check his jaw.

The gray scar had grown. At the very first, it had been a pock the size of his pinkie tip, a burn from a drop of the witch's blood, and much smaller pocks around it where the blood had spattered. Now there was just one scar, more than an inch across, and blood had leaked out of the center.

Henry licked his lips and swallowed back the beginnings of panic. He'd find his father, and they'd find the rest of the family, and his father would find the witch, and someone would find a way to kill her. The witch had to die. Somehow. What he had seen in the witch's dream wasn't real. It couldn't be. Not yet. It was what she wanted to be real. Had she sent the fingerlings into Endor? Henry picked at the blood spot on his jaw. It was awfully black. He got a fingernail underneath it and tried to break it off. It was rubbery and wouldn't break. He pinched it between his fingers and pulled.

Gasping, trying to catch his breath, Henry watched the thing lengthen, stretching, pulling more out from his jaw, sloppy and wet after the dry tip, the texture of an earthworm.

Three inches of it fell away from his face and dangled between his fingers, dead and black. He dropped it in the toilet, flushed, and turned his back quickly, again facing the mirror. A single drop of blood perched in the center of his scar. Red blood. Normal red blood. He controlled his breathing, slowly, steadily.

He didn't really want to know, but he had to check. Leaning toward the mirror, Henry let himself see, and looking at his burn, he saw it twice.

The gray, slow-spinning strands were there, ghostly, twisting away from his face. But they were no longer spiderwebs. They were the thickness of yarn.

Henry shook his head, rubbed his eyes, and turned away from the mirror.

He dressed quickly in the clothes Zeke was loaning him—an old, worn pair of jeans, striped tube socks, a Boy Scout T-shirt, and a plain black hoodie. Then he picked up the necklace his father had given him, slipped it over his head, and tucked it under his shirts. The metal was cool against his already-chilled skin. He stepped out of the bathroom and moved down the narrow hall.

In the living room, Mrs. Johnson took Henry by the shoulders and looked him in the eyes. Henry stared back into hers. She smelled like peanut butter.

"Henry York Maccabee," she said. "You all need a rest before you go and do something this crazy. Now I'm not trying to put my foot down and keep you from going. But look at you, look at the day you been through. Rest your bones for a bit." She let him go, straightened up, and crossed her arms.

Henry shook his head. "I slept a bit just now. And I slept back in the old house."

"You were unconscious," Henrietta said. "Not sleeping. You'd been crushed in the cupboard. You look horrible."

"So do you," Henry said. Henrietta rolled her eyes.

"We don't have enough batteries for the flashlights," Zeke said. "The bait shop opens in a couple hours. Rest now, then we'll pick up stuff and go."

Henry looked around the room. Exhaustion rolled over him. His bones didn't want to hold him anymore.

He nodded and walked to the other mint recliner. It felt bigger than his bed. Without opening her eyes, his grandmother reached over and felt his face.

"No dreams," he said quietly. "No dreams."

Frank Fat-Once-a-Faerie stood in the street and wiped a sooty arm across his forehead. The sun was down, but the clouds had cleared, and a sliver moon was climbing. Richard was breathing heavily beside him with his hands on his hips. He was wearing pants now and oversize boots—a gift from one of the neighbors.

Una and Anastasia were picking carefully through the rubble, along with a dozen or more of the townspeople carrying lanterns. Three of the house's exterior walls still stood.

Fat Frank had heard the story, a muddled version first from Anastasia, clarity from Una, and then again from several who had been in the crowd.

"Would you like to hear how it happened?" Richard asked.

Frank snorted. "I have heard, and no, I don't like." He rolled the kitchen knife over in his hands. The knife that had been thrown at the christening, the knife that had gotten him unfaeried. He tucked it into his cloak. He'd found the finger, too, but after matching it to the bald spot on the big corpse, he'd thrown it to a crow. Now the crow was probably dead.

There had been no bodies in the rubble. No Grandmother, no Henry, no Henrietta. No second large man in black.

Anastasia and Una picked their way back toward Fat Frank. Una moved carefully, with her hair pulled back and her face down, scanning each shadow and gap. Anastasia scrambled, tripping. She held something up.

"Raggant feather," she said. "But no raggant."

Una looked up. "Henry's alive," she said, and she smiled broadly. "And if *he* is . . ."

"How's that?" Frank asked. "The stars up and tell you?"

"Henry is capable of a great deal," Richard said.

Fat Frank spun and looked up into Richard's narrow face. "So I know, and so I've seen. But he's no fire salamander, nor a phoenix, not at my last inspection."

"It's my mother's trees," Una said. "In the courtyard. They're all alive, even Henry's sapling."

"It has some dead leaves," Anastasia said. "They're ashy, but the tree's alive."

Fat Frank puffed out his cheeks.

"When my older brothers died, that's how my mother knew. Their trees died in her courtyard." She reached out, poked Frank's cheek, and grinned. "So smile, Fat Faerie. Henry's alive."

Anastasia tucked the raggant feather in her hair and laughed.

Frank scowled and rubbed his nose. "I'll come back in the day's light."

"Do you want them to be dead?" Anastasia asked. "They aren't, so stop grouching."

"Dark truth shines brighter than lying hope," the faerie said. "And that's the dark truth."

"Franklin, formerly Faerie?"

The four of them turned. Another faerie, taller and fatter than Frank, stood in the center of the street. He was bald and had a purple patch over his left eye and a thick black mustache, waxed at the ends. He nodded at the burned-out house and moved closer.

"That your work?"

Frank said nothing.

"Franklin, formerly Faerie, now waning, sometimes known as 'Fat'?"

Frank nodded.

The fatter faerie pulled his mustache, then put his arms behind his back. "Franklin Waning Faerie, formerly of the Island Hill of Badon Chapter, who knowingly rebelled against the policies of District R.R.K., trampled upon the letter and spirit of the *Book of Faeren*—all rise—and disregarded the ruling of the queene's—may her eyes never squint—duly appointed committee? Franklin 'Fat' formerly Faerie, who is to be considered a danger to all parliamental faeren and a consorter with villains, who has been cast out from the mounds and severed from the source of his soul, the faeren peoples, and the protection of the queene?" He stopped, looked Frank up and down, and blinked his one eye.

"Aye," Frank snorted. "Keep talking if you fancy a brawl."

"I have a package for you." The faerie dropped a small wooden box into Frank's hands, took ten steps backward, and pulled at his mustache. "A response is required," he said, and turning on his heel, he walked proudly down the center of the street. He pointed up. "By moon's noon!" he yelled, and disappeared into the shadows.

CHAPTER EIGHT

Frank Willis shifted his weight in the darkness and leaned forward, trying to ease the pressure of the shackles on his wrists behind his back. And trying to breathe through his mouth. The stench belowdecks in the galley was like nothing he had ever experienced, and he'd once fallen into a septic tank. When they'd been brought on board the hulking five-tiered galley, heavy with chains, the soldiers had plugged their own noses with wool before dragging the prisoners down through the stacked rows of slaves.

More than three hundred slaves slept in five outward sloping tiers, hunched over the oars in the belly of the big ship. Chained to their benches and to the oar grips, the night moans of the slaves mingled with the popping and creaking of the great timbers as the ship shifted in the waves.

Frank stared at the men's backs and then tried to shift again. He and the others had been chained to timbers in the bow, in a small open room stacked with provisions for the slaves. Isa and James were wedged together between the sacks. Poor Monmouth had been laced up in a kelp wizard bag to contain his magic, and then hammocked from the ceiling. Dotty and Penelope and Hyacinth slept in a cluster, chained to the same ring in the same timber. Frank had his own, but with the ring and his arms behind him, he could only slump forward.

Slumping was about all he felt up to.

Had Henrietta burned? His mother? Dotty had told the story in spurts. Henrietta had been knocked on the head and thrown back into the house before the soldiers had torched it. And then Henry . . .

Somewhere deep inside Frank, wrapped up in worry and grief, there was a spark of hope. Dotty said Henry had killed the big man who'd dragged him out and then jumped right back in. She'd also said that no one had come out again.

But Henry could do things. Sometimes.

"Not like me," Frank said quietly. "Mayor for a day."

Footsteps crossed the floor above Frank's head. He listened as they found the ladder and descended. Two soldiers, white fluff sticking out of their nostrils, stepped down into the room and approached Frank. Without a word, they unlocked his chains and pushed him in front of them, out of the little room and up a steep ladder. They passed out of the slave hold, through the middle deck—a forest of hammocks and sleeping soldiers—and on up into the night and its cool salt air.

Frank filled his lungs, gasping with relief, and looked around at the easy seas, up past the loudly ruffling sails at a clear sky full of stars and a sliver moon not yet at its zenith. Sailors moved quietly through the rigging and across the deck, around the housings and barrels of the four enormous brass guns the galley carried. As long as a wind blew, the ship would not be anchoring. Land stood out in a thin shadow on the horizon.

The soldiers took Frank's arms and led him down the deck and around the monstrous sleeping guns, each scaled like brass serpents. Viperous heads gaped around barrel mouths large enough to swallow and spew men. And then they climbed up steps, and up again until they stood on the stern.

There was no wheel. Twin tillers had been joined by a beam, hinged at its ends, and two men stood inside them, guiding the ship. The captain leaned against a rail, his arms crossed and a short, fat-bowled clay pipe smoking beneath his nose.

He pulled the pipe out of his mouth. "For the smell," he said, and tapped his foot on the deck. "All that filth belowdecks."

Frank rubbed his jaw. "I don't know," he said. "I sense a bit more filth up here. I prefer dirty humans to, well, dirty humans. But that's just me."

The captain nodded at the two soldiers, and as they turned and walked back down to the lower deck, he took Frank's arm and moved him to the rail. The two faced out to sea.

The captain was shorter than Frank, though not by much. His hair, graying and long around his ears, tangled in the sea breeze. He wore no hat.

"There are times," he said slowly, "when I miss Hylfing."

Frank turned and looked at him. He looked familiar. Barely.

The captain looked back. "How old were you when you left, Francis? Thirteen? Fourteen? It wasn't too much later that your father and older brothers were killed, and your little brothers set out to trap the witch-queen. And they did, too, the little buggers. I was twelve, peeking out a window, watching your father out on the harbor jetty fighting back the witch's storm. He had this sword that was all blackened and bent, and the lightning hit it, and the windows shook, and I ducked down because I couldn't watch. When I stuck my head back up, he was still there, still doing whatever it was he did. All I could see was the rising water and the waves and the lightning striking again and again. Never have seen anything else like it. Never hope to."

Frank's eyes were hot. His throat was tight. He looked back out to sea, blinking. "I wasn't there." He took a slow breath. "I was playing baseball. In Kansas."

"Whatever you were playing, wherever you were playing it, you're lucky you weren't in the city that night. Your brothers were already dead. Lady Anastasia, your mother, was the only one on the walls, the only one who could stay on the walls in that wind, her long hair all wet and cracking like a whip. When the waterspout took your father and the waves came up over the walls, she was still there. People said she didn't budge till morning, when the storm broke."

"Roderick?" Frank asked. Roderick. He'd been a nice kid. No dad. No siblings.

The captain nodded and then dropped his head. "I sat at my window all that night. I worshipped your father. And your brothers." He puffed on his pipe and watched the smoke trail away on the wind. "And you. But you all never had much time for kids outside the tribe, did you?"

Frank said nothing. Memory was grinding. Was that true? Maybe.

The captain sighed and shook his head. "No, you didn't. Your family had no use for the rest of us except as pawns, to be thrown into the fight and lost when needed. In the morning there were your crazy twin brothers. . . . I stood outside the walls with close on a hundred other boys, and we watched the two of them march off into the hills, serious as priests, Caleb with that enormous bow over his shoulder almost as tall as he was. A few tried to follow, but they got cracked and sent home. Your brothers said they knew the old mountain doorways and were going to trap the witch in her own lair. I thought your family was done."

"Why are you telling me this?" Frank asked, and he spat over the side. Anger was growing in him, but he forced his voice calm. "Gettin' all nostalgic about my family is a bit odd, what with the chains on most of them down in the hold."

The captain turned and faced Frank. "After your brothers left, I did. I hopped on the wagon my mother had been loading, and we went south. You know what she said?" He paused, as if Frank might actually answer. "She said, 'We have to get away from this family. We have to get as far away as can be got. They're like wands to death and evil, the same as towers to lightning.'" He knocked his ash out, and Frank watched the glowing leaves flutter down to the water. "She was right. Once we got away, all the trouble your family kicked up had a different effect. Funny thing, in the south, most good things came to me because I knew your family. Got my first ship's berth easy enough as I was from Hylfing and a friend to Mordecai Westmore, the boy who'd buried the witch-queen. When her witch-dogs and wizards all scattered, he got the credit—rightly or wrongly— and I got promoted. After all, my friend had saved the empire. Learned a few parlor tricks to add to the mystique. Always said that Mordecai had taught me. That was good for free drinks. Truth is"—he tugged at a serpent on his sleeve—"when it came to the captaincy, Hylfing blood was no hindrance, and having eyes that had seen the great Amram taken into the sea, and his sons march into the mountains, well, that's been a bit more than a help."

Frank spoke slowly. "Gratitude would put Mordecai's blood and bone ashore. What are you doing?"

The captain laughed, and his laughter had a hard edge. "Why won't you say my name? Say my name. Am I beneath the great Francis? I shouldn't be. You always were the least of Amram's sons. As for gratitude, well, I took the benefits as something owed. My father was killed behind yours in one of his petty wizard skirmishes."

"Roderick," Frank said. "My mother always liked you. Caleb and Mordecai always liked you."

"They liked everyone."

"What are you going to do with us?" Frank asked.

"Take you to the emperor," the captain said. "I was told to bring Mordecai peaceably or by force. This was the only other option."

"Bait a hook with his family?" Frank asked. "Why are you doing this?"

"The emperor considers him a danger to be corralled, contained, or destroyed. I don't know which, and I don't need to."

"You don't want that," Frank said. "You don't want that hanging round your neck."

The captain flexed his jaw. "Mordecai made his choice when he angered the emperor. He chose again when he refused to come peaceably. He's the one who gave you chains."

Frank leaned over and looked closely at the captain's face. The man's eyes were scrunched, like he was staring into the sun, and he was gnawing his lip. "Call a pickle a peach, it'll still make you pucker," Frank said. "You don't want this." He turned around and shoved back his wrists. "Chain me on up. Take me back down to where you got the grandbabies of Amram of Hylfing in shackles. Take me down to my wife and the wife of Mordecai Westmore." He glanced over his shoulder. "Come down yourself. We're in the slave hold. Tell 'em all some stories about the family."

A clay pipe smashed into the side of Frank's head, and he staggered forward. The two soldiers ran up the stairs and grabbed his arms.

"Your family draws death and evil like a tower draws

lightning!" the captain yelled. "I'm not bringing you anything you didn't ask for!"

Frank twisted around in the soldiers' grip. "Tall trees get struck. Ditch weeds got no cause for fear. They can watch out the window. Maybe later, they can blame the tree."

His legs dragging, Frank stared at the captain as the soldiers lugged him across the deck.

"Give him some wool," the captain said, and one of the men shoved two clumps of fleece up Frank's nose.

He snorted them out on the deck. "I'll smell it."

The captain pointed at him. "I refused to chain your mother! I wouldn't!"

"They burned her house," Frank said. The soldiers shoved him onto a ladder. He looked back at the captain, at the boy who'd lived three houses behind him. "She was in it," he said, and he climbed belowdecks.

When he had been reshackled and the soldiers had gone, Frank thumped his head against the post behind him. "Brainless," he said. "Can't coax a turtle with shouts. He'll be shelled up now." Shutting his eyes, he breathed in deeply.

Through his nose.

Fat Frank pushed away a fourth empty bowl of what had been crab stew and licked his lips. He'd brought Una and Anastasia and Richard to an old inn on the square—The Horned Horses—and they weren't being charged for any food. A woman with red cheeks and an apron ruffled

Richard's hair as she walked by. Mordecai's people wouldn't pay. Not today. Not any day. The place was dark, the ceilings were low, and the plank floors rolled like hills, but the food was good and a fire swarmed in the hearth between the two big, black, and badly chipped stone unicorns. Some people said that the inn had been built first—by a fisherman who'd lost his ship—and then the town had been built around it, by people who wanted to be closer to his cooking. Others said that the unicorns had been carved first, and the inn built around them, and the town built around that. But what everyone knew is that the inn—in its first incarnation, and in every bit of repairing and growing that had been done through the centuries—was entirely built from the timbers of broken and wracked ships. The dark beams that carried the low plaster ceiling, the posts that braced the leaning stairs, the planks in the floors and tables, all of it had been fished from the sea, and every piece had been branded with a ship's name, the number of souls lost, and the date. Between the beams, where the walls were plaster, strange designs and scenes and sea creatures and battles had been painted by sailors long dead. The walls were covered with the faded colors, coated over with pipe smoke and the grime of years, but the sailor artists and doodlers had each left their own mark—a name or self-caricature and date—though most were smudged over. It was the first time Anastasia and Richard had been in the place, and they couldn't even look at their food. Instead, they were scanning the beams for names, or slipping out of their seats and walking to a wall to stare at some wild doodle older than Kansas.

"*Two Deaths?*" Anastasia asked. "How's that a name for a ship? And fifty souls lost." She looked down at her cousin. "It's like we're eating in a graveyard, but without the bodies."

"Graveyards are nice," Una said. "If you see them the right way. I'm always the saddest when a gravestone has lost its name. I just wish they could have listed every sailor. I'd want to memorize all of them, and try to imagine their lives and stories, their mothers and fathers whenever I looked at the sea. Sometimes I wonder how many people I was related to on all these ships. You can't ever know." She pointed at the beam. "*Two Deaths* was probably raised twice." She pushed her empty bowl away and picked up a roll the shape and color of a potato. "Two wrecks, but recovered both times. Just not the third."

Richard looked around. "That would be a great deal of memorization."

Una laughed and pushed her black hair back over her shoulders. "Isa and I counted once. We came in here with pens and paper and wrote it all down. It adds up to more than sixteen thousand souls. The oldest beam is over three hundred years old, from a ship named *Beolaf.*"

Fat Frank leaned back on his tall stool and sighed. Children were strange creatures. Humans were strange creatures. A little food, a little warmth, and they forgot their boiling troubles and let their minds go skip in daisy fields. He couldn't do the same. He wanted to drink himself into oblivion and then throw himself into the sea. He wanted the innkeeper to add one more number to the timbered ceiling in memory of his death. His magic was fading. He could feel the change. The green mound life no longer pulsed through him. He felt like a mug of scum-topped water, and every sip, every draught from the faeren strength that remained in him took him closer to emptiness. Closer to the opposite of green life. Closer to chalk bones and chalk blood, and a death more suited to a troll than a onetime faerie. His anger—at Mordecai for giving him a task in his grief, at himself for failing—was all that warred with the despair inside him. He wouldn't fade into lifelessness. He'd die fighting and green. He'd see that he did, and it wouldn't be long coming.

Now that Frank had eaten, he had to set a course for himself, and for these three. He looked at Una. There was a bit of Henry in her looks, but more of her cousin Henrietta. The same jaw, but framed with Hyacinth's dark hair. And she had her mother's strength, a peaceful mind in high winds, a thin tree that would bend when thick trunks broke. Frank pulled on his earlobe and crossed his arms. Richard would be no use to him no matter what he might decide, and little Anastasia, who didn't know how young she was, would be a gamble and come up trouble or laughs at every toss.

"So what is it, Frank, waning faerie?" he muttered. "Stay and wait? Hope for the green man to trot home early? Wait days, maybe till next week's end to tell him that fingerlings were abroad, that his house has been burned and his family sacked and shipped off on imperial galleys? That his son and niece and mother were last seen in the flames?"

Frank snorted and stuck a knuckle against his forehead. Or was it off to Endor? He couldn't take these three, and leaving them behind, well, he had a promise to Mordecai.

"A broken promise," he said aloud. "That didn't last the night."

The three children stared at him. The fat faerie stared back. Then he looked for the woman in the apron. He could eat more. Another bowl of stew. Maybe some chops or spiced apples. Pie.

"No," he said. "No being a human about this, Franklin. Make your mind and make your move. Staring at the pinch won't ease the pain."

He dug into his pocket and pulled out the box the faerie had given him. At least a message from the faeren could make him angry at someone other than himself. He dropped the little cube onto the table. The others froze, Anastasia with her spoon in the air, Una picking at her roll, Richard with a cheek bulging and a dribble on his chin. The thing was smooth, oily even, and deep brown in the firelight. The corners were rounded. Frank flipped it with his finger. It appeared to be seamless.

"Open it," Anastasia said. Fat Frank glared at her.

He turned it over again and found a faint, pale circle on one side. "Can't be," he muttered. "Not now."

Richard tipped his head back, pooling the stew in his jaw to speak. "I used to have a puzzle box," he muffled. "Perhaps I should take a look."

Frank grunted. Anastasia watched the faerie spin it, twisting, staring at each side, moving on and doubling back. It was a perfect cube. And it looked heavy for its size. Full of something.

"I really think—" Richard said.

Groaning, Fat Frank looked up. "This isn't a box." He dropped it back onto the table and shoved his fingers into his hair.

"What is it?" Anastasia asked. She scooted down the table.

"Beyond trouble?" Frank dropped to the ground and kicked over his stool. "Beyond a blight and a curse and a kick to the shins? Beyond a salty finger in the eye, and the most unhelpful, useless bit of tomfool faeren nonsensing?" He stormed to the door. "Beyond that, it's just an impossibility. A bedtime story." He kicked the wall and stomped on the floor. "A faerie tale!" he yelled, and pushed out into the street. "And not even a good one!"

Anastasia watched him go. Then she leaned over the table and picked up the box. In her hands, she knew it immediately. She knew the dark swirling grains and the oily skin. She knew the pale white spot.

Confused, she looked up. "It's a chestnut."

Richard and Una crowded around her, watching the glistening cube rotate in her fingers.

"Odd," Richard said. "Botanical geometry."

"There's writing on it," said Una. "In the grain. The grain is writing."

Anastasia leaned closer and tipped the oversize chestnut to avoid any glare. The circling grain worked into a calligraphy of sorts that traveled around the cube in lines as uneven as the grain on any chestnut. The words seemed written with smoke.

"Where's the beginning?" Anastasia asked.

Una reached down and rotated the cubed chestnut until the pale spot was down. Anastasia let go and watched her cousin. Squinting, Una began to read.

"Nudd, Lord of the Second World, monarch of Glaston's Barrow, soul of the three-mace trees, master of the earthen winds, protector of true faeren, bane of traitors and folly-coddlers, claims Franklin, infamous, hopeless, hapless, severed faerie, for his own, as is his divine right, and bids him come and prove the worth of his life. Bend and live. Stand and be broken."

"Who is Nudd?" Anastasia asked.

"Apparently," Richard said, "he is someone who believes himself to be a king of some sort."

Una dropped the chestnut on the table and sat down. "I've just heard stories. Nothing nice."

Anastasia poked the chestnut onto its side. "But what is he? Who is he?"

The door opened and Fat Frank hurried back in, white-faced. Scooping the chestnut up, he threw it into the fire and sat down, bouncing his short legs.

"A pint!" he yelled.

The rosy, aproned woman stuck her head out of the kitchen. "Dark?" she asked.

Fat Frank put his head in his hands. "Something to curl my hair."

Anastasia looked at Fat Frank's round head and then at Una.

"What is it?" Una asked.

Fat Frank took a deep breath and sat up. "They're in the street already," he said. "Thirteen of them. The moon's about perched. They'll be in in a breath or two."

A tall glass full of something the color of a pond bottom thumped down in front of Fat Frank. The chestnut popped loudly in the fire. Frank picked up his glass, sucked the froth off the top, and raised it with two hands.

The front door opened, and a wind blew in, bending the flames, setting chills in Anastasia's skin. The door began to shut but pushed back open, again, and again, and again. Thirteen times.

Footsteps drummed on the plank floor while invisible bodies surrounded the table, and still Frank drank on.

"Um," Anastasia said. "Frank?"

Richard tried to stand, but unseen hands shoved him back into his seat.

Una looked around slowly with her eyes narrowed. Anastasia moved closer to her. "You see anything?" she whispered.

"Just shimmers," said Una. "And that means faeries."

"So it do!" a voice boomed.

The inn was far from full, but the few customers

slid into corners, or felt their way along the walls to the door.

Fat Frank emptied his glass and threw it into the fire. "And what are you fancies looking for? I'd expect you lot to be off tying strings to cat tails, or maybe sucking eggs in the henhouses. Of course, the evening's fresh, you could fit it all in yet." He leaned forward and laughed. "Wait, you're all standing in a ring." He spun his finger in a circle. "Do yer little dance! Make it come up mushrooms!"

Anastasia scanned the room. She could hear breathing, and the floorboards creaked, but nothing more.

"We've come for your reply," a voice said.

"To what?" Frank asked.

Two more chestnut cubes appeared and tumbled across the table like dice. "Franklin," the voice said. "You must know they grow in threes. Burn them all and still nothing changes."

Fat Frank crossed his arms and wrinkled up his face. Anastasia tried to follow his eyes. "What is it you're called?" Frank asked.

"My name is Jacques," the voice replied. "And that is what I am called."

"Well, Jacques," Frank said. "I am a faerie what loves my queene. I'll not budge."

Anastasia blinked. The air warped like a heat mirage, and a faerie appeared. The bald faerie from the street. He reached up, adjusted his purple eye patch, pulled the ends of his mustache, and then shoved his thumbs into his wide belt.

"You are no longer faeren, or have you forgotten? And even if you were, the queene is"—he waved his hand slowly—"a decoration. Love her if you like. That is allowed. The king himself indulges in love for the queene. But she offers you no loyalty or love in return. You are out from her protection. You, Fat Franklin, are the Chestnut King's to claim, and we have been sent to collect you. Whether he keeps you or leaves you to the law of faeren decay will be entirely up to him."

"I shall have no king," Frank muttered.

Jacques grinned. "But the king shall have you." He reached into his jacket and pulled out a small book bound in leather, almost as thick as it was tall. He slapped it down in front of Frank and flipped it to the back. "Is that your signature, Franklin? Is this not your copy of *The Book of Faeren,* issued to you upon your entrance into the service of District R.R.K. and its committee?"

Anastasia's eyes were wide. Frank had turned a pale gray. He closed his eyes and puffed his cheeks.

"I was a tyke," he said quietly. "It was just a bit of formalizing. That's what they said. They said it was just fancy words and tradition. There was no king. He was a story, the same as the midnight goat. No one had been expelled, not all the way, in a hundred years."

"Is it yours?" Jacques asked.

Frank nodded.

"Who shall read it?"

Frank put his forehead on the table. Jacques straightened and held the little book high in front of him.

Anastasia, realizing that she was gaping at him, shut her mouth quickly. The faerie smiled, leaned over the table, and slid her the book.

"From the top of the page," he said. "Crisply now. Don't slur."

Anastasia looked down at the dirty little book and then back up. Frank was motionless. Richard was goggling at her, breathing heavily out of his mouth. Una nodded.

Anastasia blinked at the old typeface. It looked like each letter had been stamped, smashed on by an antique printing press, and the spelling was odd in places, just plain wrong in others. The pages were brittle, and little notes and pictures had been childishly scrawled in the margins. Clearing her throat, she read.

Being the Fifty-Second Article
Section xxxviii
Individual Incorpoarates, Loyaltys, Fealtys,
   and Threatenings

I, being born amung the faeren people and no changeling, free in mind and boddy, under no oppressions or duressings, do put my mark to this book, swearing my self in service to my district, my queene and all her hairs, all dutifly and parliamentally appointed committees and governmentors, bonded pauper-sons and allegiances, and to abide in the waking life according to the laws and regulates herein plainly stated.

If my oath be broken, may I be struck from the faeren peoples, banished from the mounds, stricken from the lively blud and all recordings, abandoned by the queene and her governmen, and stricken with a public death, or given boddy and mind to the king and his torments. Sworn to and signed in the presence of witnesses, and charm bonded with blud,

Franklin Fat

"It wasn't meant to be literal," Frank mumbled.

"Oh," said Jacques, "when the wording was agreed upon by the king, I believe that it was." He took a bite of Una's roll. "Bid farewell to your friends, Franklin. The king's waiting."

Frank's head jerked up. "They come, too," he said. "Or cut me down where I stand."

Jacques sniffed and looked around the table. "Three children?"

"I promised to look after them," Frank said.

The bald faerie winked at Anastasia. "And you keep promises, do you?"

"Poorly," said Frank. "And worse tomorrow."

Richard rose in his seat. "Perhaps we should struggle."

The ring of faeries burst into laughter.

"Bring him for certainty!" one cried.

Another reached up and poked Richard's cheek. "I could do with a bit of struggling myself. Shall we then? You struggle first, and then I'll give a go."

The laughter grew, and Anastasia watched Richard go red and then white. He picked up his spoon.

"Leave him be," Fat Frank said. "You take us all." He scooped a chestnut up off the table and looked around the room. The aproned woman and a large, bearded cook stood in the kitchen doorway.

Frank lobbed the cubed chestnut across the room. The cook bobbled and caught it with both hands.

"When Mordecai's returned," Frank said, "give him that nut right off." He pointed at Una, Anastasia, and Richard. "And remember these faces."

The big cook nodded and gave it to the woman. She tucked it into her apron.

"Mordecai Westmore? The green man?" Jacques asked. "What has he to do with a waned faerie?"

The other faeries quieted. A few shifted nervously.

Frank inflated his chest. "That," he said, "is something I think you'll be learning." He walked over to the door and stopped. Anastasia felt Una's hand on her arm, and the two girls moved quickly after Frank.

"Well," he said. "Take us to your king. I got to learn the mushroom dance and get to ruining people's gardens."

Coradin leaned against a wall, hidden from the moon in the shadows of an alley.

"A tragedy is what it is," a woman said. "My heart's achin' for Lady Hyacinth." She dumped a mop bucket at Coradin's feet and stepped back into her house.

Across the street, Coradin watched the last of the

townspeople leave the smoking ruin and walk away, taking their lanterns with them. He stepped out of the alley and crossed the street. He had roamed the city. He had watched the ships sail. He had watched the round faerie rescue three of the children in the struggle at the gate, and he had done nothing.

His task was the boy. And the boy . . . the boy was somehow still closest to the charred house.

He stood at the front door, where his blood brother had been killed, and he flared his nostrils. Traces of smoke drifted up in the moonlight. Blackened beams stood up from the ground in a jumble, like the bones of some monstrous creature.

Coradin shut his eyes. Blood. The boy had the blood of Endor in his flesh. He need only find the traces. Minutes passed. Voices grew and faded in the street behind him. A bat flitted near his head. Still nothing. And then gray. Strands of gray, the smallest hints, moved in front of him. With his eyes still closed, he staggered forward, feeling his way on all fours through the rubble, following the spiderwebs until they became strings and the strings became yarn.

He opened his eyes.

A slab of plaster and brick lay between his feet. Grunting, he gripped its edge and flipped it over. A fallen cistern, cracked and collapsed, still leaked dampness despite the heat of the fire and the warmth in the ruin.

Coradin lifted off a large, cracked piece and threw it away. Beneath, in a shallow puddle, there lay a creature, small, winged, black by nature or fire, bluntly horned. Its goose wings were bent awkwardly, and in places its feathers were burned down to nubbed quills. Coradin gripped the loose skin on its back, lifting it from the rubble. The creature dangled limp from his hand, wing tips down, unmoving, with only the breeze rustling in its feathers.

The boy's gray traces were stronger. They were in the cistern. Coradin crouched and shifted his moon shadow. There was a small door, hinged to a box, now nearly collapsed to one side.

With his free hand, he pulled out the damaged cupboard and held it up, dripping.

He grows closer.

"The way is small," Coradin said.

I will teach you.

Coradin turned and moved toward the street.

A snorting jaw clamped onto his arm.

CHAPTER NINE

Henry rubbed his head. Kansas had been crisp in the gray predawn, but here, in the old farmhouse's new world, the sun was down, and there was no moon.

The attic was as black as one of his dreams.

He was sitting on his little bed, ignoring the wall of doors, ignoring their smells and flavors and muffled noises, ignoring Henrietta's flashlight, which she kept flicking between him and the dark door on the bottom row. Door Number 8. Endor.

They'd said good-bye to his grandmother and Mrs. Johnson and then walked through Henry, Kansas, casually enough, despite Henry's oilskin cloak. At the bait shop, they'd ignored the stares of coffee-drinking farmers and bought as many new batteries as they could afford, along with a sizable stash of jerky. Then they'd trudged to the hole by the old barn and walked into a dark house, creaking in an empty world.

"We don't have to do this," Henrietta said. "There has to be another way. We could go back to Hylfing and wait for your dad."

Henry blinked and shaded his eyes from her flashlight.

She flicked the light on Zeke and then pointed it back down to the black door.

"The door to Hylfing is closed," Henry said. "Blocked or crushed or something. We can't go back without going through Badon Hill and the faerie mound. And my dad said he wouldn't be home until my birthday. If then."

"We can wait," said Henrietta. She shrugged off her backpack and set it on the bed. "Your dad might find us."

Henry laughed. "Since when do you ever want to wait? You always wanted to explore the cupboards, and I never did. You even wanted to go through that one." He pointed at Endor.

"Yeah," Henrietta said. "Well, things change. That was a long time ago—before a witch nearly killed us all and a wizard ripped the whole house out of Kansas."

Henry stood up slowly.

Henrietta turned to Zeke. "What do you think? There's got to be a better way, right?"

Zeke bent his head side to side, stretching. "Henry's got to find his dad, and he's got to do it soon. And his dad's on the other side of that door somewhere."

"Henrietta, listen." Henry picked up her backpack and handed it to her. "I have to do this. I don't want to. My head feels like it's going to split already. I'm all clammy, and I'll probably throw up again, but I have to do this." He reached up to scratch his jaw and stopped himself. "But you don't," he added. "You can stay with Mrs. Johnson. We'll come back for you. Do you want to go back?"

Henrietta crossed her arms, uncrossed them, put her

hands on her hips, crossed them again, and then tucked her curls behind her ears. She shivered.

"I almost died with my arm through that door." She sniffed. "But I'm not even going to answer that question."

"You don't want to go back?"

"Of course I do." Henrietta sniffed. "And you do, too. But I'm not going to."

Henry smiled.

Henrietta scowled. "I'm going to die in a cold black place and never be found. That's what I'm going to do."

Zeke looked at both of them. "Are we ready?" he asked. When they nodded, he crouched and pulled off the small black door. A thin gold chain dragged out behind it.

Henry felt dizzy. Dizzy and chilled. His jaw was piercing cold. His mouth felt like it was freezing shut. Gagging, he dropped to his knees in front of the door, and the wall went blurry.

He could hear his cousin, talking from somewhere far away. "Don't be sick."

And Zeke. "Henry? Henry, are you okay?"

He had to do this fast or not at all. He needed every bit of dandelion fire inside him.

Henry shut his eyes and fought to block the cold and the sucking and the awful wrongness of the door. He pulled his father's necklace out of his shirt and made a fist around it with his right hand. He flexed hard, and the metal grew warm. He needed that fire. He needed his father's strength. And his grandfather's. He needed all of it.

He could feel dandelions. There were some through

the door to Badon Hill. And another door farther away and higher. And another. He felt for them all. They were already feeling for him.

His arm warmed and then his shoulder. The gagging faded. Only his jaw was cold.

He knew his eyes were black, and he opened them.

The door to Endor drew everything to itself already. Every breath, every influence from the other open doors drifted toward the dark cupboard by the floor, graying as they came, slowly draining into nothingness.

Strands drifted away from Henry's face, twisting around themselves and snaking through the cupboard mouth.

"Now or never," Henry said, and he pointed his burning palm toward the door.

The swirling stopped. The drain became a tangle as green and gold writhed and flinched away from the hole, as the gray death retreated against the wall and scattered and splayed when the colors came close.

"Come on," said Henry, and he swirled his hand around the opening, chasing gray, forcing the influences to mingle. He would need more if he was going to widen the world-seam beyond the wood of the cupboard. He scooted closer. The cold in his jaw became a tugging. His own gray strands quickened. He grabbed at all the other doors, intercepting their flows before they died, and blended them together. He built himself a swirl that was big and alive, and then he brought it down to the dark door.

The mouth gaped. The seam, hungrier than any other,

grew, and Henry slid forward on his knees. He pushed himself back away from the wall and stared at what he'd done.

The room was gray. All the colors had died, and the seam, bookmarked by the small black cupboard, now gaped wide on the wall.

It wasn't getting smaller. It was growing. Henry blinked and struggled with the flow. It didn't have to shrink, not until they were back through, but he didn't want it to be growing while they were gone.

His little bed slid against the wall.

"What's happening?" Zeke asked, leaning back. "Is this normal?"

Henrietta jumped back through the bedroom doorway and stood in the attic.

Henry gasped. "Okay," he said. He'd slowed it down, but they'd still be able to duck through without crawling. "I'll go first. Then Zeke." He looked at his cousin. "Last chance, Henrietta."

"I'm fine," she said. "But watch yourselves. I'll be right behind you. I'm not spending an extra second in here alone."

Henry stood and stared at the swirling wall. "It's still pretty big."

"What is?" Henrietta asked. "What are you seeing?"

Henry didn't answer. There was no way he could. Henrietta's flashlight flicked all over the wall. Zeke's was steady on the cupboard. It could have been higher. Henry turned on his own flashlight and adjusted his backpack. He faced the death-drain, took a deep breath, and then two more, and he stepped through.

Henrietta jumped and bit her lip. She couldn't help herself. Henry had walked straight at the wall, hunched a bit, and disappeared. Crawling through Grandfather's cupboard at least felt like it made sense. But this, watching Henry in his cloak, groaning and wincing and dripping cold sweat, shutting his eyes and waving his hands around like a drunk weatherman? It gave her the creeps, especially with this door. She shivered again. Zeke checked her with his flashlight and then stepped in front of the doors.

"Hold on a sec," Henrietta said. "I'll go next."

She hopped in front of him, and before she could think about it, squeezed her eyes shut, ducked her head, and stepped sideways toward the wall.

It was like dropping too fast in an elevator. Her stomach rose, and everything in her stomach rose with it. And then weight, too much weight for her body, and a sudden stop.

Cold. Very, very cold. But not in the way winters are cold, or ice cream. This was cold because nothing was moving, cold because there was an extreme absence of heat, an absence of any kind of life at all. This was death.

"My nose isn't bleeding." Henry's flashlight spotted her face. "That's a first. But I did throw up. Don't walk over here. Where's Zeke?"

"This is awful," said Henrietta. She swung her beam around the room. Her knees were weak, and her skin felt like it did underwater. Zeke staggered into place beside her.

All three lights spotted their way around the room.

"I don't like this," Zeke said. "How do we get out?"

Coradin held the animal in front of him in the moonlight. Its eyes were red and rolling in its skull, and its bellow was hoarse. More than just feathers had been burned. Avoiding the teeth and the butting head and the flapping wings, Coradin slid his hand to the animal's throat. He squeezed, and the bellowing sputtered and stopped. He squeezed harder and knew that blood flow had ended. Harder and his fingertips found the spine.

Kill.

He drew a blade from his belt, turned the animal away from himself, and set the knife tip on the back of the neck. Slide it in, and the body would die immediately. The mind would live on, but only for a matter of moments, cut off from its own dead flesh.

Kill.

Hesitating, he relaxed his grip. The animal wheezed, breathing again.

Now.

He didn't want to kill the creature. It had survived much. Like himself. And it was like no other animal he had ever seen. He tucked his knife back into his belt.

A searing pain shot through his skull. Ice, cold and

sharp, pumped through his veins. A voice, angry as a water-fall, roared in his head.

Coradin!

He dropped to his knees in the rubble, still holding the raggant. His joints throbbed. His head felt ripped open, split wide in the back. His fist tightened again on the raggant's throat. Groaning, he threw the animal away into the wreckage and fell forward.

The pain grew. His body shook. And then calm. Peace. Balm flowed through his limbs. His head was numb. He had no pain. He had nothing. His mind was clean, his trifling rebellion forgotten.

Take the doorway.

He rose to his feet and picked up the cupboard.

The crypt was square. Black pillars held up a low-vaulted ceiling. They, and every other surface, were covered with scratches and etchings, strange symbols, shapes, and figures—scrawls of the imprisoned. Low, peaked doorways lined the walls, four to a side. Some were sealed, some were gapped open, and some had been sealed but now held nothing but shattered stone. All of it had been carved in shades of black. There were no cobwebs at all—those would have required living spiders—but a thin film of dust had settled over everything. A film disturbed in places.

Zeke and Henrietta moved their flashlights from doorway to doorway. Henry turned and faced the wall behind them. It held doorways as well, but it also held a shelf, small and leaning slightly to one side. On it there were rotted books, a bird skull, the bones of a human hand, and what looked like a pile of rags. He let his light rest on an odd shape beside the rag pile, a small black pyramid, ten inches tall, intricately carved. One of its sides was hinged and open, holding a seam between the worlds. He could feel the swirl on the other side, draining things into this place.

He chewed his lip. That current against them would make going back hard. But hopefully, they wouldn't have to. They would find his dad and his uncle and go back with them.

"Henry," Zeke said. "Look at this."

Henry turned. Zeke's flashlight lit up a large, flat, circular stone in the center of the room. Small symbols covered its surface. Beside it, a large circular space was free of dust.

"It's been moved," Henrietta said. "How long ago?" She turned in place, scanning the doors.

"No way to know," said Zeke. He looked at Henry. "What now?"

"Henry?" Henrietta asked. "The witch was trapped here, right? Did we think about that at all? If she couldn't get out, how will we?"

Henry shivered. His skin was tightening. Something was coming. Or someone. He shut his eyes. If there was a way out, they wouldn't find it just trying every door. He needed to see the place.

There was nothing. Nothing but still gray death and

the swirling, dying flavors through the little door behind him. And then he saw something he didn't understand. A faint web of deep purple with traces of green woven into the stone of a doorway. And another. A strand ran between them. Another strand, embedded in the stone, ran . . . he followed it over the ceiling and down the other side, down to the little pyramid, where it was frayed and broken.

Henry opened his mouth, wishing he understood. He knew that these things had to be from his father, the strength of his grapevines stitching together the seams of lifeless rock, rock from which no strength could ever be drawn. But how did it work? Could he open it? And if those doors were sealed, then they had to lead out. He crossed the room and stared at the low arch and the smooth stone that filled it.

Henrietta screamed, and Henry spun around. Through one of the shattered doorways, there peered a face. It was a woman's face, old and shorn bald. She blinked at the flash-lights, sniffed the room, and stepped in. She was wearing Henry's old long-sleeved T-shirt, the shirt that Nimiane had pulled through the cupboard a lifetime ago.

Zeke dropped his backpack, unzipped it, and jerked out his hatchet.

"No way Out," the woman said. "Only In. You have found In."

Henry slid slowly back toward the other two. "Who are you?"

"I. I. I am queens." Her shape flickered and changed, and suddenly, she was towering, tall, beautiful. "I am kings." She became a man holding a gold mace. And then she shrunk back down to her wizened, shorn self and sat on the stone floor, crossing thin legs beneath ragged skirts. "I am Nia. And you are sweet-blooded childrens." She looked up, blinking, and then shut her eyes and sniffed. Henry gasped and stepped back. She'd become a man again, tall, even seated, and broad-shouldered, with eyes like sharp holes hooded beneath a pale brow. A thin silver band studded with swirling stones sat in his night-dark hair. In one enormous hand, he cupped a small black ball, baseball-size, shimmering with white flame around the edges like a pale, eclipsed sun. In the other, he gripped three writhing serpents, all hissing and striking at each other.

"I am Nimroth, called Blackstar," he said, and the walls shook. "Devourer. Ruler of men and demons, master of the southern gin and the northern incubi. World-walker. By me were the first races cast down and the gardens burned. By me the moons were made cold." He shimmered and changed, and Henry could see beyond the image. He could see the old woman in his shirt, hunched, rocking like a cage-crazed monkey.

The man aged. His hair whitened and thinned. His eyes grew cavernous, and his cheeks clung to his teeth. He still gripped the black star in one hand, but in the other, he held only ashen snake skins.

"I am Nimroth," he said, and the voice was brittle and old. "Called Blackstar. Devourer of Death. Adam to the Undying Race." Henry could feel Henrietta's fingers digging deep into his arm, and the man changed again.

Gray sores spotted his bald head. His gums had receded, and stray white hairs drifted away from his chin and ears. His voice was high, shrill, like a sick child's. He was hunched over something on the floor—the black star—rolling it back and forth, rocking slowly and chattering to himself, almost singing.

"Nimroth, Nim, Nim's frogs. Pretty frogs need six legs. Six legs for swimming. Six for plucking. Kitten heads for throwing. Sister's kittens lost their heads, but couldn't stop their mewing."

And the man's image was gone. The old monkey-looking lady winked at Henry, and he swallowed hard. Henrietta was trying to pull him farther back. He didn't want to go. There were other open doors behind them.

"He's locked up, locked up!" the woman shrieked. "Old Mad Nim and his marble in the dark. Listen! Listen!" The woman lunged forward, sprawling on the floor. She pressed her ear on the stone circle in the center of the room. Henry pushed Zeke and Henrietta back toward the shelf.

"Shhh," the woman said. "Listen!"

Henry's pulse drummed inside him. He stood perfectly still, trying to quiet his breathing. And then he heard it. Faintly. A slow, smooth sound, almost a grinding, almost a sliding. A stone ball rolling on stone.

"He's down there?" Henrietta whispered. "Right now? Under that?"

The woman cackled. "Down. Down. No light for Nimroth." She grew suddenly serious. "No light for Niac. No light for brothers and sisters and cousins and mothers. No light for Nia." Her eyes widened with sadness. "No sweetbloods. Only Nimiane has light. Only Nimiane has sweetbloods." She scrambled back up to her feet. With hunched shoulders, she glanced around the room, as if she might be overheard. Henry ran his flashlight quickly over the doorways and then back to the shriveled woman. She winked and then whispered, "Nimiane found a way Out."

She hobbled toward Henry.

"Back," Zeke said, and he stepped to the front. The woman slid sideways, staying out of his reach, and pointed at Henry. She sniffed.

"Your blood!" she said. "Your blood! You opened the Out! She tasted your blood! Ooh, I licked it off her finger. Sister let me lick."

Suddenly, the woman lunged forward. Henry dropped his flashlight and jerked away, but she was too quick. Her hands were on his face—hands as cold as death. He grabbed her wrists, and she screamed, clawing at his hand, at where his dandelion brand pressed against her skin. Zeke knocked her backward, and she sprawled out on the stone circle. Whimpering, she clutched her knees to her chest.

"No bloods," she said. "Not for Nia. Nimiane tastes you. Her blood eats you. You will die and be ash. Ash, ash. Your face will be the moon. She drinks the souls. She is Nimroth now."

Henry coughed and shivered, trying to shake the chill

from his skin. He put his right hand to his jaw, felt his pulse slow, his breath become even.

"We need to get out of here," Henrietta said. "Right now. We have to go back or find another way out."

Zeke kept his light trained on the shaking woman. Henrietta moved hers around the walls, pausing on every open door. Henry picked up his flashlight. For a moment, the room was silent. A slow, rolling sound crept beneath the floor.

"Nia," Henry said. But the shriveled shape rocked on its side and ignored him. "Who shut you in here?"

"Sisters," Nia said quietly. "We were last. All were mad. Mother drooled. We sealed her up in stone. Brothers mad beneath their slabs. All save Nia and Nimiane. She shut me in. She closed the doors." The woman squinted into Henry's flashlight. "Your father's blood, sweet-bloods, green-bloods, opened the doors, and she came in after, she came to feed on boy bloods." She giggled like a little girl and rubbed her bald head with both bony hands. "Little boys tricked her. They shut her in, still with her strength. They sewed the stones with greens and grapes. But blind Nimiane found the Out. A little blood for strength, and down." She slapped the round stone. "Down to the old ones to learn the small ways. She broke the deep seal, the old seal. Not Nia."

"Are you hungry, Nia?" Henry asked. He unslung his backpack and unzipped the pouch.

Henrietta hit him. "What are you doing? Don't feed it. Maybe kill it, but don't feed it."

"Sweet-bloods can't kill," Nia said. "Can't kill Niac. Can't kill Nimroth or his marble. Blackstar blood won't die, can't die. Death won't die. No, it won't."

Henry pulled a piece of jerky out of his bag and threw it to the grinning woman. It hit her in the shoulder and landed on the slab. She stared at it. She sniffed.

"She doesn't even have any teeth," Henrietta said. "How's she going to eat jerky?"

Nia reached out and poked the dried meat. Then she picked it up, gripping it hard.

"Cattle," she said, and closed her eyes.

"What's she doing?" Henrietta whispered.

The jerky twisted in her hand. The ends curled and folded. The piece of meat grayed and then fell to the floor in a trickle of ash.

Nia opened her eyes. Henry braced himself, watching her closely. "The taste," she said quietly. "It has been long. Long. Too long." Already she seemed stronger, and Henry wasn't sure if he liked that.

Suddenly, the shrunken woman jumped to her feet, with her arms upraised, morphing back into the figure of the man. "I am Nimroth!" she boomed.

"Stop it!" Henry yelled. "Enough!"

Nimroth's arms dropped. His shape faded.

"Green-bloods," Nia said quietly, and sat back down. "No more Nimroth for green-bloods."

Henry bit his lip, took a deep breath, and walked around the woman. He put his hand on the smooth door where he had seen his father's vines in the stone.

"Nia?" The woman stared at him. "What's behind this door?"

"Down," she said. "Down, down, down to the tomb streets and the tomb cities. Where mad Endor lives. Dark Endor. No light for the under-streets and the dead doors."

Henry moved to the other sealed doorway. "This one?" he asked.

"Up," she said, and raised her arms. "Up, up, up to the ash."

Henry nodded at Zeke and Henrietta. Zeke picked up Henry's backpack, and he and Henrietta slid past Nia, backing toward Henry with their flashlights on the shrunken woman.

"So," Henrietta asked. "If we don't find your dad, we have to come back through here?"

"Right," Henry said, running his hands over the smooth surface of the door. "Assuming that we get out in the first place."

The stone was lifeless to him. This was not stone that had been something else first. It had not been shaped by rivers or seas or fire or time. This was not stone that had once lived and was now dead. This was stone that had always been stone. Stone that had never had life and could never have it. But inside it, someone had woven life and sealed its seams.

How had his father done it? A sealing spell? Some curse? Mordecai had said that Henry would learn words of power, that he would make his own. But there hadn't been time, not with his scar growing and the witch to hunt.

Henry ran fingers around the joints. There were scratches. From stone shards? Fingernails? He pointed his flashlight back across the room at the little pyramid. It had been sealed, too, though differently—the web was external—and he and Henrietta had broken through it without even knowing.

They shared Mordecai's blood. Could he just break through? He looked back at the door. And if he did break through, what would follow him out into the world?

Henrietta reached under Henry's cloak and pulled on the pouch of his hoodie. "Henry. I hear something."

"The rolling?" Zeke asked.

Henrietta shook her head and pressed her back against the wall beside Henry. Her light flicked around the room, bouncing between openings.

The rolling had stopped. Footsteps. Muffled shuffling footsteps. But from where? Which door? Zeke clenched the hatchet and shifted on his feet like he was in the batter's box. Henrietta jerked off her backpack and fished out a short-bladed kitchen knife.

"Can we go back?" she asked. "Is there time to go back?"

Something hard cracked against stone. The echo rattled around them.

Nia was smiling, with her head cocked and her eyes closed, seated on the center slab. "Up, up, up," she said. "Up they come." She opened her eyes. "Nimiane broke the seal. Not Nia. The old ones smell the sweet-bloods."

The slab shook beneath her.

*   *   *

Coradin closed his eyes. He was in the cellar of an abandoned house, and he had done as the voice had said. The symbol had been drawn. The small doorway had been straightened and sat against a wall. Kneeling with the backs of his hands on the floor in front of him, he felt something cold grow inside him. Another voice took control of his tongue, and a woman's words filled the room—they filled him. Painful words. Words of force, of violence. He could sense the boy.

His skin stretched, pulling away from his bones. His hair unraveled and flowed forward around his face. Something twitched on the back of his head.

And he was gone.

A surface soft and damp collapsed beneath him, and he tumbled onto a floor.

The place was all darkness, but something else was pulling him backward. He climbed to his feet and turned. He saw nothing, but cold fear swept over him. This was emptiness. But it held the boy. And sucking death. And somewhere distant, it held his blood brothers—eight fingers.

He stepped forward.

The slab shook again, and dust rattled off the walls. Henry's heart was drumming in his ears. He couldn't do this. They had to go back.

"Henry!" Henrietta spun him around. On the other side of the room, the shelf rattled, the small pyramid rocked, and suddenly, a man in black appeared on the floor beneath it. He was on all fours, and his hair hung loose. Something pale twitched on the back of his head. Coradin rose slowly, blinking, and raised one hand to shield his eyes from the flashlights.

"Pauper son?" His voice was Nimiane's. High. Sweet. Powerful. "It is fit that you should die here."

Shrieking, Nia scrambled away, disappearing into an open door. The round slab tipped up and ground slowly across the floor.

CHAPTER TEN

A hand reached up out of the hole in the ground. A hand holding a black sphere, shimmering around its edges with white flame.

Henry pressed his forehead against the smooth stone in the sealed doorway. Why had he thought this was a good idea? He flattened his dandelion palm against the door, but his little flame wouldn't penetrate. He had found a place where a dandelion couldn't grow.

"Henry," Zeke said. "What do we do?"

"Pauper son." Nimiane's voice was calm, soothing. "You rouse my ancestors. You disturb their darkness."

Henry blocked her out. He shut his eyes and saw only distant vines, a web of strength, and his own sputtering gold, struggling to reach them.

"Henry," Henrietta whispered. "Do something. The old one's coming. He's climbing out of the floor. He's sniffing."

Henry turned.

Coradin was smiling, his stiff black hair on his shoulders. He pulled a long silver blade from his belt. Henry took Henrietta's little kitchen knife and handed her his flashlight. In the middle of the room, a shape crawled slowly out of the hole. Henry's eyes left Coradin's and settled on the black ball the ancient man pushed in front of him. In it, compressed, tiny, Henry saw worlds, millions of lives, forests and generations, tangled tight in a common death.

Coradin's mouth moved, but Nimiane spoke. "The Blackstar," she said. "Is it not more potent than a weed, more precious than a dandelion's gold? Through it, my long-sire drank the world, as he will drink you. Through it, our blood was changed."

Henry jumped forward and kicked the old man's wrist. The ball rolled free, and a wail rose up like the howl of some otherworldly wolf.

The man grabbed at Henry's legs, snarling. Henry kicked him in the shoulder and jumped back. Zeke and Henrietta were beside him. Henry braced himself for another attack. While Coradin laughed, the old man whimpered and crawled slowly forward. The ball had wandered into a corner where it no longer flamed. Henry ran to it, but stopped, blinking. It was nothing but smooth stone. The same lifeless stone as the walls. It was nothing at all. Mad Nimroth's marble.

Henry picked it up and bowled it past the old man, back into the hole. It dropped, cracked, and bounced on what must have been stairs, and after a long moment of silence, it found the bottom. Dust snowed from the ceiling with the echo.

Three other pale faces were peering from the hole, blinking into the flashlights. The old man slithered down past them and disappeared. Coradin walked forward, and with one strong movement of his leg, slid the circular stone back over the hole.

He stepped onto it. Henry and the others stepped back.

"What will you do now, pauper son?" The voice was still Nimiane's. The big man stared into the light, unblinking. His three ear notches stood out like black teeth in his pale skin.

Henry licked his lips and gripped his small knife. "I think we're going to have to kill you," he said.

"Me?" Nimiane laughed. "I cannot be killed. Did you not know this?"

"I killed one of the others," Henry said. "You just have to cut the puppet's strings."

"The puppet's, yes. And then the puppet dies. But I am not the puppet. I hold the strings." Coradin stepped forward. "I do not think you will kill this one. He is strong. But even if you do, even if I commanded this fingerling to kneel before you so that you might snip his strings, there are others. Kill them, and I can make more. Can you stand against them all? The emperor has many such that he can give me, and fingers are never difficult to find. I do not make Endor new. Death cannot be freshened or reborn. I make a new Endor. I sit in the saddle of the world, with fleets at my command both east and west. The emperor's red-shirted thousands kneel before me, and the world kneels before them. Even at Endor's zenith, before the first madness, when Nimroth held the true Blackstar and looked to the corners of the world, he did not have such obedience." Coradin held his fist to his chest. "I, not Niac, not Nimroth, I shall be the greatest of the undying blood, though you shall not live to see it."

"Stay close," Henry whispered.

Henrietta, pressed against his side, was breathing loudly. "What?" she asked.

"You heard," Henry said. He didn't want to say it again. In his left hand, Henry gripped his knife. In his right, he gripped his necklace. The metal was more than warm. It was hot, and his hand throbbed more than his jaw. His eyes had shifted again, and he was watching the thick gray strands weaving off Coradin's head and down through the open black pyramid. He was looking at the vines, traces of his father, frayed and broken around the pyramid door.

Coradin took another step forward, off the slab. Henry saw his legs tense. The big man was going to spring. "Where is your defiance, pauper son?" Nimiane laughed. "You, who did not fear to enter my dreams, who entered the tomb cities of Endor? Where are your weeds now? You proclaimed yourself to be my curse, but I have seen nothing of it."

"Tomahawk," Henry said, hoping Zeke would understand. "Now."

Coradin hesitated, confused.

Zeke threw his hatchet. Henry threw his knife.

The crypt pulsed with green and gold. Coradin raised his arm against the hatchet and flinched as the small kitchen knife, a galaxy of swirling green blades, bloomed with fire in his chest, knocking him to the ground. The hatchet rattled on the floor.

Henry was already running, pulling Henrietta by the sleeve.

He slid to his knees in front of the shelf, but he didn't fight to reverse the swirl and clamber into the attic. This was no retreat. He couldn't see his own right hand. He saw only an arm that ended in blazing dandelion fire, and he felt nothing but its scorching heat pulsing in his limbs.

His fire met the frayed ends of his father's vines and lit them like a fuse. Henrietta screamed, and Zeke ducked as a vein of bloom exploded up the wall, spraying stone, chattering like a thousand mother squirrels. The flaming weeds fire-cracked across the ceiling and down to the two stone doors.

Stone shards sprayed across the room as Coradin struggled to his hands and knees. Every inch of the sealed arches had bloomed.

The room, already bright, was blazing. Each dandelion bloom spun its fire-story in front of Henry's eyes, but he had no time to thank them. "Go, go!" he yelled, and he grabbed the pyramid off the shelf.

With Henrietta and Zeke behind him, hanging on to his cloak, he dashed across the room, shut his eyes, turned his shoulder, and jumped into the blooms.

Flowers and stone fell to pieces, and Henry tumbled into a narrow hall. Zeke and Henrietta piled up behind him. Henry scrambled out of the tangle and grabbed his backpack from Zeke. He threw it over his shoulder and tucked the little wooden pyramid under his arm. Henrietta handed him his flashlight, and he pulled her to her feet.

"Run!" she said. Zeke was pushing them both forward.

The hall was only wide enough for them to run in single file, and black-door mouths lined both sides. Faces and old shorn heads occasionally peered out at them, blinked, and ducked away from the flashlights. Henry could feel Henrietta's grip on his backpack, and he knew Zeke wouldn't fall behind. Ignoring the doorways, he followed the hall as quickly as he could. He followed it around curves and up short flights of stairs.

And then it twisted, bent sharply, and doubled back.

Henry stopped, breathing heavily, coughing on the stale air and dust. The hall ran straight in front of him, straight as far as his flashlight could shine, straight and sloping down.

Henrietta panted behind him. "Henry, I have no idea what you did back there, but those were not normal dandelions."

Zeke laughed, coughing. "You think?"

"They looked like they were made of fire. And one shot some rock in my eye."

Henry moved forward slowly, shining his flashlight into doorways. He didn't want to be moving down, not even down a slight slope. He wanted stairs. He sneezed and rubbed his nose on his sleeve, and then his forehead with the back of his hand. He was sweating. "All dandelions are made of fire."

"Is the guy with the witch in him going to die?" Henrietta asked. "I'd think anyone would with fire dandelions growing in his chest."

Henry leaned into an arch. Stairs. A tight little spiral, but going down.

"He won't die," he said. Henrietta was leaning her backpack against a wall, with fingers locked on top of her head. "And we have to hurry. He'll be following us soon. He's a fingerling."

"I don't know what that is," Henrietta said. "But you should have killed him."

Henry stopped. They'd left Coradin on his hands and knees. He could have cut the finger off. The hatchet was right there on the floor. But he hadn't expected his knife to work so well, and he hadn't known what would happen when he connected his fire to his father's old vines. He'd been in a rush to get out of that awful crypt and nothing more.

She was right. Henry knew he wouldn't be feeling nearly as frantic if Coradin were dead. But he couldn't worry about that now. He spotlit a doorway on the other side. Stairs. And this time, going the right direction.

"Right," Henry said. "We'll try this."

"Henry," Zeke said, pointing his light down the hall. "Look."

Henry lifted his own flashlight. A group of shrunken

people, huddling together, were inching toward them. Henry handed his cousin the pyramid and dropped his backpack. He pulled out three more pieces of jerky and whipped them down the floor of the hall.

The little group froze, all sniffing. And then, scuffling and shrieking like gulls over bread, they began to fight.

"You know," Henrietta said, "we might need those. Next time toss one of the sandwiches."

Henry pulled off his cloak, folded it roughly, and rammed it under a strap on his backpack. Pulling the pack back on, he took the pyramid from Henrietta and pointed his flashlight at the stairs.

"Up," he said. "Hope it goes all the way up."

Henrietta put a hand on Henry's backpack, and Zeke put a hand on hers. Henry stepped into the cramped, tunneled spiral, and he began to climb.

The stairway was not much wider than his shoulders, and the ceiling, peaked in the center, was only a foot above his head. The stairs themselves were shallow, four inches each at most, but worn even thinner in the center. A coat of dust had settled over it all, and Henry swirled up a cloud as he went, quick-stepping at a pace he hoped he wouldn't have to keep up for long. Zeke began sneezing first, and then Henrietta, but Henry didn't slow down. Twisting around a central stone column, they climbed, and Henry dragged his fingers along the wall, brushing them over rotting wood doors, or flicking his flashlight into openings as they passed, hoping for some sign that they were no longer belowground. His legs felt like they were filling with sand

and grew heavier with each twist, with each new doorway he left behind, with every step and every new cloud of dust.

They wouldn't exactly be hard for Coradin to track. Not that he would need a stairwell breathing out an endless cloud of dust, or the three sets of footprints that had plowed it up. He had something better. He had gray strings that would track Henry wherever he went. Coradin would track the smell and the rot of Nimiane's blood in Henry's flesh.

Henry bit his lip and pushed his tired legs on. How far underground had they been? Six stories? Seven? He should have killed Coradin. Caleb would have. His dad would have. Anastasia probably would have. But Henry had run away, and now he had to keep running. He had to run until he faced Coradin and cut his puppet strings. Until he faced the other fingerlings and cut theirs. And then, when the witch made more, he'd have to face them. Unless his scar grew first, and his face turned gray and his eyes went glassy and the witch could speak out of his mouth like she had out of Coradin's. Unless she gave him his own finger. Henry knew that he would be running until the witch died. The undying witch. Even if his father trapped her again. Even if she was resealed back into Nimroth's foul crypt beneath the ancient streets of Endor, her blood would still send down its roots through Henry's body.

Henry lifted his foot for another stair and staggered forward onto a landing. Henrietta let go of his backpack and dug a knuckle into her side. Both she and Zeke had pulled their shirts up over their noses and mouths. Their foreheads were gray except where drips of sweat had drawn clean lines.

As the dust caught up to him, Henry coughed.

"You throw up quite a wake," Zeke said.

Henry swung his light around the room. "Sorry. You want to trade?"

"There's more?" Henrietta groaned.

Henry nodded at the walls. "Maybe. What do you think?"

The room was an octagon of black stone. The stairway down was on one face, and stairs continued up directly beside it. The other six faces held doorways, all of them open, all of them small, all of them leading down narrow halls.

Henrietta walked to the center of the small room and looked into each door. "I don't know. I don't see daylight anywhere. That's what I'm really hoping for. You think we're still belowground?"

Zeke stepped into one of the low doorways. "Long and straight," he said. "No light and no fresh air." He moved to the next one. "Same."

Henry set the pyramid down and watched the dust curl up beneath it. "Okay," he said. "I know that the undying Endorians all went crazy, and their kids and grandkids built a huge network of crypts and sealed them up so they wouldn't have to deal with them. It makes sense that Nimroth and his family would be in one of the deepest—nobody would want him around. But we've been climbing for a while."

Henrietta sat down.

"We have to hurry." Henry kicked the bottom of her shoe. "I really hope he is, but somehow I don't think Coradin can be too far behind us." He wiped his forehead on his arm. "Man, I wish I knew how to seal doors. He'd be stuck right now. And Nimroth and Nimiane's crazy sister are loose now, too, though I doubt they'll follow us."

Zeke turned back from the last door. "Coradin's the one who followed us through the cupboard?"

"Right," Henry said. "He has three notches in his left ear."

"And a dandelion in his chest." Henrietta puffed loose curls out of her face, but she didn't stand up. "How do you know all this, Henry?"

"He told me his name when he tried to catch me in Hylfing," Henry said. "And I have dreams. But we really need to decide which way to go."

"Whatever you think, Henry," Zeke said. "I don't know the first thing about any of this. We'll do what you tell us."

Henrietta snorted. "Will we?" she asked.

Zeke looked at her. "Yeah. We will."

Henrietta raised her eyebrows. "Maybe Henry should tell us a little more first, then we could help him decide."

Zeke shook his head and looked at Henry. "Which is it? Pick a doorway or keep climbing?"

Henrietta pushed herself up and crossed her arms. Her eyebrows were still high, creasing the dust on her forehead.

Henry turned around in the center of the room. Dust piles drifted around his shoes. "Up," he said. "Henrietta, you can go first this time."

"You go first," Zeke said. "Same as last time."

Henry looked at Zeke and then at Henrietta. She shrugged at him and nodded at the stairs. Henry picked up the pyramid, moved into the stairwell, and waited for Henrietta.

She stared at Zeke for a moment and then pulled the collar of her shirt up over her nose and mouth and stepped into place. "Watch yourself, Ezekiel Johnson," she said quietly.

Zeke smiled. "I'm pretty sure you'll do that for me."

Henry tried not to kick up as much dust, but it was hopeless. He couldn't move at all without ashen clouds swirling up around his legs. He felt bad for Henrietta and worse for Zeke and not just because they were breathing dust. Neither of them seemed to have a sense of what they were in for. Yeah, they'd been willing to crawl through the black cupboard, and they'd already been trapped in Nimiane's crypt, but he should have told them about the fingerlings. He should have realized that they would still be following, that he was no better than a fish on a line. He had gray strands trailing him, blood in him that they could sense.

Suddenly, relief surged over him, relief that they hadn't stayed in Kansas longer. If Coradin had come through the crypt cupboard, that meant that he'd found Henry's Kansas door in the cistern in Hylfing and gone into the attic. If Henry had stayed in Zeke's house, Coradin would have come to him there. He sneezed. How far could they track him? Through worlds? Could they find him in

Boston? How many cupboards would he have to jump to throw Coradin and the other eight off his scent? Or could he ever shake them?

Had they climbed another four stories? Five?

A window loomed in the wall beside Henry. A window filled with smooth stone, but still a window. Were they close? Another one. Henry slowed and pushed on it, but it was as firm as the wall itself.

"Are these windows?" Henrietta asked behind him.

"Yeah," Henry said. "I think we're close."

Henry dragged his fingers across three more as the stairs twisted on, and then he stopped. His hand was on a fourth, and the stone was cracked. Even better, dust was moving slowly down the stairs toward him. The air was moving. It didn't smell fresh—at least not Kansas fresh—but there probably wasn't such a thing in this place.

"What is it?" Zeke asked.

"The air's moving."

"Well, hurry up," Henrietta said. "I'd like to breathe again."

Henry forgot his rubber legs and hurried forward. Another window, and around the next twist . . . he was pushing through rubble and found himself standing on a stone octagon, a small platform. But this time, they stood beneath a night sky. There were no stars, and only the faintest hint of moonlight managed to filter through a blanket of clouds. Cool air drifted freely around them, and on every side, the walls were gapped or missing entirely. Rotten beams from what had once been a ceiling sprawled across the floor. Beneath them, bent and angled, there lay a huge bell, tarnished and green.

Henrietta and Zeke squeezed up beside Henry and stood silently surveying the situation with flashlights.

"Um," Henrietta said. "Henry, are we in a bell tower?" She climbed over a beam, walked to the edge of the platform, and looked down. She sighed and turned her flashlight on Henry's face. "We're higher than I've ever been before." She swung her flashlight around, and its light caught the spires of neighboring towers and the distant teeth of rooflines.

Henry followed her to the edge, leaned over the low rubble, and pointed his flashlight down the side of the black tower. It fell away smoothly, spotted only with dust and windows, until its rounded surface seamed into the wall of a bigger building and eventually, at the very bottom, reached a pale street. The thin gray street ran on a little ways and then emptied into a city circle, just visible from their perch. The buildings around them were a few stories shorter, and the flashlights brushed over silent windows and gaping doors.

Henry sat on a beam and put his head in his hands. "Turn it off," he said, and flipped the switch on his own flashlight. "Anyone watching will know we're here."

Henrietta and Zeke both killed their lights. Henrietta turned. Henry could barely make out her shape. Or he thought he could. "Well," she said. "On the bright side, we are definitely aboveground. And we don't have to climb any more stairs. For some reason, I thought we'd have some daylight. I'm kind of glad we're not down in those streets right now. Ouch." Henry heard rocks crack together, and then she sat beside him. "Now give me a piece of jerky."

Henry set the pyramid on the beam beside him and unzipped his backpack. "I'm sorry," he said. "This really isn't good." He handed Henrietta the jerky.

"Jerky doesn't go bad," she said, and he heard her rip it with her teeth.

"No." He smiled despite himself. "I'm sure the jerky's fine. Everyone here seems to like it."

"I think this is as good a place as any," Zeke said from the dark. "It's not exactly expected. We could stick here until daylight and then look for your dad."

"It doesn't matter," Henry said. "We can't stop. We can't stick. Not until we're ready to fight. Coradin can find me anywhere. And there's eight others who can, too."

"How?" Henrietta asked.

"The witch's blood," Henry said. He tapped his jaw. "It's in me. I shouldn't have brought you here, but I didn't want to come alone. I'm sorry."

Zeke and Henrietta were both silent.

"Okay," Henrietta said. "I need to know. What *is* a fingerling?"

Henry massaged his cheekbones. He was such an idiot. What had he been planning to do? How would he possibly find his father in an enormous, pitch-black city? It had seemed so easy, like it would all just fall into place. He pulled the necklace out of his shirt and gripped it tight. Now he was sitting at the top of a tower, waiting. Coradin was on the stairs somewhere, climbing. The only question was how far he had come already.

Henry cleared his throat, and as quickly and as painlessly as he could, he described his dream of the men in the garden and the gray strands he could see growing from the fingerlings' heads

"That's pretty sick," Henrietta said. "Are they wizards?"

"I don't know," Henry said. "Could be, but their power seems more like hers. I want you both to go."

"Where?" Zeke asked.

Henrietta laughed. "Henry, I am not walking back down those stairs. My legs are fried, and some guy with notches in his ear and a finger on his head is coming up the other way."

Henry dug through his backpack until he found his own kitchen knife, borrowed from Mrs. Johnson. He'd thrown Henrietta's. Holding the knife, he stood up.

"There's nowhere to go," Zeke said.

Henry flicked on his flashlight. Henrietta and Zeke both blinked. He pointed his light down, down on the little pyramid, then he bent over and flipped open the triangle door. "You're going back to Kansas," he said.

Zeke stood up. "Not a chance, Henry."

Henrietta laughed. "Now who's the boss?"

Henry ignored her. "Listen," he said. "The witch only cares about me. If you leave, you'll be fine."

"Or," Henrietta said, "we could throw you off the tower. Then we'd be fine, too. Right?"

Zeke crossed his arms. "We're not going anywhere." He looked at Henrietta. "At least I'm not."

"We're not," Henrietta said.

Henry pointed his light down the stairwell. "This was a horrible idea."

"There weren't any better ones," Zeke said. "You need to find your father."

Henrietta hugged herself and shivered. "Now what? Wait?"

Henry pulled his wadded-up cloak off his backpack and tossed it to his cousin. "I don't think we should wait. I think we should go down. Maybe he was slow getting out of the crypt."

"Maybe we got lucky and Nia ate him," Henrietta said. "Is this a baseball in your pocket?"

Henry looked back at his cousin. She held the ball up in the light.

"Why do you have a baseball in your pocket? That's not your handwriting. Henry York Maccabee." She grinned at Henry. "Richard wrote your name on the ball?"

Henry nodded and reached out for it. "I took it with me for luck when I went out with Fat Frank before . . . well, before everything." Henrietta handed it to him; he gripped the leather and the strings and tucked it into his sweatshirt pouch.

"I'm sure Richard would love to be here right now," Henrietta said. "He's worse than the raggant."

"Henry," Zeke said, stepping closer to the stair mouth. "Listen."

Henry clicked off his light, and the three of them held as still as the stone. A dry breeze shifted the ash and dust around their feet. Night, black and heavy, swallowed them.

Drifting out of the stairwell came the sound of shuffling feet. Henry's ears strained, and he swallowed hard. Now was the time. Coradin would die here on top of a ruined bell tower. He would have to. Henry didn't want to think about the other option. He blinked. Something about the sound was strange. There were more than two feet.

"Is that an echo?" Henrietta whispered. "Please tell me that's an echo."

The shuffling grew louder. Feet tromping in and out of sync. Lots of feet. Henry's heart sank. His skin went clammy.

"That's not an echo," Zeke said.

Voices rose out of the stairs.

CHAPTER ELEVEN

Anastasia looked back over her shoulder at the city. The pale walls and spires were glowing in the moonlight. Two galleys stood out in the silvered water of the harbor.

They were going to see someone the pirate faeries called the Chestnut King. That much she understood. But whether he was a real king or not, she hadn't expected this. She wasn't sure what she had expected, but definitely not a long walk into the hills.

The faeries had invisibly led them through the streets, through the square, and out the rear gate. She'd been surprised to see red-shirted soldiers still in the square and around the hall. She'd been surprised to see a three-bodied serpent still flapping over the city.

The climb into the hills had been long, up cattle trails, through tall grass, and over boulders. Her shoes, more useful as slippers than for what they were doing now, had already torn scrambling over rock.

Una held her hand. Fat Frank walked easily in front of them, unaffected by the climb. Richard was wheezing behind. She wondered if he had asthma. The other faeries seemed to be all around them, appearing and disappearing into shadow. Occasionally, disembodied voices called out to each other, or strange whistles—soft and almost impossible to hear, or sharp and strong—echoed in the rocks.

"I thought the soldiers and the ships left," Anastasia said. "Why are they still in the harbor?"

Fat Frank jumped onto a rock, and his round features were sharpened with moon shadow. He looked like a badly carved statue, maybe of a young troll. "The big galley left," he said. "The others are only wishing that they had."

"Why's that?" Una asked.

"Because," Frank said, jumping down, "Mordecai's still loose, and that's his town they're in, and that's his house they've burned, and that's his family what's missing. The red-shirts down there are in for it, and they know as much, too. Three heads or no, that snake's coiled in an eagle's nest."

Jacques appeared out of the shadows beside Anastasia. "Mordecai," he said, and his mustache grinned. "Again this Mordecai. Not all peoples fear the green men like the low faeren. The greens do little but tell tales of themselves and grow in legend."

"Low?" Frank asked. "The queene's faeren are low, are they? And Mordecai's a liar?" He snorted. "Who put Nimiane in her bed, then? Did the 'high' faeren?"

"I wouldn't know," Jacques said. "Not having been there. Were you, Fat Franklin? Did you stand and watch or were you shrouded deep within your mound, guarding the grubs with the other brown ants?"

"Maybe I was," Frank said. "And maybe I wasn't. Where

was the king? In his gardens, growing chestnuts? He's shown no face or fight in my lifetime, nor my father's. Where were you, Jacques One-Eye, when Endor spread its fingers through the earth, graying the green things?"

Frank stopped and shifted his belt beneath his belly. Jacques faced him, smiling, pulling his mustache.

"Men make their own troubles," Jacques said. "Let them bury their own nightmare dead. Faeren should keep to the Second World and wash their hands of green men."

"What's the Second World?" Anastasia asked.

Jacques winked at her. "Does faerie blood tickle your veins? Have you walked the ancient mounds? We faeren have our secrets."

"Mr. One-Eye," Richard said between breaths. "Does your king not stand against the villainy of Endor?"

Jacques grinned, and he scrambled up the path in front of them to the top of a small rise. "My king," he said, raising his arms, "stands against the villainies of the villainous. He stands against big-booted empires and egg-sucking snakes and over-preening queens and groveling faeren and trouble-picking green men and dead-living witches and walled cities and rules by the ruled and foxes in cages and duties and obligatings." He took a deep breath and held up a thick finger. "He stands for all laughter, aged honey, naps in the sun, and high-sky winds. He stands for troubling the troublers and freeing the foxes and liberating treasures and eating grapes. He stands for doing as he pleases and keeping to hisself. And chestnuts. He stands for chestnuts."

Fat Frank snorted and shook his head. Jacques laughed

and disappeared into shadow. Anastasia looked at Una and then back at Richard. The four seemed to be suddenly walking alone, climbing higher and higher into the hills as the moon dropped slowly.

"How far?" Anastasia asked.

Una smiled with tight lips. "Too far."

"Three more hills." Jacques's voice floated out of the darkness. "We have to be cautious magicking in the low faeren regions."

Anastasia felt a tap on her shoulder. She and Una both turned. Richard, struggling behind them, coughed and cleared his throat. "If," he said, "either of you have need of assistance . . ." He wiped his mouth on his sleeve. "I will oblige."

Anastasia laughed. Una squeezed her hand. "Do you need any help?" she asked Richard. "You don't look too well."

Jacques hopped down behind the girls. Standing on the slope, he grabbed Richard's cheeks and looked directly into his eyes. "Whelpling," he said. "We have three more ridges to cross before morning. Are you ill?"

Richard shook his head and winced. "I'm fit," he said.

The faerie ran his hands around Richard's scalp. "What is this?" he asked. "A hen lay an egg in your skull or has someone been clubbing you?"

"The street," Richard said. "Fat Frank knocked me out of the wagon into the street. I hit it then."

Jacques closed Richard's eyes with his thumbs, muttered a string of words, and blew in the boy's face. Richard went completely rigid, his mouth hanging open, his arms at his sides, and Jacques laid him down on the slope.

"The lads will bring him," Jacques said. "We must move more quickly."

Fat Frank bent over Richard and stuck his fingers on his neck. "More likely the wolves will find themselves an easy supper. Bring him along now, where I can see."

Jacques sniffed and adjusted his eye patch. "Franklin Fat, don't you trust me, an agent of your king?"

"No," Frank said. "That I don't. No more than a weasel with ducklings nor a heron with fish. This lad's had his feet on a hard path long before being grabbed by serpent soldiers, cracked on the cobbles by my own self, and dragged up here by outlaw faeren. I won't risk him being left here in the tall grass and nibbled to his death in the night."

Jacques whistled and turned up the hill. Two faeren stepped out of the darkness and lifted Richard easily to their shoulders. Pale, light, and stiff, he looked like a paper statue. The faeries moved quickly around the girls and up.

"Richard is honestly the most annoying person I know," Anastasia said.

"He is loyal," Una said. "Be kind to him."

Anastasia thought about this. He was loyal. He was also scrawny and fat-lipped and pompous. Fat Frank glanced back at her and nodded.

"Right, then!" Jacques yelled from the dark. "Quicken up, girlies, before we leave you all for the night nibblers."

The two girls climbed with the moonlight on their backs. Ahead of them Franklin Faerie walked quickly, full of nervous energy, skipping onto rocks, ruffling his thick hair, muttering to himself, and pulling at his earlobes. Somewhere, hidden from the moon by shadow and magic, thirteen faeries moved around them, and one boy, rigid as a wooden bat, bouncing on shoulders, dreamed concussedly that he could play baseball.

Henry turned in place, studying the roof and its beams, flicking his flashlight off and then back on, his mind whirring frantically. His jaw throbbed with piercing cold. He was sure sound carried well up the stone stairs, but they still couldn't have long.

"What do we do?" Henrietta whispered. "You have our only knife."

"Barricade?" Zeke asked, tugging at a beam.

"I have to think," Henry said. "Think." He grabbed at his necklace, gripping it tight. "We can't fight," he said. "Not all of them." He set down his flashlight and kicked at the rubble.

"All of who?" Henrietta whispered behind him.

Henry held up a finger to the back of his head.

"What? All ten?" she asked.

"Nine," Henry said. "I killed one in the fire." He grunted, shoving a beam, looking for he didn't know what. An elevator?

Thick rope for the bell twisted through the rubble, but nowhere near what they would need to reach any of the lower roofs, let alone the street. There were stones, bent spikes, splayed and rotten beams, an old slat-sided box—

nothing that could help him against what climbed the stairs. He needed time. A little space to think. Henry picked up the biggest stone he could find. Turning to the bell, groaning, he struggled to lift it above his head.

"Henry?" Zeke said.

Henry yelled, as loud and as long as he could. Green pulsed through his bones, gold fired in his blood, and he heaved the rock onto the ancient, tarnished bell.

The stone shattered, sparking blooms as the deep peal climbed into the sky and vibrated through the stone floor. It passed through Henry in quivering waves, and he grabbed at his ears. Henrietta dropped to the ground and curled into a ball. Zeke staggered backward.

As soon as he could, Henry straightened and kept rooting through the rubble.

"Why on earth?" Henrietta asked.

"Do it again," Henry said. "A few more times. There's no point in hiding. Make them wonder. If they think we're planning something, they might slow a bit."

Henrietta stood up. Zeke scooped up two rocks and bounced them off the bell one after the other.

"*Are* we planning something?" Henrietta yelled. She heaved her own rock, and Zeke bounced two more. One hopped over the edge and off the tower. Henry watched it fall.

"Maybe," he said. "Listen at the stairs. Tell me if you hear anything." He looked back at the old slatted box, tangled with rope, half-buried in shattered stone. "Zeke, help me."

Henry jumped over a beam and grabbed at the box. Zeke followed, and together they shifted it out of the rubble, dumping old bolts and a rag as it came.

Henrietta crouched by the stairwell. "Nothing," she said. "But you all are making too much noise."

Henry sawed at the thick bell-rope with his kitchen knife. It was dry, already frayed, and his blade went through easily. He tucked the little knife into his pouch with the baseball. Picking up the old box, Henry scrambled to the side of the tower overlooking the tiny street below. He fed a few coils of rope in quickly and then nestled the little black pyramid inside them. Then he wound more rope around it, leaving only the door exposed. He picked up the whole thing, and Zeke, understanding, wrapped the excess rope around the slats. Then Henry tipped the rope-wrapped and rope-stuffed box onto its side so the pyramid faced him, and he balanced it on the ruined wall.

He shut his eyes.

"Steps," Henrietta said quietly. "They're still coming."

The world around Henry was nothing but gray and black, slow and twisting. His own gray jaw strands mingled with it, drifting out, and then bending sharply away behind him. They were thicker and more taut than they had been. Something was pulling on them.

He had nothing to draw on. There were no dandelions here, no living wood, no living stone. The life had been drained from everything.

He had the necklace. His hand found it. He had himself. Hot life grew inside of him. He had his cousin and his friend. Reaching behind him, he found their strength, mingling with cold fear and doubt. Stretching out his right hand, he opened his eyes.

"Getting louder," Henrietta said.

Henry slid backward. "Go, Henrietta," he said. "Quickly. Dive. The seam's not big."

"What, off the edge?" Henrietta asked.

"Into the box," Henry said. "Now." He shut his eyes again and raised his dandelion hand to fight the shrinking hole. His cousin's life stepped past him and disappeared.

"Zeke," Henry said, and his own voice sounded strange to him, lost in the distance.

Zeke's settled, slow strength moved forward and disappeared.

Henry clenched his jaw and lunged into the swirl.

The flashlight, perched on a beam beside a forgotten backpack, stared across the rubble and the bell. It watched an empty sky. It watched men in black rise from the stairs carrying torches. It glinted off the long silver knives in their belts.

Henry didn't have time to wipe his bleeding nose. He groped around on the attic floor.

"Flashlight?" he asked the darkness. "Flashlight?"

Henrietta groaned.

"Hold on." Zeke's voice.

Henry felt for the wall. A light flicked on, and he oriented himself. The wall of cupboards, swirling their smells and sounds around him. His old mattress. The black door to the little pyramid perched on a tower wall in Endor. He dropped to his belly and shoved his right arm in, feeling for stone, for something to push against.

Coradin stood on the tower. The others had come as soon as they had felt Henry's presence in the dead city. Mordecai was not so easy to hunt.

Coradin's shirt was torn, but he'd ripped the strange boy's weeds from his chest. He stared at the flashlight. He picked up the backpack.

The boy still felt very close, but a sensation of extreme distance seemed stronger. He had learned what that meant. The boy had used a doorway. To the others, this was new. He could hear them sniffing. And then a cry of surprise.

He turned. Something was moving on the wall. A white hand and wrist, stretching out of a box. Young fingers. The box was tipping.

Henry couldn't tell if it was working. He pushed against stone and then grabbed at the box's edge and pulled.

A strong hand closed around his wrist.

Henry jerked back. He swung his legs around and braced his knees against the wall. There was life here in the attic, strength in the wood, in the cold air above the roof and the endless grassy plains. He grabbed his opponent's wrist and felt bursting dandelion heat pour through his palm. The man screamed and tried to tug his arm away. It was Henry's turn to hunt. He pulled hard. Air moved around his hand and whistled into the cupboard. The box was free-falling, and a fingerling with it.

Henry pulled the writhing arm all the way in and held it tight. The thick, scarred fingers splayed and twisted, searching for a grip. The arm jerked and fought to pull free. Suddenly, a splintering crash lifted Henry off the attic floor and slammed him into the wall. A cloud of ash and dust exploded into the room.

"You okay?" Zeke asked behind him. "Did it work?"

Gasping for breath, Henry sat up and stared at the now-limp arm in its black sleeve. He couldn't make the same mistake again. Taking the little knife out of his pouch, he reached back through the cupboard and felt for the fingerling's head.

Coradin watched his blood brother grab the boy's wrist. He watched the shock and burning pain when the boy grabbed back with that fiery hand. He'd felt it. The box toppled. His brother had gone with it.

Leaning over the wall, Coradin dropped a torch to the street. When the ash had cleared, the flame still sputtered on. Rope and splintered wood tangled with the body. A hand moved. The boy's hand.

Coradin flinched as an invisible tie was severed. Another blood brother had gone.

He waited for the witch's anger to burn through him.

To punish him. Nothing. He looked at his other brothers, five of the six sent to Endor for Mordecai. He nodded at the stairs.

"Down," he said, and they turned.

Far to the south and to the east, the morning sun climbed over a strip of land between two seas—one pale and bright, smooth, with white sand at its shallow bottom, and the other dark and angry, frothing deep water against worn sea walls. The sun blazed on the waters' backs and poured through the tall sea gates of Dumarre, the City of the Seas, warming the stone. In the streets, merchants and vendors called to each other, and wagons wound their way from the piers of one harbor to the piers of the other. Slaves dragged barges through narrow canals, the drivers' tongues and whips lashing them forward.

Over the walls, above the palaces, a red flag flew, forked at the fly. The three white bodies of a single-headed serpent writhed in the wind. In a great hall, the morning sun fell on a wide wooden throne, its dark legs crawling with carvings of people and armies and cities and rivers and beasts. The back was scaled like a serpent, but as it rose, instead of three bodies, it divided into three open-mouthed heads. An old man with hooded eyes sat on the throne, leaning against the broad arm. A heavy chair sat empty beside him. Crowded nobles shifted nervously in their finery, curious why they'd been called. The old man lifted his hand, heavy with rings, and the men and women parted and faced a pair of tall doors in the rear of the hall.

It was time.

A drumbeat, and a voice echoed through the vaulted ceiling. The doors creaked open.

"Nimiane, one-time sovereign of Endor, daughter to the ancient kings, queen consort to the emperor!"

A rustling wave of shock and whispers swept through the crowd, and Nimiane, tall and terrible, beautiful as a forest in flame, stepped into the hall. Her rich skin shone as she walked. Her hair towered in glistening gold-dusted braids above her. Her sleek, bare arms held a white-faced cat. She stopped before the throne and dipped herself slowly. The old emperor nodded. Facing the assembled, she sat and filled her lungs with the deep and ancient smell of power.

A man, fair and thin, with a face like the man in her garden, stepped out of the assembly and walked quickly toward the doors. Two men in black stepped in front of the red-shirted guards and blocked his way. Nimiane smiled at him, at the anger of the emperor's son. No noble blood, no matter how pure, would leave the hall without bowing before her.

She would possess the world.

A sudden bite flicked through her. She winced. A mind had been lost. A finger had been cut.

Beyond the hall, stretched between two trees, a man cried out in pain.

Henry groveled, coughing in the street's ash. He hadn't brought Zeke's flashlight, but dandelions glowed around the fingerling's body and out the back of his head. Ten yards beyond the body, a torch sputtered on its side. Henry, sniffing against his bloody nose, staggered toward it. The tower loomed high above him. Somewhere inside, Coradin and the others were descending.

Henry lifted the torch and surveyed the scene. The box had shattered, rope splayed around the street in the troughed ash. The door to the little pyramid was gone, and the wood was splintered around the hinges. Other than that, it seemed fine. He pulled it out of its rope nest and looked down at the man's gold-rimmed body.

"I'm sorry," he said, and he tucked the pyramid under his arm. "Maybe you weren't as bad as she made you." He backed slowly away, down the street toward the city circle he had seen from the bell tower. "Maybe you were."

Still holding the torch, Henry turned and ran, his feet softly thudding in the inches of ash and dust in the street. Henrietta and Zeke were safe. At least for now. He looked down at the black cupboard and laughed. Safe under his arm. Adrenaline livened his tired legs. A second fingerling was dead, and he'd escaped Coradin twice. But where could he go now to escape the pack that was hunting him? If he'd stayed in the attic, the fingerlings would have walked right to the little pyramid in the street and followed him through. He had to muddy his tracks, like a fox running in a stream to shake the hounds. He would find someplace hidden, some corner of this city, and then he would go through the cupboard and double-back quickly into Badon Hill. The fingerlings would sense him there, far to the north, but in the same world. They might not be able to find the cupboard then. And if they did, when they'd followed him, he could face them on that northern island, teeming with strength, where *his* ancestors were buried. And he could call up faeren to help him. If the fingerlings couldn't find the cupboard, then he could make quick searches out of it—in daylight—until he found his father.

Light. Why was he carrying a torch? He glanced up at the flame and then back up at the tower. They wouldn't need his gray threads to track him this way.

"Stupid," Henry said out loud, and he hurled it away, through a gaping door.

A bent and shadowy shape, shorn bald, yelped and ducked suddenly out of the way.

"Sorry!" Henry yelled, and he pushed his legs harder, past alleys and side streets, past burned-out ruins and palatial buildings, and finally, out into acres of city circle.

Henry slowed and blinked, looking around. He could see a little better now that he had thrown the torch away. Street mouths spidered out from the circle on all sides. Buildings loomed up black against a graying sky. The sun was coming. Henry jogged toward the center and sneezed as his cloudy wake caught up to him. Across the circle squatted an enormous palace. Stairs rose up to it from the street. Towers rose up from it into the sky.

Henry quickened his pace and ran directly toward it. The fingerlings would be in the streets soon. He needed to be through the cupboards before they could close any distance on him.

His adrenaline wore off quickly, and his legs were tight and stiff before he reached the stairs. A stitch was knotting in his side. He pushed himself to the bottom of the stairs and braced himself for the climb.

Barbs pierced into his shoulder, knocking him forward onto the stairs. And again. Four clusters of gripping needles, and a beating wind, swirling the ash. Yelling, Henry twisted onto his back, swinging his fists. Two huge owls lifted above him, silhouetted against the fast-lightening sky. A sharp whistle from somewhere, and the birds lifted farther, circling slowly. Muffled thunder echoed off the building behind him, and Henry sat up.

Not thunder. Heavy horses, five of them, feather-feet pounding the dust. And beside them loped an enormous dog.

Henry staggered to his feet, and he burst into wet-eyed laughter. Fear fell away from him. Let the fingerlings come. Let them bring all the red-shirted soldiers they could find and raise Nimroth and his marble. Wiping his face quickly, he picked up the cupboard and ran forward.

"Stand!" Caleb's voice rolled around the circle. Henry stopped. He could see them now, Caleb and his bow, Mordecai beside him.

"Who rang the bell?" Caleb asked, and the horses slowed, cratering ash with each hoof.

"I did," Henry said, and the horses turned sideways, prancing to a stop. The pony-size dog ran to him, knocked him back a step, and licked his face.

Mordecai leaned forward in his saddle. "Henry?"

Henry nodded, ran to his father's stirrup. Mordecai reached down, his palm glowing purple and green. Gripping his son's arm, he pulled Henry up onto the broad horse behind him.

"I'll tell you everything later," Henry said, and he pointed back across the circle.

Six figures, five holding torches, stood framed in the tower street.

CHAPTER TWELVE

Frank Willis leaned forward and watched the sweat drip off his nose. In front of him, three hundred slave backs bent over three hundred oars in rhythm, and then, with the unanimous groan of men and timber, those bare backs arched and pulled, knotting and contracting, shining with sweat, squeezing more heat, more stink, into the air of the hold.

Again, they groaned, and Frank could feel the ship crawl forward beneath him.

Soldiers with whips in their hands and fleece in their nostrils walked a narrow plank between the tiered oarsmen. The tiers were stacked in a v, the lowest groaning men sat pinched all the way in against the narrow walkway. Those on the top struggled precariously on seats cornered between the hull and the beamed deck above.

"Those poor men," Dotty said.

Frank strained to look back over his shoulder at his wife. Her face glistened red, as did Penelope's beside her. Hyacinth had her eyes shut, and her face was pale beneath beads of sweat. James and Isa were chained together, one pile of sacks over. Isa had her head on her brother's shoulder. She winced at every cracking whip. James sat as upright as he could. His jaw was set, and his eyes were angry.

"Dots," Frank said. "You hangin' in there, love? Pen?"

Penelope and Dotty both nodded. Dotty looked above Frank's head, at the dangling kelp sack that held Monmouth.

"I'm worried about him."

"He won't survive the day," James said. "Not in the heat belowdecks."

Frank cranked his head back and looked up at the bagged wizard. As the slaves groaned and the ship moved forward, the prison hammock rocked on its hooks. The laces bulged beneath Monmouth's weight.

"Monmouth," Frank said. "You still breathin'?"

The large sack creaked and swayed and said nothing.

Isa sat up. "Is he dead already?"

Penelope opened her eyes. "Who's dead?"

"No one," Frank said. "No one's dead just yet." Straining at his chains, he managed to get his legs beneath him and push up into a crouch. The shackles dug into the skin around his wrists, and he pulled harder, trying to reach the sack with his head. A dangling lace tickled his scalp, and grunting with the slaves, he got another inch. He butted the bag.

"I am alive," Monmouth said. "And, no matter what James might think, I will be tomorrow."

With a rattle of chains, Frank collapsed back down. "Next time we're guessin' at your death, try resolving the issue with a little shout. Maybe a whistle."

"How did you reach me?" Monmouth asked.

"With an impressive acrobatic feat," Frank said. "A meeting of grace and power. Like figure skating."

Dotty smiled. Penelope laughed.

"Figure what?" Isa asked.

Monmouth coughed, and the bag shook. "Do you have enough grace and power to reach the laces?"

Frank stared at the bottom of the bag and its bulging seam. He cocked his head, squinting at the loose dangling end that he'd touched.

"Maybe," said Frank. "And maybe not." He shook the chains behind him. "I'll give it my best Houdini."

"Who's Dini?" Isa asked. James shrugged.

Frank moved back into his crouch and bit his lip. Pain was all right. He could handle pain, so long as it had a point. But he was glad that he couldn't see the skin on his wrists. He could already feel blood, warm and sticky, trickling into his palms and thickening between his fingers.

"Don't hurt yourself," Dotty said.

Frank grinned at her. "That, Dots of mine, is exactly what I am going to do. If I'd hurt myself back in Hylfing, maybe we wouldn't be in the septic belly of this galley."

He jerked up against the shackles and bit his tongue in pain. "Skin," he said, and his legs shook with his pushing, "grows back."

Hyacinth sat up and opened her eyes. "Francis," she said. "Not now."

Frank looked back at her and dropped down. He followed her eyes out to the galley benches.

As he turned, a great cracking rattled down the left side of the ship. The oars had tangled. Handles bent and snapped and threw slaves against their chain leashes, against the hull, against each other. The oarsmen on the right side all levered their blades out of the water. Soldiers tumbled down the ladders, shouting. Two men stepped back on either side of Frank and stood with crossbows, watching as slaves were unchained and righted on their benches. Broken oars were shoved out through the oarlocks and given to the sea. Broken slaves, unconscious or dead or moaning over bent limbs, were pulled onto the walkway.

Frank Willis watched with a clenched jaw as five and then six and then seven limp bodies were dragged to the stern and heaved out of a hatch and into the sea. Behind him, Dotty gasped as more followed—the badly injured were knocked unconscious first. A few lucky others, gripping wrists or ribs, were taken abovedecks.

And then, with whips in hand, watched over by the bowmen, the masters rebalanced the ship. Slaves from the right were shuffled to the left and arranged. New oars were pulled from beneath the walkway and fitted in place, and the hold quieted. Oars were still, and soldiers spaced themselves evenly along the walkway.

The captain descended. He glanced at Frank and his other prisoners and then positioned himself directly in front of them to survey the balance of oarsmen.

"How many?" he asked.

"Captain, fifteen!" yelled the closest master.

"Fifteen lost." The captain adjusted the wool in his nose. "Uneven." He nodded and the man hurried forward, carrying his whip. When he stopped, the captain spoke again. "Add an oarsman to the left. The right is strong by one."

"We have no other bodies," the master said. "But one affects nothing."

Frank Willis hung his head. He knew what was coming. He had provoked it. Roderick, who had grown up in the shadow of his family, looked down at him. And then he looked back at James.

"Unchain him," he said. "And place him on the left."

"He's Mordecai's son," the master said.

The captain wheeled on him, flushing. He grabbed Frank by the hair. "And this is Mordecai's brother!" Spit flew from his mouth. "And there sit his daughter and his wife and his niece." He punched Monmouth's sack. "And here is Mordecai's wizard pupil. I will lash them all to oars if need demands! I will feed them to the sea. Mordecai is nothing to me."

The soldiers stood motionless. Slaves peered back over their shoulders.

The captain dropped Frank's hair. "Now strip the lad and chain him to an oar, or be stripped and chained yourself."

Soldiers scrambled past Frank and into the sacks. They unchained James and dragged him out. He stood, with shoulders square and head up, staring at the captain. His shirt was ripped from his back and his trousers from his legs.

Frank watched his broad nephew's knotted ribs as they rose and fell with long, slow breaths. The captain stepped closer, and the two stood eye to eye.

"Pride is a brittle bone," the captain said. "Easily broken."

"Envy is a worm," James said. "Consuming souls."

"Envy?" Roderick laughed, and looked from James to Hyacinth to Frank. "What is there to envy about your family?" He nodded to the soldiers, turned, and walked to the ladders. A whip cracked, and James flinched.

Hyacinth looked away. Isa, now chained to her timber alone, squeezed her eyes tight and tucked her face down into her shoulder.

James was taken to an empty bench, halfway up the *v*, and a new oar was fished into place.

"Mordecai's son!" a slave jeered. "We'll see you fed to the gulls!"

A chorus of anger rose to shout him down, but the whips brought silence with their cracking. Oar blades were lowered to the water, and soon, guided by shouts and lashings, they groaned in time.

In the heat and the stink and the rhythm of the galley hold, Frank leaned forward. The ship sighed beneath him with each stroke. The slaves groaned and flexed and groaned again, pushing timbers through the sea. With his eyes on the shining, striped back of his brother's son, Frank slid his wrists against the shackles and swallowed back the pain.

*   *   *

An old crow cocked its head and blinked in the sun. It had been half-asleep, letting its feathers gather warmth before heading out through the wood in search of an early lunch. But something large had just floated by above the ground. The bird sidestepped down the branch into a small patch of shade, leaned forward, and looked again.

Through the brush and around stone, three bodies floated in a line, each perfectly stiff. The crow knew stiffness. Stiffness meant death, and while the bird preferred pulling soft snails from their shells, it wasn't about to pass up an easy meal, even if it was drifting well above the ground.

Croaking loudly—this meal was too big for him alone—the bird spread its wings and dropped off the branch.

Anastasia opened her eyes and squinted into the sunlight shining down between trees and branches and breeze-fluttered leaves. Squinting was about all that she could do. Jacques had grown impatient with their exhaustion, with their human-girl speed, and now she could open and close her eyes and breathe. No more. At first she'd been able to speak, but the mustachioed faerie had adjusted that after twenty minutes of questions.

A black shape flicked through the sunlight, gliding beneath branches, and a throaty call told her what it was. A crow. She shut her eyes again. Her face was hot.

Something landed on her stomach, cawing loudly.

Blinking, she focused on the bird. It walked slowly up

to her chest and turned its head, staring at her with one large, curious brown eye. She tried to blow on it, but her lips wouldn't pucker. The bird flared its wings and hopped to her shoulder, bent over, and stared off the edge, down at the ground. Straightening, it eyeballed her again, and again bent over, searching for her legs or wings or whatever she was using to move.

Anastasia tried to laugh, but only managed a motionless snort.

The bird hopped back to her stomach, startled. Two other crows landed beside the first, both sleeker and gray-eyed. All three flared wings and bobbed, cawing. More circled ahead, descending.

Anastasia's heart raced. The faeries had to notice. And they had to notice before she lost an eye or a lip. She managed to grunt, and then inhaling over her limp tongue, she snorted. But no one set her down, and the branches still slid by quickly.

Leaves parted around her, and she was in shadow. Deep, cool shade. The sun was gone, and an enormous, dense canopy cut off the sky. The sleek crows flapped up, cawing frantically, fighting to retreat through green. The old, brown-eyed bird hopped forward, gave her a last, long, one-eyed stare, bobbed its head, gargling, and followed the others.

Invisible hands lowered Anastasia to the cool earth. Una, rigid, four feet off the ground, rocked down beside her.

Jacques's face appeared above her upside down. Sweat

dripped down his bald head, through his bushy eyebrow, and onto the purple eye patch. He smiled.

"Up, poppy," he said. "Should have toted you from the first."

Anastasia's body went suddenly limp. She coughed and put her hands to her face, opening and shutting her jaw slowly. Then she sat up.

They were in a hollow. Moss and bare dark earth spread up the sides of the bowl. Limbs as thick as any tree she had ever seen loomed out over the cool circle, dipping the broad fingers of chestnut leaves down nearly to the ground at the outermost.

In the center, three enormous trunks rose up separately and then joined together to form a single tree as big around as an old grain silo.

Una sat up beside Anastasia and looked at the strange canopy. Richard, still stiff, snored quietly.

"Where's Fat Frank?" Una asked.

Jacques, the only visible faerie, turned around. "He is being taken. We follow soon."

Anastasia looked up into the tree. The branches bulged with green spiked clusters. "Are the chestnuts square?"

Jacques laughed. "The konkers will hold triplets of any shape the king desires. This is one of the ancient three-maced trees, a gateway to his kingdom."

"Konkers," Anastasia said quietly. She looked down at the faerie. "Are we going into a faerie mound? Henry says the faeren live in mounds."

"Stand," Jacques said. "And follow."

Both girls scrambled to their feet. Richard's stiff body rose off the ground. The broad faerie moved between the girls and gripped their arms above the elbow. Together, they walked toward the triple trunk and stepped easily into its center.

Jacques turned them to the left, and they walked back out and veered right around the next trunk and stepped back in. Back and forth, they wove in and out of the great tree, twisting and looping and turning while Jacques whispered to himself, concentrating, like he was reciting the pattern.

Anastasia's eyes widened as they moved in and out of darkness, circling in the domed green world. Each time they stepped out of the tree, something had changed. The ground was more level, or even sloping down. The moss was taller, yellower. The tree's canopy was higher, the tree younger, the trunk slighter. Green konkers, ripe and cracked open, lay strewn on the ground. The tree was in bloom, perched high on a hill, and what was that beneath her? A highway? With cars? It was. She knew it was, and she could just hear a horn honking far beneath her as they turned again into the trunk and stepped out beneath bare branches and falling snow.

Una laughed. The faerie was twisting them in and out of a dozen different trees, winding them around the surface of the world, around the worlds.

And then they stopped, centered beneath the trunk, with a soft bed of loam and leaves and bark beneath their feet.

"Shut your eyes," Jacques said, and squeezing the girls'

arms tight, he pulled them backward into a cool, light, drizzling rain.

"Turn," he said.

Anastasia did, and her mouth fell open. They stood on an open plain, rolling slightly, lush with short turf, deeper and brighter in its green than Kansas in the spring, spotted in places with ancient trees. Behind them was a dense wood. And in front of them, dominating the plain, rose a round, steep hill, nearly a mountain. Its sides, emerald green, stepped up in seven leaning and off-balance terraces to the peak. And the peak was crowned with a tall square tower. Knobbed spikes reached into the sky off each of its corners. Behind the green, behind the hill and the trees and the tower, the sky swirled with the whites and grays and charcoals of the rain-bearing clouds.

Fat Frank stood staring at it with his thumbs in his belt. He glanced at Anastasia and looked quickly away. His bulbous cheeks had been wet. "Never thought I'd see it. Nor that it existed to be seen."

"What?" Jacques said. "Tears from the queene's own Franklin Fat?"

Frank sniffed. "Rain in my eye."

The bald faerie pulled his mustache and spread his arms.

"What is it?" Anastasia asked.

"That," Jacques said, "is Glaston's Barrow, the first mound of the faeren fathers, Hall of the Chestnut King." He winked. "No man has entered since Clovis, and his bones are in it still."

*   *   *

Coradin walked down a long, broad hall. He had smashed in the rotten door of a barrack on the street level and was now two floors belowground.

Turn.

He turned and faced a wide opening, closed off by an iron grate. The five men around him stepped forward. Only two still had torches. The wind thrown up by the horseman had smothered the rest. The wind had also gathered the dust and ash from the circle and forced Coradin and his brothers to their bellies in the street. When the dust had cleared, the horsemen were gone. But they hadn't gone far. Not if the boy was still with them.

The three without torches gripped the grate and forced it up, grinding ancient gears as it rose.

My fathers kept armies of your kind. You will find what you need.

Henry slipped off the broad horse's back and followed his father and Caleb up a short but wide flight of steps. They were at the rear of a building that Henry would have called a palace in any other city, but here it seemed modest—four stories of black stone, arched windows and porticoes, supported by thin, bonelike pillars and buttresses and a balustrade encircling what looked to be a flat roof. The horses stamped and snorted in the ash, and the men stayed with them. The dog flopped down panting on the steps.

Caleb whistled as he reached the door, and Henry looked up. The owls, five of them, rose higher and drifted away over the city. Mordecai stopped and waited for him. Henry hadn't been able to tell him much in all the blowing wind and galloping that had gone on since they'd met in the circle. He wasn't exactly sure where to start, and he was still carrying the little pyramid tucked under his arm.

Caleb threw open the doors and stepped to the side. His bow was over one shoulder, and two short swords were tucked into his belt. Mordecai carried no weapons. Taking Henry by the shoulder, he led him through into near darkness. Then he pulled a limp sack out of his cloak.

Henry smiled. "Faerie light?"

Mordecai nodded and slapped the sack three times against his thigh. Then he held it to his lips and—Henry strained to hear his words—hummed quietly. A snap. His father jerked the mouth open and cracked the sack like a whip. Light exploded through the house, ricocheting off walls and burrowing into cracks. There were no shadows. The light was everywhere.

Mordecai smiled and led Henry through a small room and out into the main entryway. The floor glistened white wherever feet kicked away dust. Stairs twisted up to mezzanines, three in all. It was open to the roof.

"With a little encouragement," Mordecai said, "this light may last us an hour." Henry followed him onto the stairs. His father's eyes had hardened, and his rough jaw moved slowly. "Tell me quickly what brings my son to Endor. I cannot imagine it to be good news."

"It's not," Henry said. He stopped. Mordecai turned and faced him. Henry stared into his father's eyes and saw that they were black. They were focused on his face, on the threads on his jaw. Henry put his hand up to cover it and stopped. If he needed anyone to see it, it was his father.

Mordecai sighed. "It grows quickly." He put his arm around his son's shoulders. Caleb stopped on the stairs behind them. "Come," Mordecai said. "Your uncle and I hunt for a cure. Tell us your tale while we search. There is not much time."

Henry was tired of stairs, but he hurried up them, and was led down a hall, through a doorway, and into a library piled with books and scrolls and manuscripts. Stacks filled an enormous stone fireplace and blocked the tall windows. Much was beneath dust, but much had also been recently shifted. A table, bowing beneath the weight of pages, had only one small clear end.

Mordecai lifted a stack of loose manuscripts onto the table. Caleb leaned his bow against a tattered stack of papers.

"What is this place?" Henry asked.

"When Endor was green," Mordecai said, "and Nimroth was no more than a young pauper son in his father's house with a questionable taste for wizardry, this was his home." He looked up. "And this was his room. But we wait on your story. Why do we find my son running from fingerlings? From the hills, we watched lights on the bell tower and rode in when we heard its ringing."

Both Caleb and Mordecai stopped and faced Henry, leaning against the table.

Henry took a deep breath. Looking at his father, at his

uncle, he felt a knot growing in his throat. He would not cry. He would not even let his voice waver. "The morning after you left, soldiers came. There were two more galleys in the harbor. They were looking for you. You weren't there, so they took Uncle Frank and James and Monmouth and my mother."

Caleb straightened, and his face became stone. Henry couldn't look at his father's face. He couldn't look in his eyes. Staring at his boots instead, he continued. "Fat Frank and I tried to find them, but fingerlings were in the city, too, and they came after me. When I got back to the house, more soldiers had come, and they were dragging everyone out and putting them in a wagon. A whole crowd was trying to stop them, but they couldn't. When Henrietta fought too much, they hit her on the head and threw her back in the house. Then they lit it on fire. Grandmother was inside, too."

Henry looked up. His father's eyes were no longer black. They were ice. He was leaning forward now, and his jaw worked silently.

"I got inside," Henry said, "even though a fingerling tried to stop me, and I got Grandmother and Henrietta up to the roof and then through a cupboard up there that I had from Kansas. You didn't know about that, I'm sorry."

"We knew," Mordecai said.

"What?" Henry looked from his father to his uncle and back again. "For how long?"

"Since your first bloody nose," Mordecai said. "Go on."

"Well," said Henry. "There's not much else. I mean, there is. Lots. But not important. I left Grandmother in Kansas with Mrs. Johnson, and Zeke and Henrietta and I came through the Endor cupboard to find you."

"Zeke and Henrietta?" Caleb asked. "Where are they?"

Henry held up the little pyramid cupboard. "We came into this horrible crypt." He looked at his father. "And I'm sorry, but I think I let Nimroth and Nia and everyone else out. And then the fingerlings had us trapped on top of the bell tower. That's when I started ringing it. We all went through this little pyramid cupboard into Frank and Dotty's old house, and then I reached back through and tipped us off the tower. When it landed in the street, I left Zeke and Henrietta there, and you found me in the big circle."

Mordecai stared at his son. Caleb smiled and looked at his brother.

"Lucky, too," Henry said. "I didn't have much of a plan."

Mordecai pointed at the cupboard. "Zeke and Henrietta are in there?"

"They're through there, yeah."

"Well." Mordecai crossed his arms. "You have walked the spiders' webs."

Henry grinned. His father sounded like Uncle Frank.

"Who told you that you faced fingerlings?" Caleb asked. He looked at his brother. "I cannot think fingerlings likely. Nimiane used other, newer tools—wizards and witch-dogs." He looked back to Henry. "Did Fat Frank name them for you?"

For a moment, Henry rolled through his memory. Who had told him the name? "I think the witch did," he said. "In one of my dreams."

"You spoke with the witch?" Caleb asked. Mordecai's eyes were back on his son's jaw.

Henry nodded. "And I've seen the fingers. I cut two off. But more fingerlings just keep coming." He put his hand to his cold scar. "They can find me anywhere."

Henry watched shock spread across his father's face.

For a moment, Caleb was motionless. "We must move," he said. "Now."

"Fool," said Mordecai. "I've been a fool. Nimiane positions the board while we root through a library. Of course fingerlings could find you." He turned to the manuscripts piled on the table. "Caleb," he said quietly. "We have been wasting our days."

"Maybe not," Caleb said. "But we did waste our time covering our tracks. They'll come straight to us."

Mordecai filled his lungs slowly. He looked deep into Henry's eyes and lifted his right hand to his son's jaw. Henry saw the swirling brand of grapevines on his father's palm, and then he felt it in his flesh—a slow, twisting strength, as rich as it was deep. He saw pain in his father's eyes when he touched the scar. The eyes moved away, around the room, but his hand stayed where it was, warming cold death.

"This room was my hope," Mordecai said. "We searched for a secret without knowing what it might be— only knowing what we needed it to be. But there is no time for sifting through this graveyard now, even without the fingerlings. Nimiane has struck too soon and too hard. The board is set, and now we play her game."

"What were you looking for?" Henry asked.

Mordecai smiled and put his other hand on Henry's cheek. "We search for the death of death—for the tapestry of power behind Nimroth that first fused his soul to his body and gave him eternal leeching life. We search for your life, for all our lives."

"The Blackstar?" Henry asked.

"Perhaps," Mordecai said. "Perhaps not. We have searched for it before. Nimroth hid it before his madness rose to its fullest tide. He carried only a disguised pebble in his last year enthroned, much to the disgust of his heirs. In the end, even he believed it to be real. He does still. His sons entombed him with it. But if you have seen his husk, you may know this already."

Caleb tumbled a stack of decayed books off the window-sill and onto the floor. Pages ripped free and slid through clouding dust. He rattled the casement off its hinges, threw it down into the street, and whistled.

"Notch and stirrup! They come!" he shouted. Then he turned to Mordecai. "Brother, we cannot carry books. The witch is in Dumarre, that much we know—the emperor's phalanxes would not form against us without her whispers in his ear." He picked up his bow. "We have galleys to race or I should beg to perch here and wait for the finger-men."

Mordecai straightened, dropping his hands. "I would

209

have given my sight for Eli FitzFaeren in this room, at this task. I have been useless." He looked at Caleb. "Nimiane wishes us to race into her arms, and she baits the hook well. We may yet bite." He rubbed his jaw, and Henry watched his father's eyes unfocus, staring away past the books and the walls, past the house and the life-drained land. "She has left us three moves with little difference between them. We are taken by the fingerlings, or we run to her snarling but powerless to make the kill, and her fingerlings come behind us. We defeat the fingerlings, and still we run to her. That buys time, but time is of little use. As you say, we race the galleys already." He sighed, and his eyes reentered the room. "What does she fear? Not death. The coming of her madness? We must find a way to play beyond the board. We must do the unexpected."

"Unexpected or no," Caleb said, "what we do, we must do now. Much has already been decided for us. We outstrip the finger-men on horseback, or soon, very soon, we face them on foot."

"Henry?" A voice drifted out of the pyramid. Henrietta's whisper. "Henry? Are you okay? What's going on?"

Birds screeched, and the long howl of the great dog echoed through the house.

Downstairs, wood splintered.

CHAPTER THIRTEEN

Henrietta leaned her back against Henry's little bed and stared at the darkness. He had told them to stay and had ignored their objections. By the time she really had managed to clear her head and get her bearings after diving through a world-seam on a tower wall, Henry was gone.

She flicked on her flashlight and pointed it down at the little cupboard to Endor. It was weird thinking that Henry could be carrying the other end around. It was weirder thinking that she had just come through that tiny door. She wiped her nose and checked her fingers. The bleeding had stopped.

"We should save the batteries," Zeke said.

Henrietta killed her light. "We should go after Henry."

"Let me know when you figure out how."

"If he hadn't lost Grandfather's journal, we'd be able to. We could set the compass locks to Endor and crawl through downstairs."

The floor creaked as Zeke shifted. "We're here for him. We can wait."

"Does he even need us?" Henrietta asked. "It's not like

either of us did much in there. We rang the bell. You threw the hatchet."

Zeke laughed. "Which bounced off." A backpack slid across the floor. "Henry's pitching. Slap your glove and talk him up. Pitcher throws better when a team props him, even if it's just with chatter."

Henrietta sat in the dark and listened to Zeke breathe. "You mean like, 'Atta babe, down the pipe,' and that stuff my dad would say? Then we're just cheerleaders."

Zeke yawned. "We're in the field with him. We back him up. If a pitcher's real good . . ." He yawned again, slowly. "*Then* we're just cheerleaders."

"Boys are ridiculous," Henrietta said. "You'd never call each other 'babe' after a game." She waited for a response. "Zeke?"

Zeke snored.

"Sheesh." Henrietta turned her flashlight on. Zeke had pushed his backpack against the wall and was lying flat on his back with his head propped up on it and his mouth open. Henrietta scooted closer to the little door to Endor, crossed her legs, and listened.

She couldn't hear much. More noises drifted out of the other doors. She looked over at Zeke. She could never sleep in this room, not with so many doors open. A sudden burst of wind pushed through the Endor cupboard, carrying a funnel of ash. She slid her backpack over and blocked it. After a while, she pulled the pack away. Could she hear something? She leaned closer. Thumping? Voices?

She didn't want to yell for Henry. He could be hiding.

He could be in the middle of something. There was no "could be" about it. He was sure to be in the middle of something. She bit her tongue and waited—listening to distant sounds trickle from the other cupboards, the creaking of the old, battered farmhouse, and the breeze moving through the broken round window at the end of the attic. Zeke rolled onto his side and stopped snoring. Sighing, Henrietta imitated him, lowering herself to her side and propping her head on her backpack. With her mind wandering, imagining horror after horror pursuing Henry, she stared into the dark mouth of the little cupboard.

"Atta babe," she whispered.

Time crawled by, measured by an unknown sun outside and Zeke's breathing in the attic. Henrietta blinked. Her mind was foggy. Had she been asleep? She wasn't now. She could hear voices. She rolled forward and put her ear in the cupboard mouth. Henry was talking to someone. Caleb? It *was* Caleb. She laughed. He'd found them.

She pressed her face into the cupboard. "Henry?" she said. "Henry? Are you okay? What's going on?"

No one answered.

Caleb and Mordecai both stood straight. Neither flinched. Shouts rose from downstairs, and the dog's baying grew. Caleb, breathing slowly, looked at his brother and smiled with tight lips. His eyes held no fear. Drawing one of his short swords, he held out the hilt to Mordecai.

"We stand here," he said.

Mordecai nodded, taking the sword. He turned to Henry. "Is the way open to Hylfing?"

"Maybe," Henry said. He shifted nervously. His father didn't seem to be in any kind of hurry. "But the fingerling followed us through once already."

Caleb ducked into the hall and disappeared.

Mordecai set his right palm against the black pyramid. One swift movement of his wrist sent Henry rocking backward. His father had opened the seam more than head-high with nothing but his own strength—a hole, bounded by deep purple and twisting green. "These stacks are useless." Mordecai pointed to one side of the room. "But these"—he turned to the wall behind Henry, mounded with scrolls and rotting leather and loose pages—"one sentence may mean a different world. Take as many through as you can. Store them safely in the ruined farmhouse. Get to Hylfing."

Caleb stepped back into the room. "They come cautiously," he said. "But they are armed and helmed and wear collars and chains. It will not be easy."

Henry sagged. He didn't want to get anywhere. He'd just finished getting somewhere, and it had been horrible. He wanted to plant himself firmly in the shadow of his father and uncle, wherever they might go. "Can't I stay?" he asked.

"If I could keep you with me, I would," said Mordecai. "I would keep you with me if you were weak as well. But you are not. Find Fat Frank. We will meet you in Hylfing if we can. Wait at The Horned Horse, but do not wait more than a single day. If we do not come to you, travel with your cupboard. Stay nowhere long. Enter the mounds together and demand passage to the Faerie Queene. They are stubborn now, but you have bullied faeren before. The district mounds will be no help. They will not aggress beyond their regions, and Dumarre must run mad with a plague of faeren if we are to succeed. That city must receive no galleys."

Caleb drew back an arrow on his big horn bow and leaned into the hall. He kissed the nock and held it, unshaking.

"If the faeren will not or cannot take you to the queene, and they may not—no one has received an audience in my lifetime—then you must travel into the hills to the southeast. Search for a great triple-trunked chestnut. Wait beside it, but not for long. If no faeren show themselves, then set a flame to the tree. Tell those who come that you have a treasure for the Chestnut King from Mordecai Westmore. Give him these ancient pages and tell him what we seek, what we need, and what must be. He may help you. Do not bow or grovel or apologize. Speak to him like a brother and an equal."

Henry's head was spinning. He didn't understand, and what he did understand, he didn't like. "Who is the Chestnut King?"

"He won't find the tree," Caleb said to his bowstring. "I have stepped through its shroud and seen its trunks but once. The outlaw king has little love for our blood." He straightened and whistled sharply.

Henry looked at his father and his uncle. Shouting rose through the floor. "What will you be doing?" he asked. "Where will I find you again?"

"This time," Mordecai said, "we will seek for you."

The huge black dog bounded into the room. Caleb relaxed his bow, dropped to one knee, and held its broad face in his hands. The dog froze, and Caleb stared into his brown bovine eyes. Then he whispered in its ear. The dog twisted in a circle and dropped to the floor beside Henry's feet.

"Beo shares a memory of the tree," Caleb said. "He will guide you." Rising, Caleb stepped into the hall. "Brother," he said. "We cannot wait longer."

Mordecai followed him. "Work quickly," he said over his shoulder. His face was set, his eyes black as night, faerie light draining into them. "When I call your name, do not hesitate. Pass through the doorway and set fire to the cupboard behind you."

"Fire?" Henry asked. "I don't have fire."

His father smiled. "My son," he said. "My strong son, of what are you made?" Turning, Mordecai pulled the door closed behind him. He was gone.

Henry slumped to the floor. The pony-size dog slid toward him.

"Henry!" Henrietta's voice rattled through the room. "Henry, what's going on?"

*   *   *

Coradin stood at the base of the stairs. Two others stood with him. The remaining three still pushed against the archers in the back of the house.

He had taken two long-handled swords from the armory, and he gripped them now. Both had long, slender blades, bending slightly. He had stood on many fields with swords of similar size and shape, but never quite like these. It was like every blade he had ever held had only been a promise, a taste of this pair, untouched by time and passing ages. Their weights were perfect, the silver edges sharpened into transparency. More than steel had been braided and hammered into the blades. Every life they had taken had made them stronger. Every drop of blood drawn had given up its strength and fallen away from the blades ashen. They sucked and whispered in the air now, thirsty for life, for their first feeding since the fall of FitzFaeren.

Coradin's helmet was silver, with braided brows around the eyeholes and noseguard. On the back, in place of a plume, a single black finger curled. Three silver chains bound the helmet to a black collar and ran down to a broad black belt of steel, decorated only with a circlet of white fire on the buckle. Twin scabbards hung on his back, between collar and belt.

The others wore similar helms, but each had chosen different arms, weapons loved and used in forgotten lives—an ax, a mace, swords like scythes.

The boy was upstairs. Coradin, the swords, could taste him.

Go.

He stepped forward, but something inside him resisted. An instinct. Hold. He will strike us on the stairs. He drew his foot back.

Go.

Coradin arched as fire erupted into the back of his scalp, burned down his spine, and ripped through his mind. Breathing heavily, he was blank again. As cold and ruthless as the swords in his hands. He was a sword in another's hand, a mindless tool.

His mouth opened, and a voice crawled out of him. His blood-mother's voice. "Mordecai Westmore, son of Amram!"

Coradin stepped onto the stairs and began to climb. An arrow tore through his chest, and he staggered backward, catching himself before he fell. Looking down, he saw no shaft. One feather stood out alone against his ribs, scraped off by the arrow's passing.

Nimiane's laugh poured out of him. "Death is not so easily delivered to these, my messengers! Come and see if the two brothers can stand before them."

A burst of air rolled down the stairs, gathering dust and ash, pushing the fingerlings back.

"Nimiane!" Mordecai's voice swirled with the air. "Your soul shall be shriven from the husk of your flesh, your darkness unmade. Death finds you. We shall be his guide."

Coradin laughed. His pierced body quaked. The high voice, not his own, echoed in his helmet, through the dust, and filled the ancient house. "Death? Death does my bidding. He and I are one, as fused as Nimroth's body and soul. While there is life, I will live, drinking of it, feeding on it, feasting on its death. When you have killed all living things, then I shall go hungry. Then I shall fade. Not before."

Zeke sat up. "Henrietta, why are you yelling? Just wait."

Henrietta glanced at him and then shoved her mouth all the way against the cupboard to yell again. But her lips didn't touch the wood. Her face slid forward through the wall, and suddenly, she was blinking in a lit room mounded with papers and books and scrolls. The room seemed to be shaking. With wind? Was there a storm? And someone was shouting. A woman.

A pile of papers moved toward her, staggered, and almost overbalanced. She jerked back, into the dimness of Henry's old room.

"Wow," said Zeke, and then Henry, groaning under the stack of manuscripts, tripped into the room, collided with Henrietta, and sat on Zeke.

Caleb's dog leapt out of the wall, knocking Henrietta through the doors and into the attic. The little room was officially full.

Dropping more as he came, Henry followed her with his pile. When he banged it onto the floor, the whole attic shook.

"Help me," he said. "We don't have much time." And then, ducking back into his little bedroom, Henry walked into the cupboard wall and disappeared.

*   *   *

Henry loaded his arms with books. Coughing, accidentally inhaling dust, he staggered back around and faced the grapevined doorway his father had made. Zeke and Henrietta stood on either side of it, looking around the room. The windows rattled, and the house shook. Dust drifted down from the walls.

"Over here," Henry grunted. "These piles go through into the house. As many as we can take."

The big dog knocked Zeke and Henrietta from behind and loped around the room, tipping book piles.

"Stay!" Henry yelled, shifting the weight in his arms. He'd never had much interaction with Caleb's dog, though Beo's sire still lived in his dreams and infant memories. He tried to whistle but only managed to spit. The dog ignored him, bounded around the table, snarled at the closed door, and collided with Henrietta.

"Beo!" Henrietta yelled. "Down!" The dog dropped to his belly and froze, staring at the door with his ears up.

Henry puffed his cheeks and slid back through the expanded cupboard and into the old house. When he set his pile down, Henrietta and Zeke each dropped a pile beside his.

"What's going on?" Henrietta asked, but her cousin was already running back into the little room toward the cupboards.

"Fingerlings!" Henry shouted. Henrietta and Zeke followed him. In the library, Henry shoved his arms beneath another leaning pile, the smell of dust and ancient paper filling his nostrils, sweat beading on his forehead. "Caleb and my dad are fighting them. They told me to get these through the cupboard."

Henrietta laughed. "Poor fingerlings."

Zeke smiled. Henry looked at them both and bit his lip with effort, wobbling beneath his new burden. Zeke steadied the pile with one hand.

"Caleb"—Henry groaned—"said it would be hard. And my dad"—he tripped and swayed—"doesn't have much to work with. This place is—" He stepped through the cupboard doorway and wove his way around the little bed, out into the attic, and dropped the books onto sighing floorboards. "This place is dead," he said quietly, and ducking around a wobbling Zeke, he hurried back.

Coradin looked at the men on either side of him. One was crawling slowly to his feet. Another lay unconscious, beaten down with blows of air whenever a foot touched the stairs. All lived. All had been pierced with arrows, but arrows were nothing. Somehow, he knew that to die, he and his brothers must lose their helmets. And their helmets were chained to collars and belts. The other three, also with feathered shafts in their bodies, walked into the grand entryway. The light in the house was orange and fading.

"They circle on horse," one said, and he nodded at the stairs. "They avoid us and wait on those above."

"The boy flickers," said another. "He dances between worlds. They have an escape."

Coradin nodded and twisted his swords in the air. The blades whispered with forgotten voices and quivered with stolen lives. The men on the stairs were patient and did not show more than shadows of themselves. They must be pressed on all sides. He pointed at two of the new men, his brothers. "Seek another stair," he said, and his voice was his own. Pointing at two others, he gestured in front of him. "Press here." While the others moved slowly away, he filled his lungs. He would take the prey.

Kill.

Coradin knew the voice was in all of their heads. Their mother had commanded that father and son be brought alive.

Kill, she said again.

Coradin turned, and sheathing the swords on his shoulders, he walked through to the back of the house. He would find a window.

Henry wiped his forehead. Beo the dog watched him. The bright faerie light was dying, but gray light filtered in through the windows. He wanted to take his sweatshirt off, but he knew he would regret it. It would end up like his backpack on top of the bell tower.

"Are we done?" Zeke asked behind him.

Henry looked back at the piles more than head high that still filled one end of the room. He shook his head. "No. My dad said to take as many as we could before he yelled. When he yells, we have to get through fast."

Zeke filled his arms again and moved back through the

cupboard. Henrietta stepped beside Henry, blinking and sniffing in the dusty air, running her eyes over the disturbed piles. The house was still.

"What are we looking for?"

Henry shrugged, rolled his shoulders, and walked back to another stack. "A secret," he said. "The secret to Endor. The secret to killing the witch."

"But who's going to go through all this?"

"I don't know," Henry said. "My dad wants me to take it to the faeren. I think he's hoping we'll find the real Blackstar or something." He staggered and nodded at Henrietta. She set ten more inches on top of the stack in his arms. "I don't think we will," he said. "Not in time."

Zeke stepped back out of the cupboard and reloaded. "In time for what?" he asked.

"In time for me," said Henry, and he disappeared.

All the way through his room and in the attic, Henry felt the pull of his father. He felt Mordecai grasping for strength where he could find it, and the air moved, chased by a distant rumbling.

Henrietta screamed.

Henry dropped his pile and rushed back into the little attic room and through the cupboard wall.

"Maccabee!" he heard his father yell. "Maccabee!"

The dog was on his feet, hackles up and lips curled back, a rumbling in his chest. Zeke was on his back, the load he had been carrying scattered around him.

In the window a man crouched, his eyes hidden in the shadows of a silver helmet, a long sword in his right hand.

His left gripped Henrietta by the hair, winding tighter in her curls. She stood on her toes in front of the man, biting her lip, with tears streaking down her dusty cheeks, thrashing and thumping her fists against his shins.

"Coradin," Henry said. He knew who it was, even without the notches in his ear. His shirt was ripped where dandelions had sprouted from his chest.

"Brother," Coradin said, and slid into the room. Lifting his long blade, he set the edge against the back of Henrietta's neck. "Brother, what will you do for your cousin?"

"Nothing," Henrietta grunted. She tried to twist, but the whispering sword edge against her neck changed her mind. Her eyes widened, and Coradin let her sink to her heels. Henry watched a trickle of blood appear on the side of her neck. The blood stopped, grayed, and then drifted away in powder. "Go, Henry," Henrietta said. "Go."

Henry backed up to the closed door. Beo was motionless, frozen, poised to attack if the man should step free of Henrietta. The house shook, the door rattled, and air swirled into the room from the windows. Mordecai was busy. Zeke slid backward toward Henry and then stood up.

"Brother," Coradin said, his voice crawling out from the silver helmet. "Come to me. I do not need your cousin's blood. I do not need your friend's. Our mother calls for you."

Henry slid his hand into his pouch and felt the tiny kitchen knife nestled with his baseball. Coradin's helmet was chained on. He didn't stand a chance.

"Zeke," Henry said. "Go." His mind groped around for

strength, but everything in this land had been drunk dry long ago. He couldn't reach into the sky as high as his father. He had only himself and the heat in his blood. The golden and green laughter. But there was no laughter in him. The dandelions burned in anger, and every inch of Henry's skin flushed with the heat. His eyes turned as black as Nimroth's marble, and the world shifted.

Zeke hadn't moved.

Coradin's sword was forged of lifeless steel but woven and triple-braided with gray death strands. Henry could see his own strands mingling with the death all around him. The dead woods, the dead papers, the dead stone, all gray and stiff and motionless. Only Henrietta and the dog and Coradin swirled with life. Henrietta was all fear, the dog all anger, Coradin all strength and confusion, bound by the thick gray ropes that stretched back from his head.

The heat in Henry grew painful, building to a golden explosion. He couldn't hold it. He had nowhere to put it.

"Let her go," he said. "I'll come." He stepped forward.

"No," Henrietta said. "You moron. Go. Get out of here." She jerked and tried to push back against the sword. Coradin pulled it away with her motion. "Come on, Mr. Finger! Cut my head off." She looked back at Henry. "Leave!" she yelled, and choked on a sob of anger.

Henry took another step closer. He was beside Beo now, and he could feel the dog's growling strength and anger. It fed his own heat.

"Henrietta." Henry's voice was flat and calm. "I'm dead anyway." Henry lifted his right hand and held the palm out flat. His dancing dandelion brand was huge, but it was as small as he could make it, living its anger, blazing its life, telling the story of its strength in flame. Henrietta blinked. She could see fire on her cousin's palm. Henry watched its reflection twist in the silver of Coradin's helmet.

The fingerling's sword flicked up and then slashed down at Henry's forearm. Henry jerked back in time, pulling out his kitchen knife as he did. He swung his right hand across stacks of ancient papers, and his dandelion anger rushed out through them, crackling, blazing, exploding toward the ceiling in golden flame, dancing in strange colors where the fire found charms and ancient inks.

Coradin came forward fast, dragging Henrietta and slashing at Henry.

As the blade flicked through flames, Beo leapt, his jaw cracking shut on Coradin's wrist. The sword dropped as Coradin staggered under the weight of the snarling dog. Henry lunged for Coradin's other arm, slashing the kitchen knife between Henrietta's scalp and the fingerling's hand. She fell free, her curls left behind.

"Go!" Henry yelled. Coradin's fist thumped into his cheek and then closed around his left wrist. Henry dropped the knife but shoved his fiery hand at the fingerling's head, forcing it up beneath his helmet.

The room was a bonfire. The air was disappearing fast. Zeke dragged Henrietta away toward Mordecai's opening, and the two of them disappeared in the smoke.

Beo dropped Coradin's wrist and lunged for his throat

as the man writhed beneath Henry's burning touch, skin and hair singeing. Kicking the dog, he grabbed at Henry.

The door burst open as Henry was thrown to the floor, ripping the sword and scabbard free of Coradin's shoulders as he fell. The flames, licking the high ceiling and funneling out the windows, suddenly bent toward the two fingerlings, who staggered back into the hall.

Henry slid across the floor toward his father's swirling doorway, still tall and uncollapsed. Beo snapped at Coradin's collar, pushing the fingerling farther into the flames. Henry couldn't whistle. He whooped for the dog, called his name, and crawled through into his old attic bedroom.

Dropping the sword, he spun on his knees and grabbed at his father's magic, struggling to collapse the seam, to let the little pyramid burn.

"Beo!" he yelled. The doorway was shrinking. Heat—painful, blistering heat—surged from the cupboard wall as the seam closed.

The dog leapt through, knocking Henry onto his back. Henry grabbed for the sword and drew it, expecting Coradin to follow. The seam closed, and only smoke and heat wormed through into the attic.

Henry slid farther back from the wall, panting. What had happened to his father? His uncle? Would the whole house burn? That's not what his father had told him to do. Was his father's body in the house? Would he burn, too? A tiny flame danced in the mouth of the cupboard and then died. The heat and smoke faded.

"How long does the water take?" Zeke asked behind him. Henry looked around. His friend was holding a crowbar and standing on the bed beside a small diamond-shaped cupboard. Number 18. Henrietta had fallen through it into a shipwreck. It had flooded the whole house. Now it was open again, and the wood around it was splintered.

"I don't remember," Henrietta said. "It seemed fast."

"Why?" Henry asked, still breathing hard. Instead of an answer to his question, a long blade, hissing like a snake, slid through the Endor cupboard and twisted around, searching for flesh. Zeke jumped off the bed and brought the crowbar down on top of it. The head of the crowbar tumbled off and bounced against the wall. The blade slid back through.

"Oh no," Henry said. "He saved the cupboard. It didn't burn. They can follow us."

Still kneeling, he put his head in his hands. He had burned the books and manuscripts but not the door.

"Burn this one," Henrietta said. Her thick hair, cut with the kitchen knife, stood out in uneven curls around her head. Her face was filthy. "Burn it on this side. I saw your hand. You could light anything."

Henry held out his palm. His anger, the heat inside, was gone. His mark was faint, tired, and slow. Henrietta wouldn't be able to see it at all.

He looked at the doorway. It would be dangerous. The sword could come slashing back through. Stretching forward, he put his palm down on the bottom of the black cupboard. He tried to pull strength to himself, to build up the heat that had exploded out of him in Nimroth's old library.

Dandelions sprouted between his fingers, blossoms glowing. Broad-bladed leaves twisted around his wrist.

"I'll get some matches," Henrietta said, and she ran downstairs. Henry tore his hand free and slid back. He glanced at Zeke. Beo was on his side, panting in the corner.

"Grab some of the papers," Henry said. Zeke hurried out into the attic and came back with a slim stack. Henry flipped through them in the dim light. The language was nothing he could understand, and the writing looked like something that should have been chiseled in sandstone rather than inked on paper. Where there were drawings, they all looked more like engineering illustrations than anything magical. One picture, blotchy, looked like a floor plan.

As Henrietta thumped back up the attic stairs, Henry wadded the old papers and crammed them into the cupboard around the dandelions. His cousin stepped into the little room and tossed him a small pack of cardboard matches.

She ran her hands through her choppy hair. "How about next time we don't cut my hair," she said. "Just cut off his hand or something."

Zeke laughed.

Henry lit a match and slid it into the cupboard beneath the paper. While it flamed up, he scooted back toward Zeke and the dog, laying Coradin's long, sheathed blade across his knees.

"Now," he asked, "how do we keep it from burning the whole wall?"

"She's way ahead of you." Zeke pointed at the little cupboard he had pried open. "She says water comes through that one."

As smoke crawled out of the Endor cupboard and the wood began to crack and pop, the three of them looked at the little diamond-shaped cupboard above the bed.

"Oh no," Henry said, looking back down at the growing flame. A trickle of water ran out of the higher cupboard and down the wall. The trickle grew. It grew quickly, and seawater from some distant world and distant time surged out of the wall.

Henry jumped up and grabbed the end of his old bed. "We can't let the water put it out too soon."

Zeke and Henrietta scrambled to help him, and they tipped the bed onto its side and butted it against the cupboard wall between the flood and the fire, accidentally slamming a few of the small doors as they did. The other end of the bed stuck out the doorway and into the attic.

"Papers!" Henry yelled. He slipped over the top of the bed into the splashing water and ran out into the attic. A few pages were already floating, but most of the water found the attic stairs before traveling too far into the room. Grunting, he managed to slide most of the piles down to the end of the attic, beyond the spray and the sea-river once again running through the old farmhouse.

Back in the little room behind the mattress, sheltered from the splashing, he crouched on the wet floor and watched a doorway burn, a doorway that he had always feared. Flames licked the faces of the other cupboards as the black wood crackled.

"Should we put it out now?" Henrietta asked.

Henry shook his head. Reaching forward, almost burning the skin on his knuckles, he picked up the old lid to the Endor cupboard, now damp, and threw it into the flames. The dandelions were long gone. The papers were nothing but shrunken, glowing balls. Henry blinked and picked up the handle to the broken crowbar. He could see something. Three of the papers hadn't burned. They had tightened, and the flames that danced around them were white.

Henry knocked one of the papers out of the cupboard onto the floor. It hissed for a moment, and the floor dried around it. He knocked out the other two and shoved the crowbar all the way into the cupboard. It thumped against the back. It thumped against the wall of an old Kansas farmhouse now rooted in an empty world.

Henry scooped up the three balled, burned parchments, and Henrietta slid the bed away from the wall. The fountaining salt water sent its fingers spraying across the face of the Endor cupboard. Zeke cupped his hands, filled them, and splashed the water into the ashen gap where a world-seam had once lived.

When the fire was out and steam had replaced the smoke, Henrietta tried to shut the little diamond door against the water. Soaked for her troubles, she was unable to close it. Zeke joined her. Together, the two of them pinned it to the wall, but the latch wouldn't catch. Water blew it open whenever they stepped away, and it squeezed out the seams when they didn't.

"Did I break it?" Zeke asked. His eyes were shut, and he was spitting salt water.

"You must have," Henrietta grunted.

Henry wasn't listening. He didn't care about the water. He was carefully unfolding a piece of paper in his hands. It was warm, fragile, and white. There were no chiseled-looking letters and no building plans. Ink, pure and black, formed a perfect circle. Around it, formed from the same hungry, light-eating ink, there were flames.

The flames were moving on the page, and three strange words, twisting in place, were set in a triangle around them. As Henry blinked at them, the paper fell into ash and drifted toward the floor. Quickly, he began to unfold another, but it crumbled with his first tug. The last snowed down between his fingers before he could even begin. Ignoring the water and the discussion behind him, Henry hurried out into the attic. Picking up the first dry piece of paper, he flicked another match. The paper caught fire, blackened, and curled like any other. He dropped it into the moving puddle behind him, and it floated down the attic stairs. Picking up another, he scraped a match and waited.

This page did not blacken. It shrunk in his hand, tightening around the edges first, whitening from antique yellow, to snow, to the pale fire of the Blackstar. The same circle appeared, the same moving ink flames, the same indiscernible words, and the paper fell in tiny pieces to the floor.

"Henry!" Zeke yelled. "Henry, we can't do this!"

Coradin stood in the flames of the home he had shaped with his own hands. The roof crumbled around him. The body of his wife, of his soul, lay in front of him. Death had beaten him home from war. His king was dead in the field. His family dead before him, his daughters and son, lifeless in their beds with flames for blankets.

The city was falling. The empire of the treble-serpent would consume the world. While the floor crackled, he dropped to his knees beside the body of his wife. He pulled the cloth down from his mouth and lay beside her with his arm around the one he had loved. The one he still loved.

And then shouts and hands gripping his ankles.

Coradin opened his eyes. Black smoke clouded the sky. Again he had been pulled from the flames. Two men stood near him, each helmed in silver. He wore a helmet as well, and the back of his skull throbbed with heat and pain. These men, they were his brothers, or so his aching head declared. But he had no brothers. He sat up slowly in the ashen street and watched the palace burn.

One of the helmed men looked at him. "Two of our brothers killed," the man said. "One taken. The green man and his blood escaped. The children—" The man looked away and down, at a small, smoking, wooden cupboard in the shape of a pyramid sitting in the street. "The children closed the small way with fire."

While Coradin watched, confused in mind and body, one of his brothers hefted an ax.

Black splinters tumbled through the ash. The cupboard was gone.

CHAPTER FOURTEEN

The sun hung low over the western sea, gilding crystal blue tides as they lapped high against the sea walls of the great city. The eastern sea, at low tide, already darker, already angrier, seethed in the shadow of the city.

The young man, slim and pale, could see them both from where he stood, leaning against a casement in his father's inner room. He could see the streets as well and hear the faint rumblings of anger and fear and fighting along the canals. He could see the red shirts of soldiers holding the gates, sealing in heaving crowds of the unwashed and superstitious as they fled with their possessions wrapped in blankets and balanced on their heads, or mounded on donkeys or the long-necked fur mules of the south.

The man's name was Phedon, though few called him by it. His older brother was gone, and he was now the Serpent Prince.

"Father," he said. "The city is under siege from within. You imprison your people."

The old emperor creaked in a tapestried chair. "They are cattle, believing every rumor and lie and whispered tale." He rose slowly from his chair, gripping a thick wooden cane, scaled, with three heads intertwined at the knob, and made his way to the window beside his son.

"They hear the truth," said Phedon, and his pale eyes found his father's face. "Death comes to Dumarre and is called her queen. You lose your people. Is she worth the exchange?"

The emperor snorted. "Death," he said. "She holds the keys to life. I have only one life, but many peoples remain to be ruled. New lands, new countries, new kings. New peoples have yet to spring from these street cattle. I will shrug off age and no longer fear the darkness of my bed, no longer fear that the light of morning will never find my waking eyes." He coughed violently, and then, licking his lips, he spat out the window. "No longer fear that Dumarre, City of the Seas, will fade as I rot in some sealed tomb, or that my sons' grips are not strong enough to hold it. I shall live, and with no fear of death. The kiss of Endor comes to your father."

Phedon shifted his weight and calmed the anger inside him. He had been forced to kneel, to kiss the cursed hand of the witch-queen. His voice was calmer than he felt. "Endor's kiss is a horror, and the minds held by the undying blood are driven mad and left useless in undying shells. So say the stories and the old tales. Better to die than to live forever dead." He waited for a moment, but his father merely rattled his breath through a moist and shrunken throat. "My brother would have held the city and its frontiers well. His wars would have been fierce." He looked into the shadows of his father's eyes. "Do you fear death so much? You who rode into battle with the vanguard, handled your own chariot, and commanded galleys? Does age make a coward of you? Better to have given your life up in its bloom."

The emperor twisted toward his son. Anger flashed in his hooded eyes. He had been a great man once, a head taller than his own bodyguard, shoulders broader than the throne his grandfather had set on the back of the world, eyes full of laughter, a voice to challenge thunder, anger in him to match the eastern storms. Now he was broken, a raisin of his former strength. His shoulders sagged, his back twisted, his skin hung off him like the skin of a giant, as it once had been. His slender son, born to him by a northern queen, his seventh consort, loomed above him, grass that had outgrown the oak.

"Who are you?" the old emperor rumbled. "What manner of battles and wars and weapons have you tasted? Who are you to speak of cowards? You wage wars of whisperings for position in my court and seating at my feasts and rejoiced when your elder brothers fell in faraway fields. You are not my son, nor your brother. I have no need of sons. There is no inheritance for you. Death take you both. I shall reign on."

"Where is my brother?" Phedon asked. "What has been done with him?"

The emperor laughed, the gurgling of slow-boiling water. "Your brother? Maleger knew my desires. He met my queen. I offered him life as well, but he spat at it. He wove a web for me and laced my wines with poison. His fingers have found a better use. He graces the queen's garden."

"He lives?" Phedon asked.

"He lives like you," said the emperor. "For a time."

"Father—"

The emperor turned away, moving slowly toward his chair. "She comes to me," he said. "There are rites to be performed. Begone. Begone from my court, from my city, from the world itself. Do not again pollute my eyes with your presence. Go down to the street. Mingle with the rioting cattle. They are your kind." He thumped his cane on the stone floor, and the door opened. Two men in black, hair knotted at the back of their skulls, stepped into the room.

"Escort him from the palace." The emperor slumped into his chair, coughing. "Leave him in the street."

Frank Willis licked his teeth. They ached. The lace dangling from Monmouth's sack was tattered from his chewing, but not so tattered as his wrists. He couldn't feel his hands, and he was wishing that he couldn't feel his arms, either. A black rat slipped out from beneath the walkway and scurried toward him. He spat at the rodent, but his aim was short. The creature paused, sniffed at the moisture, and then hurried on past Frank and into the sacks.

Why? Frank asked himself, slumped against the post. Why hadn't he rallied Hylfing's guard against the imperial red as soon as the soldiers had arrived? Because he had only been mayor for a day. Not even a day. One night. Because they already had a fight on their hands, and they didn't want another one, not with the emperor, not now.

Well, Frank thought, they'd all gotten another fight. Only it hadn't really been another one. It was all one fight. The heir of Endor had hidden herself in the serpent's den. The dark ones had always been power lovers. It made sense. But not enough sense that anyone could have guessed it.

Another day was gone. His chained family members were lost in restless sleep behind him, exhausted by the heat and hunger. Hyacinth whispered as she dreamed, quietly calling each of her children by name. In front of him, the slave backs bent, panting in rest over their oars, striped with red, still glistening with sweat and stink. The sun was not yet down, and its light slashed through the oarlocks on the starboard side. They had found a wind to carry them south to the great city, to where the serpent nested, listening to the lies of a dark, undying bird.

James cranked his head around, exhausted, and looked at his uncle. Then he dropped it onto his oar. Frank watched the quick rise and fall of his nephew's ribs.

The masters were gone abovedecks to feel the breeze.

"Monmouth?" Frank asked. The bag above him swayed gently. "Still with us?"

"I am," Monmouth said quietly. "For how long, I cannot say."

"Hold tight," Frank said, and gritted his sore teeth.

What good was his body? He couldn't spin magic like his brother or his father or his nephew. No strange strength branded his skin and ran through his veins. He had only bones and skin and blood and muscle. "When I'm old," Frank said, "I'll give my wrists an hour or so to themselves every day for putting up with this."

"You are old," Monmouth said.

"Older by the minute," said Frank. "But when I die, it'll be from too much livin', not the poking of some lump in a red shirt or spicy words from a witch."

"What about when I die?" Monmouth asked. "Will it be from thirst and starvation and overheat in a kelp sack?"

Frank gathered his strained legs beneath him, held his breath, and lunged. He ignored the frayed lace. Metal carved down into the bones of his hands. His teeth closed on the wizard sack. He clenched and held.

The sack bounced and swung. "Ow," said Monmouth. "Did you just bite me?"

Frank said nothing. He relaxed his legs. He let the chains pull his weight down, while his jaw tightened. He sank an inch. The wizard cloth was stretching. And then it ripped in one bursting, staggering seam. Frank landed on the ground, and Monmouth landed on top of him. Spitting out his mouthful, licking his bleeding gums, Frank laughed. Monmouth was even more pale than normal. Dirt and lines of salt had dried on his forehead and cheeks, but there was no sweat. He was out of sweat. The young wizard rolled off Frank's lap. His wrists and ankles were bound tight with rope, and his eyes were all black pupil. Frank watched the boy mutter, and he watched the ropes become silver and green. Aspen leaves sprouted from them, and they straightened and unwound from his limbs. Two slender saplings rooted into the plank deck.

Monmouth stood and stretched. His shirt and trousers were filthy. Looking around, he quickly stripped them off.

"Monmouth?" Penelope asked. The others stirred.

"Hi, Pen," Monmouth said. He turned to Frank. "Up, old man." He tucked his clothes under the seat of his rescuer. Then, pale and scrawny, with pink scars dotting his ribs and chest and shoulders, wearing only a pair of baggy linen underpants with buttons in the front, he grinned.

"Those horrible scars," Dotty said. "I'm so sorry."

"Wizards aren't kind to thieving apprentices, but everything they taught me, I learned by stealing. They didn't do too much to me when I got older."

"You stopped stealing?" Penelope asked. Frank glanced at her. She sounded hopeful.

"They stopped catching me." He kicked the little saplings. "But they found lots of trees."

"What are you doing?" Frank asked. "Won't you need your clothes?"

Voices echoed above them. Feet descending ladders. Monmouth turned and scrambled quickly down the walkway between the slaves, spotted an empty seat on the top tier of oarsmen, and clambered up like a furless monkey. Then he hunched over an invisible oar. The slaves around him straightened, looked at him, and then watched the ladders, confused.

The masters descended.

"Sleep," Frank whispered. "We're all asleep."

"Two days with this wind," one of the oar masters said. "And then the channel and the lovelies of Dumarre."

"Not for you," said another. "They'd as soon look at a three-legged goat."

Four men with wool in their noses stepped in front of Frank, all with their backs to him, swaying with the creaking rise and fall of the ship.

"We'll be weeks in the harbor, and that means weeks in the inns. Captain wants to sell off this lot at a seasoned price and bring in fresh backs. Never liked mastering new meat. They're all weepers, begging to tell you of their mothers or wee things back home. It takes a few moons before they've hardened silent."

"It's not the weeping I mind," said the first man, twisting his whip. "It's the dying and the crabbing oars. Half lost in the first week."

"We'll fatten plenty of gulls and beasties, right enough," said another. He looked back over his shoulder, then looked away. After a moment, he tapped the man beside him, and they both turned. Frank watched them through his lashes, a bead of drool hanging off his lip.

One of them thumped the empty sack with his whip handle. Dust rained down. He looked at the floor. "Trees?" he asked.

The others scanned the hold nervously. Stepping

forward, the largest of the masters uncurled his whip. "This'll be joy to the captain. The little greenie loose and leaving his mark."

Farther down the hold, a chain rattled. Then another. The masters shifted on their feet. The smallest turned and hurried to the ladder.

Henry sat at the dining room table. It was nice being out of the dim attic, being entirely out of Endor or any smell of Endor. Sunlight poured through the broken windows. The white curtains, brightened by the sun, stroked the breeze as it climbed into the room. The room echoed with the sound of water splashing down the stairs. The ceiling dripped.

He was wet, extremely wet, and so were Henrietta and Zeke, but he still kept his feet up off the floor, where seawater rippled an inch deep. Beo had splashed around in it so madly that they had finally let the dog out the front door. That had calmed things. Henry struck his last match, lit a paper, and threw it onto the table in front of the others. It whitened and shrunk. Henrietta pulled her shortened curls straight and let go. They bounced back up to the top of her head.

"What is it?" she asked. "The sun?"

Zeke scratched his cheek and watched the paper soften and gray until only a rectangle of ash was left. The rectangle grabbed on to the breeze and rolled toward Henry, disintegrating as it went.

"It looks like the ball the old man had," Zeke said. "The man who crawled out of the floor."

Henry nodded. "The Blackstar. But why is the picture hidden in the papers? The faeries might be able to tell us. At least I hope so."

"You think that picture is going to help us find it?" Henrietta asked.

Henry shrugged. "I don't know. But the words mean something, and someone put them there for a reason."

Zeke glanced at the seawater running across the floor and straightened, stretching his back side to side like he did before a pitch. "Your dad wants us to take these papers to the faeries?"

Henry braced his feet against the table legs and tipped back in his chair, brushing the ash off his lap and into the water. "Try for the Faerie Queene and then the Chestnut King. That's what we do."

"But we're supposed to wait a day?" Henrietta asked. "Where? There's no house. There's nobody."

"The Horned Horse," Henry said. "We're supposed to wait there. I don't know where it is."

"It's on the square." Again Henrietta pulled at her hair and felt it bounce. "Una took us. I don't know where you were. Maybe playing baseball."

Henry thumped his chair flat. "You don't have to keep doing that. Pulling your hair. It's not going to make it longer."

Henrietta dropped her hand. "Do you realize how short I'm going to have to cut it now? It's ridiculous. I've got these straggles on the sides and it's super short on top."

Zeke smiled. "Next time, Henry, try to cut it even."

Henrietta snorted. "Next time, Henry, don't cut it at all."

"I'll work on that," Henry said. "I really will. How's your neck?"

Henrietta turned around and lifted up her short hair. "It doesn't hurt."

Both Henry and Zeke leaned forward. A thin black scab ran across her neck where the sword's edge had parted her skin. The skin itself, on both sides of the cut, was dry and flaking.

"I can't believe you leaned back like that," Henry said. "I thought you were dead."

Henrietta dropped her hair and turned around.

"I'm glad you're not," Henry added.

"I'm glad I'm not," she said. "Your turn, Zeke."

"I wasn't worried," Zeke said.

"Ha." Henrietta kicked him, and her foot splashed water beneath the table. She turned to Henry, and her face shifted serious, the smile gone from her eyes. "What did you mean when you said you were dead already? Why would you say that?"

Henry licked his lips. He leaned forward, braced his elbows on the table, and rubbed his eyebrows. His hands wanted to be somewhere else. They wanted to be scratching. His stomach burbled and tightened. Hunger, he decided. It was only hunger. He needed to eat something. He dropped his hands and looked in his cousin's big eyes, set in her filthy face. He looked at Zeke. His friend was slouching in his chair with his arms crossed and his chin down.

The seawater stream burbled on the stairs. Outside, Beo shot past the window.

Henry pulled his ear and then let his hand drift down to his jaw. His fingernails picked at the dying skin. "My old burn scar is growing. Pretty fast."

"That doesn't mean anything," Henrietta said. "I'm sure they can do something."

"Who's they?" Henry asked, studying the tabletop. "The witch's blood got into me. I can fight it. My body can fight it. But nothing can stop it. My dad doesn't know what to do. He said that he wouldn't have survived as long as I have. Everything around the scar is dead and cold. Eventually it will reach my mind. It will shut me down. Who knows, maybe I'll go crazy, and you'll have to kill me. Maybe the witch will be able to control me. Maybe I'll kill you." He looked up. It was strange, letting his fear come out. Embarrassing. And it didn't make him feel any better. "The fingerlings can find me anywhere because of it. The witch gets in my dreams."

Henrietta's eyes bounced around Henry's face. Zeke looked up at the dripping ceiling.

"Well, then, who does know?" Her voice rose. "Someone has to. You can't just let it kill you."

"What do you think this has all been about?" Henry swallowed hard and cleared his throat. "My dad and Caleb were in Endor trying to find some way to kill the witch. If her blood wasn't in me, they could just seal her up again. That's why they weren't in Hylfing when the soldiers came. That's why everyone got tied up and taken away; that's why the house burned. If they'd been there, instead of out trying to find some way to save me, then everything would be different. But right now, everything is pretty scrambled. I don't even know where they are or what they're doing." Henry breathed slowly. "I don't want to die, but if I had already, things would be better for everyone else."

Zeke smacked his lips. "Nobody would be happier with you dead," he said quietly.

"I know that much," Henry said. "That's the problem. My dad's trying to keep me alive."

"Shut up, Henry," Henrietta said. She stood and crossed her arms. "Really, just shut up. I'm sorry about your face. I am. But I always thought boys liked scars. And if you're still alive, then act like it. It's not that hard to figure out what we have to do."

Henry raised his eyebrows. "What?"

Henrietta gave her hair one tug and dropped her hands to her hips. "We kill the witch."

Henry laughed, but Henrietta continued. "Where is she? When was the last time anyone tried? The FitzFaeren arrow worked on Darius. Why don't we see if we can borrow it?"

"It's not the same—"

"I don't care if it's the same!" Henrietta yelled. Henry

ducked his head and ran his hands through his hair. "We have to try, and we have to try everything! Can we poison her? Can we steal a bomb and bring it through the cupboards? Can we burn her? Does she melt?"

Zeke laughed. "Maybe she has a ring. All we need is a hobbit and a volcano."

Henrietta pointed at him. "Don't make fun. Henry's giving up, and he can't give up. Not ever."

Zeke held up his hands. "I wasn't making fun of anything."

"I'm not giving—"

"Shut up, Henry. I'm not finished. If I were you, I wouldn't be all mopey. My family got tied up, too, and I can't flame up my hand or turn knives into dandelion ninja stars."

"Henrietta," Henry said. "If I admit that you're better than me, will you stop?"

"I'm not better than you," she said. Her eyes shone, and she blinked the moisture quickly away. "That's the whole point. I'm not. I'd have been dead a long time ago if it weren't for you. So why don't you start acting like it."

Zeke stood up. "I think we're all hungry." He slapped Henry on the back of the head. "And Henrietta's right. You got this, Henry. You always have. I thought we were dead on that bell tower. I thought we were dead when the fingerling jumped through the library window. I thought we were dead in the crypt. That's three times wrong. This witch can't hit your heater." He smiled. "Keep it coming. Down the pipe. Straight fire."

Henry pushed his chair back and splashed his feet down in the water. "They don't die. But I do."

Henrietta stepped over beside Henry. "Yeah, well, if you die, do it trying. I don't think the rest of us will be too far behind."

"Who's depressing now?" Henry asked.

Henrietta slapped his butt. "Atta babe," she said. Zeke burst out laughing. Henry stared blankly at them both, and then, carrying Coradin's sword in its black sheath, he splashed through the water into the kitchen and stopped by the back door.

"We don't have much time," he said. "We'll just grab some food, and then we're off to Hylfing. We can sleep there while we wait."

"Henry York's got the heat," Henrietta said. "H-baby. Hot Yorkie. Comin' for ya with the Henry Monster."

"Henrietta," said Henry. "You need to stop now."

"The Henry Monster?" Zeke asked.

Henry turned the knob.

"Maccabee, Maccababe." Henrietta laughed, while her cousin opened the door. "No one hits the Maccababy."

Freckles stood nervously beside his stepfather. He'd had plenty of discussions with policemen in the past, but he liked it this way better.

He had swiped his stepfather's video camera and set it up beside the hole. Then his stepfather had tracked him down, and at first he hadn't been happy. In fact, he'd been extremely unhappy, more so about his camera and tripod being used than the cigarette that Freckles had been smoking.

And then the water had started. A trickle at first, and then a mini-waterfall a little more than two feet wide. The water spilled out of the empty air just inches above the edge of the hole and tumbled down its side. His stepfather had tasted it and declared it salty. They'd trained the camera on the water, and then they had both stood, side by side, mesmerized. Truthfully, it was the first moment the two of them had shared.

When the policeman came, he'd been angry, yelling about trespassin' and danger. But then he saw the water.

"Chiggers and ticks," he'd said, and he watched it with them. After a while, he ran his hand through the air above and behind it. And then he had asked for a copy of the tape. His wife, apparently, had been making fun of him for his firm belief in a paranormal explanation of The Willis Disappearance, as the town of Henry now called it. A few people in the barbershop had been calling it The Willis Abduction.

After a while, the water level in the hole was noticeably higher, and the radio on the cop's hip began to crackle.

He ignored it. He didn't want to miss a single salty drop.

And that was when the doorway opened in the air. More water slopped out of its base, but no one was looking at the base. Three humanoid figures stood in the sky door. One appeared to be gripping a weapon. They were laughing.

Cackling almost. A high female voice, lilting, almost singsongy, issued a proclamation.

"No one hits the Maccababy."

The door slammed. The air returned to its normal shape beneath the Kansas sky. The water trickled on. The policeman lunged forward and waved his arms through the space.

"Sir!" said Freckles, pointing down, jiggling his arm. "Sir!"

Where the water appeared, a corner of parchment now dangled. The policeman gripped it carefully and pulled it out of nowhere. One corner had been burned away, but otherwise the dripping yellow page seemed fine. Its ink hadn't even run.

"It's alien," the policeman said.

Henrietta snorted with one hand clamped over her mouth.

"Was that a video camera?" Zeke asked.

Henry nodded. Somewhere that cop had his glove. For a moment, he thought about stepping back out and asking for it, but that wasn't really an option.

Henrietta couldn't stifle her laughter any longer. She slumped against the door, shaking. "Maccababy," she said. "What's a Maccababy?"

Henry felt his smile growing. He couldn't have stopped himself if he'd tried.

"Whatever it is," Zeke said, "don't hit one."

Henry's laughter grew quickly. "I wish we could see the tape." He wiped his eyes. "Your mom might see us on the news. Do you think they'll recognize us?"

Zeke shrugged and shook his head. "Don't know. The camera was a little low. Maybe not."

"Either way," Henry said, "we're eating in Hylfing. Does The Horned Horse have hamburgers?"

CHAPTER FIFTEEN

Red-shirts marched the walkway. Cracking whips kept the slave heads down. The captain stood in front of Frank, with his hands behind his back.

"Stand up!" he demanded. "Now."

Frank smiled. "Can't. Tried. But can't."

The captain pulled keys from his belt and bent down to unlock Frank's shackles. "What have you been doing, Francis? Trying to take your hands off?"

Frank's arms fell loose, and he stood slowly, refusing to look at his wrists, though he heard Dots gasp behind him. He nudged Monmouth's clothes with his toe. "He went out the hatch. The back door for the dead."

"We are a great distance from land," the captain said. "It is only a shadow on the horizon."

"Must be a swimmer," said Frank. "Why else would he leave his clothes?"

The captain looked around inside of Frank's eyes and then scanned the hold. "Why would he leave you?" he asked. "Did he learn the lesson I did so many years ago? Was it time to shake off the horrible taint of your family? Only fools stand with you."

"Maybe," said Frank. "But here you are, right beside me, little Roderick from Hylfing. How close do you have to get before you're tainted?"

The shorter man turned and stood chest to chest with Frank, flaring wool-filled nostrils. "Your family is done. Hylfing will be just another northern port, smelling of fish and poverty. You will not survive the anger of the emperor."

"We've survived worse, but then you know that already." Frank patted the captain on the cheek. His wrist was banded with blackened blood.

Roderick knocked Frank's hand away and drew a knife from his belt. Behind him, the sound of a long chain snaking through a hook and collapsing to the deck echoed in the beams. And then another. And another. Three at once. Chains were dropping on both sides of the walkway.

Green leaves sprouted from the beams of the ceiling. Silver bark began to wrap them. The soldiers on the walkway stepped back, ducking, pushing to get out from underneath the creaking growth.

An oar slid in from its oarlock and cracked a soldier in the temple. And then, from both sides, slaves leapt from their seats, yelling, brandishing chains.

The soldiers fired crossbows into the swarm, but the bodies tumbled on. A big man, with dark skin and a bald head above his full beard, cracked bones with his blows. The soldiers were trampled like grapes, whipped with chains, and crushed with knees and feet. James stepped through the mob of skin and anger and grabbed the captain's wrists. He dropped his knife and tried to twist away. James cracked him head to head, and the big man stepped from behind James and looped a chain around the captain's neck.

"No!" Frank yelled. "No! Deal with him later."

A space cleared around the ladders. Crossbow bolts were pouring down into the hold. The slaves, still yelling, sending taunts up through the decks, stripped weapons off the killed soldiers. There was no fear. These men had forgotten to care for their lives long ago. They scrambled up the ladders like so many half-naked pirates, and Frank listened to the pounding and the shouts of victory, the shrieks of killed and killer.

James ripped the keys from the captain and jumped to his mother. Frank pulled the captain to himself, the heavy chain dangling loosely around his neck.

"Roderick," he said. "You taste this? You smell it?" He pulled the fleece out of the captain's nose. "You've been baking with death and agony for too long. Taste it now. They'll kill you, and I'm not thinking that it will be quick. More than likely you'll get eaten or made into a shirt and trousers. I'm giving you one chance, more than you gave me. Out the hatch. Swim. Die free in the open sea. Haggle for mercy with God, but you'll get no more from me. Go."

The captain stood motionless, his eyes glassy with terror and confusion. A strong third of the slaves were still in chains, craning and shouting at the others to free them. Pale Monmouth moved slowly down the walkway, bending and stroking the beams as he came. The wood livened and grew leaves. Dowels became limbs. The new life pushed out the iron hooks that anchored the chains, and more slaves leapt from their benches, armed with their own shackles.

"Go, Roderick," Frank said. "I can't save you from this storming. Reach land and take a new path with your life, or make your peace and sink. But get on. It will be worse if you stay."

A torrent of slaves rushed by, scrambling up the ladders and up each other, eager for air and the blood of their captors.

"You can save me." The captain looked into Frank's eyes. "Let me row. Chain me to an oar. Hide me. We were boys together. You can't let them kill me." He pulled at Frank's shirt.

Frank shook his head. "Swim," he said. "Drown. Both are better than what they'll be handing out, and better than what you've been giving to them." He turned the captain and pushed him onto the walkway. Monmouth stepped aside. The hold was empty of all but the bodies of the masters and soldiers and the slaves who'd fallen to arrows.

The captain walked slowly through the hold until he reached the hatch in the stern.

The struggle above had quieted. Songs and cheers had replaced the clatter of steel.

"Find him! He's below!" The voice was big, rumbling down the ladder. "His head on a pike! His skin for our banner!"

The captain opened the dead man's hatch and took one look back. He was a boy again, looking at a family that could never be his, at blood that he could never share, at courage he didn't understand. Feet pounded on the deck above. Muffled shouts reached his ears. Filling his lungs, he clenched his teeth and looked to the sea. Then, like hundreds of men before him, he tumbled out beneath the watching gulls, above the watching beasts. Roderick of Hylfing was never known again.

Not by that name.

The hatch banged on the breeze. The whole ceiling, covered with aspen leaves, flickered on the passing air. Armed slaves descended, glanced through the hold, checked the bodies, and then scurried back up the ladders.

James and the others stepped out from the sacks and stood around Frank. Monmouth walked toward them, grinning.

Penelope looked from the bodies to the rustling grove on the ceiling. "How did you do that? Is the whole ship alive?"

Monmouth laughed and looked around for his clothes. "The beams are strong. It doesn't take much to liven them." He picked up his trousers and hopped in, one leg at a time. "It would have been easier if I'd been branded with oak strength, but aspen did well enough. Your cousin would have turned everything into a dandelion patch."

James picked up the captain's knife and tossed it to Monmouth. Then he flipped over a soldier's corpse and fished a long blade from his belt.

Dotty tucked her arm into her husband's. She kissed his hand. "Your poor wrists."

Hyacinth and Isa moved farther into the hold. Hyacinth touched Monmouth's cheek. "Thank you," she said. "You've grown stronger since you first slept beneath our roof."

"Not much stronger," Monmouth said. "Not like your son. But cleaner."

"What do we do now?" Penelope asked. "Will they take us back to Hylfing?"

Frank clicked his tongue. "Now *that* I doubt. I'm hopeful that they'll let us live, what with Monmouth's tree beams spitting out their chains, but I doubt they'll pull oars for us against a wind."

"Are we safe?" Dotty asked. She needed water. Her face, so easily flushed, was now pale.

"Yes," Frank said. "Maybe. We can hope."

James moved to the ladder. "We need to get above-decks. Someone will be settling in as commander."

He tucked the knife in his teeth, and the others followed him. Monmouth and Frank came last.

When they reached the upper deck and crawled into the sunset and the air, no one so much as looked at them. The big, bearded man stood in the center of the deck, his dark skin glistening with the orange light of the sun. He held a whip in one hand and a long, curving knife in the other. The crowd had cleared a circle around him, and he turned slowly, eyeballing anyone who even approached his stature.

"Who questions me?" he shouted. "I've pulled an oar in

this hell for three years, and now it is mine to command. Who doubts it?"

Sails snapped and tugged the ship forward, but the men were silent. And then the crowd parted, and two men, twins, stepped into the circle. They were as pale as Monmouth, but tall and lean. Dirt-colored hair clumped around their shoulders, and scars crisscrossed their backs. Both had narrow faces and noses like axes. Both held short seamen swords.

"We command this ship," one of them said. "We will serve under no Southerner." The crowd shifted, muttering, clearly eager for the fight, eager for the taste of more blood, eager to see a big man fall.

James pushed forward.

"What's he doing?" Isa asked. She covered her mouth. "Oh, no. Mother?"

Hyacinth closed her eyes and wrapped her arms around her daughter. Her lips were moving.

"Is he going to fight?" Penelope asked.

Frank nodded. Monmouth tried to move forward, but Frank grabbed him. "Too many, and we'll have a war."

James stepped into the ring, flexed his back, and walked slowly over to the side of the big man. Turning, flipping his knife and catching it by the blade's tip, he nodded at the man beside him. Then he scanned the crowd.

"He commands!" he yelled. "Not a pair of hatchet-faced brothers. This is the man I'll serve. What's your name?" he asked suddenly.

"Meroe," the man said.

"Captain Meroe!" shouted James. He moved in front of his new captain, alone facing the brothers. "And James, sixth son of Mordecai, mate." He glanced back at the bearded man. The beard nodded, and the brothers moved forward, long legs spread, hands high, and blades point down, like men trained in alleys and harbor brawls. James flipped his knife again and caught it, balanced on his fingertip. Monmouth's laugh was passed through the crowd.

"I wouldn't do it," James told the brothers. "Why survive what you have and die now? For what? Who knows, we might even put you ashore."

In a flash, the brothers jumped forward. One high, slashing at the head, the other low, sweeping at ankles. James ducked and hopped to the circle's edge. His knife flicked out of his hand and buried itself in a brother's neck.

Meroe stepped forward, swinging his bladed fist like a man set to kill a bull. His opponent slid to the side and managed to gouge his hip.

James grabbed his knife and rushed against the second brother. Pressed on two sides, the man jumped into the crowd, but it parted, offering no protection. With a quick slash to the wrist, James disarmed him, and the sword clattered to the deck. The man yelped and pushed all the way back to the galley rail, flung one leg over, and jumped. The crowd sent his brother's body after him.

Before the ripples died, James grabbed Meroe by the arm and led him across the deck and up the short stairs to the helm. There, he whistled the crowd into silence.

"Right!" he shouted. "Which of you oar-dogs have done any sailing without the heavy bracelets?"

Frank turned to Hyacinth, and she smiled.

"James," she said. "James has always been James. Part rooster, part lion. He is sweetness to my soul, but I have gladness that he wasn't the seventh."

"Why?" Isa asked.

Hyacinth squeezed her daughter. "James needed nothing else."

Henry had tried to expand the opening the way he'd seen his father do it, but he wasn't surprised that he couldn't.

He knew that the way was still open back into Hylfing through his old Cleave cupboard, because he had shoved his arm through. But he didn't know exactly where he was going to end up. Was the cupboard still in the rubble of the house? Had Coradin taken it someplace?

And the water was a huge distraction. He felt bad for flooding the old farmhouse, but it seemed like a better option than letting all the cupboards burn. The water still streamed out of the little diamond-shaped door high on the wall and tumbled down the stairs and found its way to the main floor and out the doors.

How long until they created a salt marsh? How long until Henry, Kansas, was a lake? He was curious, but there was nothing he could do about it either way. The door just wouldn't stay shut.

They'd flipped the bed back down in order to reach the

Cleave cupboard, but they were still going to have to get a toehold in another door to crawl through the funneling seam Henry had made. It was holding its shape well, but it wasn't large.

"I think I should go first," Henrietta said behind him.

Henry turned around. He was standing on the bed. Coradin's sword was tied on his back, knotted to his belt and the drawstrings of his hoodie. Zeke and Henrietta stood in the splashing beside him. Beo was panting in the attic, lying down in obedience to Henrietta, not to Henry. "Of course you do," Henry said. "Why wouldn't you want to go first?"

"I'm just saying." She raised her voice to compete with the water. "If you go first, the little invisible thing we're supposed to be crawling into might disappear. Then we'd be stuck."

Henry laughed. "Invisible things have already disappeared."

"Whatever," Henrietta said. "I just think you should come behind us."

Henry looked at Zeke. He shrugged.

"Okay," Henry said. "Go for it. Climb on in." He stepped off the bed and gestured for Henrietta to go first. "You know which one."

Henrietta hopped onto the sponge bed and tossed her backpack at the cupboards. It disappeared before it reached them. "I don't think I'll ever get used to this," she said, and she stuck her toe into an ax-shaped door, pushed up, bent, and wormed her way into the wall. Her shins and feet dangled for a moment, and then she kicked forward, and they were gone.

Henry nodded at Zeke. "Go for it."

But a whistle shot back through the wall, and Beo bounded into the room and onto the bed. He turned in a circle, looking for Henrietta, and then barked, confused. The whistle came again, and he faced the wall. The dog sniffed and then jumped. His head and front legs vanished, but his hind end scrabbled and clawed at the wall. Henry and Zeke both jumped onto the bed and shoved the dog up and forward, tail-beaten for their trouble.

"Okay," Henry said, panting. "Now you go."

Zeke stepped onto the bed, shoved his pack forward, and in one fluid motion, he was up and through the door-way, leaving Henry alone in the flooding house.

Henry double-checked everything. He had his base-ball, a few folded-up pages as samples, and some kind of ancient death-sword strapped to his back.

He really wanted his baseball glove. He needed it.

"Oh well," he said aloud. "I could lose worse things." Maybe someday he would knock on that cop's door. Maybe not.

Henry scurried up the wall and slid into the cupboard, grateful that it wasn't shrinking on him. His toe slipped, and he dangled, halfway into someplace dark and musty that smelled like fish and wet dog, and halfway in the air of his old bedroom. With a kick and a scooch, he made it in, not so gracefully as Zeke or even Henrietta, but at least better than the dog.

Coughing, he sat up. A door creaked and let in the last light of a sunset. He was in a small shed. Zeke was on his feet, opening the door. Beo was whining about something, and Henrietta—

Where was Henrietta?

"Oh, Henry," she said in the darkness. "It's Rags. He's here. He was trying to find you."

After looking carefully, Zeke opened the door all the way and stepped outside. They were down by the harbor, in a wharf shed. Nets hung on the walls. Henrietta was sitting cross-legged, and Beo stood beside her, sniffing and whining. On her lap, there was a tangle of burned feathers.

Henry slid forward. The raggant was still, his rough skin burned in places, his wings patchy.

"Oh, Rags," Henry said. He took the drooping animal carefully from Henrietta and settled it onto his lap. Henry hunched over and pressed his forehead against the animal's blunt horn. "I'm so sorry," he said. "I'm so sorry. I should have made you go through the cupboard first, but you know you wouldn't have. What happened? I wondered where you were."

Henrietta cleared her throat. "I think he's dead, Henry."

Zeke leaned back in.

"No," Henry said. "No. He can't be. I would have known. I would have felt something."

"You really think so?" Henrietta asked. "With all that's been going on?"

Henry stood up, carrying his animal, if it really was his.

He was sure that the raggant thought of himself as the owner.

"C'mon," he said. "Let's get to this inn. Go, Henrietta. You know where it is."

The three of them walked through the streets of Hylfing, wet and unrecognized, with Henrietta leading. Beo paced beside Henrietta, somehow aware that his city wasn't as cheerful as when he had left it. Zeke carried the little cupboard crammed into his backpack. The sun was just hidden behind the sea, and most of the townspeople were inside, muttering their anger and sorrow over evening meals. The cobbles hid in shadows, and a cool breeze clipped in from the sea with the tang of winter storms to come, ruffling the feathers in Henry's arms. Two galleys still squatted in the harbor, and that meant soldiers might be in the streets. Worse, how many fingerlings had been accounted for? One had died in Hylfing and one in Endor. Six more had been in Endor, including Coradin. That left two. Where were they?

Henry began staring at shadows as they passed and glared angrily at every alley, trying to squelch his nerves. If they could feel him, why couldn't he feel them? Maybe he could? He'd have to try. It would definitely be useful when walking through cities at twilight.

"Can we go faster?" Henry asked.

Henrietta looked back at him, slapping Beo's neck. "Are you that hungry?"

"I wouldn't mind being inside already," Zeke said. "With lots of light. I've had enough dark for a while."

"We're almost in the square," Henrietta said. "Hold on."

They wound their way down a gradual hill, passed three cross streets, and stepped into the square. It was well lit on the other end, in front of the hall. Six fires burned in wire cages around the building, and soldiers were posted beside each of them.

"This way," Henrietta said, and sticking close to the edge, she led them across the corner of the square to an old building that had forgotten how to stand straight. Black timbers, angled with age, held up the low-slung inn. The front door was closed. Lanterns on either side of it hung dead and empty.

Henrietta grabbed the center knob and pulled. It clanked in place. The door was locked.

"Hey!" she yelled, and knocked on it.

"Closed!" The muffled voice filtered through the door.

Henry stepped forward. "No, you're not!" he shouted, and he kicked the door's base three times.

After a moment, a heavy bolt slid, and the door opened a crack, revealing a tiny slice of golden light.

"Password?" a man whispered.

"We were told to meet someone here," Henrietta said.

"Wrong," said the man. "Password?"

"Let us in or we'll burn it down," Henry said. "Does that work? Mordecai, my father, told us to wait for him here."

"Is that Henry? But you blazed in the house. You're ash." The door opened and emptied the inn's light into the dusk. The big cook hooked them all easily and dragged them in. Beo was forced to his belly on the mat. The door slammed, and the bolt slid.

Henry looked around the room. It was full of faces: hard sailor faces, leathered by the sea; shepherds and guardsmen with sharpened eyes; even shopkeepers, soft in their middles. He had never been in a room so full of anger, so full of . . . humans. Women were sprinkled throughout the room, and others moved quickly with trays bending beneath drinks, but most of the eyes on him were male. They were glad to see him. Faces smiled, but not in any way that calmed the fury beneath the surface, and in some cases, the fury on the surface. Forehead veins twitched. Knees bounced. The place was sweltering with breathing, and the windows had all been covered with blankets.

Henry began to notice weapons.

The cook yelled, and the wall-to-wall whispering died.

"This here's Henry York Maccabee and his dead raggant—you'll be knowin' who sired him—and Henri-etta Willis, daughter to the mayor, both thought to be burnt to soot." He glanced back at Zeke. "And their friend," he added. "And Beo, their uncle's dog." He turned to Henry. "I'm Zebudee. Call me Zeb. Knew your father since we were weaned. This is my inn."

"I'm really, really hungry," said Henry. "Is the kitchen open? And I need someone to look at my raggant."

"Who will make a trencher space?" the cook yelled. "Give a seat to Mordecai's blood."

Men shoved their way clear of a table, leaving space

enough for Henry, Henrietta, and half of Zeke on a bench. The three of them levered themselves in and sat quietly in a silent rainstorm of stares. Henry stroked the raggant on his lap.

Three bowls of thick stew were dropped in front of them, along with spoons. A hunk of meat, bone in, was thrown to Beo.

Henry ignored his bowl, and the stares became questions. The rain became a flood.

"Where's your father?"

"You burn up?"

"Where you been hiding?"

"Where's you father?"

"When'll he be back?"

"You think we should strike?"

"Where's your father?"

"You think we should burn the ships?"

"What would your father say?"

"How you live in all that fire?"

"Shame on us if one red-shirt still breathes in the morning. What say you, Henry?"

Henry couldn't answer anyone. His story was too big, and his eyes, his mind, his heart were on the pile of sagging flesh and feathers in his lap. The men from the table all leaned in, facing him, watching him watch the raggant. Rows of others crowded behind them, drinking, fuming, chewing on threats and questions.

A small, steaming glass was slapped onto the table.

Zeb nodded at the raggant. "If he's got a spark of life, that will shake him up. Works on sailors pulled from the wracks."

Henry rolled the raggant onto his back and picked up the little glass the innkeeper had given him. The liquid was brown and as thick as syrup, cool to his touch despite the steam.

Squeezing the raggant's lips, he tipped the glass.

"Just a drop there, lad," a gruff voice said. "Don't be melting his tongue."

One fat, slow, string-trailing bead fell into the raggant's mouth. The questions stopped while every man watched. Henrietta chewed slowly. After a moment of silence, the gruff voice spoke again. "Right then, two drops, and then give him up. More than three would kill a plow horse."

Biting his lip and swallowing hard, fighting his own tight throat and hot eyes, Henry eased two more drops into the raggant's mouth. After a few seconds, men began to shift and whisper with disappointment.

"He's gone, lad. Noble beast. Pity."

"No," Henry said. He tipped in two more drops, and then a third. "No." He set the glass back on the table and bent over his raggant. It was his raggant. His. His mother had bonded it to him. It couldn't be dead. He wouldn't let it. Henry looked up and around the room, at all the stern and angry faces waiting to see if he would cry. His eyes went black, and the room became a bedlam of influence, traces and strands and histories and breaths pouring from

---

every man, mingling together into a single mob of anger at the ceiling. He turned his eyes down to the raggant.

It was still. A translucent gray web pooled limply around it.

"No," Henry said again. He ran his right hand, his glowing burn, around the rough animal's face. He sent his heat into its belly. There was something there. Something pulling at his palm from beyond the skin and bones. The bond between the two of them had not been broken. The animal couldn't be dead. Not yet. The room was full of life and strength, but Henry needed none of it. He poured his own heat into the animal; he let the pull take his strength; he let the bond grow.

The raggant's back arched. His nostrils chuffed and flared. Writhing, his wings thumped into Henry's chest. The creature sneezed, again and again, and on the seventh sneeze, two clouds of dandelion down erupted from his nostrils.

The raggant opened his eyes. Then, levering his front legs onto the table, he flared his damaged wings, knocking Henrietta's bowl onto her lap and thumping Zeke in the face. Eyeing the men around the table, he bellowed, long and loud and furious.

The gruff sailor laughed. "Vicious, isn't he. He'll be wanting a drink with that fire in his belly." The man slid his dark, foam-topped pint forward carefully, watching the raggant's eyes as he did.

The raggant quieted, dangling his black tongue out of

his mouth. He dipped it through the foam and into the sailor's draft. His lips followed, and he slurped noisily.

"Innkeep, water!" the sailor shouted. "In a bowl for the beast!"

When a wooden bowl full of water banged onto the table, Henry tried to pick the raggant up. The animal flapped hard and shook, kicking and butting, rolling his eyes and looking for something to bite. But Henry didn't care. Blinking against the beating wings and grinning happily, he dunked the raggant's head in the water.

Immediately, the animal went limp, burbling. Henry let its rear sag onto the table, and then he let go completely. Tucking his wings back, the raggant kept his face in the water with his tongue lolling out. His horn and nostrils peeked above the surface, and he sprayed sailors with every breath.

Henry sat down and sighed.

"I thought he was gone," Henrietta said.

"That he was," said the gruff sailor. "That he was. Your cousin here's got a bit of spark."

"No." Henry shook his head. "Rags had a little life left."

"Either way," Zeke said, "I'd say he's got a lot now."

Henry plowed through his stew, dropped his spoon, and puffed his cheeks. Now that he was done and the raggant was calm, the men around him expected answers. A barrage of the same questions poured down on him.

Henry held up his hands. "Hold on, hold on!" he yelled, but no one so much as paused for breath.

Behind him, the innkeeper whistled sharply, and the room died.

"Okay," Henry said. "I'm alive, and my cousin is alive." He patted Henrietta's shoulder. "You know that much. My grandmother is alive, too, and safe in another city. My father and Caleb are in Endor searching for a way to kill the witch. They will be coming here if they can. The witch is somewhere far south in a big city." He looked at Henrietta. "What's it called?" She shrugged, and he looked back at the group. "The emperor's city."

"Dumarre?" a sailor asked. "Mordecai knows this?"

Henry nodded. "He thinks she's controlling the emperor."

"And why does he think that?" someone shouted.

"The emperor's got enough evil of his own," said another. "They'd make quite the pairing."

"Have you heard of fingerlings?" Henry asked the room.

Voices died. Finally, someone cleared his throat. "My gran told stories. Gave me night sweats."

"Aye," said another. "Old Endor tales—fingerlings and witch-dogs."

"Well," said Henry, "there were fingerlings with the soldiers here. More in Endor tracking my father."

The first sailor scrunched up his face. His eyes looked young, but his skin looked like worn shoes. "With the finger and all? Really?"

"Really," Henry said. "I killed two of them. They were wearing black, and they keep their hair knotted to hide the finger."

The room was silent. After a moment, someone shouted. "Hoy, he's got a knot!" A group scuffled in the corner, and a man was passed forward. Rope-hardened hands doubled the man over and pressed his face to the table.

"Name's Harold!" he yelled. "Only ten fingers and all on my hands!"

His hair was brown and knotted in the back. A long knife appeared in someone's hand and the hair knot was gone.

"See!" Harold yelled. "Nothing! I'm no witch-finger, you clods!"

Hands released him, and he straightened, his hair falling unevenly around his face.

"Do I look that bad?" Henrietta asked.

Henry snorted.

"Yes," said Zeke.

"To the ships!" a sailor shouted, and a dozen voices joined him. "Burn the serpent galleys!"

"Wait!" Henry yelled. "Just wait! If the witch is killed, then the ships and soldiers will leave!"

"And if she isn't?" a man asked. His skin was softer than the others, one of the shopkeepers. "What then?"

Henry scratched his jaw. He didn't like to think about that option. If she wasn't killed, then everyone could figure out what to do after he was gone.

"Right!" the shopkeeper shouted. "Up, Hylfing! Two moons of credit to any who stand on the galley decks with me tonight!"

Gradually, the shouts and laughter died. Lanterns around the inn were snuffed out, until only a few flickered through the mob of shapes and voices. The doorway opened, and cloaked and hooded whispering men slipped out in clusters, moving down toward the harbor.

When the inn was empty, an aproned Zebudee moved through the room, relighting the lanterns and wiping tables. Henry sat quietly between his cousin and Zeke and watched the still-panting raggant blow bubbles.

"Not a good idea," Henry said quietly.

"Why?" Henrietta asked. "After everything else, why not burn the ships?"

"Some of 'em will die," Zeke said. "And if the ships burn, nothing changes."

The innkeeper wiped the table in front of them, steering well clear of the raggant and his bowl. "Oh," he said. "Don't blame them for rushing to a fight, not with what they've seen. Old Amram's house burned. You lot left in the flames, and the rest marched off like slaves to market." He pointed at Henry. "You see the board from end to end. They see only red-shirts in their city with sword and torch. Let the bulls charge; they'd buckle under guilt if they didn't."

"What about you?" Henry asked.

Zeb winked. "I sees a bit more than most." He straightened up and flipped his rag over his shoulder. "You'll be needing rooms."

"We don't have any money," Henry said. "We can't pay you."

"I think I have a dollar in my pocket," said Zeke.

"I don't know what a dollar is," the big man said. "But you can keep it to yourselves. I have more than rooms and food for you lot." He dug into his apron pocket and glanced around the room. The place was empty, but he still leaned forward and whispered. "Given this for Mordecai, but you're like to do as well." He dropped the big chestnut cube on the tabletop. "Fat-Faerie gave it to me."

"Franklin?" Henry asked. He slid forward and grabbed the glistening cube.

Zeb nodded. "And he was with your sister, Miss Una." He looked at Henrietta. "And your little sister, too, the spunky lass. And the fish-faced boy."

"They weren't taken?" Henrietta asked. She leaned over Henry's shoulder.

"Well," the innkeeper said. "It seemed that they were. But not by the red-shirts."

"Writing?" Henry asked. He squinted and rotated the cubed nut. "Nudd," he read. "Lord of the Second World, monarch of Glaston's Barrow." He looked up suddenly. "Is this from the Chestnut King?"

"Straight from the tales," said Zeb. "And no other."

CHAPTER SIXTEEN

Henry York Maccabee, seventh son of Mordecai, lay flat on his back in his bed. He was physically exhausted, beaten, and drained. He was also physically unable to relax. His toe bounced beneath the blanket. The fingers of one hand ran gently across the burn on his jaw, refusing to scratch. The fingers of the other rubbed and twisted the metal square on its leather string around his neck.

The raggant snorted and snored and butted against Henry's hip. Every so often, Henry reached down and gently massaged the animal's coarse skin, tracing lines between the burns, reassuring himself of the life beside him. He needed to find someone to take care of the animal. He needed his mother and her balms. Or Aunt Dotty. Where were they? The window was open, and a crisp breeze carried in the rumbling lullaby of distant surf. Zeke was snoring lightly in his bed, and Henrietta was silent on her trundle, arms around Beo. The dog occasionally twitched or moaned and dragged a toenail across the plank floor, but was generally quieter than the raggant.

Henrietta had absolutely refused to sleep alone in a

room and then had absolutely refused to take either one of the boy's beds.

Gently shuffling the raggant off his side, Henry sat up and crossed his arms. For a while, he'd waited and listened for an attack on the galleys in the harbor, but the men had either given up on the idea or were waiting until deep in the wee hours. He hoped they'd given up. The fight seemed pointless to him.

Henry wondered if the innkeeper was still awake. He could creep down and beg for more stories of the wild faeren and their king, the faeren that had shunned the green men and incorporation into districts and *The Book of Faeren* entirely—the faeren that had disappeared into shaded woods. He replayed the man's description of the faeries that had taken Frank, the two girls, and Richard. If Frank hadn't put up a fight, he had to have been radically outnumbered. But the innkeeper's stories—stolen babies, scorched cities, missing herds, curses, vanishings—none of them made the Chestnut King seem like the kind of someone that Henry would like to approach for help. But then, all of the stories were old. The innkeeper said that he hadn't believed the Faerie King existed, not until he felt the strange chestnut in his own hand and read the writing in the grain.

Filling his lungs with the fresh breeze, erasing the smell of dog and burned raggant feathers, Henry glanced at the little table where he had left his baseball, his leaning sword, his folded stack of Endor papers, and the Chestnut King's bizarre message. He claimed Fat Frank for himself? Why? Henry scrunched his lips, suddenly wondering if Frank had been happy about it, about belonging to faeren again. Was that why he hadn't fought? Or was fighting just hopeless?

Henry shut his eyes and envisioned the writing on the chestnut, the smoky, swirling letters. The message had sounded a little like faeren messages Henry had received, but shaping letters in a grain was much different than using a typewriter. Henry knew he wasn't supposed to go straight to the king. His father had told him to try the queene first. She was more likely to be helpful. But his father hadn't known about the chestnut. He hadn't known that Anastasia and Una and Richard and Fat Frank were already with the Chestnut King. And he *had* told him to find Fat Frank. The two of them were supposed to try for the queene together, but what chance did they really have? Frank wasn't even faeren anymore, and Henry was just a kid with a problem. Of course, he was Mordecai's kid with a problem, but who knew if that would help?

What would the queene look like? Fat Frank with curls? Did the faeries think she was beautiful? Did they ever get to see her? Or maybe she looked just like any other queen but shrunk down in the wash? What did any other queens look like? It's not like Henry knew. He'd seen Magdalene, Eli's sister, Queen of FitzFaeren. Maybe she would look like her—small and hard, but lovely. Lots of very white hair.

Henry's mind drifted away, again watching the Arrow

of Chance, relic of FitzFaeren, flying from Caleb's bow. He was again pulling it out from beneath a floorboard in the old attic. Only this time, he couldn't, because the stupid little diamond-shaped door wouldn't shut, and the whole attic was under six inches of water, and the diamond-shaped door grew bigger than the entire wall, and the empty grass world was a sea, and the old house was floating away, sailed by gerbils.

The empty world was gone, and it had taken the gerbils. Henry was in darkness, bodiless, a dandelion flame and a slow-moving gray rope. He couldn't run from that rope. He knew that. It followed him, and others followed it. He was tired of running, tired of scrambling away. He wished that he had stayed with his father. Mordecai would not be running away. He was looking for ways to advance, ways to surprise, ways to win, not ways to survive. Everyone was surprised that Henry had survived, as if not dying was victory. He didn't want to survive anymore. He wanted to play baseball in the sun. He wanted to sit with his mother in her courtyard and listen to her voice and feel her hand on his head and hear stories of his brothers, the three he could never meet, and James and the two who still sailed faraway seas. He wanted time with his father, time enough to do nothing but watch the world and wander the woods of Badon Hill, time enough to learn how to be what he was. He wanted to teach Richard baseball.

Sensing nothing but two floating influences, golden and gray, Henry ached. He couldn't have those things by running. He couldn't have those things by hiding.

His dreaming mind turned and focused on the gray trail that streamed out from him and away into the darkness. Paths can be followed two ways. Prey can double-back on the hunter.

Henry, nothing more than a spinning dandelion soul, began to move, and the emptiness brightened around him. The world filled in, and his body took shape around the golden fire. He stood on the cobbled hill in front of the charred ruins of his mother's house beneath the moon's silver. His nostrils filled with the stink of burned histories, the walls that had known generations. Was he really here? Was he dream-walking or imagining? He didn't know. His body felt less than tangible, but at least he had one.

The gray strand was floating away from his face. He turned to follow it, but someone pinched his cheek. Grandmother Anastasia smiled at him, her full white hair braided back from her smooth, sun-darkened skin. In dreaming, only her eyes seemed old, the spark inside them sharpened by all they had seen, all they had struggled against, all they had searched for, all they had found. Looking at his grandmother, Henry knew that Magdalene of FitzFaeren was not the only queen he had ever seen. And this one shared his blood. She took Henry's left hand in hers, kissed it, and stood beside him. Interlocking her fingers with his, she pointed at the trailing gray thread in the air, and the two of them stepped forward. The world spun into a blur of color. Only the dead rope remained clear to Henry's eyes. He let his right hand, his burning hand, trace it through the confusion.

And again the world was still. Henry and his grandmother stood hand in hand at the peak of a large hill. A ruined watchtower gaped jagged teeth at the sky behind
them. Loose stones were scattered over the hilltop eaten
and half-eaten by green turf. The air was warmer here, and
beneath them, spread out miles into the distance, lit only
by the moon, the land fell away and narrowed, dropping
until it was all that separated two great seas, and then
widening, growing back into a continent, rising into hills
and distant mountains.

Long, gated walls guarded both ends of this land
bridge, the outposts of a great city. The city itself looked to
be rooted in stone, rising like a mountain range broader
than the land itself, its walls and gates staking claim to the
seas on either side. Ten Hylfings could have nested within
its walls, twenty within the harbors. Towers and palaces
competed with each other for precedence. Great statues
straddled the battlements, and red banners flew at their
heights. Ships and galleys and barges crowded within and
without the harbors.

Thick smoke rose up from the gates. Fire danced
around the canals.

"What's happening?" Henry asked. "Is this Dumarre?
Is it burning?"

His grandmother shrugged, pulled his hand, and again
led him forward through the dream, down into the city.

The two of them stood on a city wall wider than a
Kansas street. Above them loomed an enormous statue of
a man, straddling the wall, a dolphin beneath each foot. He

wore a helmet and a loincloth, and in each hand he held a ship. Henry stared up at him and then down inside the walls. Soldiers in red rushed by, carrying double-bladed pikes. Bodies lay scattered in the moonlit streets, bodies of men and women and soldiers, bodies of oxen and horses still hitched to shattered wagons. Phalanxes of soldiers blocked the gates, and archers stood behind them. Men ducked through the shadowy streets, hurling stones or torches at the barricade and slipping away again as arrows rattled in the streets and off the walls behind them.

Henry ignored the gray trail he had been following. Dropping his grandmother's hand, he turned and moved along the wall, scanning the city, watching canal barges burn and rioters creep in silent mobs through the streets. He looked up at the towers with their lamp-lit windows, and out at the sea, crowded with anchored merchant ships, corralled by galleys. The harbor within the sea gates was full of smaller craft, crawling with anxious sailors. The gatehouse on the wall was surrounded by soldiers standing firm against the knife-armed anger of seamen.

Henry didn't understand. Did they know about the witch? What had she done? And then he froze. Walking tall through the streets, unarmored and unafraid, came two men in black, both with oiled hair knotted in the back. Four broad men walked behind them, with swords at their belts and whips in their hands. They wore wizard robes, brown with hoods hanging large on their backs. Each held a wolf on a chain. Where they went, crowds scattered. And when they didn't, the wolves ran free, maddened by the whispers of their masters.

The witch was no longer hiding herself, and the lovers of darkness had crept out from their corners. They had found their queen.

Even in his dreaming, Henry's skin was cold. Everywhere, he could feel the witch and her endless leeching, her theft of life and strength. She had no need to hide her traces now, no need to shrink in shadows. This was her new Endor. Her game had been played and played well. This was no imagining of Henry's. He knew that his dreaming eyes saw truth, just as he knew that his stomach had curled into knots inside him. Fingerlings and witch-dogs patrolling the emperor's city. Citizens dead in the streets, held in by their own defenders. How long until all life was gone? How long until the streets were paved with ash?

He turned to his grandmother. Her eyes were wet, but as hard as river stones.

"This is real," he said.

She nodded.

"This is where they are bringing my mother?"

She nodded again.

"Where is the witch?"

Henry's gray strand was thicker here, and taut. They followed it down off the wall, and together they stood in the carnage of the streets. From his jaw, the trace of the witch stretched away from him and up into the towers.

"How do we find our way?" Henry asked.

His grandmother took his hand.

"Do I really want to?"

She half-smiled and pulled him up through the dream, up through the city, above the shouting and the ducking and the torch-carrying panic. They stood on a small, un-railed balcony, hugging the shoulder of a tall palace tower. Across from them, a greater tower strained for the sky. Be-tween the two, suspended from chains thicker than trees, there hung a walled garden.

Henry blinked. Treetops stretched above the walls of the hanging garden. A narrow rope-bridge led from the balcony to a small, peaked door. He could feel the pulling now, the pulling at everything, though the walls and trees in front of him were still. He knew what lay inside those walls. There would be a pool and a fountain. There would be four trees set around a couch where the witch slept. He knew what would be hanging between two of those trees. He moved forward onto the bridge, expecting it to sway beneath him, expecting to feel fear, but his dream-body was not heavy enough to move anything. He could have walked across the gap without the bridge, or jumped un-harmed to the courtyards below.

When he reached the door, he hesitated, and then shut his eyes and stepped through the heavy planks.

The garden was as still as it had been in his earlier dreams, and a little different. The fountain of the tortured man was larger. The black pool was smaller. The trees were alive, but not with their own strength. They were ungrowing, undying, unchanging, and their branches were overdelicate—real trees, corrupted and molded and filled until they were hardly trees at all.

Not one cricket chirruped as Henry walked, not a leaf rustled. He walked past the pool and through the trees, into the small clearing where fingerlings had been made, and beyond, to Nimiane's grove, her bed.

The pale man hung limp between the trees, sleeping. Where his hands were buried into bark, Henry could see gray strands growing, twisting like lazy smoke into the sky. There were only six, two from one hand and four from the other. Something inside Henry smiled. Four had been killed now. His father and uncle must have ended two in Endor. But there was something odd about one of the strands. It was thicker than the others, stiffer. And it wasn't all gray.

Henry moved closer, letting his eyes relax on the trunk where the strands emerged like ghost branches. One of them was a braid, gray blended with tendrils of green and purple. In places, tiny leaflets sprouted. Grapevines. Panic rocketed through Henry. Did one of the fingerlings have his father? Was his father being made a fingerling?

He stepped around the tree and stood, seething with anger, above Nimiane's bed. His grandmother grabbed his arm from behind, but Henry pulled it away.

The cat was asleep in the witch's arms. Nimiane, the beautiful horror, lay on her couch, limbs and fingers re-laxed while the streets of Dumarre ran with blood. Her eyes were shut in sleep, but her brows contracted. Her lip curled in dreaming anger. She was emptiness. Life, drifting in from the city, lost its colors and piled and coiled around her, graying, and then falling into her. Fading. Disappearing completely. The man between the trees was tied to her, and a tangle of lives—his own, the trees', the fingerlings', and hints of Mordecai—stretched out from his spine and into the sleeping witch, into the dark, empty hole that was her soul.

Henry bent over her. He could feel pain building inside him, building inside his distant, sleeping body. His own gray strand, his rope, felt like it had been set in his jaw with hooks of ice. The pull was strong, and he watched as flickers of gold passed from himself and into the witch, into the back of her head—as if she were herself a fingerling—where Zeke's bat had once been ruined saving Henry's life, or at least postponing his death. The witch had been weak then, freshly released, barely able to maintain her false appearance for all her coughing. Tensing, Henry leaned closer, ignoring his grandmother's hand squeezing on his elbow. How could he kill something like this? Where any other creature—fish, bird, bug, plant, or man—would have a soul, a glory, even if twisted or damaged, she had only devouring nothingness. Would she feel it if he touched her? Would she feel a brush, a breeze, a whisper? Would she know he had come, that somehow his dreamwalking self, his soul, had found her roost, had bent over her? Her breath, as cold as death itself, as cold as loneliness, brushed against Henry's face. The hooks in his jaw pulled harder. The tie between them grew faster, broader, more golden than gray. Henry closed his eyes.

His body, his grandmother, were gone.

He was looking at himself back in Nimroth's library. He was looking out of Coradin's eyes. In her dreams, the witch walked the minds and rememberings and visions of her fingerlings. Henry, nothing but consciousness, walked with her.

Henry saw the blade part the skin on the back of Henrietta's neck and felt the witch's goading, her frustration that Coradin had not taken her whole head. He watched his own flaming hand, the little kitchen knife, Beo's snarling attack, and he felt pitiful. He was so small next to the fingerling, small even next to Zeke and the dog. The room burned, and as Coradin's own memories crowded in like old pain, the dream faltered and disappeared.

Coradin and two others, all of them armed, were climbing through the moonlit hills. Ahead of them, set in a looming cliff, there was an ancient wizard door. Henry felt his physical heart jump. Where would they come out? How close would they be to Hylfing?

But he calmed himself. Something strange was pulling the witch's dream, something she at first resisted.

And then they were behind another fingerling's eyes, in a big room bursting with a light whiter than the sun. It was a circular throne room, vaulted, domed, ornate even in its dust. A white throne of pale, nearly translucent stone sat in its center.

On it, with his legs sprawling and his arms draped over the sides, sat Mordecai. He smiled and leaned forward slightly. Caleb stood beside him, leaning on his black horn bow.

"Nimiane," Mordecai said. "I have been waiting. Such an old friend should have come sooner."

The fingerling twisted. He was on his knees, and his arms were tied. A hand gripped his jaw, and another gripped his hair. He was being made to look at Mordecai, Henry could feel it. And he could feel something cold, a blade, pressed against the back of his head, just beneath a lump. A lump that moved. A finger.

The fingerling opened his mouth, but it was Nimiane who spoke. Henry felt her thoughts shape themselves into words, and he heard them with the fingerling's ears.

"Friend?" the witch asked. "Your father's jests were not so weak. You are not even an enemy. You are a blister soon to be lanced, one weed in a field ripe for the harvest."

"A blister? At what age did I imprison you in lifeless stone? How many years did you spend with your sister, your own flesh that you betrayed, dwindling in strength?" Mordecai straightened, filling the throne.

"What are years to the immortal? Decades in stone or one night's drowsing are of equal burden. But your own son released me and brought about his death. He opened the door that leads to my new kingdom, my new throne. The great Amram was worthy to face me, but you? You fell short of his mark, and your own son is a soft and hollow husk of what your line once was. The breed weakens and fades." The witch laughed, and Caleb shifted in his stance.

Mordecai was motionless. "Tell me, Mordecai, does Henry know what awaits him? My blood roots within him. It reaches for his mind. My grip on him grows stronger with each rising sun. Does he know that your hand will be the one to cut his throat when the madness comes, or will it be his mother? For madness it will be before his death, and the death of the northern green men. So ends the true line of Iothric and Amram. So ends the line of the Old King— in the death of a weakling."

"Look to your own madness, Nimiane." Mordecai's voice had grown an edge. His smile was gone. "These eyes will see your end."

Again the witch laughed. "Is that all you desired to say? What fear can you give me? Capturing a fingerling and flopping in a throne make you no danger to me. Do you want me to grieve for this dog from my pack that you hold? Kill him. Take his finger. Strike him down. I have no fear of you or any of your kind. Come to the emperor's city. Face me and see if I quiver. Watch me take the eyes from your wife as your father took mine. Sit by and await your audience with Dumarre's new queen while your sons are fed to birds."

"Nimiane," Mordecai said. "I have the Blackstar. I hold its power for myself. I will come. I will strike you down."

"You lie," said the witch. "You have nothing but words and false hope."

Reaching behind him, Mordecai brought out a stone, black and smooth, bordered by a halo of white fire.

"Death stands by your door," Mordecai said. "So it is. So it shall be."

Henry, shocked, watched his father stand and his face harden as he stared at the fingerling. He expected the execution. He expected the finger to be sliced, the vision to end. He felt the blade press harder on the back of the skull, the edge slid up.

Again, the witch laughed. "Order it, green man. His death will bring no harm to me. Play at the great king! Sit on Nimroth's throne. Execute your first victim."

"Blindfold him," Mordecai said, and hands slid a cloth in front of the fingerling's eyes.

"You will never rival me," said the witch. "You haven't the stomach."

Pain seared through the fingerling's world, nothing but pain. Somewhere far away, Henry's body writhed and arched its back in agony. The scream that echoed through the throne room was not Nimiane's. The fingerling found his own voice, and his own memories, stifled by the witch's influence, came rushing back. An old man, a smiling woman, girls laughing, treetops rustling in the sun outside a high bedroom window.

And death came with silence. His life was consumed, even the strength of his final twisting shout, swallowed back into the witch.

Mordecai was gone. The world was gray emptiness. Henry would have gasped if he'd had a body. There was nothing to feel—nothing but the witch's boiling anger and, strangely, the beginnings of fear.

The green filth lies. He cannot have found the true stone. He cannot hold it without being consumed.

The anger calmed. The witch's voice quieted. Mordecai, misty, flat, and imagined, knelt in the gray fog. Coradin appeared behind him and raised his whispering sword. Henry could not look away. He had no eyes to shut. His mind was within the witch's. The sword dropped, and Caleb appeared, kneeling, and then Frank, and then an old man with a crown and baggy skin. Illness crept through Henry's mind as execution followed execution. And then the shape of his own body appeared. The witch watched as Henry's scar grew, as his skin dried and peeled away and his eyes rolled. His mouth hung open, drooling. Gray strands coiled around him like a dozen serpents.

And then something changed. The false Henry raised his hand. A single dandelion bloomed on his palm, and the gray snakes twisted away from it. Dandelions bloomed on his wrist and up his arm, and then in a rush, the fiery weeds exploded down his torso and up around his head, crawling out of his ears and eyes and nostrils and mouth. Only a gray circle remained on his jaw, untouched by the fire. And then, from its center, there rose a tiny green bud, struggling, straining to expand, to root, to grow.

The false Henry disappeared.

Pauper son, the witch said quietly. *How long have you been with me? Have you learned nothing? Are you such a fool as to try and walk my dreams again? Do you seek for death to avoid your madness?*

Henry said nothing. He tried to think nothing. He

pulled away. He tried to retreat, to walk, to redream himself standing in the garden.

You wish escape? It is too late. You have journeyed too deep. You have let too much of yourself go . . . your body dies where it sleeps.

The gray world went black. His mind slowed. It wanted to stop, to let itself fall forever into cold nothing.

Mordecai slumped back into Nimroth's seat, the first throne of Endor.

Caleb sighed beside him. "Will she believe?" he asked.

Mordecai dropped the plain, small stone to the floor and watched it roll away. "Maybe through a fingerling's eyes. Never through her own."

An ashen body lay facedown in front of them. Three men stood behind it, waiting. Caleb nodded at them, and they turned and walked out of the throne room, back toward the street and their horses.

"What now, brother?" Caleb asked.

Mordecai stood slowly. "She is right. It is time. We have no answers, no other moves. I must seek her in Dumarre. I must stand against her storm as our father did."

"You will die," said Caleb simply.

Mordecai nodded. "As our father did."

"And I beside you."

Together, the two brothers walked from the domed room, leaving behind the ash and the throne and the vaulted ceiling, alive with faerie light. Leaving behind the rock that had, for a little while, glimmered like the Blackstar.

"What of Henry?" Caleb asked. "And the others of our bone?"

"May the faeren find them," Mordecai said. "May they keep them."

CHAPTER SEVENTEEN

Henry drifted. Where was his body? He wasn't sure he had one. He didn't need one. Not for anything he would be doing.

How would he play baseball?

He didn't want to play baseball.

Yes, he did. Of course he did. Where was his body?

You need nothing.

I need hands. I need feet. Am I blind?

What is blind?

I . . . I'm not sure. The umpire is blind. I need to see the ball.

Your body is nothing to you now. Stay here. This is peace. Here, you will never need to eat.

I like to eat.

I will feed you.

What?

Souls. Your brothers and sisters. Your mother and your father. You live within me now. You are my strength. You are part of me.

No. I'm not. I have legs and eyes.

No. You do not.

No legs?

No.

No eyes?

No.

I like the sun. Where is the sun? It is warm. I am like it. Where is the dirt? I jump from it. I explode.

You do nothing. Be at peace.

I have a long neck and green fingers. I reach for the sun. He is my cousin. I have a thousand tongues of fire. I shout for him. He warms my leaves. We share our heat. Where is my heat?

I have taken it. It is in me.

It is gone.

Be still. I can hold you. Stay with me.

I am dying.

Yes. You die.

I am a thousand deaths. We are beneath the earth. We are cold.

Rest.

We rest. We will explode.

No.

Henry drifted. He wasn't Henry. He was feathered ash. He was a secret, hidden in the cool darkness. He was a joke. He was pressure building.

He was fire.

Cold ice pressed in around him, and he weakened. He faded. And then something else, something clean and white, silk like his grandmother's hair, hung above him. It pulled at him, and his heat rushed into it. He was rising, bursting from the ground and the cold. He had eyes and hands and legs. The air cracked, and he was out, standing in the witch's garden, glowing with orange light, for a split second blinking at his grandmother's face. Her hands gripped his, pulling him away, pulling him from something stronger than she was.

Gasping, coughing, choking, Henry woke, still sitting up in his little bed. Sweat as cold as ice water beaded on his forehead and dripped off his nose. His body rocked, struggling to fill his lungs with air. Weak light drifted through the window, and Henrietta and Zeke still slept. Beo's black pony head was up, with ears lifted, staring at Henry. The raggant was on Henry's lap, staring at him with one eye wide open and one eye closed.

As Henry's breath leveled, he touched the animal's coarse, doughy skin and leaned his head back against the wall.

What had happened? He had lost all track of himself. He'd been nothing but a cold breath, a breeze inside the witch. He could remember his thoughts, his confusion. In the end, the only thing left of him had been, had been . . . he looked down at his palm and his eyes darkened. Twisting slowly, smaller than he had ever seen it, bent and pale, his dandelion story sat above his skin, rooted in his burn.

He thumped his head against the wall three times. He should be dead. Henrietta and Zeke should have woken up to find him as cold as Nimiane's breath. His grandmother had saved him. He shouldn't have shaken her off. She knew what she was doing. She'd been damaged by dream-walking too far and too dangerously in search of Mordecai. She knew what could happen. He hoped she was all right. He'd apologize the next time he dreamed. But at least he knew his father was no fingerling. He had captured a fingerling and invaded its mind to challenge the witch. Maybe his father had found the Blackstar. Maybe he knew what that meant and what to do with it. Somehow, Henry didn't think so. If his father did have it, he wouldn't have warned the witch. He would have just done something.

Henry reached up and scratched his jaw. Dry powder, as fine as flour, snowed down from his face and coated his fingers gray. His throat tightened in sudden fear. His ears began to ring. Swallowing, breathing slowly, he touched his face again and watched the falling death. He slapped at his jaw, and kept slapping until no more fell. Then he traced the outline of the scar. It wasn't much bigger, but half of his face felt cold. His cheekbone and jaw were both numb. He looked at the little table by the window, where his sword leaned and Nimroth's pages rested beneath a square chestnut and beside a baseball.

He needed to get to the faeren now. Dumarre was in chaos, and his mother and family were on their way. But he didn't want to try for the queene. Una and Frank and Anastasia were with the king. And Richard.

Henry, slipping quietly out of his bed, pulled on Zeke's borrowed jeans and his hoodie and moved over to the table. The raggant snorted. Henry looked at him with raised eyebrows and put a finger to his lips. The raggant snorted again. Louder.

"Okay, Rags," Henry whispered. "You'll come, too. But we won't be gone long."

He started to sling Coradin's sword onto his back, but then he froze, looking at the raggant's tattered wings and weakened legs. He grabbed Henrietta's backpack and emptied it quickly onto his bed. He buckled the sword to the side of it and then opened the main pouch as wide as it would go.

Behind him, Beo whined. "We'll be back," Henry whispered. "You're taking us up to the wood today." Then he stroked the raggant's head and rubbed the knobby joints where his wings attached. The animal went limp on the bed, sputtering deep in his chest. Henry folded his wings tight and picked him up as he had dozens of times, with the creature's hind end dangling loose like a paralyzed basset hound's. Only this time, he set the raggant down in the backpack.

"Good boy," he whispered. "You know you're coming. Nobody's leaving you behind again." Henry zipped the pack up slowly, until only the raggant's head stuck out. Then he stepped back and smiled at the strange picture. The raggant, apparently completely comfortable, shut its eyes.

Henry grabbed the papers and his baseball off the table, but left the chestnut. Looking around, he finally drew Coradin's long sword and stared, almost horrified, at the blade and its edge.

BACK SOON. H

When he was gone, Beo, who knew about early-morning needs, rested his chin on Henrietta's side and watched the door with nostrils flaring. He would not sleep again. Not with Henry gone. But he could track him if he needed to. Even through the smells now rising up from the floor below.

Henry moved quickly down the creaking hall and found the stairs.

Lamps glowed below him. Low voices and groans climbed up the stairwell. At the bottom, he stopped and tried to take in the scene. The innkeeper had his sleeves rolled up and his apron on. He was covered in blood. Seven tables held bodies. Only two were moving. Five more shapes were in a line by the front door, all beneath old sailcloth. Two women helped the innkeeper as he worked on a man's tattooed chest with needle and thread. One of them looked up and into Henry's eyes. Hers were empty, despairing. Henry walked toward them, toward the table and the groaning man. He recognized the gruff sailor from the day before. His eyes were shut, and he was whispering to himself.

Zeb glanced up at Henry, at the raggant on his back, and then back down at his thick fingers. They moved quickly and easily with the heavy needle.

"You sleep hard, lad," he said. "Though you look no more rested."

"What happened?" Henry asked.

"What happened is that one of the galleys was taken, and then burned and rammed and sunk by the other, which now sets to a little beyond the jetty. The wharf and harbor were all swords and flaming arrows for a while." Zebudee looked up and dropped his needle and thread onto a corner of the table. "They're still fighting in the streets."

"How many were killed?" Henry looked around the room. "What can I do?"

"Ten dead within these walls," one of the women said. "Who knows how many in the gutters."

Zeb nodded and wiped his brow with his forearm. "Can't say how many souls were on board that galley, nor how many mothers' sons reached the shore. And I don't need to tell you what to do. You know that already."

"What?" Henry said.

The sailor groaned on the table, and a woman squeezed his hand. Zeb patted the man's cheek, then looked into Henry's eyes. "You said it yourself. The witch-queen dies, the ships and the reds are gone, and that was true enough, though these brave lads couldn't wait on it. But there's two barbs to that hook, Henry Maccabee. She dies, and this storm lifts, but if she lives, tonight's blood will look a picnic next to what comes, in this city and every other within the serpent's strike. Wars, Henry. Wars that can't be won. Wars to plow cities under and peoples into the sea."

"War," the sailor whispered.

"Do you need help?" Henry asked, and he began to shrug off his pack, forgetting what he'd been planning to do.

The innkeeper grunted. "Haven't you been listening?

A rook can't play the pawn. Leave that for us. Go. You have your own game—and a dangerous one. Hurry to it."

Henry backed slowly away, pulling the straps of his pack up. He felt guilty leaving the room, and worse because of the man's words. This fight wasn't just about him. It wasn't just about his own life, or whether or not he would go mad, and it wasn't just about his family. He'd seen the streets of Dumarre.

Turning, he pulled the door open and stepped out into the cold predawn.

Nimiane lay on her couch, angry, breathing slowly, stroking her cat, her eyes, and watching Maleger, the emperor's son, groan and twist between the two trees. She had convinced him to poison his father. She had promised to be his queen. And then, when the emperor had been saved from his son's vile plot, she had asked for him. And she had asked for the ten most dangerous men in the city. The emperor had offered her soldiers, but she had chosen only three. The rest had been prisoners, much harder men. Only five remained to her now. Four strands trailed away from Maleger's right hand, but only one from the left. That was Coradin's thread, the deadliest of all and the hardest to hold, but not so hard as the boy. Coradin resisted too much; he was still too human. And the boy had escaped him three times. But with only five fingerlings to focus on, control would not be so difficult. He would become as deadly as she knew him to be. She needed him to be. She needed Henry dead.

Sitting up lazily, she looked around her couch between the four trees. Dandelions surrounded her in a thick ring, carpeting the ground with gold, running away through the gardens. The closest dandelions were dead, withered up in curls. Farther out, they were tall, gray-headed, and seeding. The rest of the weeds were bright and thriving. He had been here, not merely in her dreams. He had dream-walked so far from his body and then entered her mind, and still he had lived, still he had escaped. And the woman. Nimiane had forgotten that she still lived—old Amram's bride. But she would join him now. The damaged dreamer had reached too far. Nimiane's anger grew, and she filled her nostrils with the foul scent of the blooming weeds. And she drank them in. In one sweeping motion, the fiery blooms withered, curled, and dropped into dust. Nimiane savored the taste. It was the taste of the boy, the slippery, fiery boy.

Shutting her eyes and leaning back onto her couch, she wandered through Maleger and into Coradin. He was standing in the hills, well outside of Hylfing. She whispered into his mind.

The boy dies today. Bring his head and right hand to me.

Henry hurried through Hylfing's streets. Soldiers were moving in tight groups, cold and stiff beneath the gray predawn sky. Their boots were loud, and it wasn't hard for Henry to avoid them. He ducked into alleys or doorways and watched them pass. Some looked confused and freshly woken. Others were already marked with the spattered blood of angry townsfolk. Henry was making his way to the rear gate. He needed to reach the faeren, and the closest place was the outpost mound just beyond the city walls. He had used it before, but not since he had set up his own doorway to Kansas.

Henry stepped into a straight and very empty street. Tucking his thumbs through the pack straps, he began to run. The raggant bounced against his back, grunting.

"Sorry, Rags," Henry said. "You wanted to come, and we've got to hurry."

Six armed soldiers stepped cautiously out of a side street, looking around themselves. All of their eyes fell on Henry where he had stopped, rooted to the cobbles beneath his feet. They moved toward him.

"Hey," Henry said, taking a step backward. "Sorry about the ruckus. Hope you all survive."

One of the men, young and blood-spattered, opened his mouth. "You're the boy. I was at the fire. I saw you. You should have burned."

"Yeah, well," Henry said, still backing up. "I didn't. But my mother's house did. Look on the bright side."

"You killed Croese when he rescued you."

Henry forced a smile. "It wasn't exactly a rescue."

"Lay down your sword."

"My sword?" Henry held out his hands. "I don't have a sword."

"The one on your back."

"Oh," said Henry. "Right." He reached back with two hands and drew the blade out of its sheath. His pulse quickened. He was holding a sword, facing six soldiers. He wiggled the thing in his hand, feeling its weight, testing it like a baseball bat. The blade sucked at the air.

The soldiers stopped. All of them seemed to be measuring him up. Two of them had actually seen Henry at the burning house. They had seen a cobblestone explode into dandelion seeds, and they had seen Henry somehow kill Croese, the old, scar-faced mercenary and assassin. The other four had heard stories of Henry, son to the green devil, and the stories were vastly more frightening than the truth.

In the silent morning air, a young but large trash-eating beetle smelled something on the other side of the street, something damp and heavy. Something he could crawl beneath to find moist happiness. The creature spread its shiny green wing casings and decided to fly. Flying was always faster.

He thrummed between Henry and the soldiers. The sword twitched in Henry's hands, and the beetle parted in two. The beetle halves bounced and rolled on the cobbles and came to a stop. Curious what had gone wrong, the beetle looked around. He twitched his antennae and tried to flap his wings. He felt lighter than he had since he'd been a larva, and suddenly, he wanted to sleep. Sleep would be nice.

Henry looked at the beetle, and he looked at the soldiers, all of them perfectly still, glancing from the halved insect to Henry.

"Okay," Henry said. "I need to go." A bit nervously, he

sheathed the sword over his shoulder, and while the soldiers watched, unmoving, he ducked into a side street and again began to run.

He couldn't afford a fight right now, and he didn't want to draw the sword again. He wasn't sure what exactly had happened. The blade had moved in his hands before he'd even noticed, jumping when life had passed in front of it. Henry heard more boots and then shouting and the sound of fighting. He turned into an alley away from the noise, straightening back toward the gate at the next street. He could see it ahead of him now. It was open, but more than a dozen soldiers stood around it.

Slowing down, evening out his breath, Henry pulled up his hood and ducked his head. He didn't want to be recognized again. The raggant bellowed loudly, and the red-shirted gatekeepers all turned. They were as on edge as Henry was. How could they not be with one of their galleys on the bottom of the harbor?

"Name?" one asked.

Henry glanced up. "Ezekiel Johnson."

"Johnson?" the man asked.

"John's son," Henry said slowly.

The soldiers all studied him—his shoes, his jeans, the hoodie, the sword, and the backpack full of raggant. "Your clothing is strange," the soldier said.

"Yes." Henry nodded. "Yes. My dad's a tailor." He wasn't sure how that would help, but he stopped himself from saying more.

A few of the soldiers whispered to each other. The one

who had been doing the speaking, a thick-chested man with a black mustache, moved forward.

"What is this creature?" he asked.

"A raggant," Henry said. "It's, uh, sorta like a pig. I'm going to look for mushrooms. He's good at it."

The raggant bleated loudly and scuffled around inside the pack. Henry could feel the short legs thumping and pawing at his spine.

"The sword?" the soldier asked.

"For wolves," Henry said quickly. "They like raggant."

"Wolves," the man said. It wasn't a question. He stuck his thumbs in his belt and looked Henry up and down. Then, reaching out, he pulled back Henry's hood.

Wheezing through its nostrils, the raggant lunged up and snapped at the soldier's fingers. The soldier jumped back, yelping and shaking his hand.

Henry ducked his head and hurried forward, trying to ignore the eyes that were on him, trying to pretend like there was no reason in the world that the soldiers would want to stop him. He was in the gate. He was through, trying not to break into a run, straining his ears for any footsteps, but all he could hear was the raggant's irritated breathing.

As soon as he could justify it, Henry slipped off the road and into the brush and trees that would grow quickly into the wood that climbed into the hills and mountains behind the city of Hylfing. He wasn't far from the little faerie hall, he knew that, but spotting it was never easy. It wasn't supposed to be, not even for a green man.

After one hundred yards or so of brush and pocket groves, Henry stopped and looked around himself. He thought he recognized some of the trees. After his first trip, he had carved a big *H* into a trunk to mark the spot, but the next time back, the faeren had healed the bark.

Henry whistled and then stood quietly, waiting. The raggant sneezed on the back of his neck.

Henry grimaced, wiping the moisture off. "Rags, c'mon now, be a help. Let me know if you see something." He turned in place and whistled a tune his mother sang in her garden. Then he walked slowly forward and whistled again.

The raggant sputtered its lips, and Henry turned just in time to see a bush shift at the root. Henry hurried to it, grabbed the branches, and pulled it out of the hands of a round-faced faerie squatting in a low, arched door set in a mound of brush-covered earth.

The faerie's cheeks were puffed out, and his face and neck were purple. The air shimmered around him and around the doorway.

"What's your name?" Henry asked.

The faerie blinked, but was otherwise motionless.

"I can see you," Henry said. "What's your name?"

The faerie didn't move. Henry leaned over and pinched his nostrils closed. "What's your name?"

The little man slapped at Henry's wrist and jumped back through the doorway. Henry shoved his leg through the shimmering, supposedly invisible opening before something physical, wooden or earthen, could be used to close it. When nothing slammed on his shinbone, Henry sat on the ground and slid down inside.

The room had changed little. It was long, with its peaked earthen roof and walls covered with muddy sculpture. Committee proclamations and guidelines were pinned to the dirt wall on one side. A table—dotted with cards and dirty mugs—and barrel chairs were positioned in the center. It could hold a number of faeries, but right now, there was only one. He was on the far end of the room, rubbing a mixture of mud on the wall between some sticks that had been pressed into it in the shape of a door. One bucket of charmed water and one of charmed earth sat by his feet.

"Little faerie," Henry said. "Do you know who I am?"

The faerie glanced back and then continued trying to make himself a doorway back to the Central Mound. Henry squeezed past the table and barrels, grabbed the faerie's shoulders, and pulled him back to the table. Pushing the small, terrified faerie onto a barrel seat, Henry wedged himself down across from him.

"One more time," Henry said. "What's your name?"

"Thorn," the faerie said. His fat face was smooth and hairless. The hair on his scalp was brown and fine, static clinging to his forehead in places.

"I'm Henry York Maccabee," Henry said. The faeries always liked the full name. "I'm a green. My father is Mordecai."

Thorn nodded.

"You knew that?" Henry asked.

Again, the faerie nodded.

Henry felt anger climb up inside him, but he pushed it down. "Well, then, Thorn," he said. "Next time you hear me whistling and peek through your bushes, you holler and let me in."

The faerie didn't move.

"Okay," Henry said. "How old are you? You look pretty young."

"Thirty-two," the faerie said. "Last moon."

Henry scrunched his lips. "Right. So why don't you tell me what's happening? Why are you here alone? Why did you try to hide? Also, I'm going to need a pen. I have to write a message."

"A pen?"

"Yes," said Henry. "With ink. For writing on paper."

The faerie's eyes lit up. "Is the message official?"

"What? What do you mean?"

"Is it for official businessings?"

Henry thought about this. If any message of his was ever going to be official, this was it. He nodded. "It's for your queen."

Thorn's mouth fell open. He seemed unable to catch his breath, inhaling in useless spurts like he'd been kicked in the stomach. He jumped off his barrel and rushed to a stack of shelves in the corner. He returned to the table, glowing, carrying what looked to be a box wrapped in a potato sack. He set it in front of Henry, pushed his plump cheeks up with a wide smile, raised his eyebrows, and whisked away the sack like an amateur magician.

Henry blinked and cocked his head. He was looking at a typewriter—a wooden typewriter.

"The design is my own," Thorn said. "I started on smelting kits and repairings when I was young, but those horrible contraptions the district uses have no life, no flavoring. They are all hard grindings and clumsy hammers."

Henry leaned to one side and then the other. The thing was truly amazing. Perfectly smooth, nearly black wood with a solid band of pale inlay, nearly white. And inside that, a band of glistening silver. The word *Thorningtons* had been engraved in the side. Polished black keys with sparkling white letters lay below an army of silver hammers and a wooden roller. He ran his hands gently over the keys.

"Are they stones?" he asked.

Thorn sighed happily. "Yes. Shaped by a mountain stream—I will not tell you which one under any torturings. It took me a heavy week to find enough of the proper body and heft. The letterings are needled pearl mother." Thorn straightened, suddenly serious. "I must ask, beseech, and demand that you use this inscriptor for your message."

"Um . . . ," Henry said.

Thorn raised a plump hand and nodded. "Inscriptage is hard learned, true, but I can assist in difficulties."

"Thanks," Henry said. "Really. You can watch, but I should be fine." Thorn was now breathing in his ear. Henry leaned away and pointed back at the barrel seat. "You sit and tell me what's going on. I'll type."

Thorn narrowed his eyes and slipped onto his seat. "Type?" he asked.

Henry fished one of Nimroth's pages out from his pouch and shifted the raggant's weight on his shoulders. "Type," he said again. "In the world where these were invented, they're called typewriters."

"You have been? You have seen them?"

Henry nodded, smoothing the paper flat on the table, and then studied the wooden machine for a place to insert it.

"Are they . . . ," Thorn began. He cleared his throat nervously. "Are they more beautiful than this?"

Henry laughed. "Not that I've ever seen. Not even close. This is unbelievable." He held up the paper. "Could you put this in?"

Thorn, glowing bright red with elation, carefully wound the page around the roller for Henry. The side he had to use was only partially blank. The other was covered with scrawl. When the faerie was content with the page's positioning, he sat back down, put his elbows on the table, and propped up his chin.

"Go ahead," Henry said, trying to think of how to start his letter. "Tell me why you're the only one here and why you didn't want me in."

Thorn's joy clattered to the floor around him. His skin reverted to pale, and even though he couldn't take his eyes off his typewriter, the extreme sparkle of love was gone.

"It was all Franklin Fat's fault," he said. "Not that I was there to see, but I heard enough. As did we all."

"What?" Henry asked, staring at the yellowed page in front of him. Smiling, he pressed down a key, and a silver hammer swung forward—an actual hammer-shaped hammer. An *a* appeared in purple ink on the page. Henry spaced and punched on.

"The hearing," Thorn said, watching Henry's slow hammering with glazed eyes. "Fat Frank was unfaeried. No one wanted it, but if the rules don't hold, then you may as well be human. No offense."

"And?" Henry asked, more than a little distracted.

"And Mordecai Westmore, your father that is, bonded as he is to this district and others, stood against the rules. He made slighting remarks about the committee's enforcement, and, well, rules is rules as the rules say someplace, or at least as all the oldies say they say. And even when the committee had banged the hammer, he still kept on calling Fat Franklin a faerie." Thorn slipped off his seat and moved to Henry's shoulder, examining his work. "*Queen* takes a third *e* at the tail." He pointed at the page.

Henry looked up and pointed back at Thorn's seat. "Well, why can't he be? Frank, I mean. Why does his magic have to yellow?"

Thorn sat back down. "Is it yellowing already? Some faeren thought he'd be chalk by morning. Others said it'd be a moon."

"Chalk?"

"The words were spoken," Thorn said seriously. "I heard them. He is no longer of the mound, and its magic will run out of his blood, out of his body, until he has no spark and no color and no . . . life. His breath will leave, and he will harden."

Henry paused and stared at the little faerie. "Really? You're serious? Frank will turn into chalk? They're killing him?"

"Oh, the oldies said there were charms. He could live a while bonded to a tree, so long as he stayed close to its roots. With the right wizarding, he could even live a year or two as a common dwarf." Thorn shrugged. "Not Fat Franklin. He hubbubbed and name-called and swore he'd stay in Hylfing when the committee had district-banned him, and Mordecai, your father, called him a friend and invited him to stay as long as his pleasure kept him."

"So?" Henry asked.

"Rules is rules," Thorn said. "The committee reduced the Hylfing hall to token."

Henry looked into the faerie's eyes. "But they didn't close it?"

"They call it closed and collapsed," Thorn said. "But I'm here to keep an eye, sent on account of failure in other duties."

Henry couldn't hide his surprise. After everything the last committee had done, they wouldn't give even a little on Frank?

"I can't believe that," Henry said.

"Well, it's only for half a moon," Thorn said. "Out of respect for rules and no slight to your father."

The raggant snored on Henry's shoulder. Henry shook his head. "I wasn't talking about closing the hall. Faeren are ridiculous."

Thorn sagged on his barrel.

"No offense," Henry added. He looked down at his page. "And I have a job for you."

"Can't," Thorn said. "Hall's closed."

"Can," Henry said. "And it's not really for me. It's for the queene. I'm almost done."

A few minutes later, Henry sat back. His purple message seemed passable.

"What kind of ink is this?" he asked.

"Ink?" Thorn asked. "The silk ribbon soaks in blackberry juice. I would like something darker but have found nothing."

"Catch an octopus," Henry said, pulling his page off the roller. "They'll squirt ink at you when they're mad."

The little round faerie cocked his head. "Is this what the other world uses?"

"Honestly, no. I doubt it," Henry said. "But their inscriptors aren't so lovely as this."

Thorn crossed his arms and grinned. "I shall gather octopi. I shall milk them for my ink."

Henry smiled and read through his letter one final time. Unfortunately, all of it was lowercase, and he'd slipped up on a word or two, but the queene could overlook that. After all, it was in purple ink, and he'd managed to make it sound especially faerie-pompous.

a lert
to the queene of all faeren, with deep respect,
admiration, and hopefulness from henry york
maccabee, dandelion green man, seventh son to

mordecai westmore, sevnth son to amram.
nimiane, one-time witch-queen of endor, maddens
dumarre with her evil, and her witch-dogs and
fingerlings walk the streets. mordecai humbly,
politely, and urgently asks the queene of all
faeren to dispatch her strongest and most
cunning soldiers to resist, stifle, an thwart her
witchery. also, a galley carries some family of
mordecai to the witch in chains. he asks the
great queene to prevent galleys from entering the
harbor. he will come as soon as he can free
himself from struggles in endor. gratitude, love,
and fondness to the queene, our friend and ally.

henry york maccabee for
  his father mordecai westmore

p.s. i inscript this lert on a page stolen from
nimroth's own library.

Henry handed the letter to the faerie. "Take it to the
queene. I don't know where she is, but you have to find her
and give her this. Only her. No one else. From your hands
to hers, nobody in between. Okay?"

"I, uh . . . the committee. . ." The poor faerie's eyes were
crowded with worry and confusion.

"Put your typewriter back in its sack and go right away,
as fast as you can. Get it to her. If you don't, the rules might
just go away. All of them."

Thorn clenched his jaw, but his face was still pale, his eyes terrified. "Right, then," he said. "To the queene."

Henry slapped the faerie on a soft arm and smiled, standing up carefully. He moved to the door. He had his own trek ahead.

"Thank you," he said over his shoulder and the raggant's nose. Then he climbed up into the morning air and the brush.

After a moment, he shoved his head back down through the doorway. The little faerie was still standing where he'd left him with the letter in his hands.

"Thorn," he said. "You get this done, and my father will always stand beside you. Always, no matter what a committee or a king or an emperor or a rule might say. Just like he did for Frank Fat-Faerie. And so will I."

Thorn nodded and tried to smile. He couldn't quite get his face to work.

Henry pointed at him. "Octopi," he said, and the faerie grinned.

"Octopi."

CHAPTER EIGHTEEN

The ship rocked slowly, climbing the swelling waves, driven by a steady wind. Frank filled his lungs with the sea's breath and leaned on the rail in front of him, over-looking the lower deck.

Monmouth stood beside him. Behind them both, James discussed charts with Meroe. The view in front of Frank Willis was as unlikely as any he could have imagined.

The deck was covered with sleeping bodies. Despite the chill, despite the lack of clothing, not one slave had set foot belowdecks in the night. Between the bodies and around the big, serpentine guns, slender aspen saplings had shot up, and the planks, where visible, had barked over with silver and seamed their grooves together. It was from the grooves, and any knots in the planks, that the saplings now grew. Every spindle in the galley's rails sported the heart-shaped, silver-bellied leaves of the aspen tree, and the masts were barked and boughed with slender limbs. The ship creaked as it rose and fell in the water. The sails ruffled and cracked in the wind. These things were normal. But now the ship's deck rustled in the wind like a forest grove, and the living leaves danced in the light of the early-morning sun as it rose over a jagged coastline. Meroe's course had taken them closer to land in the night, but that wasn't likely to last long, not with their new captain's plans.

Frank rubbed the thick bandages on his wrists and lifted his eyes from the aspen grove sprouting up between the bodies of freshly freed slaves, to the bow, where his wife and daughter leaned together, watching the ship plow through the sea. Hyacinth stood tall beside them, the wind pushing her dark hair forward over her shoulders, with one arm around Isa, a younger picture of herself.

He sighed. Where were his other daughters? His brothers? Where was his nephew? What, exactly, could he and the others hope to do now?

"I didn't expect this," Monmouth said quietly, with his eyes on the flickering leaves. "I wasn't trying to turn the ship into a grove."

"Can't imagine that you were," Frank said. "Can't imagine anyone would."

"Aspen send up saplings from a common root. I only livened a few timbers to push out the chains. The rest just happened."

Frank smiled. "Don't go sounding like an apology. By the time we put in someplace, we'll be a floating forest, not a slave galley. And that's an improvement to my mind."

"I will not sail north," Meroe said behind them. His voice was raised, drumming in his broad chest. Frank and Monmouth turned. James was holding his hands up defensively. The huge, bearded captain leaned toward him, resting his fists on a chart and table. "I will not send men below to pull oars into the wind. And I could not if I willed. They would have my flesh in stew first, for all of your knife tricks."

James smiled. He was wearing clothes stripped off a dead soldier, minus the red overshirt. Meroe wore the same, though the sleeves of the dirty white shirt were snug on his forearms and fell several inches short of either wrist. His broad shoulders kept the shirt neck spread wide. Blood from the wound in his side was seeping through its bandage.

"What, then?" James asked. "South to Dumarre and fresh berths on the emperor's galleys?"

Meroe tugged fingers through his thick beard. "Open sea, out of the eyes of Dumarre, and south beyond."

James clicked his tongue and then whistled a few bars, staring at the chart between them. He looked up into the big man's dark eyes. "A foodless voyage. How much stock remains to you?" He pointed at the men sleeping in the young deck-forest. "Every cask tapped, every sack torn. At the least, put in and provision."

"Even if I had gold for provender," Meroe said, "I would watch my crew disappear into the hills. We sail south, and we pirate."

"Your crew," James said. He raised his eyebrows. "Your crew? Look at them. They are not sailors; they are slaves. The sun rises, and they still sleep with bulging bellies and heads swimming with liquor dreams. Will they obey if it comes to rowing or any other labor? You cannot keep them on if they want only to be put ashore. Not unless you use the shackles and carry a whip."

"South," Meroe said slowly. "South and only south. We will pirate supplies or gold for supplies and put in when Dumarre is no more than a filthy dream over my shoulder and in the past. Any and all will be free to seek their own course then."

James stood quietly, his jaw clenching.

"Am I captain or no?" Meroe asked. "What says Mordecai's son?"

James nodded and looked to the sea.

"Not sure it much matters," Frank said. He picked a handful of leaves off the rail and let the breeze carry them down to the deck. "Monmouth here freed you a crew but gave the ship back to the forest."

Meroe grunted and looked at Monmouth. "We are free, and it floats. I am grateful."

"It floats," Frank said. "But not fast enough for your pirate dreaming."

Meroe rose to his full height and stretched his back. Frank watched his shirt seams stretch.

"We shall see," the big man said. "Let us wake the crew. More sail could be spread, and this forest must be cut back."

Frank and Monmouth watched James and his new captain wade through the bodies and saplings, kicking and shouting and thumping as they went. A few men sat up, and two rose to their feet, staring at the green leaves around them in groggy confusion. The rest groaned and complained and rolled to their backs and bellies, covering their heads with their arms to protect their dreams.

After a moment, Monmouth spoke.

"I made it all leafy and green." He looked at Frank. "But I didn't make the ship slower."

Frank laughed and slapped Monmouth on the back. "No more of this tone. You embarrassed that you can turn dead oak trees into the strangest aspen grove that's ever been seen? Don't be."

Monmouth laughed. "I'm not embarrassed. It's just a little strange and unexpected."

"And slower," Frank said, grinning. "If I could dive under and check the keel, how many roots you think I would find draggin' behind us in the sea? You did do the first livening business in the lowest hold."

Monmouth shut his eyes and grimaced.

"When we're done with this galley," Frank said, "I think we should find some elephants, haul it up out of the Hylfing harbor, and plant it between the river and the baseball diamond."

Two-thirds of the men were now awake and up. All of them were either complaining loudly or examining the growing ship with worried looks.

Three men, led by James, were clambering up rigging onto the central mast. A dozen more stood watching with open mouths until Meroe drove them to the other masts. Someone else was shouting about breakfast.

Under James's direction, a topsail unfurled and snapped to.

"Monmouth!" James shouted. "Even up here?" He plucked the few leaves that had sprouted that high and dropped them. The wind carried them forward as they fell, all the way to Dotty and Hyacinth and the girls, where they stood watching the bustle.

James hooked his legs on a crossbeam and dangled upside down, smiling at his mother. She smiled but shook her head. Isa covered her mouth. And then the expression on her brother's face changed.

Frank watched James swing upright, hop onto the crossbeam, and shinny up to the very top of the mast. There was no barrel crow's nest. He hung with one leg and one arm hooked around the pole and held his free hand out from his temple to block the sun.

The mob below, for the most part, didn't notice. A few had begun to climb rigging to the other masts. Others were ripping at the deck saplings and throwing them overboard. Meroe was still shouting and bullying men into wakefulness.

A long, sharp whistle from James drew Meroe's eyes up.

"Sails!" James shouted. "A pair!"

For a moment, the deck calmed, and then a mob of shouting men rushed to the rail to strain their eyes at two shapes on the horizon.

"Empire red!" James's words carved a silent moment into the crowd below him.

Meroe's voice ripped through it. "All backs, belowdecks!" He moved through the crowd like a giant, slapping heads as he went. "Pull oars for open sea!"

Men ducked away from him, but no one moved toward the ladders.

"Below!" he roared again.

A tall, slender man jumped onto the leaf-covered rail. He scowled at Meroe and then looked back to the coastline.

"Enough of oars!" he shouted, and dove into the sea. More men followed quickly after, and more after them. The press at the rail grew, and bodies tumbled, dove, and somersaulted off the ship in dozens. All the while, Meroe raged, and as those who had at first held back saw how few their numbers were, they, too, ducked beneath and around the anger of their bearded captain and lunged out into air and then the sea.

It was the closest thing to a stampede that Frank had ever seen, and all of it took no more than a minute. James and Meroe stood together in the center deck, and only slender aspens stood with them. The rail had given way under the rush, and now it leaned, split in places, off the side of the ship. Hundreds of bodies flailed and splashed in the water, struggling toward land that was farther away than it had looked from the deck.

"No more than half will reach it," Meroe said. "Less."

"How many would have lived free if they'd stayed?" James asked.

Meroe said nothing. His hope was splashing away.

Frank turned to Monmouth and nodded toward the stairs. Dotty and Hyacinth and the girls were already descending from the bow.

Standing at the rail, with the rustling of leaves and the snapping of sails to fill the silence, the small group looked at each other. Meroe stared at the sea and the distant cliffs.

"This is trouble," Frank said. He reached out and took Dotty's hand. "Hot and fresh and that's for sure." Meroe looked back at him, and his eyes were empty. He lifted one leg to the rail.

"Hold now," Frank said, grabbing his arm. "Jump if you like, but you have a head as well as your bulk, and you're not built for swimming. Where will our wits get us?"

"Chained, like as not," Meroe said. He flared his nostrils and looked from the water beneath him to the sails on the horizon. He lowered his foot from the leafy rail. "My first craft, and captained for a single night." He turned to James. "Spread every thread of sail. We run straight at them."

Henrietta sat up suddenly in her blankets, unsure of where she was. Beo was whining, scratching at the door. The inn. The little room was even dingier in the daylight than it had been the night before. Zeke was already gone. So was Henry. And her backpack. **BACK SOON, H** was carved into the door.

"No, they didn't," she said, and jumped to her feet.

She pulled the door open, and Beo tumbled into the hall, sniffing.

Zeke was walking up the stairs, wiping his hands on a rag.

"Where's Henry?" Henrietta asked. "What's going on?"

"Not much now," Zeke said. "But a lot last night. A galley got burned and sunk, and there was fighting in the streets. Zeb says the townspeople will lay low until tonight and then go for the other galley. Everyone's hoping Caleb will show up and get the city guard organized. I don't know where Henry is."

"You don't know?"

"I don't know." Zeke reached the hall and stood beside her, scratching Beo's ears. "I saw the note, the same as you."

"Back soon?" Henrietta sneered. "What kind of note is that? He could be doing anything."

"Could be," Zeke said. "Are you going to take the dog out, or should I?"

Henrietta looked down at Beo, her pillow through the night. He seemed frantic. Clearly in need.

"I'll do it," she said, and she walked down the stairs, whistling for the dog. Whining, with his nose in the air, Beo thumped down behind her. At the bottom, she stopped. The front door was open, and two men cautiously slipped out, carrying a long shape wrapped in cloth—man-size and bending in the middle. Outside, the men trundled it quickly into the bed of a wagon and tucked it beneath a canvas tarp. More shapes waited in a row beside the door.

Blinking, she hardly noticed that Beo had slipped past her until the black pony-dog shot out the front door and was gone.

"Beo!" Henrietta yelled. "Sorry," she said to the men loading the wagon, and she ran out of the inn just in time to see Beo galloping across the square.

Slapping bare feet on cold cobbles, Henrietta began to run after him. Henry had said that Beo knew the way. They were supposed to follow him into the hills to the Chestnut King. He couldn't just run off.

"Beo!" she yelled again, and then slowed, panting. The dog disappeared into an alley mouth. This was her fault. Henry probably wouldn't say it, but he would think it. Why hadn't she paid attention? Not that she could have stopped a dog that size anyway, if he really wanted to be somewhere else. But he'd always obeyed her, ever since her long trek with Caleb and his men.

Maybe he would come back. Henrietta raised her hands to her face and pushed back her hair. It fell forward again, too short to stay tucked behind her ears. She had the horrible feeling of having slept in her clothes, along with the stiffness of having slept on the floor, combined with the loud smell of dog. And now she was sweating, and her hair was awful, and Beo was gone.

She shaded her eyes against the low sun and stared at the other side of the square, hoping to see a big, galloping Beo erupt from some street or other. Hoping that he'd just needed to stretch his enormous legs.

The sun glinted on a tall man's silver helmet. She

turned. It glinted on three silver helmets. The men in black entered the square, and each turned in place, looking for something, sensing. Smelling. One held an ax, another carried a long sword on his back. After a moment, the three walked quickly across the square, toward the street where Beo had gone.

Henrietta's feet staggered backward. "Oh no," she said quietly. "No." Biting her lip, she turned and ran to the battered inn.

Henry tromped slowly around the outside of the city wall. He didn't want to try to get back in through the same gate, past the same soldiers. Most of the day, this side of the city would be cool and damp, a place for moss to grow in shadow. But now the morning sun pounded against the smooth stone face of the wall, and Henry walked beside it.

He hadn't eaten anything. He hadn't had anything to drink, and his back was soaking with sweat where the pack, bulging with a warm breathing body, pressed against it. And the tip of the black scabbard banged into his thigh with every step. He stuck out his tongue and caught a drip of sweat off the tip of his nose. His father had said to wait no more than a day. But Henry wanted to eat breakfast and leave. It was taking every inch of his willpower to keep from clawing at his jaw, the only cold—painfully cold— spot on his body. He hoped Zeke and Henrietta were up and ready. He could leave a note for his father with Zeb.

The raggant bellowed in his ear.

Henry stopped and looked around. Crickets were

buzzing in the tall grass, but he could hear nothing else. And then Beo appeared from around a bend in the wall, running like a giant greyhound. The animal overshot Henry, turned, and looped around, rolled onto his back, writhed for a second, and jumped to his feet. Henry waited. Henrietta and Zeke had to be behind him. Where were they?

Beo nosed Henry in the belly, forcing him to stagger backward. Then the dog turned and began to trot away from the city toward the hills. He stopped and looked over his shoulder at Henry. His tree-branch tail wasn't wagging. He wasn't playing. After a moment, he trotted back, sealed his lolling tongue in his mouth, and stared up into Henry's eyes with his ears forward.

"Where's Henrietta?" Henry asked. "What's going on?"

Beo walked behind Henry and butted into the back of his legs. Then he bit Henry on the ankle.

Henry jumped forward and spun around. "Ow! Beo! We can't start now. I have to eat something. We need Zeke and Henrietta. I want to bring the cupboard."

Beo crouched and curled back his lips, ready to bite again. But he didn't need to. The raggant bit Henry on the ear and didn't let go. Yelling, Henry twisted and slapped at the animal. He tripped and fell to his knees. With his mouth open in pain, he managed to get his hands back around the raggant's head. Gripping its blunt horn and lower jaw, he pried the creature off. Furious, he began to shrug off the pack, but Beo filled his mouth with the hood of Henry's sweatshirt and tugged him onto his side. Knocking the dog away, Henry stood up.

"Fine," he said, keeping his head away from the squirming raggant on his back. "Fine. I'll come. And let's hope you know what you're doing."

Beo bounded away through the tall grass, toward the hills. Henry stuck his thumbs in his pack straps to keep the raggant from thumping against him and began to jog after the dog, watching his feet, picking his way around stones and boulders and the occasional scrub tree as he went. Beo never let him get within fifty yards. He would perch on a bank or a log, sniffing at the air while Henry struggled to catch up. And then he would jump down and tear away.

By the time the pitch of the ground had finally steepened into a true slope, Henry's legs were burning, and twin knives were digging into his sides. The pack straps were digging into his shoulders, and his thigh was tender where the sword tip had been counting his steps. Henry staggered to a stop beneath a tree and whistled at the dog. Above him, the trees thickened, and a track of rubble like a creek bed lined the fold between the two halves of the hill.

The raggant was wheezing in his pack. Henry unslung him and set the thing in the shade.

"What's your problem?" Henry asked, rubbing his legs. "You're not doing anything."

Beo appeared well above Henry on the hill. He barked.

"Hold on!" Henry yelled. He pulled his sweatshirt over his head and double-tied the arms around his waist. Then he turned and looked back down the hill at the city of Hylfing, sitting on its small plain between the mountains and the sea. Were Zeke and Henrietta down there? What were they doing? Probably eating breakfast. They had their own plan. He remembered the first time he had ever seen the city—in a blustering storm, pounded by lightning, unbreaking. Parts of it were still blackened from that struggle, and one spot, on one of the city's hills, was blackened from a newer fight. But this time, Caleb and Mordecai were not within the walls, and red-shirts ruled. Hylfing had fallen.

Again, Beo barked. He kept barking. He was coming back down the slope. Henry picked up his pack, and the raggant grunted. He eased his arms into the straps, raised the weight slowly to his sweaty back, and turned away from the city, his city.

"I'm coming, Beo." His legs weren't easy to start, but he did it. "No biting. You, too, Rags." He glanced over his shoulder. Something moved on the slope below him. The sun had glinted against something bright. While Henry watched, a man rose from behind a large stone. He stood, realizing that he'd been seen, and the sun shone on his helmet. A sword handle like Henry's sprouted above his shoulder. Two other men rose beside him. They couldn't have been more than three hundred yards away.

Henry's blood ran cold. They'd been stalking him. What had happened to Zeke and Henrietta? Anger and frustration and fear and humiliation all throbbed inside him. He was sick of making mistakes, sick of being surprised and hunted and beaten. He was sick of surviving. He could draw his sword and run back down the hill. Beo would fight with him. He could die right now. No more dreams, no more fear of death. Death itself might be better. His father would find some way to beat the witch. Henry reached up and gripped the sword strapped to his backpack. The fingerlings watched him do it.

Beo thumped to a stop beside him, and a growl rolled out of his chest. Henry couldn't do it. Not yet. Not unless he had to, and he still might have to. He had no idea how far away the chestnut tree was, only that it was probably much farther than he would like. His father had given him a job. His mother and family were on their way to the witch. He couldn't just die to get it over with. He wanted his death to hurt the witch; he wanted it to push her that much closer to the brink of her own nothingness.

Turning, Henry dropped his hand from the sword and began to run. His legs, which had felt like mud, fired with adrenaline. The knives disappeared from his sides, and hunger was forgotten. Beo loped in front of him, slashing back and forth across the hillside to cut the angle. But Henry, chin down and lungs pumping, gutted his way straight up the hillside, over rocks and logs. He could never keep up the pace, not for more than a few minutes, if that. Even adrenaline runs out. But now, with fury and fear fanning the flames, the only race he could run was a sprint. They wouldn't catch him. Not now. Not ever.

The trees were growing closer together, the spotted

hillside was becoming a ridge, and the ridge was becoming a wood. Henry threw up his arms and plunged into brush, behind the black shape of his uncle's dog.

Antilly Johnson hurried through the streets of Henry, Kansas. She didn't know what else to do or where to go. When she turned toward the old Willis barn, she stopped. Patrol cars surrounded the property with their lights flashing. Beyond them, enormous news vans blocked the street, and a burned-out wheat field had been turned into a parking lot. A crowd hundreds strong blocked her view of anything more than the swirling lights, but there was water running in the street.

Tilly would have normally ducked away. She hated crowds. But she couldn't. Not now. She moved around a line of cars parked against the curb—a few of them with out-of-state plates—and shouldered her way into the back of the crowd.

She tried saying "excuse me," but no one noticed; no one moved out of her way. So she dug her arms in between laughing, shouting, or tiptoeing people and forced herself through the seams.

The ground became softer as she went, and soon mud was slopping over the tops of her shoes and sucking at her feet when she lifted them. The front of the crowd was being held back by a blend of cop cars and cops, yellow tape, and camera crews. Some fat kid with freckles was standing in front of a very proud-looking father, staring into a camera lens and mumbling into a microphone.

The Willis property was a swamp. From the road to the irrigation ditch was sloppy with water. The hole where the house had been was invisible. A short waterfall splashed inches above the swamp's surface, spreading ripples in every direction. The old barn looked like it was floating.

Behind the barn, a mob of farmers was arguing with state troopers while two backhoes worked to keep the water out of the irrigation ditch.

"Salt water!" an old farmer screamed, and he threw his cap into the flood. The crowd laughed.

Tilly pushed her way toward the closest state trooper. "Sir," she yelled. "I'm sorry. I tried to call."

He put his hand to his ear and moved closer to her. "What's that?"

"I tried to call—"

The trooper dropped his hand and nodded, smiling and pointing at the news vans. "Channel Four took out a pole."

"I tried to call the hospital!" Tilly yelled. "My mother won't wake up, and she's having trouble breathing. I need an ambulance!"

CHAPTER NINETEEN

The captain stood on deck, watching the green and leafy galley chop methodically through the waves toward his own pair of ships. The galley was moving slower than he would have expected with so much cloth spread to the wind, but then he didn't know what to expect from a five-tiered craft sprouting with branches and flickering leaves. He was an old man, a sailor almost from his birth. His beard was whitened with sun and salt, his eyes had bleached to a pale blue, and his bones were as toughened as the ship's beams beneath him. He had been a ship's boy, a hand, a gunner, a mutineer, a merchant, a galley slave, a commander of fleets, all before he had become the pirate that he now was. He had gone down into the sea with a ship's wreckage more times than he could count, and had seen more of the sea's secrets than he cared to tell about. But he had never seen anything like this.

His ship was a three-tiered galley, pirated in one of the southern seas. Two black guns, roughly forged, burdened its upper deck, and a crew of thieves and murderers and men conscripted from the harbor inns of three continents pulled oars for him.

His other ship was a little merchant vessel taken only the day before, sailing with a sparse crew until a new crop of men could be gathered in the harbors. Both of his ships flew the imperial flag. He could think of no reason why they shouldn't. It was his business to do to ships what the emperor did to countries. And he did not think of himself as a pirate. He was simply a servant of the sea, and he took whatever it gave him.

He nodded slightly, and a young sailor beside him began to twitch and swing the signal flags at the little merchant ship. It was the faster vessel and nearer to the strange galley. After a moment, bright flags waved on the merchant's stern.

"Deck clear," the sailor said. "They think we should do the boarding, sir."

"I can see their flagging," the old captain said. "No one wants first foot on a demon ship?"

"Must we board, sir?" the sailor asked. "A five-tier galley shaped of living trees? It's bewitched."

"Aye," the captain said. "And empty of souls and under full cloth to a gusting wind."

"Let it sail on, sir, please. Or gun its hull and send it to the bottom."

The captain inhaled slowly and then looked at the sailor. The young man's face was white with genuine fear.

"The sea has brought her to me," the captain said. "And she comes with brass guns worth more to me than a dozen petty merchants. Put alongside. Prepare hooks and boarding crew. Alert the oar masters."

Orders were shouted above and belowdecks, and the small galley began to turn—backing water with one side of oars while the other stroked on—preparing to come alongside the forest ship that sailed toward them. Sailors scrambled through the rigging, unfurling more sailcloth. Arms clattered beneath them as a boarding party assembled.

When the two galleys finally moved side by side through the growing waves, another order was given. Oars were drawn, and three-pronged hooks on chains were thrown across the gap, catching in the rail or the rigging. And then the chains were pulled tight, drawing the hulls together, heavy timbers groaning with the friction.

"Boarders weg!" the captain shouted. A team of armed sailors moved tentatively toward the rail, staring at the leaves and limbs that lined every joint between the bigger galley's planks. Not one man touched the ship.

"Boarders weg!" the captain shouted again, but he knew already what must be done. His boarding party did not budge, paralyzed by the flickering aspen leaves.

Before simple fear could become rebellion and rebellion could become mutiny, the old captain stepped forward. He grabbed ahold of a boarding chain, and as his silent crew watched, he scrambled up the face of the bigger ship, pushed through the quivering branches, and disappeared over the rail.

Alone on the big galley, the captain tried to take it in. A young forest, nearly up to his waist, covered the decks. The masts had grown silver bark and slender branches up almost to their tips. With gaping reptile mouths, the four scaled brass guns looked like beasts wallowing in a bed of reeds.

The captain drew a short sword and turned slowly in place, looking for the hatch belowdecks.

"One man," Monmouth whispered. "An old man." He dropped off the ladder and landed softly next to the others. Meroe and James and Frank were all armed with sea-swords, short-bladed and curved. Hyacinth held a slender knife, but Dotty and Isa and Penelope hadn't wanted anything.

"Only one?" James asked.

"One can become many," Meroe said. "We should have used the guns."

"That we shouldn't have," said Frank. "Can't be handing out death with no cause."

"They fly the serpent red," Meroe muttered. "That is cause enough."

Above them, footsteps echoed across the deck, and the group pushed back into the leafy shadows.

The hatch banged open, and for a long moment, no one breathed. Then a pair of boots found the rungs of the ladder, and a man began to descend.

Halfway down, he paused, ducked his head beneath the deck, and peered around the space. The ship's timbers creaked. The young forest rustled, and then his eyes caught the glint of steel.

Meroe leapt forward and gripped the old man's ankle,

pulling his leg free of the ladder. As a blade slashed down, James jerked the man's other leg loose, and the wiry body crashed to the planks below. Twisting quickly, he somersaulted away, leapt to his feet, and faced the group with blade raised and chest heaving.

Frank stepped forward and cleared his throat. "Welcome aboard, sir. Wish we could offer you some refreshment, but we're in a bit of an odd circumstance."

The captain's narrow eyes took them all in—the girls, the women, the men with swords, Meroe with his blood-seeped side.

"Who bewitched the galley?" he asked suddenly.

No one moved.

"Is one of you a witch? A wizard? What curse is on this place?"

"No curse," Monmouth said. "Only life. Dead things have begun to live."

"I can think of no greater curse." The man's voice was flat, revealing nothing. "Who captained the vessel?"

Meroe stepped forward. "It is newly mine."

The old man looked the big man up and down. "I'm afraid," he said, "that now it is newly mine. At least until I have given it back to the sea."

Meroe snarled. "And if I spit you now?"

"Then your hull is shattered, and your sailing grove finds the bottom."

"And if we accept?" Frank asked. "Will you take us aboard your craft and carry us north to Hylfing?"

"Hylfing?" The old man smiled. His eyes flitted over the living beams around him and then back to Frank. "Are you the one called Mordecai? This is his breed of faerie witchery."

Frank shook his head. "I'm his brother."

The old man sheathed his sword. "You are here, in the belly of an empire galley, so you must know that Hylfing has been taken. No doubt your eyes were there."

"We were there," Frank said.

The old man pulled his beard and sighed. "I cannot take you north. I can only put you in at the next port. But you must not show your faces abovedecks. I will not have this witchery cast upon another craft, or my crew addled with fear. If you are seen, then my guns will send you under and I will sail on without a care."

"Could we have any food?" Dotty asked. "Water?"

Footsteps pounded on the deck above them. The captain looked up.

"Cowards," he muttered. He stepped toward the ladder, and no one moved to stop him. "I will have food lowered through the hatch. Do not let them glimpse you."

Frank watched the old man scramble up into daylight. The hatch banged shut behind him.

With a yell, Meroe buried his sword into a beam.

"Better than chains," Frank said quietly.

Meroe slumped to the floor and thumped his head against the ladder. And then he laughed. "The gods have no love for me," he said.

Hyacinth looked at him. "Your tale has not reached its end." She smiled. "Nor has ours."

Beneath them, the sea beat slowly against the hull. Above them, feet drummed and voices shouted.

The captain threw his leg back over the ship rail and slid quickly down to the smaller galley. He'd left just enough terrified sailors aboard the green galley to guide it behind his own.

"Dumarre by morning! Full cloth, lads!" He walked into the bow, and his young signalman hurried after him. Together, they watched the stern of the little merchant heaving along ahead.

"We'll strip guns north of the harbor," the captain said. "Then claim reward on the galley."

Bright flags waved.

Henry tripped and fell panting against a tree. Grabbing at its branches, he just managed to keep himself from tumbling back down the steep slope. His head was swimming, and his body felt light and out of his control. Beo stood beside him, his ribs rising and falling quickly, his thick, foam-covered tongue dangling out the corner of his mouth.

Henry reached back for his sword but couldn't even manage to grab it. He pressed his face into the tree trunk, gasping, and shut his eyes. Something hard, the raggant's horn, thumped into the back of his skull. He didn't care. *Thump away, Rags. Thump, crack, and split.* His head was already useless—hot and spinning everywhere but his jaw. An anchor of ice was hooked into his scar, pulling his head down, trying to pin him to the earth, to keep him from moving.

Where were the fingerlings? Henry groped for his gray trail with his confused mind. Could he feel them? Maybe they were walking. He could rest.

Pauper son. Sleep. Rest.

Henry jerked up and opened his eyes, blinking away stinging sweat. She couldn't be in his head. Not like that. He was awake. It wasn't her. He'd imagined it. Was that better? Was he starting to imagine things? How long had he been running? Too long. At least a week. He couldn't see Hylfing. He couldn't see the ocean. He could see rocks and trees and hills, or at least their blurry shapes.

Beo stopped panting and began to growl. Henry looked down the slope, trying to focus his eyes. Nothing. No fingerlings. No moving shapes. But the trees were close. He couldn't see far, and his eyes were blinded with sweat, his eyelids sticking with each blink. And then his vision shifted. He could see the wind. Like a great snake, like a river dividing and uniting, climbing the mountains and resting in the valleys, the breeze surrounded everything beneath the sun. The trees, an army of life, shouting their glory and their strength, grabbed at the wind, the sun, the air with uncountable twisting, growing, laughing fingers. And rocks stood in it all, anchors of history, their stories towering and slow, patient and unforgetting. Henry's head, already weak, throbbed like it had the day he had first seen the dandelion fire. His eyes widened, trying to understand it all, to see through the living storm that was reality. He could see three shapes, struggling through the trees, surrounded with a gray twining fog, avoided by every bright spinning strand around them.

Your brothers come for you.

"Go, Beo." Henry turned and looked up the rocky slope, through the roaring life of trees and the mumbling of stone. He wished that he could learn every detail, smell every leaf, slap every boulder, that he could catch more of the thundering waterfall in the small bucket that was his body.

He clambered up onto a rock and savored the feel of the wind on his skin. His legs were moving, carrying him higher, pumping and pushing. And his vision faded. The pack straps were rubbing his shoulders raw, and the raggant was groaning in his ear. He was Henry, tired and hungry, chasing his uncle's dog up a mountain with death on his heels and a cold hole in his face. But he was a weed, a lion. His legs had fed on the strength of trees, and his heart pumped fire.

Nimiane sat in the emperor's throne, her head resting against its back. Her eyes were shut, and one hand scratched the cat on her lap. She could feel the boy. She could taste him, almost as well as when he had first reached into her tomb and left some of his blood on her hand, and she had taken the shirt off his back. This was the smell of that shirt, the strength of that blood. But it was something else, too. His blood had always been strong, but now it was hot and quick. He had changed in many ways since that first meeting in the doorway between worlds. His taste was better now. And the blood-tie between them was growing stronger every time he tried to face her. How long until she could shape words on his tongue and see out of his eyes? Days. Hours. Perhaps tonight. Where he was running, she did not know. Neither did she care. Her fingers would catch him. Coradin would not fail her again.

"Majesty, the emperor's throne . . ." The chamberlain's voice trailed away. Nimiane did not open her eyes, but the cat raised its head.

"His magnificence has asked me to preside," she said quietly. "Do not approach your queen again."

Half of the emperor's nobles stood uneasily in the hall. The other half, the stronger half, had fled the city, been killed in the streets, or burned in their beds. A smoky haze still hung over the city. Her witch-dogs had done well. But they had not brought her Phedon, the emperor's proud son. He had not escaped the city. He would be found. The wolves had been given his scent.

Nimiane slowly filled her lungs and savored the tinge of smoke and the smell of nervous, fearful nobles, spattered with their gaudy perfumes. She would keep a few of them in the end, those men and women in the crowd who were already dressed in black and stood nearer to the front—those who were willing for darkness, blood, and conquest to be the latest in court fashion.

The witch smiled. It had been long since she had been surrounded with courtiers in a living city. Tomorrow she would tint her gown with scarlet. How many of these bleating sheep would imitate the wolf?

A man pushed out of the crowd and approached the throne. She did not open her eyes, did not lift her head or stop her fingers from their slow combing of the cat's fur. The man was tall, taller from where the cat looked up at him. His face was pale with fear, his jaw chewing methodically on an empty mouth.

He had once been strong, broad-shouldered, and simple. Not one of the court preeners, he wore no high collar, no tall boots or jewels. He was staring into her face, not the cat's, waiting for her to open her eyes, to look at him. She waited for it, knowing what would come. Let him strike at a sleeping woman. After a moment, while the silent crowd watched, he drew a knife from his belt and lunged toward the witch-queen.

The crowd gasped, at first in shock and then in horror.

The lowly aristocrat, not much better than a farmer, froze with his hands raised. His legs buckled, and he dropped to the floor like a limp rag. His knife clattered across the stones.

The witch pulled every drop of him to herself, every crackle and spark of his life, his strength, his final courage. Only his soul escaped her as his body faded to ash within his clothes, like a young bird in the witch's hand, like a country beneath her feet. The crowded hall was silent. Wind from the open window shuffled the ash across the floor beneath the cat's watching eyes. Wind. The wind had been good. The galley would reach Dumarre beneath tomorrow's sun. She inhaled slowly. The boy's mother would be savored, a punishment for father and son.

Mordecai would come to her soon. His pride would bring him. The son was within her grasp even now—struggling in the brush.

Tonight, she would attend to the emperor.

Henry slipped between two rocks and fell to his back, sliding down a bank into cool shade. The raggant bleated and squirmed beneath him. Beo licked his face.

The ground was soft. Henry squinted at the air above him. It shimmered like a heat mirage but was too close, beginning just a few feet from him and climbing high, blurring the blue sky and fast-passing clouds together in a rippling sludge. Henry sat up.

Beo was exhausted, too. His back sagged. His head drooped, panting. Foam had dried around his mouth. When he barked, his voice was hoarse.

Henry crawled to him and threw an arm around his neck. The muscles in his legs quivered, spasming. Beo dropped to the ground. "Good dog," Henry said. "We're here, aren't we? You brought me." He looked up, blinking at the shimmer. "What do we do now?"

The dog forced himself slowly to his feet and walked forward. Henry shut his eyes and crawled after him. The air cooled around him. The sun's heat was gone from the back of his neck. He tried to relax his eyes, to let them see the real, and then he opened them.

He was kneeling on dark earth beneath the canopy of

an enormous chestnut. The faeries had hidden it the same way they hid themselves, but the magic was much stronger, much bigger, and . . . ancient. Henry felt a pressure building in his ears while the shimmering faded from his eyes. He couldn't tell if the tree was actually three trees with trunks grafted together well aboveground, or if it had been one, split and reunited. Regardless, the trunk was tripled, leaving arched entrances to a dark, hollow center.

Bracing himself, Henry staggered up to vertical and walked forward to the trunks. The enormous leaves above him moved slowly, like fans, and the branches were heavy with the spiny green casements of ripening chestnuts. The dangling maces grew in clumps of three, and each urchin-like shell looked big enough to hold a baseball.

Henry reached the trunk and slapped it. "Hey!" he yelled. "I'm here to see Nudd! I have a message for the Chestnut King!" Nothing happened, so he stepped into the darkness between the trunks. It was like standing under a water tower—a water tower older than most civilizations. Beo flopped onto the ground outside. "Hello?" Henry shouted. "Hello?"

His father had told him to wait and then to light a fire. He wasn't sure that he could wait. He wasn't sure that he could light a fire. He couldn't just do things like that. Not always.

With his foot, Henry scraped together a pile of dry leaves. Then he knelt beside them, shut his eyes, and looked down at his right palm. The dandelion fire was slow, spinning alone in darkness, but larger and brighter than it had been after his dream-walking. He needed some of the tree's strength.

"Little brother," a voice said. And Beo began to bark.

Anger lined with fear rushed through Henry, and he opened his eyes. His hand flamed from gold to white. The leaves crackled. Dandelions swarmed up the inside of the trunks and met above Henry's head. He slid out of the trunks and jumped to his feet. Coradin, helmed and collared and holding his sword, stood beneath the sprawling limbs, his silver helmet green from the canopy above them both, the eyeholes pure emptiness. Beo, hackles up, crouched with his belly low to the ground. The other two fingerlings stepped beneath the tree beside Coradin. Their breathing was soft and slow. They weren't even winded.

Henry wobbled on his feet, and the raggant bellowed in his ear. Reaching back, he managed to draw his own sword. Gripping the handle with both hands, he turned sideways and faced the fingerlings like a batter. Leaves crackled behind him. The cool, damp air carried smoke into his nostrils. A three-mace cluster of chestnuts dropped to the soft ground.

It was time to die.

"This far?" Coradin laughed, moving forward. "This race through mountains to set a flame beneath a tree?"

Henry nodded, blinking. Beo growled.

"It is time for you to come," Coradin said, pointing his sword tip at Henry. "Your head and right hand must travel to our mother. The rest may stay behind."

Henry savored one last breath, blowing it out slowly.

Then, with his sword still held high, he walked toward the fingerlings.

Above him, the tree shivered. It shook, and chestnut clusters drummed to the ground. Shouting thundered from the trunk, and the sheltered chestnut world was full of faeries—big faeries with red angry faces and green maces in their hands. Henry lowered his sword, laughing as the flood rolled around him. The fingerlings stood back to back, but the wave of faeren broke them apart, and they were swept out beyond the boughs.

A large bald faerie with a purple eye patch leapt at Henry and brought a heavy mace down onto his head.

There were too many dreams that wanted to be. They struggled with each other, images colliding. Shapes twisted and colored and disappeared. Stars stared down at Henry, daring him to stare back, to see who would blink first. Trees grew, bent beneath a storm, and were gone. Hyacinth smiled at Henry, reached for his face, and cried. Fire grew around her, and she became sky-climbing smoke.

Coradin stood over Uncle Frank in the cathedral, his knife raised. Dotty was on her knees, too, beside her husband. Her hair was straggling away from her head like it always did when she baked. There was flour on her face and a bowl of peaches beside her. She was rolling dough on the floor. The girls were lined up as well, all of them kneeling, and Coradin's knife grew into his sword. Monmouth was yelling for Henry, telling him to run. Where was he in the darkness? Two bright aspen trees stood in a garden and

Monmouth hung between them, his fingers gone, his hands grafted into the silver bark. Ten men in black lay on their faces in front of him. A city was burning. Henry was kneeling in a Kansas field, ripe for the harvest, watching a storm building above him. Green lightning struck him, and he was fire, running through the fields, burning the world.

Henry tried to make it stop. He tried to direct his mind, to focus on a single thing, even a nightmare. But the barrage didn't slow. The images quickened, the horror grew, until Henry sat alone in a cold, dark crypt, sealed in, undying, consumed by madness. A stone slid on the floor and a shape crawled out, carrying a ball circled with white fire. The shape was Mordecai, laughing, stroking the Blackstar, gibbering in a woman's voice.

Stop. Stop. But Henry had no eyes to squeeze shut, no way to shut it all out. Grandmother? Where was she? Everyone Henry loved died or became evil while he watched, and she didn't come. He suffocated on his own dandelions, and she wasn't there. The scar on his face gnawed at him like a creature digging into his mind, draining his life, his sanity. And Henry began to cry.

He woke suddenly, sobbing in a dark room. Hot tears cooled on his jaw while his body quaked and his lungs struggled for air. Lights hung on the wall, three small, glowing circles in a cluster. Where was he? The bald faerie had hit him on the head with a chestnut. The fingerlings were gone.

His body calmed, his breathing leveled. He tried to sit up, and his head nearly exploded with the pain.

"You are a dreamer," a voice said. "But in this room, any horror is your own. No mind or spirit can reach through these walls. No mind or spirit can escape them."

The light on the wall grew, and Henry squinted around the room. It was a small bedroom, and it held exactly one bed and one chair, with the lights on the wall between them. There was no door. The light was a steady flame burning three large chestnuts, or burning around the chestnuts. Nothing was happening to them, and there wasn't any smoke. The large, bald faerie sat in the chair across from Henry. Leaning back with his thick legs crossed, the faerie adjusted his eye patch and pulled on the ends of his mustache. His head glowed almost as much as the chestnuts.

"I am Jacques," the faerie said. "Green whelpling, you are where you should not be."

Henry pressed his fingers against his temples and tried hard to keep his eyes focused. What had his father said? *You have bullied faeren before. No bowing.* "I am Henry, and I am where I'm supposed to be. I have a gift for the Chestnut King from Mordecai Westmore, green man to the northern faeren."

Jacques snorted. "Green man to the lesser faeren of several districts, and a seamstress, too, no doubt. Has he made the king a scarf?"

"I must see the king," Henry said.

"You must see me," Jacques said, smiling. "And that is all the must you need."

Henry leaned forward, trying not to look like his skull was screaming pain. "I don't think you understand. I'm not asking to see the king. I'm telling you what will be. The king must see me. I have a gift for him."

This time, Jacques laughed. "The sparrow thinks himself no smaller than the rooster and cocks his doodle-doo. The potatoes are in need of composting. You are more likely to offer up your life in their service than to offer up your gift to the king, or even see his face. The child acts a bravado, but I have seen him weep."

Henry pushed himself up off the bed. The little light in the room vanished as the blood drained from Henry's head. He braced himself against the wall as it returned.

"I wept for the faeren people," Henry said. "I am fond of chickens."

Jacques stood as well, facing Henry, his glistening scalp almost reaching Henry's shoulders. His one eye sparkled. "You set a flame to one of the ancient three-mace trees, little greenling. You owe us gratitude for every breath your lungs draw."

Henry looked down at the faerie. "Thank you for not murdering me while I slept. And thank you for knocking me over the head. I only set the flame to draw you out." Henry smiled. "Actually, I really am grateful you came, even with the head-knocking. I had raced those fingerlings from Hylfing."

"Fingerlings?" Jacques cocked an eyebrow. "Truly?"

"Truly," Henry said.

The big faerie tugged at one end of his mustache. "Their resilience is explained. We were unable to kill them, and several of our own were struck down."

"I'm sorry," Henry said. "They've been after me for a while. They might even be able to find me here."

Jacques shook his head. "No. No one finds here. Not even the lesser faeren. Not you. Not your father. All are brought."

"Is my dog okay?" Henry asked suddenly. "And where's my raggant?"

"Your dog? We believed it to be your uncle's."

"Right," Henry said. "Beo is my uncle Caleb's, but he sent him with me."

Jacques nodded. "We have a fondness for your uncle here, though none for your father. Caleb, Amram's son, has a love of the wilds, and all growing and breathing things obey his kindness. His dog has been made happy. The raggant's injuries have been tended, though he has been made to sleep or he would have broken his skull on these walls in search of you."

Henry crossed his arms and blinked slowly. The faerie's face was blurring. "Where's my sister? And my little cousin?"

Jacques turned away.

"They were with my friend, a skinny kid named Richard," Henry continued. "And Fat Frank. I know you brought them here."

A doorway opened in the wall, and Jacques stepped

into it. "They are as well as you," he said. "Rest now. It is late. The moon climbs high. You have slept long but not well. Your head is weak. Give it peaceful dreamings. I and others will return."

"The king," Henry said. "I need to see the king. And Nudd needs to see me."

"Do not speak his name," Jacques said. He waved a hand at the chestnuts, and Henry blinked as they snuffed out.

"Leave the light," he said, swallowing down a faint taste of panic. "I prefer the light."

"You fear the darkness?" Jacques laughed. "Your grandfather's line has truly failed. From the great Amram to Mordecai to you, a weed at the foot of a mighty tree."

Henry leaned against the earthen wall. "Give me light!" he yelled. Anger hammered at the inside of his skull.

The dim outline of the doorway began to vanish, but not before glowing dandelions rimmed it and spread through, surrounding the big faerie. Jacques blinked in surprise, and the door was gone. Henry sank slowly and carefully back onto his bed, watching the dandelions line the walls and cover the ceiling. Their sweet smell replaced the scent of dirt, and each one spun and swung in the same bright dance that sat on his palm. The light was better. Even when he shut his eyes, knowing that there was light was much better.

His ears were ringing like his old doorbell in Boston, and he pressed his knuckles hard against them. With his eyes shut, he breathed slowly and tried to think. He doubted that the faerie was right about all dreaming in this room being in his mind, but it was definitely an attractive idea. That meant he could change things. There would be no horror. Just his grandmother, and if she couldn't make it, baseball.

His eyes shut, and his mind fell into nothingness.

Tilly Johnson sat nervously in her vinyl chair, twisting the sleeve of her oversize sweater with one hand and holding Grandmother Anastasia's cold hand with the other. The old woman's skin was smooth to touch. Her wind-weathered face now seemed soft and strangely young, even beneath the plastic mask and the terrible, flickering hospital lights. Her white hair was bright, whiter than the hard, bleached pillow beneath it. Her breaths were slow and small and far apart. A heart monitor drew pictures of low mountains, one lonely peak at a time.

A glass door slid open, and a nurse in pink scrubs slipped in. "Mrs. Johnson?"

Tilly sniffed and looked up. The nurse gave her a sympathetic smile and cocked her head.

"How old is your mother?"

Tilly shrugged and shook her head slowly. Reaching up, she gently brushed back the white hair with her fingers and fanned it over the pillow. "I don't even know."

"Has she lived a good life?" the nurse asked. "Clearly, she's loved."

Tilly's eyes shot up to the nurse's. "What are you saying?"

"The scans are all clean. No clots, no blockages. Her lungs are fine. Her heart is strong."

"Then what's wrong? What can you do?"

The nurse sat down on the end of the bed and put her hand on Grandmother's leg.

"All lives end," she said. "We can make her comfortable for as long as she holds on."

Antilly Johnson began to cry.

CHAPTER TWENTY

Henrietta shivered. Clouds sailed in silhouette across the face of the moon. Distant white lines of surf crawled toward unseen cliffs.

"Do you think he made it?" she asked. "We should have followed him."

Zeke looked at her. The two of them sat on the roof of the inn. They were supposed to be watching the square, but Henrietta's eyes kept drifting toward the sea and the galley in the harbor. Zeke was holding a bow that Zeb had given him, and a quiver hung over his shoulder. She had wanted only a small knife, now tucked into her belt.

"We couldn't follow him," Zeke whispered. "I'm no Indian tracker, and we don't know where he went."

"We should have followed the finger-men."

"If we had, we would both be dead in the hills."

"With Henry," Henrietta said slowly. "Dead in the hills with Henry."

Zeke shook his head. "He's tough. And he had Beo."

"There were three of them." Henrietta sniffed and twisted a finger in what she now thought of as her horrible hair.

Zeke elbowed her and pointed. A group of soldiers were moving across the square. More than fifty. They'd come out of the hall and had almost reached the fountain.

"Just patrolling," Henrietta said.

Zeke shook his head. He tucked one leg up and baseball-slid down the roof, grabbed on to a dormer, and swung his legs into an open window. He tossed his bow through, then leaned back and stuck his arm out for Henrietta. She slid down and caught his hand, and he dragged her halfway into what had been their room. A candle burned low on the table. **BACK SOON, H** was carved on the door. A rickety cupboard peeked out of a backpack on one of the beds. Together, Zeke and Henrietta tumbled down the stairs and into the crowded dining room.

"Soldiers," Zeke said. "Fifty, maybe more. Coming from the hall."

Tonight, the men were harder. No one was drinking, and the anger crackled ice-cold. Men, friends and brothers, had been lost as well as the city. Sailors and guardsmen and merchants had spent the evening sitting quietly, whispering quietly, sharpening swords and small boarding hatchets, fletching arrows and oiling bowstrings, waiting for the appointed time.

"Lanterns," Zeb said. "Archers to the windows."

In an instant, the lights in the dining room died. Bowmen crept to the blanketed windows. In the blackness, Henrietta felt Zeke begin to move forward, but she grabbed his arm.

"What are you doing?" she whispered.

"Archers," he said quietly, and crept to a window where one man already crouched, painted with moonlight through the barely lifted blanket. Henrietta followed Zeke carefully, and when he crouched, she crouched beside him.

Gray shapes moved silently to surround the house. Crossbows, pikes, and swords spread themselves in a fence. Sparks stood out in the dark as someone struck a flint, and then an oily flame came to life on the end of a torch and quickly spread to a dozen others. A man walked to the door.

The pounding of his fist echoed through the inn.

"Rebels and traitors!" he shouted. "Weapons to the floor! Crawl out in a line or burn together!"

The voice of Zebudee, strengthened by years of bar-room ballads, boomed a reply. "Servants of the snake! Back to the sea on your bellies, or a merry good-bye to you and your souls!" And then quieter, to the room, "Torches first, lads."

While Henrietta watched the torch-bearing soldiers step forward, the room filled with the sound of shattering glass. Zeke and the man next to him both forced arrow-heads and fists through panes and then let fly. The torch-men in the ring all fell, but while the flames flickered on the cobbles, a swarm of crossbow bolts ripped through the windows and blankets and rattled through the beamed room. Glass and wool fell onto Henrietta's head as the soldiers rushed forward, pressing at every window, forcing the door. Throwing the blanket away, she saw the flame and moon shadow that was Zeke draw his bow and release it inches from a climbing soldier's belly. The man folded over and tumbled into the inn, two others still alive behind him. Henrietta staggered backward, pulling her knife.

It was then that she saw the three shapes beyond the rushing soldiers, the three men in black with the moon-silver helmets. One of them drew his long sword and began to move forward through the clattering mayhem. It parted around him like so much mist.

"Zeke!" Henrietta yelled. "Zeke!"

As if he knew her voice, the fingerling turned and walked toward her window. The others walked behind him.

Throughout the dining room, the shouting grew triumphant. The soldiers had broken. Armed men leapt out of the windows, running survivors down. Three men jumped out over Zeke where he knelt, shrugging off a soldier's body. All were cut down with the fingerling's long blade. The dark men had reached the window and were climbing through. Zeke found his feet and staggered backward, notching another arrow, drawing his bow. The long blade flicked, and Zeke's bow leapt out of his hands in two halves. The man raised his sword above Zeke like an executioner, and Henrietta ran forward, yelling. She jumped into the man's chest and threw her arms around his neck. For a moment, she hung on him, groping with her little knife, trying to slide the blade up the back of his helmet. And then, for the second time, the man's fingers found her hair and forced back her head. The butt of his sword cracked against her temple, and she slipped away, floating in a pool of darkness.

When Henrietta opened her eyes, her body was folded over something big and moving, squeezing against her stomach and chest. Her breath wasn't coming easily, and her ribs ached. Her quick pulse drummed in her temples. The only light came from the moon and some distant orange flickering.

Groaning, she tried to straighten up, but she couldn't. She was draped over the back of a horse, and a tight rope ran between her hands and feet beneath its belly. A man rode bareback in front of her. Craning her head, she could see a broad metal belt and silver chains running up his back to a collar, and from the collar to the rim of a silver helmet. A long sword was sheathed on his back. Two other horses rode nearby. A second shape drooped behind one of the riders.

"Zeke?" Henrietta said. "Zeke?" The man in front of her shifted slightly.

"If that is his name," the man said, "the queen knew him. She requires you both."

"Who are you?" Henrietta asked. "Why are you doing this?"

"I am called Coradin. My father was also Coradin. We have always carried swords."

"Did you want the finger?" Henrietta asked. "Does she make you do everything?"

When the man said nothing, Henrietta arched her

back as far as she could and tried to see where they were. Hylfing was below her, at the bottom of a long, smooth slope. The square was full of tiny torches, and a huge bonfire blazed near the center. While she watched, the bells began to ring. She knew this slope well. She and Eli had galloped down it on Caleb's horse, with lightning falling around them. The fingerlings were taking her to the wizard door.

"What happened in the city?" she asked.

"Do the bells not tell you? The soldiers were slain or captured. The galley was taken. The slaves were freed."

"Did the inn burn?"

"How many more questions await me?"

"Did it?"

"No."

Henrietta wished that she could laugh, that she could be happy, that she could taunt the man with failure. But she didn't think that he had failed. If he had wanted to burn the inn, it would have burned. He had wanted her. And Zeke. Why? What did that mean about Henry?

"My cousin got away, didn't he?" Henrietta strained to look up at the back of the man's head. "I mean, the witch wouldn't care about me if she had him."

Coradin said nothing.

Henrietta forced more air inside her aching ribs. Talking hurt, but she didn't care. "We're going to the old wizard door, aren't we? I've been through it before. With my uncle. But where then? Where are you taking us?" Pausing long enough to know that the man wasn't going to answer, she continued. "You know you're going to die, don't you? When my uncles kill the witch, you'll probably go, too, right? Because of that finger. My uncles *will* kill the witch. She might make a big mess first, but they'll kill her just like they killed Darius."

"I do not know Darius," Coradin said. "But the queen has no life to lose. Still your tongue. No more words."

"She has some kind of life," Henrietta said. "And she'll lose it."

Coradin drew the sword over his shoulder and twisted in his seat, setting the butt against the back of Henrietta's head. He raised it.

"Okay, okay," Henrietta said. "I'll be quiet."

The man began to resheath his sword.

"You are going to die, though," Henrietta added.

In one motion, the big man's arm came down and around. For the second time that night, the sword hilt cracked against Henrietta's skull. For the second time that night, she forgot that the world existed. She forgot who she was or *that* she was. She knew nothing.

Frank sat cross-legged watching the flames dance in three galley lanterns on the planks in front of him. Beams popped, and aspen leaves brushed against his arms as the ship rode the sea's uneven back. They were all gathered around, all watching the lights. And they had all eaten, but not much. Crusts and cheese had been dropped through the hatch before dark. Most of a night had passed since then.

Meroe groaned. His shirt was off, and the wound in his side had already begun to seep through the fresh bandage Hyacinth had bound tight around his middle. He pressed a fist against it and inhaled deeply. His face calmed.

"Dad," Penelope said. "What's going to happen to us?" She was leaning on her mother.

"Couldn't say," Frank said.

"Nothing good," said Dotty.

Frank leaned over and kissed Dotty on the cheek.

"Frank Willis," she said. "I can't remember when we've been in worse trouble."

"Can't you now?" he asked. "I think that I can. Dots, love, we've held hands a little closer to death's brink than this."

James plucked himself an aspen sapling and stripped off its leaves. Monmouth yawned and stretched out on his back.

"I should swim," Meroe said. "Out the death hatch below. This captain will not free us."

"Trailing blood out of that wound?" Frank asked. "You'd be chumming for sharks and every other meat-eater."

Isa sighed and leaned her head on Hyacinth's shoulder.

"How long since we heard a sailor's tread?" James asked. "We should go above."

"Soon," Frank said.

"We are still sailing south. South." James bent the aspen, but it did not break. He cinched the slender trunk into a knot and threw it into the shadows. "The morning will see us in Dumarre."

"What will they do with us in Dumarre?" Isa asked.

"Nothing good," Dotty said again.

"Monmouth," Penelope said. "Do you have another forest in you?"

The slight wizard sighed and tucked his hands beneath his head. "I don't know. I didn't know that I had the first one. What good would it do?"

Hyacinth began to hum quietly. It was a song from her own childhood, a song her mother had sung, standing on the roof of her house, watching the sea, waiting for the return of her father.

Frank leaned his head back against a timber and breathed slowly. He reached out and pulled his wife and daughter against him. The tune was distant and familiar. When Hyacinth began to softly sing the words, he knew their meaning, though the language was long forgotten, nothing more than a painful memory of childhood lessons. The song was full of sweetness, thirsting for reunion, sorrowful, bending beneath separation.

Frank shut his eyes and listened to the creaking ship. He listened to the gentle lilt in Hyacinth's voice and Penelope's breathing as she sank into sleep.

James stood up, and Frank opened his eyes. His nephew looked at him and then looked at Meroe. Frank nodded. Meroe nodded.

"Monmouth," James said quietly. He tucked a long knife into the small of his back. "Come with me."

The wizard quickly found his feet, and the two of them moved away. They did not climb the ladder. They both disappeared down into the floor, down into the slave hold, down to the death hatch.

The water was barely cool, and its temperature told James just how far south they had already come. Too far. The currents were mixing. Before long, the water would be warm. He bobbed beneath the surface, filled his mouth, and then spat out the salt water against the ship's side. Monmouth slid through the water beside him. The moon was low, scraping its light across the sea and painting the aspen galley silver. In the east, the horizon had begun to gray.

Kicking his legs, James surged up against the hull and grabbed two fistfuls of young aspens. He twisted them quickly around his wrists, braced his feet against wet wood, and began to climb.

For Monmouth, it seemed easy. The aspens never gave way in his hands. But James struggled, constantly slipping as his slender holds tore free from the ship's side. By the time one hand had reached the rail, he was fighting to keep his breath even and quiet, praying that he wouldn't fall and rouse any sailors with his splash.

Monmouth slipped over the rail like something part snake and part cat. Clenching oak instead of aspen, James pulled himself up in time to see Monmouth lowering a body gently down beside the double tiller. James rolled softly over the rail and sat on the deck, breathing hard.

Monmouth held up four fingers and pointed down the length of the ship. In the moonlight, James could see two bodies stretched out in sleep, and two more sitting beside the deck hatch, swords across their knees.

Drawing his knife, James crept forward to the stairs and moved silently down to the center deck.

Henry sat in the sun. His dream was fuzzy around the edges but crystal clear where it needed to be. The baseball diamond was almost perfect. Almost. The infield was grass, and the reddish earth of the base paths was freshly combed beneath crisp chalk lines. The outfield fence was boarded and painted with local sponsors. Those kept changing for some reason. His subconscious mind was having trouble settling on endorsements. The bleachers were changing, too, from a few aluminum rows behind home plate to stands that would work better in a minor-league park and everything in between.

The dandelions were a bigger problem. At first they'd sprouted everywhere. He'd worked at it, and now they disappeared whenever he looked at them. But as soon as he looked away, he just knew the outfield was erupting with gold.

He was standing on the pitching mound.

Three more problems. He had no glove. He had no ball. He had no players.

He tried to make a glove appear, but his mind wasn't buying it. The stupid cop had his glove, and no dreaming could get it back. And he didn't know where his baseball was. The bald faerie had probably taken it. Again, his mind knew the ball was gone and wouldn't help out with any imagining. And players . . . why couldn't he conjure up players? One of them could bring a ball and some bats, and he could borrow a glove.

He stared at the plate and tried to imagine a catcher. Something moved in his periphery, off in the completely golden left field. He turned, and the dandelions rushed into hiding.

It was his grandmother. She walked slowly, and her eyes were closed. The sun was on her face and playing in her braided hair.

Henry smiled, watching her face while she walked toward him. She stopped on the grass beside the mound and opened her eyes.

"Your hair is really white," Henry said. "Are you actually here?"

She smiled at him, and for some reason, both joy and sadness mingled in her eyes. Then she nodded.

Henry laughed. "The faerie said no one could dream-walk into this place."

"Nothing could keep me away," his grandmother said. "Not from this. Though I do not dream-walk."

"Not from what?" Henry asked. He stepped off the mound and sat down in the grass.

His grandmother smiled. "Thirteen years ago, at this dark hour of the morning, a boy child came into the world. Your mother, Hyacinth, sang over you, weak from the struggle but flushed with the triumph. And when I saw you in your father's arms, I wept." She lowered herself to the grass beside Henry. "You fought your mother long, but when you came, you were as swift as a sunburst."

"Today is my birthday," Henry said. Sadness rolled over him. He'd forgotten. And he'd pictured a feast like the one at his christening. Aunt Dotty had promised him pies. "Wait." He looked into his grandmother's face. "You're talking. Are you sure you're real? You've never been able to talk in a dream."

"For me," his grandmother said, "this is no dream. I am as real as I have ever been."

Henry sat perfectly still. Something heavy sank inside him. Something he refused to look at or think about. "What's going on?" he asked, and his voice was quiet.

His grandmother squeezed his hand. "A dream-walker returns to the body when the dream is done."

Henry shut his eyes. He wanted to wake up. He didn't want to hear any more. It wasn't true. He was making it up. The faerie said no one could come. Suddenly, he could see his grandmother's face as it had been in the witch's garden—weak and pale. He opened his eyes, shocked.

His grandmother's eyes were wet.

"I did this," he said. Grief surged up inside him. "Oh, I'm so sorry. I shouldn't have gone into the garden. I shouldn't have gone into her dream. You didn't want me to; you tried to stop me." He shoved the heels of his hands into his eyes. "I'm sorry. I'm so sorry."

"Shhh," his grandmother said, and she slid closer to him. Her arms went around his shoulders. "You were right to challenge her. I am an old woman, fearful for her grandson. I forgot who you are. I should not have tried to stop you."

Henry opened his eyes and sat up, breathing hard. "But you died."

His grandmother smiled. "I die."

"Then we can stop it," Henry said. "You can go back to your body. The raggant almost died."

"Henry," his grandmother said. "Long your grandfather has waited for me. He was taken by this same witch, when your father was young. And when your father was imprisoned by the faeren, I wandered too far in search of him. My soul and body were torn. In life I am blind; in dreaming, mute. My waking mind staggers along its road, and my speech is cloudy. Look at me, am I not becoming whole again? The last strand stretches between body and soul, it is tearing even now. I must journey after my husband and elder sons and all those who have carried my love and gone before."

"But you'll be dead," Henry said.

"In one world," said his grandmother. "But not in another. Would you have me for another Nimiane? Flesh afraid to pass to dust? A seed fearful of the flower?"

Henry shook his head. "But what will I do?" he asked. "How can I tell my dad? Will I ever see him again? I can't even get through a dream by myself."

Grandmother smiled. "You have gotten through more

than dreams. You have done well, and your blood suits you. Do not do as I did. Do not forget who you are."

"Who am I?" Henry asked. "I'm a boy with nightmares, a burned hand, a witch's blood in my face, and her voice in my head."

Henry's grandmother tipped up his chin and stared into his eyes. "You are Henry York Maccabee, seventh son of Mordecai Westmore, seventh son of Amram Iothric, in the line long faithful to the Old King, bone from my own bone, blood from my own blood. You are the pride of your father and the glory of your mother, a fire green and gold and a curse to darkness." She dropped her hand. "May you never need to be told again."

Henry sat silently, trying to find words, trying to feel like anything more than a beat-up kid.

"Henry," Grandmother said quietly. "I have already visited your father this night and kissed his hand and kissed his head. I have wiped his tears."

Henry fought back a sob and bit his lip. "Where is he? What's he doing?"

"Caleb and Mordecai, my two sons of thunder, look down on the city of Dumarre. But you shall see them soon enough."

"I will?" Henry asked.

Grandmother nodded. "You will. But now it is time for your birthday gift, and then you must wake."

"Why?" Henry asked. "I don't want to wake up. I want to stay with you. I don't want a gift."

Grandmother's eyebrows rose, though she smiled.

"You must wake because your name awaits, and your blood is called. You must have a gift because I must give one."

She stood and pulled Henry to his feet. The field was all dandelions, but Henry didn't care. Again Grandmother took Henry's face in her hands and smiled into his eyes. She wiped his tears with her thumbs, and then she leaned forward and kissed him on the head. Turning his face, she stared at his jaw, and then bent and pressed warm lips to his cold burn.

Straightening, she lifted his right hand. "Sweet boy," she said, and then laughed with beautiful, wet eyes. "You are a prince among weeds." She kissed the back of his hand and then his palm where the dandelion bloomed. "It is your birthday, and here is your blessing. For you may the weak have love and the strong have fear. For you may the darkness break. May your life be a truth, and your death a glory. It is your birthday, and here is your gift." She lifted his necklace from his shirt and gripped the worn silver pendant. "What strength I have left in this world is yours. What love I have left in this world is yours. What courage, what sight, what joy, what hope, all that remains of me and in me, all that remains of your grandfather now becomes yours. You are heir to it all. May it strengthen your arm and brighten your fire."

Henry felt heat rush into him, the heat of a lifetime of summers, the laughter of a lifetime of feasts, the love of wind and grandchildren. He felt old, like ripened grain, like the burned field, and young as the morning.

His grandmother was gone, gone from his dream, gone from the world. He opened his eyes and blinked up at the empty blue sky.

"The young green wakes with tears on his cheeks," a deep voice said. "I am impatient for my gift."

CHAPTER TWENTY-ONE

Henry sat up, blinking. He was on the crest of a very large hill. A landscape of emerald pastures divided by hedges and streams and lanes was spread out beneath him. Beyond the pastures, sprawling to the horizon, there was a forest of finger-leaved trees. Behind Henry, a square tower loomed, crowning the great hill. It seemed empty at its base. Each face was arched with a doorway, meeting in a hollow, vaulted center.

Across from Henry, seated on a living chair plumed with broad-fingered chestnut leaves, a huge faerie with a beard on his chest and a belly on his lap was fingering Henry's baseball. His hair and beard were deep brown, and wrinkles traced lines on his skin like a wood grain. He looked up at Henry, and his eyes were long tunnels that led through lifetimes. He pulled a red handkerchief out of a pocket and flicked it into the air. It flared its four corners and settled slowly onto Henry's lap.

"Dry your eyes, little green," the big faerie said. "And then we will speak of your father's gift."

Henry took the red cloth and set it on the couch beside him. He felt no shame in the tears on his cheeks. None at all. They would dry themselves. Sorrow still ached inside him, but there was more than sorrow. He felt full, crowded with blood and heat. And he felt calm. There was new strength inside him, and he was wealthy with a love for the world, for the smell of the breeze and the texture of the stone, for the height of the hill and the deep moss green of the fields that spread beneath him, for the gently journeying clouds wandering far from their mother the sea. He had smelled his aunt Dotty baking bread and heard his mother singing in her garden, he had stood beside his father and his uncles, he had seen his sisters smile and heard his cousins laugh, he had felt a ball hit the sweet, sweet spot on a wooden bat, and he had held a breathing frog in his hands. He had seen the raggant fly. These things and a thousand others made him rich. A quiet song was pulsing through him, a dandelion telling its story of ash made green and green made gold. A story of death and separation, of strength and reunion and death again. The story was his name.

Henry couldn't move. He couldn't speak. He could only sit, and with every sense and more straining inside him, he could feel.

"You, lad, have a strange look about you," the faerie said. "The world is in your eyes."

Henry blinked and inhaled slowly, and filling his lungs was like walking through a quiet, whispering crowd.

"You are Nudd," he said. "The Chestnut King."

"You would call your king by his name?" a voice said

behind Henry. Jacques stepped into view, and his bald head was flushed with anger.

"He is not my king," Henry said, looking up. "He is my brother."

Sputtering, Jacques raised his hand to slap Henry, but the big king laughed.

"Jacques, begone with you and your anger. I would speak with my little brother."

The bald faerie froze, and the color faded from his face. He sniffed and adjusted his eye patch.

"Jacques . . . ," the king said, and the faerie turned on his heel and walked silently back into the tower. He wound quickly through three of the doorways and disappeared.

When he was gone, the king set the baseball down on a low table beside him and laced his fingers together on his belly.

"Jacques is right," he said. "You do thieve a liberty. But my faeren underestimate your weed. The little golden lion can do more than roar, as you have shown many."

Henry's eyes were on the low table. The baseball sat beside Nimroth's remaining tattered pages, two or three at best. Coradin's sword was leaning against the table, and Henry's hoodie hung from its hilt. But it was something else that really held his attention—a folded piece of paper, loosely open, with a wilted dandelion draped around it.

"My letter," Henry said. "How did you get my letter?"

"Ah," the king said, looking down. "How do I acquire many things? Few among the lesser faeren believe that I ever lived, let alone that I still draw breath. There is little difficulty in sending my own among them. Even less when they are slight, such as Thorn."

"But," Henry said, "I need that to get to the Faerie Queene. I need her help. My family needs her help."

"So Thorn told me, and so I read." The king stroked his beard. "But the queene is no more than a girl, controlled by committees, though few even know that the elder queene, my own bride, has passed from this world. The queene has no strength."

"Then you have to help me," Henry said. The king raised thick eyebrows. "You read my letter. You know what Nimiane is doing. She'll make a new Endor, and it will be Nimroth all over again. You have to help us stop her."

Nudd sighed. "Nimiane. Nimroth. Endor. What does a green boy know of these things?" He leaned his bulk over the side of his chair and came back up with a small basket. He held it out to Henry.

Henry took it and looked inside. There was bread and crusty cheese and a small corked bottle. His hunger, a day and a night without food, flooded back over him. He tore off a chunk of the bread and held it.

"I have been to Endor," he said. "I have seen Nimroth in his crypt and held his marble. I burned his house. Nimiane's blood is in me, and she must be killed or I will die. That is what I know." He shoved the bread into his mouth.

The big king chuckled. "Little green, you please me. I will tell you more of Nimroth, but first, I grow weary of waiting for my gift."

Henry swallowed. "I stole thousands of pages from Nimroth's library before I burned it. They are all gifted to you."

Nudd chewed slowly on his lip. His stiff beard wobbled as his jaw moved. "Where would these pages be, and why should I want such a gift?"

"They are stored in an empty world. I brought a few with me. They might help us learn how to kill the witch-queen."

"Ah," Nudd said. "We are back to killing the witch-queen. You who have been to Endor and held Nimroth's marble. You who are dying with Nimiane's blood in your face. Do you not know that the Endorians cannot be killed?"

For the first time, Henry felt irritation toward the old king. He looked at the broad belly and the big beard. He looked into the deep eyes. "That's what everyone says." His voice was flat. "But their power started somewhere. If we knew where, then maybe it could be stopped." He pointed at the pages on the table. "Burn one of those."

Nudd stared at Henry, then picked up the pages with thick fingers. There were only two. He held one out by the corner and whispered a single word. The page burst into flame and crumbled in black ash to the grass.

"The other one," Henry said. While the king held up the other, Henry took a deep breath, hoping that he hadn't messed up again, that he hadn't burned too many. The second page floated away like black feathers on the breeze. The king brushed off his fingers and looked at Henry.

"Burn my letter to the queene," Henry said, pointing. "It's useless anyway."

Nudd peeled off the limp dandelion leaves and held up the page. This time, the parchment tightened in the flame and grew white. Black lines took their twisting shape on both sides of the page, and the three words appeared and faded as the paper fell to ash.

Rubbing his fingertips together as if they'd been stung, Nudd looked at Henry, and his eyes were empty of their laughter.

"It's the Blackstar," Henry said. "I don't know how to read those three words. Do you? What do they mean?"

"Son of Mordecai," the king said. "I know a little of your story. Your father betrayed by low faeren, and you a foundling in another world. I know of your christening and a spell broken, your father's release. I know that Fat Franklin betrayed the magicking of his people so that a knife might be thrown. More than that, I have heard in the praise and the boasting of your sister and the insults of your young cousin." Nudd smiled. "Your small friend, the one called Richard, even threatened me with your coming."

"Where are they?" Henry asked, but the king held up his hand.

"These charmed words around a cursed image are not new to my eyes. They will help you with nothing."

Henry puffed out his cheeks and slumped. "But what do they mean?"

"*Putul Animisti Evrihilo*—the well of daimons, of

undead souls. The incubi. The Blackstar was like a mother to Endor and to Nimroth a father. It was used for the change in their flesh."

Something was happening. As the king had spoken those three strange words, the ash had stirred at his feet. Now the feathery particles were climbing, drifting around the faerie's knee. Henry watched Nudd blink in surprise. The ash quickened, tightening and winding around itself until it looked like a ball of gray string floating in the air. Its surface smoothed and darkened.

Henry's mouth hung open, and Nudd's chestnut face flushed red. He muttered a quick curse, and the sphere shattered, snowing ash gently across his knees.

Henry dropped his basket of food back onto the couch beside him. "Was that the Blackstar? Will the ash show us where it is? Can we find it and smash it with a hammer or something?"

The big king sighed and shook his head. He lifted a heavy finger and scratched his cheek. "My little green brother, the Blackstar cannot be destroyed. Not like that."

Henry stood up and put his hands on his head. "Why? Why does everyone keep saying that? I'm sick of hearing it." He looked up into the sky and watched the clouds slide by, and the wind they were riding brushed against his face. He hadn't realized that he was sweating, and the breeze chilled his skin. He dropped his arms and looked down into the grained face of the Chestnut King. "I'm sorry," he said. "I have to try. I can't just believe you. If I went straight back to Endor, if you sent a thousand faeries with me, and we found the Blackstar, how do you know that we couldn't destroy it?"

Henry looked at the king's knees. The ash was moving again, reassembling.

"You might destroy it," the king said. "With enough strength. I cannot say how much. More, at least, than I can hold. But you should not destroy it. There is great danger there."

The ashen Blackstar was complete. It drifted toward the king's right hand. Nudd moved it quickly, and the image of the Blackstar followed. Henry watched, confused and curious. Finally, the broad faerie levered his bulk up and sat on his hand. The ash spun against his thigh.

"Curse me for a fool and farmer," Nudd said. "I'm a nit and no faerie king."

Henry sat back down and leaned forward. The two of them were eye to eye, the faerie unblinking.

"Why is that ash following your hand?" Henry asked.

For a moment, Nudd was still. His chest rose and fell, and his eyes searched Henry's. Suddenly, sputtering frustration, he leaned back in his chair and held his right hand out for Henry to see. The spinning ash found his palm.

"Know the truth and no twisting," Nudd said. "Henry York Maccabee of the little gold lion, the ash reveals a thief. I possess the Blackstar." He pointed at the basket on Henry's couch. "Eat. You set your feet on the darkest of paths. I have much to say to you."

Henry blinked in surprise. His mind raced, and his mouth fell open. The Chestnut King had the Blackstar. Or he was lying. Henry bit back his flood of questions. He tried to settle down, to find the calm that his grandmother had given him.

Nudd shifted in his chair and dangled his right arm over the side, trying to keep the spinning ash out of view.

"I'll not be telling you everything," the king said. "Everything is not mine to tell. I do not have eyes to see it all, nor a mind to grasp it. But I'll tell you what I know, and I'll speak the sweetness of truth—even if it grinds hope to mush beneath its heel. And I'll tell you as quick as I'm able, for time is not your friend.

"There are evils older than Endor, green Henry. Evils as old as the stars." The king tugged on his beard. "The old stories call them many things—devils of influence, powers, forces, thrones, dominations, gin, daimon, and incubi. They were said to be fleshless—dark spirits—and many even muddled them with imps and faeren. The first sorceries were built on their powers. Men made alliance for the dark strengths and paid those tutors with what they lacked—flesh, blood, the service of minds and souls that can grow and change. The old kings struggled against them, and paupers and greens and prophets bound them in lifeless stones or glass or gems and sealed them in with names of power, for they could not be destroyed, merely bound and sealed up."

"The Blackstar," Henry said.

The king nodded. "That was all long ago, before the First World first died. Wizards and sorcerers, evil and tame and half-good, lived on, but the great source of their first power was chained and lost and forgotten, at the beginning by purpose and plan, and then by the short rememberings of flesh.

"Ages crawled by on their bellies, and civilizations rose and fell to dust before Nimroth was born to a cursed mother. He was a seventh and a green. Poison vines brought the morph to his flesh, though he'd have been as evil if his palm smelled of roses. He had no contentment in his mind or body and searched the world for old secrets and buried murderings to find what he wanted—a prison of incubi.

"Have you heard the stories of gin, Henry?" the king asked.

"Gin?"

"Aye. The spirits in jars or lamps or stones that will set you on a throne if you only grant them freedom."

"Like genies?" Henry asked. "You mean like three wishes?"

"Wishes?" The king laughed. "All lies. If you freed yourself a gin, you'd find your skin turned outside in and an evil cloud on your family and clan. Nimroth sought the incubi, and he found them in a stone, fallen from the sky and polished to a prison, by who can say what triumphant hand. In it, he found his evil.

"Henry, death comes to us when soul is stricken from body. Nimroth struck his own soul down and imprisoned incubi in his blood. He had no life of his own, but the strength to forever live on the lives of others. For those he claimed to love, he did the same, parceling out the blood of death that could not die from his foul well of evil. Between those of the undying breed, litters—I will not call them children—were born of a new race. And so Endor grew, even while the world around it drained to gray and the people in the streets and markets faded and fell, sucked to nothing by a thirsting swarm. Princes and queens flocked to Endor to purchase the incubi blood and immortality at any cost, and the nobles stored and flavored lives in their cellars like so many bottles of wine. They were holes, devouring holes, draining life and releasing it into nothing.

"In that day, I was a new king, and I thought to take the ax to the root of that evil tree. Four of us set out to steal the Blackstar from Nimroth's own hand. Only I returned with life still in my blood and bones, the well of incubi in my hands." Nudd paused. "I have spoken, and now you are the only soul that knows it. But in the end, it meant nothing, and I had stopped nothing. Nimroth denied his loss to his court, but went mad searching for the thief—torturing and imprisoning family members, executing every mortal servant in his palace. Death was impossible, but minds still decayed. Endor, empty of all life, became the city of undying madness. The evil devoured itself. They bound and sealed their own children and parents and lovers when madness came, just as the incubi themselves had once been bound, only now the flesh was sealed in as well—in crypts and coffins and beneath the streets of Endor in the tomb cities."

The king shut his eyes and held perfectly still. He

looked grown from living wood, an addition to his chair, with lichen for his beard.

"How long ago was that?" Henry asked.

"You ask my age," the king said. His eyes were still closed. "I have been king for more than three centuries." He snorted. "And only now have I walked into one of Nimroth's snares." Opening his eyes, he once again lifted up his hand. "A charm to identify a thief. How many pages did he burn, I wonder, before the madness came? How much ash did he sprinkle on the wind? But I have been discovered in the end. Even here."

"Here?" Henry said. "Where is here?"

"The Second World, the world of faeren, where we do not hide ourselves from men." The king's cheeks puffed. "The world you should not leave."

"What?" Henry asked.

Nudd gripped the arms of his chair, and it sank a little lower. He stretched his legs out in front of him, then reached over to the table and picked up Henry's baseball. He slapped it through the ash against his palm.

"The Blackstar is no bigger than this, but if you found the strength to shatter it, I cannot say how much evil you would free. Perhaps nothing. Perhaps the blood of Endor would turn to dust, and the undead would die. And perhaps a thousand incubi would ravage the world. Better to let the evil run through Nimiane's blood and addle her mind. In the end she will gibber, but her flesh in any rot and stink will still be prison to a darker thing."

"But I'll die," Henry said. His tongue thickened in his

mouth, and his stomach turned slowly before he could speak again. "The same blood is in me." He touched his face, the place where ash had fallen.

"Stay here," the king said. "And that hole will never grow. Stay as I have stayed, and your life will be as long."

"But my father," Henry said. "My mother."

"You will never see them again. But you will live." The king's voice was hard. His eyes were pointed and narrow.

Henry shook his head. "I can't."

"Why is this? Do you not fear death?"

Henry's head was spinning. "Of course I do. I don't want to die. But my father, my family . . . the witch will kill them."

"She will. But you will live."

Henry blinked. His mouth sagged open. "That's awful."

"Is it?"

"Yes, it is." Anger was returning. "My grandmother gave me everything she had left. My father will die for me, because he wants to save me, even if it means doing something impossible."

"What will you do for him?" The king's face was still. His eyes, piercing. "Will you die?"

Henry swallowed and shifted in his seat. Where was the strength his grandmother had given him? He felt clammy and foolish. "If I have to," he said.

"You do not have to," the king said. "I have said that you do not have to. You can stay in this world."

"If I stop the witch," Henry said quietly, watching his feet, "I can die. And I'll keep trying until she dies or I do."

The king let out a long breath. "Your grandfather said the same."

Henry looked up. His hand slid toward his collar and the necklace beneath his shirt. "When?" he asked.

"Before he was swept into the sea."

Henry shut his eyes and knuckled them hard. "Why hasn't Nimiane gone crazy? What's different about her? And don't tell me she's stronger."

"She's smarter," the king said. "She has better control of herself. She saw the madness in others. The more they consumed and held in themselves, the faster their minds splintered apart. She has gathered more strength and drawn more life than any, but she stores it up in tools and men like clouds full of lightning. She used wizards and witchdogs and filled them to their bursting destruction but held for herself no more strength than her mind could master. Even so, it, too, will shatter in the end."

"Will you help me?" Henry asked suddenly. "Believe what you want, but help me."

"Help you walk to your death?" Again the king's heavy brows rose.

"If you were going to try to kill her, what would you do?"

The king picked up Coradin's sword, and for a moment, the ash scattered. "Was this your only plan?" he asked. "A fingerling's sword?"

Henry nodded.

The Chestnut King drew the blade and squinted at its

vicious edge. "Nimiane is a guttering hole. This blade is like her. You cannot fight a hole with a hole, nor outdevour the devourer without becoming a greater evil. A hole must be filled and sealed." He stuck the sword in the ground in front of him and watched it sway. A gray circle grew in the grass around it. "In the land of my childhood, there was a story of a great armored beast, trebly scaled, with fangs the length of a man's arm. Its armor could not be pierced, and it devoured whole villages and dozens of knights and soldiers who thought to slay it. But one man, a farmer, took nothing but his scythe and went to face the beast. When it rushed at him, he leapt into its mouth, curled into a ball, and was swallowed. There was no armor on the inside of the beast's belly, and the farmer slew him from within."

Henry smiled. "I think I heard a story like that. And then he cut his way out?"

The king shook his head. "Perhaps when it was told to children. The farmer died within the carcass."

"Right," Henry said. "But he won."

"May you do so well."

Henry stood up. "Will you help me?" he asked again. "I mean really help me."

"What is it that you want?"

Henry looked down the steep hill and across the green pastures. He turned and looked at the tower that spiked its corners into the sky, parting the wind as it passed. What did he want? What didn't he want? He wanted the witch dead and his family safe. He wanted Endor forgotten. He wanted his mother's house back and her voice in the courtyard. He wanted to know his brothers and love his sisters. He wanted to live. He wanted to play baseball.

"I want you to send faeren to Dumarre. Put Fat Frank in charge of them. There are witch-dogs and fingerlings and thousands of soldiers for them to handle. I want you to take care of my sister and cousin and friend until I get back or . . . as long as you need to. I want you to give me a better idea than jumping inside the witch's mouth and curling into a ball. I want a sword that might work and . . ." Henry trailed off. He stared into the king's eyes. "I want the Blackstar."

"Son of Mordecai." The king raised his voice. "You ask me to send faeren to die in a world that is not their own, under the command of one formerly of the lesser faeren, cut from his magic, now in chains in the mound beneath us for disrespect to their king and their ways. You ask me to violate the law of this world and keep humans beyond the time allowed without bonding them to this world. You ask me for an answer that does not exist and a sword that cannot be, and for an ancient relic, the missing star of Nimroth, devourer of souls, purchased to myself with the lives of friends and brothers."

Henry nodded.

"You are a fool," the king said.

Henry nodded again.

Nudd, lord of the Second World, Chestnut King, snorted into his beard and then sighed. "Little green brother," he said quietly. "I find that I have love for you."

He cursed the ash ball, again scattering it into the grass. "Despite the gift you brought to me from Mordecai."

Henry laughed. "You'll do it?"

The king looked up. His grained cheeks were flushed. His eyes were angry. "There will be a price," he said. "Your sister, cousin, and friend cannot stay beyond another sunset if they hope to see their world again. That magicking is beyond my strength to control and is a protection to our world. As for the rest, I shall do as my strength is able, but the cost may be too great."

Henry waited, and the anger in the king's eyes became a sparkle. Laughter lined his temples.

"What is it?" Henry asked.

"If you live, in success or failure, you will return with Nimroth's star. You will sit at my right hand, and, when to meet my death I return to the world where you and I were born of woman, you will be the Chestnut King."

CHAPTER TWENTY-TWO

"What?" Henry asked. "No. I can't do that. You're human?"

The big man smiled. "A moment ago, you were ready to die, and you will not do this? I once was human. By birth I was a green like you. But I have long been faeren."

He held out his right palm, but Henry saw nothing. The king whispered, and a burn appeared. Henry watched the king's brand spread green leaves. In the center, purple bloomed in a bulb.

"A thistle?" Henry asked.

The king nodded. "But in the end, in this mound, the chestnut rules it all. If you did not know, why did you call me brother?"

"Because my father told me to treat you like a brother. Do the faeren know?"

"They did, but it has been long. Many will have forgotten. I was a young man with a young wife, burdened with our first child, when the faeren took me. I have walked free of this world once since that time, called by the naming of my son. I saw him christened, but no one threw the knife that would have freed me. My bonding to this world drew me back. Now I must go again. Death waits for me, and long have I put him off."

"But," Henry said, "why does it have to be me? Why not Jacques? Anybody. Don't you have any kids?"

The king smiled broadly. "You ask as I asked before you. Clovis was the first green king of faeren. They were rogues then, haters of the human world, curses with legs and arms and spite. He tamed them, though they have never noticed, and when I came, he made me king after him. The lesser faeren ran after their book and their committees and their rules so they might stay in the human worlds. The queene bowed her head to them and broke from me. Now I fade, but not before another comes."

Henry was trying to grasp what the big man had said, but none of it was making sense. "Why me?" he asked.

"Because I swore an oath to Clovis before me. I would be the guardian of the Second World and the ruler of faeren until I met another, my equal, and no faerie."

"I can't do it," Henry said.

"Why?"

"Well, would I have to stay in this world?"

"After your second sunset, yes, as I have, until you have crowned your equal and seek your death."

Henry shook his head. "No. I can't do that."

"You would rather die now? You would rather face the witch without my help, without the strength of faeren around you?" The king turned away and walked slowly to where the hill fell into its slope.

"No," Henry said. "But it doesn't have to be that way. You can help me and stay the king."

"I will not send one from among the faeren to give his life for you without the gift of your life in return. If you want my help, if you want the Faerie King to risk the Blackstar returning to Endor's hand, you will do this."

Henry looked down at his right palm and then down the steep hill at the chestnut groves. What chance did he have of living, anyway? And if he did, well . . . he probably wouldn't.

"Okay," he said. Nudd turned. "How long do I have to do it? I know you said until I die, but how long until I get to do that?"

"You will be king until you find your equal, not from among the faeren. Then you will see your own world again and draw your final breaths."

Henry swallowed, then nodded. "Today is my birthday," he said suddenly.

The Chestnut King smiled. "Then let us prepare you a sword and arm your faeren. A feast, an oath, a crown await your return. A song of sorrow, your loss."

Henry shoved his fingers into his hair. He wasn't exactly sure what he'd just done. "I hope you have a tree close to Dumarre."

"Oh," said the king. "I can do a prince of this kingdom better than that."

Coradin walked his horse through the quiet streets. He had ridden through fallen cities before. Dumarre felt no different. Faces peered out of windows. Doors shut silently. The markets were empty. The bodies of rebels lay in the gutters with only the birds and the dogs to tend them.

The girl behind him was awake again but silent. The air was flavored with smoke. The higher he climbed in the city, the more the wind from the sea cleared it away.

The brothers are inside the walls.

"Yes."

They will go first to the harbor.

"Yes."

Henrietta groaned. She had been in and out of consciousness since the finger-man had hit her on the slope above Hylfing. They had come out of another door in a hill, beside a ruined tower. By moonlight, she had seen two seas fenced apart by a long bridge of land. And now the sun was up, and they were in a city. An empty, smoky city.

"Yes," the finger-man said. She didn't know who he was talking to, and she didn't care. The other two horses, and Zeke's body, were behind them.

"Yes," the man said again, and he kicked his horse forward.

The pain in her bones with each bouncing clip of the horse's iron shoes on the cobbles was more than she could handle.

She twisted, but got only more pain. The horse's rump bounced against her ribs, and she wanted to pass out, to find that blackness again, but without being brained by a sword hilt. Henrietta bit her lip and squirmed and clamped her eyes shut. And then she held her breath. If she went long enough, she knew she would black out. Gasping, she failed and tried again. Her lungs burned, and she forgot her other pains. Her vision wavered, and the animal below her slowed and stopped, stamping its rear foot, sending shocks up its leg and into her body. The fingerling slipped off the horse, and Henrietta let her breath explode out of her.

"Where are we?" she asked. Looking down the street behind them, she could see the first ten feet of buildings but nothing more.

The rope between her wrists and ankles was cut, and her arms and legs swung free. She slid backward, falling off the horse. Strong hands gripped her, and she was handed to men in red shirts.

"To your queen," the fingerling said, and the red-shirts carried her through a gate. Henrietta tried to kick, but her legs were useless, and her arms were worse. She saw the fingerling climb back onto his horse and turn away. She saw Zeke hanging limp over a red shoulder, and then they were in a courtyard, surrounded by heaped-up columns and statued walls. They were carrying her beyond a fountain and into the shadow of intricate ceilings. They were climbing stairs, climbing and climbing, and then huge black doors were thrown open, and they were in a room. A cold room. A cold she had felt before.

"Prisoners, Empress. Children!" a voice shouted.

Henrietta's legs were dropped down to the floor. Hands gripped beneath her arms and dragged her forward through a silent crowd. Men with pale faces and tall collars, dressed in black. Women with ash for skin and gold dust in their hair, and gowns layered thick with night.

She was nearing a throne, nearing the cold. Henrietta shut her eyes as she was dropped onto her knees.

Something else crumpled onto the stones beside her. Breathing slowly, untying the knot in her stomach and wrestling the horror in her mind, she opened her eyes.

Zeke lay on his back. One of his eyes was swollen shut; the other was open, staring up at the ceiling. Black dried blood was crusted in his hair and around his ear.

Henrietta looked up at the throne in front of her. It was small, too small even for the old man who sat on it. He slumped over one of the arms. His eyes were shut, and drool dangled from his mouth. His clothes looked like they'd been stitched together from sacks. A delicate crown, a queen's crown, perched in the oily knots of his hair. Behind him, there was another throne, higher and bigger, intricately carved, with three serpents rising from its back.

On that throne, with a heavier crown on her head, sat Nimiane of Endor. She wore a gown colored like an angry setting sun, and her ringed fingers held her white-faced cat. The cat's eyes met Henrietta's.

"The first birds are caged," Nimiane said. "The others come. A new world comes."

Henrietta struggled to her feet. She looked from the cat's eyes up to the witch-queen's face. "You're a ghoul, not a queen," she said. "You look like a great big scab."

The queen smiled, but not quite at Henrietta. Then she

pointed at the wall. A soldier grabbed Zeke's ankles, and two others grabbed Henrietta by the arms. Iron cages lined the side of the room. Zeke was dragged into one, and Henrietta was thrown in after. A door banged shut behind her, and chains rattled into place.

She slammed her hands against the iron slats and shouted, "Mordecai will come for you! He'll find you!"

Laughter trickled through the watching crowd.

"Little wretch," Nimiane said. "Mordecai is already here."

Henrietta drew another breath, but the witch spoke again, a strange guttural tongue, and silence fell around her. The crowd was still laughing—she could see their eyes and open mouths, straining to seem more comfortable than they were, fighting against their own terror. But she could hear nothing. And she knew she could not be heard.

Slumping to the floor, she crawled over to Zeke.

"Ezekiel Johnson," she said. "You had better not be dead." His eye was still open, goggling at the bars above them. She closed it with her thumb and stuck two fingers on his neck. After a moment, she found his pulse, the beat of life, slow and soft. His heart still throbbed, but barely. "No dying," Henrietta said. "That's a rule."

Frank Willis crouched on the deck beneath the morning sun. Monmouth was at the tiller. Meroe was crawling around the guns. The others were all clustered with Frank, squatting in the aspens on the bow.

When the four sailors had come to, James had cut their

bonds and sent them out the death hatch. Land was not so far away now. The towers and walls of Dumarre climbed up out of the sea in front of them. Red banners were just visible, flicking on the wind. Empire galleys were clustered around the enormous sea gate.

The cry of orders crawled across the water from the small galley ahead of them. Oars were out and pulling. Signals flickered on the stern. The merchant ship seemed to be holding back, pushing farther out to sea.

"What is it?" Dotty asked. "Why haven't we turned?"

"We've tried," James said. He began to crawl away, back toward Meroe. "He cabled our galley to his," he said over his shoulder. "Couldn't see it in the darkness. Just beneath the surface until it climbs up into his stern."

"We cannot cut it?" Hyacinth asked. "We will go into the city?"

Frank tightened his lips into a smile for Hyacinth. Her hand was smoothing Isa's auburn hair. Her eyes were wet.

"Hy," Frank said. "It ain't over yet."

She looked at Frank and blinked slowly. "Your mother," she said. "Francis, your mother. I heard a whisper in my sleep."

Penelope straightened. Isa twisted and looked at her mother. Dotty pulled her knees to her chest and leaned against Frank.

"What did she say?" Frank asked.

"Good-bye," said Hyacinth. "To us all, but to you especially. Her recovered son."

Frank sighed. In Kansas, he had said good-bye to the

memory of his mother long ago. But that mother had been younger, and strong. He put his head down. He'd never expected to see her again, to find her alive, even if broken and blind. Mordecai spoke to her in dreams. He never could. He had the wrong kind of mind. But he'd had her smell again, her touch, her pinch, her kiss. For that, he had ached with gratitude. And now it was gone. What of his daughters, Anastasia and Henrietta? What of Henry? What of his brothers and his niece? How many had already gone ahead?

Looking up, he narrowed his eyes and stared past the wooden bow, past the sky and the world. And he saw nothing. He could feel Dotty's touch and Penelope's squeeze. He could hear Isa's tears.

James slid back up beside him. "It's time for a fight. Mother, you should take Isa belowdecks."

While Dotty and Hyacinth took their daughters below, Frank crept with James back to Meroe and the guns.

When Meroe nodded to Monmouth, the young wizard drove the tillers as far to the side as he could. The big green galley began to creep starboard.

"Farther!" James yelled, and he scrambled onto the stern to help Monmouth. Meroe and Frank put their backs against one of the big guns, trying to shift it in its housing. They needed to come almost perpendicular to the smaller galley if they wanted a shot at it or the cable that pulled them toward Dumarre.

The ship strained, moving forward awkwardly. And then the tension seemed to relax, and the green galley began to turn. The smaller galley had reversed oars and was doubling back.

James jumped down to his uncle and Meroe. The big man lowered a lit brand to a small hole in the brass serpent's back.

"Hold," James said. "Hold." Meroe lifted his hand while James bent over the big gun.

Smoke burst from the side of the smaller ship. Thunder boomed across the water, and something shrieked through the air above the green galley.

"Now!" James yelled, and he jumped to the side and covered his ears.

Meroe lit the charge. For a mere moment, the serpent hissed. And then it was a dragon. Fire erupted from its mouth. The galley shook, and planks popped free of the deck. James tumbled backward, and Frank staggered and fell. Only Meroe kept his feet, eyes on his enemy.

The smaller galley's center mast spun into the air. Sails toppled, but the oars stroked on.

The three men moved to the next gun.

"Which way?" Monmouth shouted.

"Straight on, lad!" Meroe boomed. "And keep your head down."

Again, smoke and thunder burst from the smaller ship. This time, the green galley rocked as its upper bow exploded. Wooden shrapnel whistled across the decks, but James clung to his brass serpentine gun.

"Now!" James yelled again, and he ducked away.

This time, there was no hiss. The gun belched its thunder, and its housing shattered in the blast. The brass beast kicked and cartwheeled over the side, taking mast and rail and Meroe with it. James slammed into the other gun. Frank rag-dolled up onto the stern and cracked into the ship's rail.

Monmouth dropped to his knees between the tillers. Only he saw the smaller galley crumple around a gaping hole at its waterline. Men streamed off the ship while it rolled to its side, taking in the sea.

"Frank?" Monmouth crawled to Frank's body and felt for a pulse. It was slow, but it was there. Jumping to his feet, he ran down the stairs. Before he reached him, James flopped onto his face, sputtering.

The deck hatch opened, and Hyacinth peered out.

"Come up!" Monmouth said. "Hurry. We got them, but Frank and James are hurt. Meroe's gone."

Beneath them, the galley began to tip. Timbers, cabled to a sinking ship, groaned in panic.

Coradin shifted on the back of his horse and looked around. Five hundred red-shirts—more than a third of them archers—held their positions around the wharf as the galley stroked closer. Only one had reached the sinking green ship before it had vanished beneath its bubbles, and he did not know what they had found. Hopefully, what his mother needed. Living bait.

Most of the soldiers stood in rank along the water, but smaller clusters had been placed in each street and along the city wall. Two dozen men with dogs and wolves on chains kept their own command, but Coradin watched them and knew what they sought. They would be the first to know when the green man gathered strength or prepared to strike.

And he was here. Somewhere. Waiting with Coradin, to see what the galley had salvaged.

Coradin looked at his brothers, also on horses, two with silver helms and chains like his, two with the black helms and the three-snake horn of the emperor's cavalry. He looked at the iron-plated wagon between them, hitched to two armored stallions, rippling, stamping warhorses. Ropes anchored the horses to cleats on the pier, and they strained against them. They knew their home and their path. There would be no driver.

The queen thought much of these Hylfing brothers. How could she not?

Breathing slowly, Coradin shut his eyes. He felt something greater than he could ever remember feeling, greater even than the rush of his first battle and the triumph of his first kill. She had made him strong. She had poured the strength of a dozen men inside him. And now she was feeding him more. He felt no pain, not from the burns beneath his helmet or the weed that had rooted in his chest or the weariness of his journeys or the agony of the mountain race the boy had run. When he turned or bent, he could still feel the steel tips of two arrows within his chest and belly. But they felt only curious and out of place. The others had come out easily.

Strength. It was good to be full. To be painless. To be the earth, ready to quake. He needed to feel a sword in his hand, to release some of the pressure within him, to clench a hilt.

As he drew the blade, the wind changed. It lost its salt, no longer crawling in on the back of the sea. And it was colder, the breath of mountains climbing down from the wilder heights of the sky.

The witch-dogs were moving, turning in place, straining wizard senses, tracking a stronger power.

Oars were in on the galley. Cables had been thrown, and sailors hurried to lash it to the end of the pier. A plank slid from the deck, and red-shirts, ready for their task, climbed aboard.

Coradin turned his horse away from the ship and scanned the walls. The wind was growing. Chop sprang up on the harbor's surface, and serpent banners snapped along the great seawall and above its gaping gate. The huge portcullis crept down toward the water. The harbor was closing.

The prisoners were on the deck, limp and dripping. Seven. He'd been told seven. They were on the pier.

Coradin nudged his horse forward.

Frank watched the silver-headed horseman move toward them. He saw half a thousand red-shirts on the wharf and in the streets and on the walls, and his heart sank.

Dotty sniffed. "I want all my babies to see Kansas again."

Frank opened his mouth. He wanted to make her promises, to tell her lies, but he couldn't. Instead, he leaned his face over into her wet, straggling hair.

"Dots," he whispered. "You're my life, and I've loved it." He drew in her smell, and she leaned her head against his lips. "Every kiss, every dirty look, every night we slept between clean, starchy sheets, and every night we didn't. Every nag and needle and nudge."

He sat up. "Your peaches," he said. "And your applesauce. How many pies do you think I've eaten in my life?" He looked down at her. "Not enough." He smiled. "If we get out of this, there needs to be more pie. That's all the complaining I've got."

"Stop it, Frank Willis," Dotty said. She sniffed and held Penelope tight.

No more pie, Frank thought. *No more anything.*

The horseman in silver approached, sword in hand. Sailors and soldiers retreated as the horse clopped around the red-shirts and reached the end of the pier, stamping.

Yells rose up from the city. A downburst of wind tumbled soldiers and raised a billowing plume of dust. Wolves were howling.

Coradin's horse reared while a dust cloud surrounded him from behind. Two of the prisoners had broken free and were running toward him. One was thin and pale, the other built like a young bull. Coradin brought his sword down at the bull, and his blade met and severed a shackle but found no flesh. From the other side, a knife dug into his back. The smaller man had ducked beneath the horse's pawing hooves.

The horse screamed and tripped, collapsing to one side. Coradin fell to the pier while the horse crashed into the water. A foot pressed down on his sword hand, and he grabbed the ankle and jerked the young man to his back. As he leapt to his own feet, the other, slender, with a blade twined somehow with green and silver light, slashed at his throat but found only iron collar and chains. Both struggled, but neither were a match for him. Their lives were his to take. With his boot on one throat, his blade went to the other.

Bring them to their cages.

Coradin clubbed the slender one on the head and ground the throat of the other, while the man kicked and slashed at his leg with a knife.

Red-shirts pulled the two young men up.

Walking easily against the wind, Coradin turned his back on the silent crowd of sailors and followed the prisoners toward the iron wagon, his blade still in his hand. The skirmish had only slightly eased the pressure within him, and while he walked, he could feel more funneling in, pouring through the finger on his skull. He looked at his blood brothers on their eager, prancing horses beside the wagon, and the witch-dogs, pacing the streets with wind-ducked heads. The archers would be useless in the wind. Perhaps that had been the point. Red-shirts even bobbed in the harbor where they'd been thrown by the first exploding gust.

Where was this green man? His would be a life worth taking.

Mordecai knelt on the rooftop with his eyes closed. The house was halfway up the harbor street, along the quickest path between ship and palace. He could feel his wife and his daughter, the struggling of his son. But his mind stretched elsewhere. He groped in the sea, and with its strength, he pulled down winds from the sky's roof, where storms are laziness and hurricanes are sleep.

"They have reached the wagon," Caleb said. "Pray Phedon and his men are ready. The streets all swarm with red."

"Signal," Mordecai said quietly. Straining, with sweat on his head beading and drying and beading again, he drew the strength of another gust and piled it down into the street. Opening his eyes, he watched Caleb draw his bow, a bundle of quivers hanging on his back. The flaming tip of an arrow kissed his knuckles, and he let it fly into the storm.

A moment later, a shout rose up from the streets. The doors of houses and merchant stalls and warehouses were thrown open. Men with sword and pike poured into the red-shirts, and Phedon, the emperor's son, in full armor, was at their head.

"All are in the wagon," Caleb said. "They will cut the

horses. Witch-dogs lead, red-shirts, pike and bow, sur-round. The finger-men press close to pace the stallions. The horseless one climbs onto the wagon. He rides a stal-lion in its harness."

"To the street," Mordecai said. "It is time." Breathing slowly, evenly, he stood. "How much would I give for an army of faeren?"

Caleb didn't answer. He walked in front of his brother to the stairs. Four flights down, they found their horses and the three men of Hylfing who had ridden with them in Endor. Mounting, Mordecai and Caleb took up their posi-tions in the street, the others beside them. The animals shifted their weight on the cobbles and whickered at the blowing dust, but the men said nothing. They sat, and they waited. And then, staring down the bent harbor road, they heard the feet and the howling and the heavy wheels on stone.

Caleb whispered to an arrow and then fitted it to his string. All but Mordecai held bows.

The first chained wolves came into view, and four of them tumbled whimpering in the dust. The rest were slipped from their chains. The wolves came snarling, one after the other pierced and falling, tumbling, dying, and the horses pawed the street. One reached Caleb. Twisting, his horse put a hoof into its skull. Arrows flew while wiz-ards flung their curses to bend the shafts away. The wizards were clumsy, weak city dwellers, but there were enough of them, and strength pushed from behind. The wizards parted, and a swarm of crossbow bolts flew up the street, breaking in the green man's wind, rattling against houses and twisting onto roofs. But not all of them.

Beside Mordecai, one of the horsemen collapsed into a wall, his horse with a bolt in its shoulder and a wolf on its rump. Mordecai poured all that he had gathered from the sea into the street in front of him. Cobbles exploded beneath the wizards, and the bearded men tumbled and flew backward into the red-shirt archers, slashed and beaten by whistling shards of stone. A wind, dragging plaster from the walls of houses and ripping away awnings, roared into the men with bows, shaking the iron wagon and blinding the horses.

From where he rode, with the stallion's anger beneath him, Coradin watched the green man work. He leaned forward against the wind and felt his body shake. He watched the wizards fall, but he had known they were weak. He watched the archers waste flights of arrows until the first horseman fell. The red-shirts pressed forward too slowly, afraid of four men on horseback barring the way. Afraid of one man who brushed their bolts aside.

You are wasting time.

Coradin slapped the horse beneath him with his sword. He urged it forward into the archers, butting and trampling through the red rows. His brothers stayed close beside him.

The stallion was mad beneath him, lips curled, neck writhing. An arrow glanced off its skull plate, and another sliced into its shoulder. Gripping his sword, Coradin guided the pair of horses toward the green man, and the two struggled to a gallop, the wagon bouncing behind them, four horsemen in black beside them.

It was the brother who came to meet them—the archer—drawing his horn bow as he rode, a knife blade in his teeth.

As they neared, Coradin raised his sword. The archer turned from him, and his arrow, lightning from the string, found the other stallion's eye. The horse staggered and tripped, dead even as it fell to its side.

The wagon began to twist. It would topple. Coradin's own horse leaned, turned.

With one slash, Coradin cut the dead horse free, and the wagon rumbled on. Two of his brothers had fallen to the street, and another of the horsemen. They had reached the green man, and Coradin raised his sword to throw.

Come, and he will come. Reach me.

Arrows flew for Coradin's horse, but its armor held. Its rider's sword flicked shafts away.

A burst of heat from the green man lifted Coradin from the horse. He hit the wagon and spun, bouncing in the street. Red-shirts swarmed around and over him. The wagon raced on.

The fight left him behind, and he stood slowly among the bodies of whimpering wolves and wizards. Red-shirts, motionless or groaning, lay on the cobbles. More smoke was swirling in the air. Turning, looking down the hill toward the sea, Coradin saw flames rising above the roofline.

The wharf was burning.

CHAPTER TWENTY-THREE

Henry sat in the room where the king had left him. Shelves heavy with books lined the walls. The room was bright, thanks to the yellow glowing chestnut clusters that covered the earthen ceiling. He was deep in the mound, in the Chestnut King's personal chamber. Behind him, the king's bed began as a tree, but branches flared out from a trunk base and held up an enormous mattress. Thinner limbs and leaves rose to the ceiling around the edges. Henry wasn't exactly sure how or where the broad man would get in. But right now, he didn't care.

A rectangular box sat in front of Henry, grown from a chestnut. He had not been able to see any seam or hinge, but a lid had fallen open at a word from the king. Now Henry sat alone, staring at its contents. Brittle leather was packed tight inside, and in that nest there was a single egg, smooth and round and black as emptiness. Faint white light wavered around its edges like flame. Nudd's ash had left him here, swallowed silently by the flame.

Henry held out his left forefinger and stuck it in the white light. He felt nothing. And then, gently, he touched the Blackstar.

He had expected cold, but nothing like what he felt. The blood in his finger stopped moving, and he felt the skin on its tip begin to harden.

Jerking his hand back, Henry squeezed his finger. It hadn't felt evil, not the way that Nimiane's cold had felt. It hadn't pulled at any of his life or strength. But it had stopped both.

Henry tucked his cold finger underneath his leg and held out his right hand. He watched his dandelion grow. It had no fear of the white light or of the stone. The star was a prison to evil, and evil lurked within it, but it was not evil itself. Henry pressed his palm against it, and his heat remained. He gripped it and picked the stone up. His dandelion surged and bloomed around it. The white halo of light mixed with the gold, and the green leaf blades flattened against it, twisting over its surface.

The door to the room opened, and Henry quickly dropped the stone back in the box.

"Henry?" his sister's voice asked. He spun on his chair.

"Henry!" Anastasia ran toward him, bouncing. She threw her arms around his neck and then jumped back and laughed.

Una walked toward Henry, smiling. His small sister looked tired but happy. She looked like their mother. Her arms went around him, and she squeezed hard and long. His ribs popped.

"I know you're not," she said. "But you seem bigger."

"I feel smaller," Henry said, but he wasn't sure if that was true. Not right now.

Richard had come in behind her. He stood stiffly in front of Henry, nodded, and stuck out his hand to shake.

"Henry York, I am greatly relieved to see you alive," he said, and spread his thick lips in a wide smile.

"Henry Maccabee," Anastasia said. "His name is Maccabee, Richard Hutchins."

Henry laughed. "I'm glad to see you, too, Richard."

Anastasia grew suddenly serious. Henry's laughter died.

"Is Henrietta alive?" she asked. "You went into the fire for her."

"Yes." Henry grinned. "She's in Hylfing with Zeke."

"Zeke?" Richard asked. "What is Ezekiel Johnson doing in Hylfing?"

"It's a long story," Henry said. "Too long for right now."

"Grandmother?" Anastasia asked.

Henry looked at her. "What?"

"Did you save Grandmother?"

"I did," Henry said. "For a little while."

Anastasia's eyes widened. "For a little while? And then what?"

Henry looked from his cousin to his sister. Both were very still.

"And then she saved me," he said. "And she's gone."

Anastasia slumped into Henry's chair. Una stepped beside her and put her arms around her little cousin's shoulders.

"My condolences," Richard said. "I am very sorry."

Through the doorway, the sound of voices and feet and yelling tumbled into the room.

"I'll be a wizard first!" a voice shouted. "Before I'll be made a jigging little chestnut farmer!"

Jacques stepped into the room, followed by four large faeries carrying a stiff-bodied but shaking and shouting Fat Frank.

The limb-locked Frank was tipped onto his feet and stood rocking like a jostled bowling pin about to fall. "Your fat-faced king has claimed me, and that's his right! But I'll not be swearing any oaths or dancing through your ritualing!" Frank's eyes shot around the room. "Henry?" he asked. "Poor lad, the chesty nuts have trussed you as well?" His eyes widened. "Have you been a day? Do not be staying another." He nodded at Richard and the girls. "Get that lot gone and hop to, or they'll be bonded. It'll be this world and no other until their hearts break or their minds crack."

"Let him go," Henry said.

Jacques snorted, tugged his mustache, and stepped dramatically toward Henry.

"Greenling," he said. "Hold your tongue if you'd like to keep it."

Nudd, the Chestnut King, loomed in the doorway. He carried Coradin's sword in one hand and a bundle in the other. "Jacques," he said. "Arm yourself and form up the ranks in the hall."

Jacques blinked, opened his mouth, and then shut it again. Turning, he and the other faeren stepped out through the doorway. The king shut the door behind him. Breathing heavily, his face shone with recent effort.

"What king holds children?" Frank asked. Nudd turned slowly. He gestured with a single, thick finger. Frank's limbs fell loose, and he staggered forward.

"Put these on," the king said, handing his bundle to the faerie. "And quiet your awkward soul or I'll be forgetting a bargain made."

Turning to Henry, Nudd held out Coradin's sword. "I have not labored so hard in my long memory. The blade has been turned. The hole has been filled. No longer does it gutter and suck, though it will kill you no queen."

Henry took the sword. Heat rushed up his arm when he gripped it. Drawing the blade, he blinked. It was the same curve, the same vanishing edge, but it whispered with gold, and as it moved in the air, it took on some of Henry's life, tracing fast-vanishing colors as it passed. Henry laughed and sheathed the sword. He handed it to Una and turned, poking the drawstrings of his hoodie back over his shoulders.

"Could you tie it for me?" he asked. "And at my belt."

"Henry?" Anastasia asked. "What's going on?"

"I'm going to Dumarre," he said. "I have to kill the witch."

Una tugged the first knot tight and then turned Henry around, looking into his face. "Why you?" she asked. "Where's Father?"

"I don't know," Henry said. "I hope he's there, and Caleb, too."

"Excuse me," Richard said, facing Nudd. "I'm going to need a sword."

The big king laughed. "I have no other. You must carry arms like Franklin." All eyes turned to Frank. He was adjusting a smooth breastplate, glistening like glass but grained like the shell of a chestnut. It looked like it had sucked on to his shape. A tree-grown chestnut mace, triple-knobbed on top with green spiked konkers, hung in his belt. He looked up and scrunched his face around his knob-nose.

"Henry York," he said. "You and I have been a-brawlin', but going for the witch is something else then. You've a surety about this?"

Henry nodded. "Yes. Well, maybe. I hope so. But you don't have to come. I mean, I assumed you would. But I'd forgotten about your magic."

Frank glared at him.

"You don't have to," Henry said. "That's all I'm saying."

The former faerie faced Henry and put his hands on his hips.

"Fat Frank don't have to? Just because I'm yellowing? Don't be forgetting that I saw you yammering in your first fight, nothing but a lump waiting for death to sit on him. Now you think you'll go a-warring without me? You wouldn't make it as far as I can fall."

Muttering, Frank turned away and cinched up his belt. "What do I have to lose, then? Come good or ill, I'll be chalk in a ditch before the moon wanes."

"Brother green," the king said, ignoring Frank. "You have your sister, your cousin, and your friend beside you.

You have Fat Frank and a blade remade. You have the Blackstar, and a faeren troop awaits you. Is our bargain binding?"

"It is," Henry said, and his heart beat cold.

"The Blackstar?" Fat Frank looked from the king to Henry, his big eyes wide. "The Blackstar?"

"What bargain?" Una asked. She squeezed Henry's arm. "You made a bargain with faeries?"

"Excuse me," Richard said. "When do I get my mace?"

"I want one, too," said Anastasia.

Something thumped against the door.

"The Blackstar?" Frank asked again. "Nimweasle's Blackstar?"

Una stepped around in front of Henry, forcing him to look into her eyes. "Henry, what bargain?"

Again, the door thumped, and the Chestnut King threw it open. The raggant walked into the room, and Beo leapt in beside him. Behind them both, two rows of bizarrely armed and helmeted faeren stood stiffly. Jacques stood in front.

"Rags," Henry said, and he turned to the king. "He looks great."

"We tended to him," the king said, and nodded. The two lines of faeren moved into the room, crowding Henry and the others back into the wall. Richard pressed up against Henry on one side, and the girls on the other. Fat Frank stood defensively in front of them. The raggant climbed up onto the table and sat beside the Blackstar. Beo sat in a corner and watched with ears up. The faeren each wore a breastplate like Frank's—deep, glossy, grained, and sucked on to their different shapes. And they each carried an oversize chestnut mace, though only Jacques and Frank held maces with three knobs. And they were all—all but Frank—wearing green spiked helmets to match their maces. The room was restless with breathing, and the faeren lines still overflowed into the hall. The king waded through them like a great, bearded, floating island until he stood beside Henry. He set a green disk covered with spines on top of Frank's head. It molded and shaped itself to the faerie's skull, flaring out below his jaw and rounding above and around his eyes. A long spike crawled down above the faerie's nose, almost to his lip. When the helmet had stopped growing, it creaked and crackled and hardened in place. The tips of every spike tightened and browned.

Richard cleared his throat, but before he could speak, the voice of the Chestnut King boomed over the spiked helmets.

"Soldiers, faeren of Glaston's Barrow, brothers to the king, we go to war, we cross boundaries into the territory of the queene."

The faeren cheered, and the king raised his hands. "We cross boundaries between worlds. Again, Endor rises. Nimiane, witch-queen, enthrones herself an empress in Dumarre. We will strike her down."

The room was silent but for Beo's panting and the sound of faeries shifting on their feet.

"King," Jacques said. "Is this our fight? Can her evil reach us here?" Mutters and whispers moved through the room.

Nudd's face flushed, and his beard rose and fell with the heaving of his chest. "Silence! Jacques is in the right. Her evil cannot reach us here. Let us burn the ancient three-mace trees and close off the ancient ways. Tear down the tower, the crown of our barrow, and let us hide ourselves from evil. Let no one leave the mound, and if evil grows, we shall flee farther."

The king chewed on his lower lip, glowering at the room. Every pair of faeren eyes was down. Jacques, where skin peeked out of his helmet, was pink.

"No!" Nudd roared. "Let evil hear the pounding of our feet! Let evil hear our drumming and our chanting songs of war. Let evil fear us! Let evil flee! In any world, may dark things know our names and fear. May their vile skins creep and shiver at every mention of the faeren. Let the night flee before the dawn and darkness crowd into the shadows. We march to war!"

Nudd threw his arms up toward the ceiling, and the chestnut lights surged into a blaze. The shout that rose up with the king's thick arms forced Henry back into the table. Fists and maces climbed with the yelling voices, and the faeren of Glaston's Barrow began to stomp in time. Henry blinked in shock and felt his sister and his cousin grab at his shirt. Fat Frank's cry rose up louder than any other, and his mace swung laps in time with the drumming of his feet. The raggant's wings were flared, and

Richard, flushed red with shouting, pounded his fists against the earthen wall.

He was the last to quiet when the king raised his hands. The room was more than restless now. Helmets bounced and feet tapped. Maces rolled across breastplates.

"An age ends," the Chestnut King said. "As you have known, I will not be with you long. My centuries have past, and another rises to lead you. You see before you Maccabee, called Henry, dandelion green, seventh son to Mordecai Westmore, seventh to Amram Iothric—before him may the witch-queen fall and Endor green! Beneath him may the roots of Glaston's Barrow deepen, and the faeren peoples bloom, for he will be your Chestnut King!"

Fat Frank spun around and looked at Henry. Una grabbed two handfuls of his shirt. Richard, Anastasia, and half the room cheered.

"He's human!" someone yelled.

"Human by birth," said Nudd. "As was I, and the king before me. But he will not be human long, and this world will be his own." Reaching beneath his beard, Nudd removed a necklace and held it high—a solid ring of silver with simple hooked ends for a clasp. Pierced in the center, with its eye out, there was a single, perfect chestnut. Nudd hooked it around Henry's neck. "He is my heir," he said. "And he leads you to war."

"To war!" a small faerie yelled, raising his mace, and Henry almost laughed, recognizing Thorn. No one joined in.

Nudd took Henry by the shoulder and led him through the quiet crowd to an overloaded bookshelf.

"In happier times," he said, "there was a door connecting the royal chambers in the barrow of the king to the same in the palace of the queene. There is a three-mace tree in the hills north of Dumarre, but this will bring you there with greater speed. The former queene was a lover of courts and cities, and her palace has a doorway into Dumarre."

Nudd gripped the side of the bookshelf and pulled it, grinding, away from the wall. A wooden door, nearly black and covered with cobwebs, was inset into the hard earthen wall. It was covered with dusty carvings of rabbits and flowers, trees heavy with fruit, and two people who were apparently in love. Henry thought they would have looked better if they'd been wearing a bit more, but he had much bigger things on his mind.

"We're going into the Faerie Queene's bedroom?" he asked.

Nudd nodded. "That you are, lad."

The faeren eventually reformed their double column, beginning at the cobwebbed door. Jacques and Frank stood at the front, ignoring each other. Richard had been fully armed, and Anastasia, who had been given only a knife, stood between him and Una. At least she had Beo. The dog had always liked Henrietta better than anyone, but Anastasia seemed to be the next best thing. His big head was under her arm, and he was tall enough for her to lean on his shoulder. She had already told Richard that his lips and his helmet made him look like a puffer fish, and even though she'd been right, Una had made her apologize. Everyone was waiting for Henry. He had left the room with the fat king, and when he walked back in alone, he looked pale, and he'd tucked his new necklace into his sweatshirt. A chestnut breastplate had been sucked on to him, but he'd refused to wear the helmet. Watching him move toward the door, Anastasia felt pride bubble up inside of her. It was hard not to be proud. He was her cousin. They shared blood. And he'd been smart enough to realize that he'd look stupid in one of the faerie helmets.

Henry reached the front of the double faeren column and looked back. He'd thrown up in the hall, but only the king had seen him. Twice. But he hadn't cried. There wasn't any point, and he'd felt too sick. This was it. Win or lose, dead or alive, he was done with his world. He puffed out his cheeks, looked at Fat Frank, wished he had a mint or some gum, then looked back at all the waiting faeren. He cleared his throat. He couldn't just open the door and march in. What were all these faeries thinking? He was supposed to be their king? He was nothing next to Nudd.

"I don't want to be your king any more than you want me," he said. "But I made a promise." He swallowed. "I just want to fight beside you. And I want to kill the witch."

"Up, Henry!" Thorn shouted, and this time, voices joined in. Fat Frank began to stomp, and every foot found the time. Henry smiled. He had one hundred and sixty-four faeries, armed and marching. If he had to die, it was a good sight to end on. He looked at his sister and his cousin and Richard, the faeren warrior. He wished there was somewhere safe for them, somewhere better than a battle. But he'd left fingerlings in Hylfing, and there was nowhere else for them to go. If he had his cupboard, he could send them to Kansas. If he lived and one of them didn't . . .

Fat Frank began to sing, chanting as he stomped, and while Henry had never heard the song, the faeren knew it well. They all joined in—even Jacques—and dirt rained down from the ceiling.

> *How mighty were the faeren kings*
> *who cropped the wizards' beards*
> *and stole away the giants' rings*
> *and pierced Behemoth's ears?*
> *Old Alfred fell, but the faeren stood,*
> *run plead for help in the wizard wood,*
> *the faeren go to war, to war,*
> *the faeren go to war.*
> *Hide all the beasties,*
> *warn all the priesties,*
> *the faeren go to war.*

"Henry!" Una yelled beside him, as the walls and ceiling shook. He turned and looked into his sister's worried face. "Happy birthday."

He tried to smile, but couldn't.

She shook her head. "That was no bargain."

"I know," he said, and he shouldered open the door.

Wood splintered and snapped, glass shattered, and Henry staggered into a bright yellow room before tripping on a toppled hutch and falling onto soft carpet.

Rolling onto his side, the voices and the stomping grew louder, and the faerie column marched in after him.

Henry reached his knees and looked back at the wall. The door had torn through some kind of plaster and knocked over a hutch full of crystal. Henry sneezed. By the smell of it, there had been perfumes.

"Hello? Who are you? What's going on?"

Henry turned and saw, sitting primly behind a delicate desk, a young faeren girl laced up in one of the most awkward dresses he had ever seen. Her face was pretty but powdered to a shade of death, and a gold lace crown looked bolted to a coil of red braids on the top of her head. An old skeletal faerie, with big glasses on his nose and wearing a long black coat, bent over her desk, pointing at papers. He must have been more than deaf—neither Henry nor the crash nor the chanting, stomping faeries seemed to draw his attention.

"Here, Majesty," he said, tapping the desk. "Your seal here as well."

"Excuse us!" Henry shouted. "Where's the door to Dumarre? We'll just get out of your way."

The Faerie Queene stood up and walked out from behind her desk. The old faerie didn't notice. He turned over another parchment and began tapping his bone finger.

"Who are you?" the queene asked again. Henry stood slowly. Fat Frank leapt in front of him and dropped to one knee, tugging at his helmet, but it wouldn't come off his head.

"Majesty," Frank said, "I am humbly, and often faithfully, your servant. I have had some difficulties with a district ruling . . ."

"Rise," the queene said, and tapped Frank's helmet. "With whom do I speak?"

Frank stood but kept his chin down. "You speak to the future Chestnut King on his way to war."

"King?" the queene asked. Her eyes grew. "War?" She looked at Una and Anastasia and then back to the armed faeries.

"Yes," Henry said. "I don't really have time to explain, but we need a door to Dumarre. I heard there was one in your palace."

"There are several," said the queene. "Long out of use but not so long as the door you have just entered. What part of the city?"

Henry tried to think. What parts were there? But the thumping and shouting were too much. "Hey!" he yelled back at the faeries. "Hold off for a minute." The columns quieted, and more than a few of the spiny-headed soldiers looked disappointed, especially those standing on the back of the broken hutch. "The harbor." He'd leave some of the faeries there to stop the galley. If they'd beaten it.

"Which harbor?"

"The one, on . . ." Henry scratched his jaw.

"The western sea, Majesty," said Fat Frank.

She looked at him and smiled. "My name is Alma."

"And mine is Franklin, Majesty."

"Okay," Henry said. "We need whatever doorway is closest to the western harbor."

Small, armed faeries in puffy, short pants thundered up a flight of stairs and into the queene's room. They stopped, panting, staring at the columns of faeren sticking out of the wall.

The queene turned to her guard. "Escort them to the second courtyard, the southeastern door."

Confused but obedient, the guards turned.

"Here, Majesty," the old faerie clerk said. "Set your seal here."

"Wait." Alma, the queene, smiled at Una and Anastasia. "Do they go to war as well? Will you return this way? I am not often allowed the pleasure feminine guests can provide."

"They can't stay," Henry said. "They're human. They'll get bonded, won't they? Stuck? Can't ever go home?"

The queene laughed. "Maybe in the Old World but not here. This palace is built with common mound magic, hidden in the human world, attached to the old. No one wants to snatch them up."

Henry looked at his sister.

"Please?" Anastasia asked. "Henrietta's met a queen before."

There was no joy in Una's eyes when she nodded at her

brother. Even less when he nodded back and began to turn away. She knew what he faced, and she knew the cost of losing. Now she knew the cost of winning.

"Brother," she said, and he stopped. Beo turned in a circle around him. "You are strong, Henry. Like our father." She raised her hand, and he raised his.

"Good-bye, Franklin," the queene said, and Fat Frank nearly burst off his breastplate, folding himself in half, bowing as he backed down the stairs.

The line of faeren moved through the room, smiling, waving, and hopping, while the queene and the two girls watched.

Una sank to the floor. Anastasia looked down at her and then dropped beside her. She knew the risks, too. Or she thought she did.

"Henry will win," she said. "He'll be back. Zeke beat the witch once with a baseball bat. I saw him do it."

Una smiled at her cousin.

"You know," Anastasia said, "we should have just killed the witch then. I had a knife. I could have done it. Penny wouldn't let me."

"It wouldn't have worked," Una said. "The witch isn't like us."

"Maybe," said Anastasia. "Maybe not. I shouldn't have listened to Pen. I should have tried."

"If you'd gotten her blood on you, you'd be dead."

Anastasia sniffed. "Henry got her blood on him, and he's not dead."

"Henry's strong," said Una.

"Up," said the queene, smiling above them. "I can't have ladies as guests talking about blood and death on the floor of my chambers. What shall I show you?"

In the second courtyard, three fountains burbled. The queene's palace had been a strange cross between the wildness of the mound Henry had explored and escaped with Fat Frank's help—bending passages, swirling confusions of stairways, magically tangled—and something orderly and marbleized, more like a museum than anything else. At least it seemed like it was supposed to be orderly, but that wasn't really something that worked for faeren. Even the straight hallways had a little rise and fall or bend or narrowing. And the second courtyard was actually on a slope. Two different doors could have passed as the southeastern, but only one of them had smoke trailing in at its sides.

Henry nodded at the puffy-panted guards, and the door was opened. Coughing, tugging his sweatshirt up over his mouth, he stepped out of the doorway and onto a narrow cobbled street. Below him, the harbor was surrounded by flames thrashing in the wind. Every building around the wharf was burning. A dozen barges, loaded down with goods and people, poled toward the sea gate. Others, too slow, sank in flames. The water was full of swimmers. Bodies of red-shirted soldiers were scattered in the streets. From all over the city, alarm bells rang.

Jacques and Frank stepped beside Henry while the column filed into the street.

The galley, even if they had beaten it, wouldn't be coming here. But the galley had already come. The fight had started, and he knew his father's wind.

"The war begins without us," Jacques said.

"No matter," said Frank. "We bring the finish."

Henry turned up the street, and he began to run.

CHAPTER TWENTY-FOUR

Frank banged his aching head against the side of the wagon as it bounced through the streets. Wind whistled in the gaps, shrill enough to be heard above the clatter and the shouting and the howling. Monmouth was unconscious but breathing. Hyacinth held her son's head on her lap while he dragged in painful breaths, and Isa ran her hands through his hair. Frank's arms were around his wife and daughter. He'd tried to fight when James and Monmouth had attacked the fingerling, but he hadn't done much good. He'd blackened a soldier's eye and received a cracked rib for his trouble. He bounced again and slammed his back into the wall, and then the wagon was tipping, leaning to the side. With a crash, their box-cage hopped in the air, then shook and rocked as it landed. They'd been righted, and the wagon raced on, even as an invisible body tumbled across the roof.

When the wagon stopped, the shouting lessened and then finally faded completely. Someone thumped on the outside, and chains rattled loose. The small hatch opened in the back, and two helmeted men in black, fingerlings, grabbed Monmouth's ankles and pulled him out. When he was gone, they reached for James and pulled him away from Hyacinth and Isa.

A silver helmet with black eyeholes leaned into the wagon. "Out," it said. "Quickly." He reached for Penelope's leg, but Frank kicked his arm away and slid himself toward the hatch. The fingerling grabbed his feet and jerked him out of the wagon. He bounced on cobbles, and for a moment, with his vision blurring, he lay still, staring at the smoky sky. They were in a walled courtyard. On one side, the mounded roofs of a palace grew into broad-shouldered towers. Two red-shirts gripped his arms and lifted him to his feet. The girls and their mothers were lifted from the wagon and handed to soldiers. Penelope kicked a fingerling and landed her other foot in the stomach of a soldier before her arms were pinned behind her back.

As they were dragged through the courtyard, Frank looked back over his shoulder at his wife and his daughter, at the wagon and the arched gate beyond it. An iron portcullis had been dropped, and men in red lined the street. Huge wooden doors were closing from the outside.

The soldiers dragged them up stairs, down corridors, and up again.

Black doors were thrown open, and a crowd of terrified, pale-faced courtiers scrambled to clear a path.

Frank's eyes hardened, and he forced his mind to calm. Nimiane sat on the emperor's throne in a blaze of scarlet. A drooling old man sat in front of her. Frank straightened and managed to get his feet beneath him, trying to walk tall between the soldiers.

"Francis," the witch said, and her laughter was sweet. "And Dorothy. Again we meet." Her eyes lifted. "Lady Hyacinth," she said. "Lovely Hyacinth. Has your bloom faded?"

The crowd of courtiers was shifting, moving back toward the doors. With a crack that rattled the windows and stirred ash on the floor, the doors slammed.

"Nobles and ladies," Nimiane said. She leaned back and shut her eyes. "You shall not leave. I prepare an entertainment for you. Before your eyes, an ancient line shall be expunged. A tree felled, the root pulled, the ground plowed and salted. Are you not accustomed to seeing beasts encaged?" She waved her hand, and the soldiers dragged Frank toward the wall and a row of iron cages.

His daughter Henrietta, with a filthy face and lopsided curls, was standing at the door of the closest one. A battered Zeke sat with his back against the wall behind her.

"Henrietta!" Dotty tried to pull forward, but the soldiers held her back. "Henrietta!"

"Queen," one of the courtiers yelled. "The city burns!"

"Does it?" Nimiane asked. Noise died. A cage closed, and Frank was wrapped in a spell of silence. Monmouth breathed softly beside him.

Leaning against the bars, he stared at the witch-queen and the motion of her laughter—noiseless to him. She did not turn her head, but his eyes were drawn down into the eyes of a cat. He pulled back and watched Dots and Penelope hold hands with his missing daughter between metal bars.

She was alive. Even in all this darkness, that spark brought him hope. Henrietta looked up, and he smiled at her, the little girl he'd raised in the Kansas wheat.

Penelope cried, but Henrietta smiled back at her father. She'd gone into the fire and come out alive. The blaze was bigger this time, and they all were in it.

"Dots," Frank whispered to himself. "My beauty. Now, this is the worst trouble we've seen. Death's brink might just come and go."

Frank Willis sat down to watch his daughters and his wife. He felt heavy, ripe. A field of memories was ready for harvest.

The canals were crowded with barges making for the eastern harbor and the sea. The streets alongside them once again bustled with citizens, families, and merchants, come up from their cellars and down from their attics to make one last attempt to flee the city.

Coradin could see them from where he stood in the hilltop street outside the palace. They looked like ants dragging eggs from a ruined nest. Smoke filled his lungs, and faintly, muffled by the storm inside him, he could feel his eyes burning. He wanted to help them, to bring some order to their exodus or command the eastern sea gate raised. Why must the city burn? Why flames?

It shall be remade. The fire cleanses.

His two finger-brothers had moved ahead, pacing the wall around the palace. The Hylfing riders had been pulled down, struggling to reach the passing wagon. Five horses and three bodies. The green and the archer had escaped.

They will come.

Coradin knew this already. They would not stop coming, not while breath remained. His sword was drawn while he walked, and his eyes roamed the walls and roofs around him, studying every haze-clouded street. The wind should have lifted the smoke and cleared the air, but it didn't. It was pushing it down, trapping it low to the ground. Smoke. Fire. Grief. An ache inside him grew. He reached for it, a memory, but another mind, his queen's, forced it away from him.

When he comes, leave him to me. He knows what he must face.

Coradin reached the palace gate and stopped beside his two brothers, in front of the red-shirt ranks, crowded in formation with their backs to the gate and the empty street in front of them. The men seemed nervous, like animals stirring in a barn.

Smoke. Fire. They watched their city burn. They listened to the bells.

"Fingerling!" The voice echoed in the street, climbing palace walls. Coradin turned and saw the archer standing in an alley mouth, leaning on his bow. The man was tall and wore no armor. A short sword hung at his belt, and feathered flocks of arrows stood out above his shoulders.

"Am I expected?" he asked. "Do these bells peal for my arrival, or shall I knock on the door?"

Coradin stepped forward. "Where is your brother?"

"My brother?" Caleb laughed. "Must I always bring my brother? Am I not welcome alone?"

Coradin turned, scanning the walls on both sides of the street. He opened his mouth to speak but said nothing. Something else, an overwhelming presence, grabbed at his senses. The boy had come. The tie between them, thin and distant, suddenly thundered into place.

"Fingerling?" Caleb asked.

The boy was nearing.

Stone cracked and rumbled, and the soldiers leapt out of ranks. Vines as thick as thighs rose slowly up from the cobbles beneath them, and a thousand curling tendrils gripped the palace walls and climbed the wooden gate. The gate sprouted its own vines, leaves spread, grapes exploded in bunches, and planks popped and splintered.

As the soldiers ran, the gate and arch fell into the street.

Sweating and pale, but with anger in his eyes, Mordecai stepped out of the alley beside his brother, a short sword in his hand. The wind, dressed in smoke, roared down around them, and blind arrows rattled on the cobbles.

In the dust and the smoke, the brothers ran forward. Phedon, the emperor's son, and one hundred former red-shirts poured out of the alley behind them.

The faeren moved easily around Henry while they ran. Pairs ducked into side streets or buildings, slipping through doors or leaping in and out of windows. Breathing hard, but not as hard as Richard, Henry felt like he was surrounded by a flock of birds, darting and bobbing and circling and weaving, but always returning. Even Beo seemed to struggle with their pace, and the raggant, bleating angrily, had been forced to fly. The sun was high and blazing red, a bloody pearl beyond the smoke. The same smoke burned in Henry's lungs, and sweat rolled down his back beneath his hoodie. There hadn't been time to take it off.

Most of the buildings were empty, and they'd found no soldiers—no living soldiers. About halfway up the long street, there had been plenty of dead. Wolves, horses, redshirts, and wizards. Henry's heart had stopped when he'd seen his uncle's horse, and then farther up, his father's, but there had been no fallen uncle and no fallen father. More than that, he could still feel the wind changing, the wind being changed. And a moment ago, the ground had shaken. His father was alive and stretching himself, perhaps too far.

Jacques, well ahead, turned back and whistled at the mouth of a large cross street.

"Come on now, Henry York." Fat Frank loped beside him. "Grow some legs, lad. I'd forgotten how slow the tortoise runs."

Frank jumped in front of him, ran backward for a moment, and then turned and wound quickly up to Jacques.

When Henry reached them, both faeries pointed the knobbed heads of their maces up the sloping cross street. They had reached the highest elevation in the city. One hundred yards from where they stood, the imperial palace loomed. Its gate was gone, as were great slabs of wall on either side. Through the haze, Henry could see thick tangles of broad-leafed vines around the gap. There were no soldiers to be seen. The bells were louder here, drifting up from the eastern slope of the city. In the west, the peals had faded.

"That's your father's work," Frank said. "And worthy of the Old King himself."

Jacques looked at Henry. The faerie's eye wasn't even bloodshot from the smoke. Henry's eyes were dumping tears onto his cheeks, mixing with his sweat. Beo stood in the center of the street, with his nose on the ground. The raggant settled heavily beside Henry.

"You have your father's strength?" Jacques asked.

Henry shook his head and held up his forefinger and thumb an inch apart. "A little."

Fat Frank laughed. "Henry's strength is Henry's own. You'll see it blazing soon enough."

"Do we just go in?" Henry looked down the cobbled hill, down at the canals. The streets there were crowded. Here, only faeries jumped and twisted and hopped on windowsills.

"Was there another plan?" Jacques asked. "Or did planning have no part in this?" The troop of faeren had already moved forward, and Beo with them.

Henry didn't answer. He began to jog up the final slope, between high walls and through shadows thrown by spires. Fat Frank glided beside him, and the raggant's shadow led the way. Henry had seen this palace before, but in moonlight, and from the eastern side. Maybe. He remembered the witch-queen's hanging garden more than the palace. Squinting up while he ran, he couldn't pick it out anywhere in the groves of thick-trunked towers. In his dream, he'd followed the gray blood strand. He hadn't needed to see it.

"Tell them all to wait," Henry said to Frank. "Stay in the street. I go through first."

Fat Frank shot ahead, and when Henry reached the gap, all the faeries had gathered in a secretive mob, perched on the rubble and pressed against the wall. Even Thorn had beaten him, wheezing in the front. Two faeries propped up Richard between them. A few in the back were picking grapes from Mordecai's vines while they waited.

Henry stopped and put his hands on his hips while he caught his breath. "Right," he said. The faeren stared at him from beneath their spiny helmets. "From here we go as fast as we can." The back row began to snicker. Henry held up his hands. "Okay. From here we go as fast as I can. Inside, there will be fingerlings, five of them, I think." The faeren quieted. "And there are probably a lot of soldiers, and I don't know how many witch-dogs."

"We'll count them after," Jacques said, and Fat Frank grinned.

Henry continued. "And my family is in there, too. And the witch-queen." The ground shook, and more rubble tumbled into the street. Henry tried to ignore it. "Jacques and Frank," he said. "You find my family, wherever they are, and when you find them, you get them out. You don't stay one minute longer unless Mordecai or Caleb tells you to."

Jacques scrunched his lips and poked a finger into his helmet to scratch his mustache. "With all respect due to the necklace the little greenling wears, we came to a war, not to play at paddy grabbing." He turned to the mob behind him. "Lower mound!" he yelled. "Flax, command." A stout faerie lifted up his mace. "You get the family out." He looked back at Henry. "As for the rest, we stay to the finish."

"Fine," Henry said. "Once my family is free and Flax gets them out, the rest of you can fight where you will or go home." He pointed at Fat Frank. "Make sure they find my family."

"No, lad," Frank said, shaking his head. "That's for Jacques and his chestnut mob. I stay with you. We find the witch and pluck her beard."

"Frank," Henry said. "I don't even—"

"Hush yourself," Frank said. "Listen to those lions roaring in your blood. Even I can hear them. I know this wager. I know the odds, and I know the stakes." He pointed up. "By the time this bleeding sun has bubbled in the sea, the game will be played and the tale told. Where your feet stand when the sun has set, there will be mine. If your blood pools, it won't be pooling alone, and if there's nought left but a pile of ash, it will be the ash of Henry Maccabee and Fat Frank Once-a-Faerie." He thumped his green mace against Henry's breastplate. "We've stood the storm before, son of Mordecai. Now draw that faerie sword and let's to war. Your father labors."

Blowing out a long breath, Henry nodded and climbed onto the ruined gate. He stood surrounded by his father's vines as he stared into the courtyard spotted with bodies, more in red than not. He shoved his right hand down his shirt and gripped his father's necklace. With his left, he drew his sword. Heat flowed into him. Strength came to him through every sense and climbed up through his feet. His lungs and eyes forgot their burning—no fire fears the smoke—and he looked up past his father's leaves, up at the towers, up at the sun. He felt like he had at Badon Hill, first seeing the roar and glory of life. Beyond the sun, he felt darkness, and cold, and further light, worlds spinning, constellations laughing, galaxies whipping around their poles. Behind him, in front of him, the seas rocked in their beds. He could feel their vibrations; he could touch their strength. They offered it. He was an island in a storm. He could feel the witch drawing on his strength, digging in his jaw. He looked across the courtyard at the palace in front of him. He could see two storms warring inside. One building and growing and pounding, the other a great hurricane of gray, swallowing it all.

This world was not the witch's. She did not own the stars; she had not shaped the seas. Her storm could break. Somehow. It had to. Henry stepped down off the gate and into the courtyard battlefield. Beo ran ahead, and the faeren, shouting, chanting the war songs of their fathers, poured in after. Scanning the other side of the courtyard, Henry picked a corridor and turned toward it.

Coradin stepped out from behind the fountain, his blade arcing down.

Henry staggered to the side and threw up his own sword. The blades sparked, and the force of the fingerling's blow knocked Henry to his back. Two other fingerlings were with him, and already faeries, shimmering in the air, danced around their waists.

Whooping, Fat Frank leapt on Coradin's back and gripped his helmet by an eyehole, pulling it against the silver chains. The fingerling's sword flashed, and Frank tumbled, his helmet bald a few spines.

Coradin slashed at the shimmering air while one of his brothers fell behind him. Richard was there, swinging his club while a black helmet was ripped free. A finger was gone. Henry felt the witch's pain and saw Coradin waver and strengthen again, surrounded by the faeren mob. Two faerie bodies tumbled to the ground, visible and motionless. A cry of anger echoed in the courtyard.

Henry turned and ran. He had a bigger fight. But now men in red were pouring out of corridor mouths. Fat Frank settled into stride beside him.

"Wasps in the anthill, that's what we are," Frank said. Grabbing Henry's arm, he veered. Henry almost matched his pace, and they reached the side of the courtyard before the wave of red reached them. Jumping through a small door into a long hall, Frank slammed it shut and slapped his hand on the wood. Henry watched the grain harden and root its strength into the stone around it.

"Wizards'd walk through, but not these dullards," Frank said. "Up now, and over, I'd say."

Henry nodded. Jogging down the corridor with his sword in front of him, he looked in every door until he found stairs. They were wide, and he and the faerie began to climb side by side.

One floor up, the stairs ended. A window overlooked the war in the courtyard, and a broad corridor ran in both directions. As they turned to run, Henry jerked and fell, his sword clattering on the floor.

Needle-sharp cold shot into his head.

Pauper son, your father waits for you. Your mother waits for you. I wait for you. Why won't you come?

Henry forced himself onto all fours.

Come. I will not drink you here.

"Henry!" Frank yelled.

Blinking, Henry looked up. Soldiers were running down the corridor toward them. He pushed against the cold. He squeezed his heat around it. It lessened. It was leaving.

I will lead you.

She was gone from his head. He'd pushed her out. Or she'd left. Henry managed to stand and look down the corridor. The soldiers had all crumpled to the floor for some reason. Fat Frank was nudging them with his foot.

"What happened there, Henry?" he asked. "You yowl

like a kicked kitten, and then this lot drops over dead."
While Henry walked toward him, Frank bent over and
flicked a soldier's cheek. "All dried out, too."

Henry stopped and looked down at the soldiers. Six of
them. What had happened to their world, their lives? Had
they been cruel, kind, before the witch came? Frank
reached up and slapped at Henry's jaw. A cloud of ash
drifted down.

"Can't say I care for that," Frank said. "But hop along
now, Henry. Split the lickety, and we might still help your
father."

"She's got him," Henry said. "She's got all of them."

Glass shattered behind them, and the raggant tumbled
to the floor, snorting back to his feet.

Henry looked at the stubborn animal and then back at
Frank, just as stubborn, just as strange.

"Onward, Henry," Frank said, and Henry nodded.

The two trotted down the corridor, with the raggant
puffing behind. Henry didn't need to look for doors or
stairs. There was a hook in his jaw and a line to reel him in.
He could see it now and feel it tug, harder than it had in
his dream.

Henrietta stood. She was no longer kicking the cage door
or shaking the bars. Everyone had been standing, even
Zeke. Her father had Monmouth propped up, the wizard's
arm over his shoulder. But now most had slumped back to
the floor.

The fight had ended.

When the black doors had fallen in, she hadn't heard a thing, though the floor had shaken. Two fingerlings, one in a silver helmet, one in black, stood like statues beside the high throne. With one motion of her long arm, the witch swept the crowd against the far wall. The old man fell out of his chair.

Mordecai and Caleb stepped through the doors beside a pale man in armor. Mordecai's face was white and glistening with sweat. Caleb's left shoulder was dark with blood. A mob of red-shirts rushed in after them, but the witch raised her hand. Some of the soldiers crumpled awkwardly; the rest pushed back out of the throne room. The fingerlings didn't flinch.

And then the queen in scarlet smiled and turned to the cages. Her hand moved, and the silence lifted. "You should hear them," she said. "They should hear you." The witch laughed. "Long ago, I walked into the snare of boys. Now they step into mine. What choice did they have?"

When the attack came, she didn't move from her seat. Caleb's arrows were clouds of ash before they crossed the room. The windows rained glass down on the tangled courtiers, and the roof shook. Stones in the floor cracked, and more tumbled from the vaulted ceiling.

The pale man in armor fell first, and his body spun across the floor.

The queen laughed, and her face was flushed and full and eager. And when she finally stood, her scarlet gown quivered and flapped in Mordecai's winds, and white light, too bright, too thin for fire, danced around her out-stretched arms and crawled around the walls.

Mordecai fell to his knees.

Caleb rushed the throne.

Henry paused halfway up a flight of stairs. Frank stopped beside him. Behind him, the raggant snorted and flapped its goose wings.

"Rags, I wish I could make you stay." He turned. "You should go to Una and Anastasia. It's going to be awful for them."

"This place is . . ." Frank lifted up one foot and then the other, looking down at the floor. "It's almost alive."

Henry nodded and started climbing again. She was close. Very close, and she knew where he was. Stone throbbed around them, crowded with stolen life and lives. The walls were ready to crawl or explode. Henry tried to breathe evenly, to keep his stomach calm, but it was hard, and fear of what he would see didn't help.

At the top of the stairs, they stepped into a broad corridor. A tall, arched doorway had lost its doors.

A dozen soldiers turned and raised their weapons when they saw Henry.

"She'll kill you if you fight me," Henry said. "Go. Leave. Find your families and leave."

Henry and Fat Frank moved forward, and the soldiers lowered their weapons. But none of them left.

Standing there with red-shirts watching, Henry took

three long, slow breaths. He shut his eyes and listened to the raggant puff. He could smell Frank. He could feel the necklace hot on his chest and the sword warm in his hand. Reaching into his pouch, he dumped a smooth black sphere out of its bag and left it loose. And then, with his eyes still shut and his soul quiet, he walked into the ruined doorway. The throne room was silent.

"Pauper son," the witch said. "I grew impatient."

Henry opened his eyes.

The throne room was long. Men and women, mostly in black, huddled against one wall. A row of iron cages lined the other.

Henry saw his mother and his brother. He saw his sister and his cousins and his friends. His aunt and uncle. Henrietta was standing.

"Henry!" she yelled. "Go, Henry! Run!"

The others of his family turned their faces toward him and began to climb to their feet.

Henry shook his head. As his pulse beat slowly in his frozen jaw, he looked at the witch-queen, Nimiane, last in the line of Nimroth, blood daughter to the incubi. She sat on an enormous throne with a cat on her lap. She was dressed in the color of the smoke-red sun, her face was flushed, and her slender neck stretched long beneath it. She wore the emperor's crown, and her hands, hanging over the arms of the throne, flickered with white light.

On a smaller throne in front of her sat Henry's father, his body rigid, his head limp. Caleb lay at her feet, stretched out on the floor. Two fingerlings lay dead behind Caleb's body. One without a helmet, the other with a short sword rammed up the back of his.

An old man lay on the floor as well. A younger pale man, like the man Henry had dreamed between the trees in the garden, lay crumpled beside him.

"You bring your pets?" Nimiane smiled. "A faerie and a northern raggant. What has happened to you, little faerie? Where has your life gone? Your magic has dried?"

Fat Frank snorted.

Shouting echoed in through the doors. Faerie voices and the clatter of weapons.

"Pauper son," Nimiane said. "I am afraid that I must kill them all. I have killed too few today. All these lives collected, your family assembled for a final feast—I have shown too much restraint." She tipped back her head and inhaled slowly. The light from her hands danced around the walls. The cat's eyes found Henry's. "Tell me, pauper son, before I harvest the faeren, before I rouse your father to watch his seventh son die, why did you come? You have many portals. You could flee through the worlds and live a while. Why come to your death?"

Henry shifted, clenching the grip on his sword. "You know why," he said. "I come because of the words spoken when I received my name. I come because you are the darkness, and I am dandelion fire. You have seen me in your dreams. You know what I can do to you."

The witch-queen laughed, opening her eyes and leaning

forward. "What you can do? You who grow weeds? A drop of my blood kills you. What can you do? Mordecai! Wake!"

Mordecai's head snapped up, and his eyes opened. He gasped in his chair, unable to move.

"Here is your son," Nimiane said. "The first of many deaths that you must witness. Let us see what it is he hopes to do."

Cold, rushing sharpness burst through Henry's body, sucking at his soul. Henry's legs gave out, and he dropped to his knees. Pain screamed in every nerve of his body. His life was emptying in a rush, flooding out his skin, his eyes, his jaw.

Curled in a ball, Henry slipped his right hand into his pouch and wrapped his dandelion brand around the Blackstar as the world went dark.

Henrietta yelled when Henry fell, and then she stopped. Something was happening. A wind was rushing from Henry and swirling around the queen. The stones around his knees began to burst. Fat Frank grabbed on to Henry's back, ducking as shards rattled through the vaulted ceiling and against the walls. The raggant nosed between Henry's legs. Dandelions bloomed like fireworks around Henry, a ring of gold. The queen rose from her throne, and the blooms began to die. Yet more burst out of the floor around Henry. The ring died as fast as it grew, the edge flickering like a thousand tongues of flame.

Coradin backed into the throne room, and the doorway filled with faeren.

*   *   *

Coradin had felt the death of each of his brothers. The chains of his own helmet swung free from his collar and belt. They were still hot from the curse of a large, one-eyed faerie. His blade was black with their blood, but there seemed to be no end to them, appearing and disappearing as easily as they breathed.

He had held a flight of stairs against the faerie press, and when the soldiers around him had been cut down, he held it alone. When he gave up the stairs, he held the hall, where more soldiers had joined him and been cut down.

Battered and burned, he had backed his way through the palace, closer to the boy, closer to his blood mother.

And now he held the door to her throne room. Fewer of the faeries disappeared, and more of them were bleeding. The big, one-eyed faerie landed a blow on the side of his helmet, and Coradin staggered back. The faeren were past him, but their leaders tumbled to the floor in a wave, stiff and gray and motionless. More pushed in, and more fell, and the big faerie was screaming in anger, raising his arm to hurl a triple mace, but his body stiffened, slipped, and fell. The faeren were falling back. Racing down the stairs. They were gone.

Turn. Kill.

Coradin turned. The boy was on his knees, curled in a ball, with a faerie clinging to his back. Heat poured out of him in golden flowers and flame. Coradin looked up at his blood mother. She had left her throne. Her arms were raised, her face strained. Suddenly, she flickered and changed. Her beauty was gone. She was shrunken and old, skin hanging off bones beneath filthy rags. Her head was shorn and spotted with sores. She had no eyes, and her lids were raw with scratching. She was burning the boy and the faerie alive. Gasping, she lowered her arms and was again tall, again lovely, and her rags were again a gown of scarlet.

She pointed. "Kill."

Coradin moved to obey, his feet crushing soft flowers. The boy and faerie were still but flickering with golden flame. He raised his sword in front of him and set the whispering tip on the back of the boy's neck.

"No!" It was a woman's voice. A mother's voice. "No!" she screamed again, and a chorus of voices joined in with hers. Coradin shut his eyes.

Kill.

He raised his right hand to hammer the hilt down. He had done it before. He knew what it would feel like.

And he was in his house, surrounded by flames, by burning, surrounded by the death of all he loved.

"No," he said.

A mind ripped into his. Pain, more pain, too much pain. Smoke and fire in the back of his skull. He opened his eyes. His sword arm shaking, he reached up and tore off his helmet, and it bounced and rattled in the dandelions, silver on gold.

The faerie was stirring beneath him. The boy moved his head. His little blood brother was still alive.

Henrietta saw the witch shrivel, struggling against the dandelions. She saw the shape she had first seen in Kansas, the husk of undying evil. She saw the wave of faeries die in the doorway and flee. She saw the fingerling straddle Henry and set his sword on her cousin's neck. She heard her aunt Hyacinth yell, and she yelled with her. She watched the fingerling hesitate and the witch scream. She watched the helmet bounce, then she looked into the big man's face. Three notches stood out in the top of his ear, and tears glistened on his cheeks. While the witch shook with anger, the fingerling stepped toward her. He raised his sword to the knot of hair on the back his head. With his jaw clenched, he jerked the blade up, slicing himself free. His body crumpled forward. His blade clattered to the floor.

Henry opened his eyes and straightened. A weight slid off his back. He was surrounded by dandelions, and the witch, tall and furious, stood below her throne. Her cat sat by her feet.

Coradin lay on his face in front of Henry, his sword beside one hand and a finger, half-hidden in a tangle of hair, beside the blade.

"You cannot drink me," Henry said to the witch. Fat Frank groaned beneath him. Henry picked up his sword and rose to his feet. He drew his right hand from his pouch and held up the Blackstar.

The witch smiled, and her face wore surprise and relief. "I have drunk nations. You are just a boy with weeds in your blood. But why should I drink you, when you bring me a great gift, the seed of our people? Bring it to me, and

I will make you like Nimroth, undying. Together, you and I will rule the worlds."

Henry shook his head. His mind was quiet. His soul was quiet. Strength and weariness raced through him. His jaw tightened against the cold, he walked toward the witch. Fat Frank limped beside him.

Nimiane took a step backward, her white light crackling through the room, drawing the strength she had stored in the stones. She became a storm, a devouring hole, and the storm turned on Henry.

Henry felt the pain and the cold, but his legs did not buckle, and his eyes did not close. Henry's breath stopped, but he didn't need to breathe. He sent his soul's roots into the stone and the sky and the seas, and they burdened him with strength. Finally, he had stuck his bucket in the waterfall. He had opened his body to Niagara, but his body had grown. It had strengthened. His grandmother had reinforced it. He had the strength of his fathers', he wore the necklace of the Chestnut King, and his hand gripped the prison of a thousand incubi. He had a soul of green life and gold fire. He had a name.

The witch drew his flooding strength out, but still more poured in. His hand tightened on the cold Blackstar, and his heat closed in around it. The strange, cool prison in his palm was a still anchor in the madness.

Henry pulled his strength back from the witch. He sealed his roaring flood behind a wall built on the Blackstar. The thick gray rope between his face and the witch became a strand and then a string. It shrunk to a spiderweb.

And still the witch pulled, straining, fear and confusion on her face, and still Henry's roots grew. Life, the roaring, spinning, rushing life of the world, passed through him, and he dammed it up. It built a reservoir of pressure inside him. He felt his bones quiver and his tendons writhe. He was going to fly apart, shatter like glass. He could not hold himself back a moment longer, and yet he did.

Henry shut his eyes. He was a farmer with a scythe. He would leap into the beast's mouth, and he would take the world with him.

Henry exhaled and threw himself open to the witch. His body shook, and his jaw split, erupting life. The gray thread burst into a raging river. The river went gold. Henry's sword shattered, and he just managed to cup the crackling Blackstar in both of his hands. The star was alive, no longer cold. It was raging, thirsting, pulling at the witch with the strength of ages, long quiet but now awake inside the golden roar, yearning to imprison and destroy. Henry's mouth spread open, and his yell was swallowed up. With the last of his racing strength, he lifted his leg, his arm came around, and he pitched into the whirlwind.

The Blackstar flew, ringed with angry light, trailing fire. It flew with Henry's strength into the devouring storm. It flew blink-fast, and it flew straight. Lightning cracked. The star was buried in the witch-queen's chest. Thunder shook the walls, and splintering stones fell from the vaulted ceiling. The Blackstar exploded, rippling reality like still water, tearing a white hole in the world's seams. For a single moment, one thousand evils roared in freedom, and then the explosion folded in, devouring it-self, devouring the roar, devouring the witch's gray.

The hole healed. The ripples smoothed. The world went dark.

The city of Dumarre quaked. Walls shifted and cracked. Great bells fell from their towers, splitting in the streets with their final peals. The eastern sea rose above the wharf and climbed out of the canals. The western sea threw up great waves, and the seawall fell beneath them. Foam washed the streets.

The walls of the palace and the streets and the court-yards around it were mortared with dandelions, and the tower roofs bloomed with gold.

Inside the throne room, Henrietta blinked and shook her head. She was on top of Zeke, and they were piled against a wall. She sneezed. The air was sweet. And heavy.

Sliding off Zeke, she sat up. The bars of their cage were bent and split. She couldn't see anything else—the room was too bright. It was made of yellow fire.

"Wake up, Zeke." She slapped his leg and squeezed her eyes tight and opened them again. Again she sneezed. And again. The room was all dandelions—up the enormous walls and across the beamed ceiling.

She stood up. Where was Henry? Had the witch killed him? She'd seen him shake and pretty much explode. And he'd thrown something. Where was the witch?

Henrietta pushed out of the cage, still blinking. Her uncle Mordecai was dropping to his knees beside a body, and Fat Frank and the raggant were with him. Frank was sniffing loudly and sobbing. Henry, his arms spread, lay facedown in the dandelions.

There was pain.

There was sorrow and emptiness and loss. There was fury.

There was a single, twisting dandelion.

Take it away.

No.

Weed.

Yes.

You've died. You killed yourself like the finger-fool. You gave yourself to me. Me, me. I drank the world. Drink. Drank. Little fool. Little green fool. I want the marble. Bring it back. We don't die. Can't die. Bring it back.

The dandelion grew, and others grew beside it. The darkness faded, and the voice was lost.

Henry opened his eyes, and he pulled in a long breath, a breath that slowed and surged but wouldn't stop until his ribs creaked and his chest was bursting.

Lips touched his forehead. His mother's lips.

Hyacinth was smiling at him. He tried to sit up.

"Don't," she said. Her fingers were on his jaw.

Fat Frank's face loomed into view, pale and blood-less. "It's not over," he said. "Let him up. The witch scram-bled."

Henry was pulled to his feet.

"Can you stand?" Mordecai asked. Henry nodded and looked around. Dotty was beaming beside him. Uncle Frank had a wide grin, and he and Penelope were propping up Monmouth between them.

James, with a huge purple stripe across his throat, stood beside his father.

"Little brother," he said. "You and I are nothing alike."

Caleb and Zeke were both sitting, pale but smiling, with their backs against the lower throne. Beo's head was on Caleb's lap. The fair man was slowly peeling off his armor beside them. Henrietta and Isa both glowed behind filthy faces.

"I know you don't like us to hug you, Henry," Isa said. "But this isn't about you." She threw her arms around him. "Can I squeeze, or will you break?"

"A little," he said, and then he groaned with the pressure.

Henrietta grabbed his head and kissed his cheek. "Even though you cut my hair."

"How did you get here?" Henry asked.

"Later," Fat Frank said. "Later. Henry, where did she go?"

"Where's Richard?" Henry looked around. "Could someone find Richard? He was with the faeries in the courtyard, but that's the last I saw. And Anastasia and Una are with the Faerie Queene. I felt sick leaving them, but I thought we were all going to die."

"Now, now," Fat Frank said, pulling Henry's arm. His

fingertips were white. "That was a marvel, truly and for sure, but the witch ain't dead."

"Peace, Franklin," Mordecai said. "Let the boy breathe. The finish can wait a moment."

"But where is she?" Fat Frank asked. "She'll fly. She'll grow again and take another root."

"She can't," Henry said. "She's broken. But I'd rather find her now."

A few courtiers were picking themselves up out of the dandelions. Henry pointed.

"Make them help pick up all the faeren. And someone find Richard." Sighing, he turned to Fat Frank, but Mordecai took his shoulder.

"Must you do this?" he asked.

Henry nodded.

"Alone?"

"I'll go with Fat Frank." He pointed at the fair man by Caleb. "And he should come if he can."

Phedon picked himself up carefully and bowed. "I owe you the empire. I will come."

The climb was grueling. Henry's bones felt like paper. His eyes hurt, and his right hand felt run over. His jaw was burning, and the baseball thumped in his pouch. The gray strand that trailed faint gold from his face was thinner than a spiderweb and hard to follow. He kept losing it. Fat Frank was still impatient, but dizzy and weak on his feet. Phedon insisted on expressing his gratitude and running out of breath on the long spiral stairs. And then, near the top of the tower, Henry realized that he'd gone too far. The thread was no longer leading up, and they had to walk slowly back down the stairs, trying to find where they'd missed a turn.

The turn was a small window. Or it looked like one. When they opened the window, a door appeared, and they stepped out onto a small, unrailed balcony. Slung on its enormous chains, the hanging garden now leaned a little forward. Across the rope-bridge, a wooden door in the garden wall had been left hanging open.

They crossed the rope-bridge one at a time. Fat Frank hobbled out first, bouncing, testing its strength, and then Henry. Inside the garden, Henry couldn't help but be surprised how nothing had changed from his dream. He didn't know if he'd expected it to be in ruins, but he hadn't expected it to be the same fake-perfect place.

"Well, this is a bit of evil," Frank said. "These trees aren't trees at all, and they're not living on tree life, nor the grass. It's all stolen and stored and shaped into a wicked wrong perfect."

"It is very well balanced," Phedon said, and Fat Frank wheeled on him.

"Well balanced, like a slaving ship. The right number of lives to a bench and the right number of chains. Only this is worse. A slave on a chain is still human. I wouldn't be surprised if some of your slaves what went missing or fell down stairs are stuffed in these trees."

Henry had already begun walking through the grove, and the others hurried to catch up.

"Why did you want me to come?" Phedon asked, ignoring Frank's loud muttering.

"Your brother's here."

"Maleger? Is he alive?"

"I doubt it," Henry said. "But we'll see."

The black pool had overflowed to one side because of the garden's new angle, but nothing else had changed. Nothing, until Henry reached the little clearing and Nimiane's bower.

The two trees that had held the man's hands had both died. The trunks were ashen and peeling. In between them, in an awkward pile, his feet still in the earth, was Phedon's dead and fingerless brother.

Phedon dropped to the ground beside him. Fat Frank and Henry moved into the bower.

On the couch, with her legs curled up and a dead cat clutched to her chest, was Nimiane, witch-queen of Endor. She was tiny and shriveled in her rags, a blind and hairless monkey.

"Pauper son," she whispered. "Pauper son grew fire inside us. Fire. The marble ate our blood. It drank it up. Where is our blood? Make the marble give it back." She coughed, wheezing.

"She's dying," Henry said. Frank moved closer, staring at the witch's head, at her swollen sockets. Suddenly shivering, he backed up.

"Not dying," the witch hacked. "Don't die. We don't die."

"Nimiane," Henry said. "You are."

"No!" the witch shrieked, and she lunged from her couch. Her nails dug into Henry's chest and groped for his throat. "No! There are drops left. They will grow. Give me yours."

Henry gripped the witch's wrists and twisted her down to the ground. He felt her, even now, gathering the strength she had stored in the garden. That was her life, all that was left of it. Her skin began to chill, and Henry's jaw ached.

"Nimiane, peace," Henry said, and he gathered himself. He pressed his blazing right hand to her skull. Her mouth opened in a silent scream as her arms dropped to the ground, limp. Her breathing was even. He'd been wrong. She was shattered, but she was still dangerous. She was an evil seed.

Henry poured more of his life into her flesh. Her leathered skin softened and feathered, and her breathing stopped. Henry stood, breathing hard, and wiped his forehead on his sleeve. He wanted to wash his hands. At his feet, a pile of dandelion down lay in the shape of an old and shriveled woman, unmoving in the stillness of the garden.

Fat Frank sighed with relief and sat on the witch's couch. Phedon had come at the sound of the shrieking, and he stood, horrified, with his mouth hanging open. "I loved her," he said. "I met her first, I thought by chance, and introduced her at court. My brother won her love, or so I thought, and I envied him. I wanted him dead." He put his head in his hands. "This is my fault. My brother, my father, she took them both. I brought her in. I thought her lovely."

"I broke the seal on her tomb," Henry said, and he walked out of the bower into the clearing.

He couldn't leave the garden, not as it was, with all its stolen life. He reached for it, but there was so much. Henry shoved his hand into his pouch, and his fingers closed around his baseball. Pulling it out, he began to pace the garden. Where he walked, the false trees died and the grass shriveled. Phedon, with the body of his brother over his shoulder, stood by the gate and watched Henry work. Franklin Fat-Faerie leaned against the wall, breathing loudly.

In Henry's hand, the baseball grew hot, and it grew heavy. The old leather smoothed beneath his touch, the core crackled, and every inch of string wound tight within it crawled with life. When he was finished, the garden was a graveyard of fake trees and carpet turf.

"Now what?" Fat Frank asked.

Facing the west, Henry could just see the falling sun above the garden wall. He pulled at the wind, and it bent down and rustled through the ashen garden. Filling his lungs and hardening his bones, Henry rocked back, hopped forward, and brought his left arm around.

The air cracked as the ball left his hand and climbed the wind's back, sailing for the bloody sun and below it the western sea.

The great chains groaned and popped as the garden

sagged and tipped. The black water from the pool ran through the grass and slopped against the wall. The three hurried across the swaying, jerking rope-bridge and scrambled into the tower. They turned and watched the chains slip and the hanging garden fall, rolling to its side, trailing ash, trailing down, thundering in its death.

CHAPTER TWENTY-FIVE

Henry York Maccabee sat in a chair beside his father. His uncle Caleb sat beside him, and his uncle Frank beside him. James stood behind Henry. He'd been offered a chair, but he was too angry to sit. Henry could hear his mouth opening and shutting, but he hadn't spoken. Mordecai had told him not to.

Across from them all, filling his living chair, sat Nudd, the Chestnut King.

Henry hadn't eaten or slept in two days, not since the throne room. And he hadn't wanted a birthday party. His day had passed. He'd catch the next one, and his family could visit him in his dirt room at Glaston's Barrow. Richard, between telling his war story and explaining how he'd been stabbed in the thigh and exactly how it had felt, insisted that he would live with Henry, and Henrietta had suggested that they all move to the faerie world and pretty much live forever. Una and Isa had simply cried and hugged their brother. Anastasia had wanted to fight the faeries. Zeke had told Henry he was sorry, but he thought he'd make a good king. That was before Caleb had taken him back to Kansas. Hyacinth had said nothing. She had simply sat with her son on the roof of a smaller house in Hylfing, overlooking the sea, and when he asked, she sang.

He'd asked a lot.

"Nothing moves in Endor," Mordecai said. "The tombs are still. And dandelions spread in the streets. It will green. You should have destroyed the star many years ago."

"I told the boy there were risks," Nudd said, pulling at his beard. "And it was a true telling. I could not say which king or prophet faerie crafted it. It might have released a more ancient evil and returned us all to the world's first death."

James's teeth clicked.

"But," the king continued, "the fuller truth is that I tried and failed. I had not the strength, nor had Amram, your father. He struggled with the star on this very barrow and called down lightning beneath the tower. Those days before his death, risks were worth the taking."

"And in these times?" Caleb asked.

Nudd shifted his weight. "They were again. Who placed the star in the boy's hands and sent it to the last striking serpent of Endor? Was that not a risk?"

Mordecai smiled. "It was, to my mind, a bargain. Your closet world is secure enough. What did you risk for yourself? And what punishment did you heap on my son's courage?"

Nudd chuckled. "No risks? A third of the barrow troop has fallen. Jacques One-Eye fell at the last in the throne room, along with twenty others. Punishment? Being a king is punishment? Counting centuries like men count decades is punishment?"

"It is," Caleb said. "As you well know. Jacques we honor as we honor those others, and those among our own city's fallen. But my brother asked what risk you took for yourself, not what risks your bold faeren fighters took. You left Henry no choice."

"He had a choice," Nudd said. "And he made a promise and said his word was binding." He smiled. "He'll be crowned tomorrow, and then I'm away from this world and from my life."

James snorted.

Uncle Frank cleared his throat. "I had a little taste of entrapment once. I found love in that world, but I never stopped being lost in it. I was just a weed in the wrong ditch. If you intend to hold Henry to this, I have to say, I'm likely to work myself into an almighty spite."

Nudd laughed and held his belly while it shook. "Henry gave me his word. And Henry it will be who holds himself to it."

Henry picked slowly at the bandage on his jaw. The raggant snored beneath his chair. "I did make a promise," Henry said quietly. "And I'll keep it."

Nudd raised his eyebrows and held out his hands. "Behold the boy," he said. "He keeps a promise."

Henry put his hands on his head and leaned back. Faeren were so stupid. At least some of them were. All of them were petty. Fat Frank had never been like that. Which is why he was in serious trouble, too.

Frank's sorrow hadn't lifted. Henry knew his friend was proud of him, and swollen with the praise of the queene, but that seemed to be the only spark of life left in the former faerie. His joints were hardening, and his eyes were cloudy. His breathing was brittle and mechanical. When Henry had looked for his friend's wild green strength, he had found only yellow and cream and, worst of all, rigid white. Not one ounce of the mound magic still flowed within Franklin Fat, and he hadn't allowed himself to be bonded by the Chestnut King. He wouldn't until he found out what was happening to Henry.

Henry jerked up. Someone was talking, but he didn't care. He pointed at Nudd.

"But what did I promise you?"

Nudd's brows sank low in confusion. "To be heir to my throne. To be the Chestnut King."

"Right," Henry said. "And I will. But for how long?"

"As long you like," Nudd said. "Or until you pass the crown to an equal, not from among the faeren."

Henry grinned, really grinned, for the first time in two days. "Well, I've found him," he said. "You can crown me if you like, that's fine, I said you could, but then I'm turning right around and crowning him."

"Who is it?" James asked.

Mordecai was looking at Henry. His eyes were skeptical.

Henry jumped out of his chair. "Hold on." He turned and ran over to the carved door in the wall. The bookshelf still stuck out awkwardly beside it. Henry knuckle-tapped the door and opened it quickly.

"Hey," he said. "Could you come in here for a minute?"

Behind him, Caleb burst into laughter.

"What?" James asked. Uncle Frank rubbed his jaw and sent half a smile at the Chestnut King.

Henry stepped away from the door and held out his hands.

Fat Frank limped into the room on one crutch. His clothes were sharp and new, and his face had actually been washed. But his eyes were heavy, and his nose and fingers were white. He turned and stuck his head back through the door. "Yes, Majesty," he said slowly. "I'll just be a moment."

Nudd snorted. " 'Not from among the faeren' was too confusing?"

"Frank," Henry said. "Are you a faerie?"

"No," Frank said. "Not but in my spirit. And good riddance, I begin to think. Struck from the mound magic— all legal and binding. Used the last of it in Dumarre. Look at me if you have the eyes. You'll see no green." He held up his pale fingers. "The toes are worse. Can't much balance. I'm a common dwarf, and I'd be a chalk road-marker within the week if I let things go. Alma, Her Majesty, even put in a recommending as to a reinstatement, but she couldn't help herself and squashed in some extra bit demanding an apology. The district said it wasn't in good order or had an improper seal or some such."

"Frank," Henry said. "Have you joined the faeren of Glaston's Barrow?"

Frank leaned on his crutch. "You know the tale. I was seized, thrown in the cellar, and then Henry here freed me by hook and barter, and I joined in battle. But I haven't been bonded, nor fed by any of the chestnut life, as you can see. I was waiting until Henry was the Chestnut King to do that. No offense."

"As for being my equal," Henry said, "I can do better. He is my brother. Without Frank, the witch would still be on her throne in Dumarre, and Endor would still be crawling with the undying. I used his courage more than mine, and whenever I ran out, he gave me more. We fought side by side, and I listened to his directions and followed his orders to the end."

Mordecai's eyes twinkled. He turned and gave Nudd a tight-lipped smile. "If the faeren had been more like Fat Franklin, you would have walked free in your world long ago, chains broken at the naming of your son. My father called you Robert Kirk. Was that your name? Your son would have lived with his father, your wife with her husband. Your bones would have long been in the ground and your mind at rest."

The Chestnut King sputtered his lips and tugged sharply on his beard. After a silent moment, he flushed and nodded.

Laughing, Henry turned to the confused faerie.

"Franklin Fat Once-a-Faerie, how would you like to be the Chestnut King?"

Frank's eyes widened and then narrowed. He swallowed hard and sat down on the floor. He looked into every pair of eyes in the room, checking for any hint of jest.

"Well?" Mordecai said.

Fat Frank sputtered and began to blink. Tears filled his eyes, and his lips scrunched up tight. "I haven't been long without a people, but it's like not having a head nor a body. I'd be a faerie again?"

Nudd nodded. "The king of faeries."

"Franklin," Uncle Frank said, smiling. "I'd get right down to the business of a royal family."

James laughed. "And a few royal words for the district committees."

Fat Frank spun on his heel and hobbled back through the door, slamming it behind him.

That night in Hylfing, bonfires blazed in the square, and while men plucked strings and swirling women drew them out to dance, the Faerie Queene came on the arm of Fat Franklin, surrounded by strange little women laced up in prisons for dresses and guards in puffy pants. Henry took off his solid silver necklace and hung the chestnut around his fat friend's neck. Then, while Frank and Dotty danced with the faeren, Henry ate plates of fish until he thought he would burst, and while the fires died and his mother hummed and sang, he stretched himself out in the street beside her, beside his sisters and his laughing cousins, his brothers and the tall shapes of Mordecai and Caleb, and, tucking a folded hoodie beneath his head, he slept, his mind dreaming only of the sea and tall wheat and a baseball field full of gold.

Hyacinth woke him when the moon was high and the faeren were gone and the fires were dim beds of popping coals.

And all them rose and went into The Horned Horse and carried lanterns through a doorway Mordecai had prepared.

The attic of the old farmhouse was still damp, and the floors were covered with silt. The water had finally torn apart the small cupboard and closed its own gate. Pieces of it were scattered through the little room full of doors and out in the attic, where stacks of wrinkled papers rustled.

Downstairs, the plaster had collapsed from the ceiling and burst in fragments on the dining room table and in the kitchen.

"I liked this house," Anastasia said. "I feel bad for it, all alone here."

"It'll be fine," Frank said. "It might just be happy to see us go. And it has itself a prairie to watch as good as any Kansas wheat."

"Not quite," Henrietta said. "But almost."

Mordecai opened the back door a crack. The camera crews and crowds were gone, but two people remained, asleep in the back of Frank's old truck, one camera on a tripod beside them. An unusual wind came in over the burned fields, gentle but firm. A little gust peeled off and climbed for the sky. A tripod tipped, and a camera filmed the mud.

They waded through the marsh in a line, the girls holding hands, the women braced by their husbands.

Monmouth, with his head still bandaged, between James and Caleb.

Richard squelched along beside Henry, limping proudly on his bandaged thigh. He hobbled closer to Anastasia, and beside her, he felt tall.

"A sword went right into my thigh," he said. "All the way in. I watched it come out."

Anastasia had heard. Listening, Henry smiled.

"And the whole time, I kept banging the soldier on the head." Richard sniffed nobly. "With my mace. You should have seen it, Anastasia."

"I wish I had," she said. "Do it again. Next time I'll watch."

Henry filled his lungs with the cool air and listened to the wind. Broad wings sifted the air overhead, but the raggant was invisible in the darkness.

"Go ahead," Henry whispered to the knot of cousins and sisters around him. He wanted to walk alone.

They hurried on, but Henrietta wasn't so easy to push away. She walked with him through the mud and into the street, and she stayed beside him, saying nothing, all the way to the small slope that was the Henry, Kansas, grave-yard.

Tilly and Zeke were waiting for them, huddled beneath a blanket.

As the line approached, Tilly stood, shifting nervously, her son's shoulder anchoring her to one place.

Hyacinth and Dotty walked to her, and they hugged her, and the three women wiped their eyes.

"I'm sorry," Tilly said quietly. "I didn't know what else to do. There wasn't any money, and I already had the plot." Three sons stood at the foot of the grave and held up their lanterns. The earth was freshly turned, like a newly plowed field, and a small cross at the head of it said simply, Mother. Beside it, there was a thicker cross. The name on it was the name of Zeke's father—Timothy Johnson. Tilly suddenly laughed through her tears. "I couldn't even afford all the letters in her name. We can do a new stone."

"You have done much for us," Mordecai said. "You named her well."

Tilly sobbed, and Caleb set down his lantern and wrapped her in his arms.

Hyacinth and her daughters sang, and their song made sorrow sweet. Little Anastasia sat in the grass with Penelope and wept. Henrietta cried, too, and she didn't care if Henry saw.

When the song had finished, and the lanterns faded, and everyone shivered in the crisp autumn night, Caleb took the last gift his mother had given him, and he gave it to Tilly. It was a blue gem set in a band that matched the moon.

And then Dotty and Hyacinth and all the girls cried, because they loved Antilly Johnson, and Henry and Zeke laughed, because they would be cousins, and Frank and Mordecai slapped their brother's shoulder, and James shook his hand, and Monmouth grinned beneath his bandage, and Richard laughed and hopped in place and said that being happy made his thigh hurt. His wound. From being stabbed with a sword.

And farewells were said, but not to each other. They were said to Grandmother, and to the Kansas sky and to the Kansas earth, to the wind that dried tears, and to a spot in the soil that marked an end.

The group walked slowly, whispering, to a little green house on the edge of town. Bowls of cereal were poured to take the edge off the darkness, and bags were packed. When the sun rose, the house was empty, the door was unlocked, and the old car was in the driveway.

In Hylfing, there was a city to build, a fat king to visit, and a new emperor sending lots of invitations. Mordecai and Caleb stayed at home, and their hands blistered from working with stone. Frank laughed at their softness, and it was under his eye and guided by his hands that Hyacinth's house rose from the ashes, and beside it, a house for Dotty. But Tilly wanted something set higher and closer to the sea.

Henry and Henrietta spent days on their aunt Tilly's roof, leaning against the wall beside Zeke. And when Henry was with his brothers, or walking the hills with his father, Henrietta went alone, and she and Zeke said nothing, but kept their eyes out past the jetty, where white lines rolled toward the shore, and the sea beat out its pulse against the cliffs.

CHAPTER TWENTY-SIX

Kansas doesn't change much. Times change. People change. Towns change. But Kansas keeps an even keel. People and towns are decorations—summer reading. But the seasons, the plowing and the seeding, the harvest and the burning, those run deeper.

Tornadoes are more permanent than towns.

Four falls faded into winters, and those four winters, those deaths, were reborn in springs and ripened into summers. Storms came, and blizzards blew, and combines rolled to keep the timing of the years.

It was early in the fifth fall, still late in the summer by some people's clocks, while the fields were burning, when a door reopened. A door that Kansas had not forgotten.

Henry York Maccabee stood in the dust-blanketed kitchen and looked around at the broken plaster from the ceiling and the sink with no plumbing. He looked out the window at the flat sea of green prairie, rolling gently in the wind. Mordecai and Hyacinth stood beside him. Uncle Frank nudged the plaster and dust with his foot and stared at three fat gerbils who peered out from beneath the fridge.

Aunt Dotty leaned against the door with her hands over her mouth, taking it all in, scrolling through her memories.

Henry was lean and as tall as his father, though not as broad. He was taller than Frank. His skin was dark, but a white scar stood out on his jaw.

"Oh my," Dotty said. "I thought I'd forgotten so much, but I hadn't."

Henry smiled at his aunt. Her smells, her pies, they were in Hylfing now. They were connected to her, not linoleum or countertops.

When they were all ready, and small bags dangled from their shoulders, Mordecai stepped aside and let Henry open the back door.

He opened it slowly at first, confused by what he saw. There were no people, so he pulled it wide and slipped through. The others followed quickly.

Henry's mouth hung open while his brain tried to process what he was seeing. Where he stood, the floor was glass, but that ended quickly. The rest of it was orange, waxed and polished. Large photos lined the walls between pedestalled displays in glass boxes. A rack of T-shirts was just in front of him. It was half souvenir shop, half museum.

He pulled out a black shirt. In white letters across the chest, it read, **I GOT LOST IN HENRY, KANSAS.** He pulled out another one. A flying saucer, and beneath it: **GIVE FRANK BACK.** A matching design said simply, **WHERE'S DOROTHY?** There were tiny sizes for babies and oversize sweatshirts for the extremely large. Some of them incorporated a bizarre and unrecognizable version of Henry's school photo from third or fourth grade. An entire rack held **WHERE'S HENRY?** in different colors and styles. A little map on the back of the shirt had a star on Henry, Kansas.

Behind Henry, Uncle Frank began to laugh. Hyacinth and Mordecai were simply confused. By all of it.

A tall, heavily freckled boy stepped around the corner with his arms full of shirts. He was wearing **GIVE FRANK BACK** in blue. "I'm sorry," he said. "How'd I miss you all coming in? Can I help you? Have you been here before?"

Henry nodded.

"I thought so," Freckles said. "You look familiar. We have a few new displays. And of course the sea window." He pointed at the glass spot on the floor. Beneath it, a pipe sprayed an even seam of water down into a brown pond. "We keep it all filtered and salt-water treated so the crabs and shrimp don't die. In the front, you can buy copies of different shows about the place." He smiled. "I'm in most of them as a fat little kid."

Henry moved past Freckles. At the other end of the shop, a television was mounted to the ceiling, and it was playing a looped tape. As he got closer, he bit his lip so he wouldn't burst out laughing. The screen was black, and then suddenly, a rectangle of light appeared in the sky, and there he was, from the lips down, and Henrietta and Zeke with him.

"No one hits the Maccababy," Henrietta's voice said

quietly—the sound was turned down—and then blackness swallowed up the light with a crash, and it began again.

"That tape paid for all of this," Freckles said. "You wouldn't believe. Of course, now this all pays for itself. My stepdad and I have a barn out back full of stuff that we sell online and ship all over the world."

Henry laughed and nodded. "It's a cool tape."

Freckles pointed to a picture of a fatter version of himself on the wall. Beneath it, a long printout had been framed. "That's my story right there. Read it if you want to."

"Thanks," Henry said, and he moved on. He moved past mugs and key chains, and alien dolls wearing **WHERE'S HENRY?** shirts. And then he stopped. In a glass box in front of him, a mannequin's disembodied hand was wearing his first baseball glove. A plaque beside it was labeled **HENRY IN HIDING?**, and it had a picture of a thick cop holding the glove. Another picture was a close-up of Richard's handwriting. *Henry Yo*.

Freckles looked over from his shirt rack.

"That's not really his glove," he said. "The cop is full of it, but we try to represent every theory."

"It's not his glove?"

Freckles shook his head. "No way. I knew Henry. He wasn't here long, but we got pretty close. Always playing ball. That's not his glove."

Henry raised his eyebrows. "Huh."

Somewhere, a phone started ringing, and Freckles hurried away.

Henry's mother gripped his arm. Frank and Dotty were already outside. Mordecai stood in the door.

"Henry!" Hyacinth whispered. Henry had sprung the lock, and the case was open. He shut it quickly and shoved the glove down his pants while his mother dragged him out of the air-conditioning and into the sun.

"I need one of those shirts," Frank was saying.

"*Need* is the wrong word," said Dotty.

Mordecai looked at his son and smiled. "What did you thieve?"

"Nothing," Henry said. He grinned and lifted his shirt, flashing the top half of his glove. "But I found something."

There was a large parking lot beside the souvenir shop and the little saltwater hole. There were signs about the paranormal salt lake and alien crabs. As the five of them walked on, heading for the bus station, they saw stranger things. The Kansas Crab Shack. The old antiques store on Main Street was called Frank's Trading Post. There was a little storefront called Dorothy's Pies. There were two bed-and-breakfasts and, in the distance, a brick outline of a new school. The old gas and bait shop had managed to turn into the Tumbleweed Motel and Galaxy Steak House.

The bus station was entirely remodeled, and the first town fathers would have been proud of themselves for not putting it on Main Street. They'd known something like this would come, and they hadn't wanted the extra traffic.

The restrooms were still the color of a swimming pool. But in one of them, someone named Greg said that he loved someone named Tiff. And he had said it with spray paint.

Henry didn't use the benches. He sat on the curb in the sun with his bag on his knees. His uncle sat beside him. Henry, Kansas, was still a quiet town. A fat, lazy fly circled above the street, buzzing and riding tiny updrafts and buzzing again.

"Henry York," Frank said, and his eyes were staring at something even Henry couldn't see. "I reckon we've grown some, you and I."

Henry smelled the warmth of the street, and he nodded.

"We wear life a little better now," Uncle Frank said. He put his hard arms behind him and leaned back on the sidewalk, squinting at the blue sky. "It's almost like it fits us."

Henry laughed and looked at his uncle. "Almost," he said.

The rumble of the diesel engine arrived long before the bus, and when the bus finally did pull up and air roared out of it, kicking up dust, and the driver levered that heavy door open, everyone was on their feet.

Henry climbed on last and settled into a seat beside Hyacinth. It was a long ride to Boston, but there was a woman he had long called mother, and he wanted to see her. And meet her new husband. If his dreaming told him no lies, she had changed a great deal. And there was a small boy to meet, too. A boy almost three years old, who played ball with his father with a giant red bat and could hit like a champion.

Hyacinth was talking, chatting with Dotty. Henry stretched over and kissed his mother's cheek, and then he leaned his head against the window. A new park crept by, with six permanent barbecues and two separate pavilions. Boys were playing ball.

He smiled and yawned, wondering how many miles one nap could handle. A large sign, blue with bright red letters approached. It told him what to do.

SAY GOOD-BYE TO HENRY

He did. And then he shut his eyes.

EPILOGUE

Wallace Merten liked to keep his feet on his desk. He was a coach, and he wanted to feel like one. Even if he didn't have a team to coach. A desk got in the way. Unless he tipped back in his chair and pried his inflexible legs out from underneath it. Right now, with his legs crossed and his arms behind his head, he was staring up at the photos still on his wall. The ones he'd taken down were already in boxes.

Opening day was in a week, and he was done. Not officially. The team was taking batting practice out the window behind him. No pink slip had been nailed to his chest. But his tires had been slashed three times in a month. It worked out to the same thing.

"Dad?" Mary stepped into his office. Her dark hair was pulled back tight. He didn't like her hair that way. It made her look stark, and she scared people already, being tall. Especially boys. "These boys want to play for you. I told them your roster was full." She cupped her hand and whispered loudly. "A little full of themselves."

Wallace swallowed back a laugh, dropped his feet to the ground, and stood up. Mary was gone, and he was left with the two boys, both wearing jeans and T-shirts. They were tall, about the same height, but the one with the squarer head and the gray eyes had more muscle to his body. The other kid was lean and had a nasty scar on his jaw. Wallace blinked. His eyes were strange. They were green, but the centers were flecked with gold. As he stared into them, his brain paused, and he felt like he wouldn't be able to look away. The boy stuck out his hand, and his palm was scarred, too. Wallace shook it and shook his head at the same time. The boy's grip was hot.

"I'm afraid my daughter's right. My roster's full. The season kicks off next week. You could give one of the assistants your names, and we'll check you out for next year." He gestured toward the door.

The two boys sat down in chairs facing his desk.

Wallace put his hands on his hips. He didn't sit down. His daughter had been right. Too much confidence. "I don't have any scholarships," he said. "And if I did, I wouldn't just hand them out to anyone who walked into my office."

"We don't need scholarships," the lean one said. "We just want to play. Watch us play."

"Your team's taking BP right now," said the bigger one. "Name your bet. Not one of them will hit his heater."

"You pitch?" the coach looked back at Henry. "Right-hander?"

Henry smiled and held up his left.

"Okay," the coach said. "I'll give you ten minutes. I'll watch you throw." He turned to Zeke. "And you?"

Henry straightened up in his chair. "He can hit my heater."

Twenty minutes later, two boys in jeans stepped onto the diamond. An hour after that, they were back in the coach's office, while he giggled and rubbed his temples.

"You didn't play high school ball?" he asked again.

Zeke and Henry shook their heads.

"Do you have any more players for me?"

"One," Henry said. "In a couple years. Great second baseman. Placement hitter. Kid named Richard Hutchins."

The coach sat back and crossed his arms. "Why me? Why this school?"

The two boys looked at each other. "You're in Kansas. We like Kansas."

"It's a hard school." The coach shook his head. "I've lost great recruits before. We have language requirements. A tough math core."

Zeke laughed.

"We'll be fine," Henry said.

Henry, Kansas, was dead in the moonlight. Henry Maccabee guided the car slowly through town and pulled into a parking lot.

"You did not get me dressed up to bring me here," Mary said. "You said it was formal."

"It is," Henry said. He hopped out of the car and hurried around to Mary's door.

She stepped out into the silver light, holding her skirt up off the asphalt. Her hair was pulled back tight. He loved that. He loved everything.

"Do you know what I think?" she said. "I think you can

throw harder, and you just don't. For some reason, you don't want to."

Henry shut the door and took her arm. "I throw hard enough."

"You do," Mary said. "But not your hardest."

Henry sighed. "My hardest doesn't go straight."

"Why are we here?" Mary asked suddenly. Henry had led her to the dark little shop. "This is the town where that kid and the family disappeared, and all that weirdness."

"Just trust me," Henry said. He put his hand on the lock, and after a moment, it popped open.

Mary looked at him. "Do you know the owner or something?"

Henry laughed and led her in. "He says I do."

The door locked behind them, and they began to move through the shirts.

"This is creepy," Mary said. "What are you thinking?"

They stopped on the glass above the pond. Henry shut his eyes, and breathing slowly, he put out his right hand.

"Where'd you get that scar?" Mary said. "Or am I still not allowed to ask?"

"Ask me in an hour."

"And why does my dad think I'm going to meet your family?"

"You are," said Henry. And a door opened in the air.

GRATITUDE

Spenser for *The Faerie Queene*
Robert Kirk for Disappearing
Kansas for Being
Henry for Winning
Rory D. for Loving
Jim T. for Scrubbing
Heather Linn for Waiting
Baseball

Don't miss the first book in
N. D. Wilson's next series!

THE
DRAGON'S
TOOTH

Turn the page for a sneak peek!

From *The Dragon's Tooth*

THE YELLOW TRUCK sat where Cyrus had parked it, immediately in front of the two adjacent motel doors—110 and 111. Both rooms had curtains drawn over the windows, but both rooms still glowed.

Dan's room was out of sight, all the way down by reception, opening onto the courtyard. No light trickled through to the walkway from Mrs. Eldridge's room. She had checked out two hours ago, showering Dan with a barrage of shouted warnings before dragging a single suitcase toward the road.

Cyrus took a long breath of the cool night and stepped over to 111—his bedroom door. For a moment, he listened to the neon buzzing of the Archer Motel's sign, and then he knocked.

On impulse, he raised his thumb and covered the peephole. A mosquito drifted past his ear and settled on his extended arm. He slapped at it and waited. A few slow seconds ticked by, and he knocked again.

Muffled footsteps approached. A dead bolt slid. A chain rattled.

The door opened, and William Skelton, smoking, leaned against the frame.

Cyrus took a step backward. The man was wearing jeans and a tight, stained tank top. His face was pale and sickly, but his bare shoulders and arms could have belonged to a thirty-year-old lumberjack, a lumberjack with a taste for morbid tattoos.

The man's skeleton had been crudely needle-etched onto every visible part of his body from the neck down. Scrawled collarbones stood out above a cage of blue ribs. Ink bones marched down his shoulders and arms. Even the backs of his hands and the tops of his bare feet were detailed with every joint and knuckle. Slanted notes and calligraphies filled in the remaining space on his arms and shoulders.

Cyrus couldn't help but trace every bit of ink with his eyes. He'd never seen anything like it. Fear was trying to crawl up his spine. He wouldn't let it. It was ink. Nothing but ink.

Looking up at Skelton's sweating face, Cyrus dug into his pocket and pulled out the heavy ring. "I brought back your keys. You know you can't smoke in here."

William Skelton turned and walked to Cyrus's bed.

"Hey." Jingling Skelton's keys, Cyrus stepped through the doorway.

His room had been destroyed. His shelves and their usual burden of animal skulls, comic books, license plates, and dozens of other relics had all been torn down off one wall and piled on the floor. The wall itself had been ripped open from end to end, revealing a row of hollow cavities and cast-iron plumbing. On the side of the bed, a small but bellied man was sitting with his legs primly crossed. He was wearing a gray suit, and half-moon glasses were perched on the end of his nose. Large sheets of yellowing paper were mounded around him.

"What?" Cyrus scanned the carnage of his room, his life. "You trashed my room."

Fear was gone. He could feel his pulse in his fingertips as his mind scrambled for some kind of explanation.

"You know what?" Cyrus kicked a shard of drywall at

Skelton's legs. "I'm keeping your keys, old man. They're going to disappear. All of them."

The small, fat man clicked his tongue and cocked his head. "This is the boy?" he asked Skelton. "This is the best you could do?"

William Skelton nodded and pulled at his cigarette. He had chewed the end almost flat.

"Who are you?" Cyrus asked the man in the suit. "Did you rip into my wall?"

Peering over his glasses, the little man examined Cyrus's shorts, his shirt, and finally his face. "You're sure about this, Billy?" he asked.

"About what?" Cyrus asked.

The room was chilly with air-conditioning, but William Skelton wiped sweat from his forehead onto the back of his tattooed arm. "Kid," he said quietly. "How do you feel about Death?"

"What?" Cyrus took a small step back.

"Death," Skelton said again. "Dying. How do you feel about it?"

"How do you think I feel about it?" Cyrus asked. "Death sucks. I don't like it. How do *you* feel about it?"

The old man stared at the end of his cigarette. "People say you can't run from Death." He shook his head. "People lie. Running's all you can do, kid. Run like Hell's on your heels, because it is. And if you're still running, well, then you're still alive."

Cyrus opened his mouth, but he had nothing to say.

Skelton examined the blue bones on the back of his hand. "You know what happens when you run too long?" The old man looked into Cyrus's eyes. "Death becomes . . . a friend, a companion on the road, a destination. Home. Your own bed.

The place where your friends are waiting. You stop being afraid. You stop running."

He dropped the stub of his cigarette onto Cyrus's carpet. "Tonight," he said, grinding the butt out with his bare foot, "I stop running. Someone else is gonna start."

He looked over at his small friend. "What does he have to sign?"

"Him? Nothing." The small man began sorting through the papers. "You've signed the appointment already, and I've found the paperwork to demonstrate that you have the necessary relationship to do so, though leaving it with me in the first place would have been wiser than hiding all of this in the walls. I can supply the guild notary and testimony of fitness and volition. As a Keeper, I can witness the declaration."

He reached into his breast pocket and pulled out a small, heavily creased paper card. Unfolding it, he extended it to Cyrus. "Read that aloud, please."

Cyrus looked at the slip, then back at the strange scene in his room. "What's going on? Those papers were in my wall?"

"It was my wall first," Skelton said. "I gave this place to your parents years ago."

"Just read it," said the little man. "They haven't enforced the original oath in generations, but I'd like to cross all the i's and dot all the t's in this situation."

"It's the other way around," Cyrus said.

"We'll cross and dot both. Read it, please."

"No thanks," said Cyrus, backing toward the door. "I'm gonna go now." He tossed Skelton's keys onto the bed and felt for the doorknob behind him. "See ya."

The keys smacked into Cyrus's chest; Cyrus caught them at his waist.

Skelton smiled and shook his head. "Those keys should have been your father's. It doesn't right old wrongs, but they're your burden now, Cyrus Smith. The race is yours. The world is yours. Run until Death's your friend, and then set those keys in another's hand. Not before then, hear me? And not a soul should know that I'm setting them in yours. I've got more to give, but that's a start."

Cyrus looked at the little man on the bed, and then back into the empty eyes of William Skelton.

"Don't worry about Horace here," Skelton said. "His family's kept more secrets than a dozen graveyards. And as for me, well, dead men tell no tales. At least, not usually."

Horace scraped the stack of papers off his lap, hopped to his feet, and slid the card into Cyrus's hand.

Skelton nodded. "Now read, boy. We're doing what we can to make sure you'll have the help you need."

Cyrus swallowed and looked at the keys. His hand closed around them, and they felt suddenly cold and heavy. The old man was crazy, no question.

"I don't want these," he said.

"Don't you?" Skelton asked, creasing his forehead. "I've seen enough of you to know you're no coward. You want to walk away? You want to live a life without knowing what those unlock?"

Cyrus looked around his ruined room. He wanted the men to leave. He wanted his wall back. He wanted his parents back. He wanted time to spool backward onto itself and erase the last two years of his life. But backward wasn't an option.

The keys had a strange kind of current to them. Exhaling slowly and ignoring the old man's eyes, he dropped the keys into his pocket and moved quickly across the room toward the warped mirror door to his closet. He could always give them back in the morning. In the right kind of mood, he could even throw them into one of the pasture streams.

He pulled out a pile of fresh clothes and turned around.

Antigone, wide-eyed, was standing in the doorway.

"What on earth," she said, looking at the wall. She turned to the sweating old man, her eyes taking in the tattoos. "I hope Dan has your credit card."

"The sister, I assume?" Horace straightened his suit. "If both are present, only one needs to declare; the other can offer assent. Are you sure you want both included? You have the right to name two, but I can see definite benefits in selecting only one." .

"Both," Skelton said. "They'll need each other."

"Who are you?" Antigone asked the little man. "What are we talking about?"

Cyrus slipped back to the door and held up the small card. "It's in another language," he said.

Antigone took the card from him and squinted at the printed letters. "No, it's not. 'Please declare aloud . . .' What is this?"

Horace stepped forward. "Excuse me, miss," he said. "If you don't mind, the Latin is actually preferable in the current situation. We're going above and beyond."

He plucked the card from Antigone's hands, flipped it over, and returned it. "Pronunciation isn't important. Do your best."

Stepping back, he tucked his thumbs into his vest and waited.

Antigone stared at the words in front of her. "Are you serious? What is this supposed to be? I'm not saying this." She handed the card back to Cyrus.

Cyrus looked at the words and then up into the tired eyes of

William Skelton. "You really want us to read this?" he asked. The keys were heavy in his pocket. Antigone didn't need to know that he was keeping them. Not yet.

The old man nodded.

"Okay," Cyrus said. "I'll read it if you answer our questions."

After a moment, the old man nodded again.

Cyrus swallowed. For some reason his throat was tightening. "How did you know our parents?" he asked.

William Skelton sighed. "For a while, I was their teacher. For a while, I was their friend. I met them before they married. Helped them through some tough times. Made some tough times tougher."

His eyes dropped to the carpet.

"And?" Antigone asked. "What happened?"

Horace coughed loudly.

Skelton nodded. "It's late," he said. "You can hear the whole story tomorrow." He pointed a tattooed finger at the card. "Do an old man a favor and read the paper. Soon enough, I won't be keeping any secrets."

Cyrus and Antigone looked at each other. Antigone nodded. Cyrus cleared his throat, raised his eyebrows, and began to read: *"Obsecro ut sequentia recites . . ."*

Pausing, he glanced up. William Skelton was staring at the ceiling.

Horace was pursing his lips expectantly. "Go on," he said.

At first, Cyrus read slowly, stumbling and tripping as his tongue attempted to string the odd syllables together. But after two lines, his voice found a rhythm, and he could almost believe that he understood his strange chanting. He smeared words, blended, missed, and guessed at words, but he got through it, and when he did, he held the card out to the little suited man.

"Keep it with you," the man said. "Miss Smith, do you offer assent?"

"Um, sure," said Antigone. "I guess."

Hunching over the bed, Horace checked his watch and made a note of the time on a large piece of paper. Then he signed the bottom with a flourish.

"Billy Bones, that's all I need," he said. "Know that I am risking a great deal for you."

He scraped all the papers into a pile, then shoveled the pile into an enormous leather folder. When he had finished, he shook hands with Billy, shook hands with Cyrus, bowed to Antigone, and picked a bowler hat up off the wreckage of Cyrus's shelves and popped it on his head.

"Good luck and good night to you all," he said. Leaning to one side, he lugged the enormous folder out into the night.

"Establish the time, Billy!" he yelled back. "Establish the time!"

Billy Bones slumped onto the end of the bed and put his head in his hands. "Go now," he said quietly.

Cyrus and Antigone backed slowly through the doorway.

Cyrus fingered the key ring in the lamplight of room 110—his sister's bedroom. There had to be at least a dozen keys, each dangling from the ring on its own small link. A couple of doo-dads dangled as well. A pearl, or something like one, moon white and gripped by a tiny silver claw. A piece of reddish wood, worn smooth and polished with handling. And what had looked like some kind of heavy charm at first—a silver animal tooth. On second glance and third handling, it had become more interesting. The silver tooth was actually a small sheath on a tiny hinge, hiding a real tooth within.

He popped it open one more time and ran his thumb along the edge of what he assumed was a petrified shark tooth—black, smooth, and cold. It could have been stone.

Antigone sighed loudly. "Tell me I'm not hearing keys. No. Don't tell me. Just turn off the light."

"Fine," Cyrus said. He dropped the keys on his bed. "But I'm reading the card first. There's a translation on the back. Listen."

Antigone filled the room with a fake snore.

"'Please declare aloud: I hereby undertake to tread the world, to garden the wild, and to saddle the seas, as did my brother Brendan. I will not turn away from shades in fear, nor avert my eyes from light. I shall do as my Keeper requires, and keep no secret from a Sage. May the stars guide me and my strength preserve me. And I will not smoke in the library.'"

Cyrus looked up at his sister. "'Translation approved, 1946.'"

Antigone flopped onto her face. "Now you've done it. No more smoking in the library."

She pulled her blankets over her head. "Turn off the light."

Cyrus set down the card, clicked the lamp off, and sat bouncing his knees in the dark.

"Whatever it is you're tapping," Antigone said, "feel free to stop."

"What?" Cyrus asked. "I'm not tapping anything."

He held his breath and listened. Someone, something, *was* tapping. Faintly, beyond the window.

Three taps. Scrape. Three more. Scrape.

Antigone sat up. "That's really not you?"

Cyrus shook his head. Both of them slipped out of their beds and crept toward the window. When they were on their knees with their noses above the sill, Cyrus hooked one finger in the curtain and peeled it back.

A large, dark shape was moving slowly through the parking lot, sweeping the white cane of a blind man in front of him. He reached the yellow truck, felt it with his hand, and then kept coming, finally stopping six feet from the pair of motel room doors. He was wearing an enormous coat and a heavy stocking cap pulled down snug around his skull. His eyes weren't covered, but they were closed. He turned his head from side to side, sniffing at the air with a flattened and crooked nose. His jaw was broad but uneven, visibly scarred even in the dim golden light. He held his long, slender cane in his left hand, tip down, bouncing it slowly beneath the weight of his arm.

"What's he doing?" Antigone whispered. "He's not really blind, is he?"

Cyrus put his finger to his lips.

"He can't be," Antigone said. "He walked right to Skelton's room." She nudged her brother. "Open the door. See what he wants."

Cyrus looked at her. "Yeah, right," he whispered. "You're crazy."

"He's blind. He might need help." Antigone tried to stand, but Cyrus grabbed on to her wrist and yanked her back down.

The blind man had pulled something out of his coat, and it looked a lot like a gun. It had four short, gaping barrels—two on top of two—all big enough to fire golf balls. It was pistol-gripped, with an extra handle sticking out to the side of the bundle of barrels. A small cylindrical tank was screwed into the back of the gun above the grip.

The man tapped his rod on the ground three more times, and six inches from Cyrus's face another shape slid against the window toward Room 111. And another.

The blind man stepped forward, raised a heavy arm, and cracked the butt of his gun against the door to 111.

"Bones!" the man yelled. "Friend Billy! Give it up. The good doctor doesn't take kindly to thieves."

Cyrus pushed his sister away from the window. "Call the cops. Go!"

Antigone dropped to the carpet and crawled away.

Skelton's voice drifted through the wall. "That you, Pug? Maxi's letting you do the talking now? Come on in. I'll get the door."

The floor under Cyrus's knees shivered as a high-pitched whine vibrated the glass in front of him. Then the door to 111 exploded off its hinges, slamming the big man into the nose of the truck before spinning up onto the roof of the wooden camper behind it.

Smoke snaked out into the golden parking lot. For a moment, the world was still. The blind man's arms were draped on the old truck's bumper, and his head lolled against its grille, blood dripping from his nose and lips.

His hat was gone. His cane was shattered.

Turning his back to the window, Cyrus slid down beneath the sill.

"Yes," Antigone said. Her eyes were on him, peering between the beds. "An explosion. And guns. That's what I said. The Archer Motel, room 111. No, I won't hold."

She hung up the phone. For a moment, Cyrus, breathless, stared into his sister's frightened eyes.

Then William Skelton's voice roared through the wall. "Come kill the killer!" Something heavy crashed to the floor. "Betray the traitor! Rob the thief! Who wants to die with Billy Bones?"

Antigone crawled back beside Cyrus and lifted the curtain. "Is he dead?" she asked. "Did Skelton kill him?" Her voice was low, but her body was shaking.

Cyrus swallowed. "I don't know," he said. His sister was hanging on to his leg. He could barely feel it. "I don't know," he said again.

He blinked, trying to clear his head. He couldn't be like this. This was how animals became roadkill. He had to do something. Wake up. Should they get under the beds? Should they run?

"Come on now, lads!" Skelton bellowed. "I know you can take more than that. Or can't the doctor's puppets kill an old man?"

Cyrus pulled himself back up to the windowsill. The blind man was on the ground beneath the yellow truck's bumper. He wasn't dead. His left arm still held a piece of his broken cane. His right hand still gripped his gun. He raised it slowly.

There was no sound of gunfire, no exploding black powder. Each of his barrels belched a burning white sphere, corkscrewing forward, braiding flame, tracing spirals in the air like racing sparklers.

Two other shapes jumped into view, both wearing tinted goggles, backing away from the motel, hip-firing searing white flame. Another stepped out from behind the truck's camper.

Four men, each with four barrels, filled the air with swirling magnesium and sulfur. Flaming spheres, infant meteors, exploded against the doorjamb, the wall, the window, and poured through the door into 111. White fire erupted into sizzling rings. The walls shook. The window in front of Cyrus warped and wobbled as pale rivers of flame raced across its surface.

Cyrus couldn't look away. He couldn't move. He couldn't breathe in the sudden heat. He didn't feel Antigone's hands. He didn't hear her screaming at him to get down. Not until she threw an arm around his neck and slammed him onto his back.

Blinking, he watched his sister sprawl across him, covering her head with her arms, trying to cover him with her body.

He watched the ceiling boil and crack. The walls surged and split, and Antigone's shelves avalanched to the ground. The first flames crept into the room.

A high-pitched whine was building somewhere—piercing, painful. Cyrus pushed his sister off, grabbed her wrist, and tried to crawl toward the bathroom. The bathtub. They needed water. His sister's books were burning. Her photo albums.

Boom.

The noise was simple enough, big enough, fundamental enough, that all the other noises became part of it.

Cyrus felt his bones ripple like rubber as he fell. His gut twisted and flipped. The closet mirror ran down into the carpet. The glass in the big picture window liquefied and collapsed, splashing on the sill.

A moment's slice later, the sound was gone, and the window had refrozen, paralyzed in its fountain before hitting the floor.

Cyrus lay gasping, gripping his sister's tense arms, watching fire dance on the wall, listening to distant sirens.

No more shouting. No more belching guns. He pulled, crawling for water.

Antigone pulled back. "No!" she yelled. "Up, Cy! Out!"

Reaching her feet, she dragged him toward the door.

"Your stuff," Cyrus said. He tore his hands free and stood, hunching in the smoke. "Get your stuff."

"I will, I will," she said. The top third of the wall was in flames. "We have to get Skelton out!"

Cyrus forced his sister away from the room's door and pressed his eye against the peephole. The glass had dripped out.

"Are they gone?" Antigone whispered.

"Maybe," Cyrus said.

"Just go," Antigone said. "Go!"

Wrapping his hand with the hem of his shirt, Cyrus jerked quickly on the sizzling doorknob, and the two of them staggered into charred air.